JILL SHALVIS

New York Times and *USA TODAY* bestselling and award-winning author Jill Shalvis has published more than fifty romance novels. The four-time RITA® Award nominee and three-time National Readers' Choice winner makes her home near Lake Tahoe. Visit her website at www.jillshalvis.com for a complete booklist and her daily blog.

KELLY HUNTER

Accidentally educated in the sciences, Kelly Hunter has always had a weakness for fairy tales, fantasy worlds and losing herself in a good book. Husband...yes. Children...two boys. Cooking and cleaning...sigh. Sports...no, not really—in spite of the best efforts of her family. Gardening...yes. Roses, of course. Kelly was born in Australia and has traveled extensively. Although she enjoys living and working in different parts of the world, she still calls Australia home.

Kelly's novels *Sleeping Partner* and *Revealed: A Prince and a Pregnancy* were both finalists for a Romance Writers of America RITA® Award in the Best Contemporary Series Romance category.

Visit Kelly online at www.kellyhunter.net.

New York Times Bestselling Author

JILL
SHALVIS

Aftershock

⟨H⟩HARLEQUIN®BESTSELLING AUTHOR COLLECTION

Recycling programs for this product may not exist in your area.

ISBN-13: 978-0-373-18087-5

AFTERSHOCK
Copyright © 2014 by Harlequin Books S.A.

The publisher acknowledges the copyright holders of the individual works as follows:

AFTERSHOCK
Copyright © 2001 by Jill Shalvis

EXPOSED: MISBEHAVING WITH THE MAGNATE
First North American Publication 2010
Copyright © 2009 by Kelly Hunter

HARLEQUIN®
www.Harlequin.com

Printed in U.S.A.

CONTENTS

Dear Reader,

It's always so much fun for me when Harlequin reprints one of my titles. *Aftershock* was written a long time ago, and it came from a "what if" dream of mine. What if you were stranded, alone in the dark, with a perfect stranger? So many possibilities! I hope you enjoy the look back at a favorite story.

For a look at what I'm doing now, join me at my blog, www.jillshalvis.com/blog, and on Facebook.

Happy, happy reading!

Jill Shalvis

AFTERSHOCK

New York Times Bestselling Author

Jill Shalvis

CHAPTER ONE

THE PLACE WASN'T what she expected. Though she was alone, Amber Riggs kept her features carefully schooled so that nothing in her cool, serene expression reflected dismay. Control was everything. A deal couldn't be made to the best advantage without it, and she did love a good deal.

She got out of her car without checking her makeup or hair. She didn't need to. It wasn't vanity that told her she looked crisp and businesslike. It was just fact. Her careful facade was purposely created with clothes and makeup so that people took her seriously.

If she were vain, she'd still be basking in the glow from the write-up she'd received in this morning's paper: "A go-get-'em real estate manager." "Best in San Diego county." "No one gets the better of Amber Riggs."

Great for business, but the praise meant little. Amber loved her work, and because she did, she didn't need anyone's approval.

That's what she told herself.

She looked at the deserted warehouse in front of her and frowned. As good at her job as she was, making money from this building would be like bleeding a turnip. It was too far out of town.

Still, stranger things had been known to happen. At least the owner hadn't cared whether she found a buyer or a renter, and that would give her some options.

Her heels clicked noisily on the rough asphalt as she moved closer. The place was two stories and mostly brick, which gave it definite character. That was good. So was the basement that held the offices. She had to sigh as she noted the deterioration of the roof and the decay of the old brick walls. That wasn't good. And no windows, which meant that the client she'd contacted this morning, the one who wanted to convert an older building into an antique mall, wouldn't be happy.

She could fix that, Amber decided, by going inside and finding *something* interesting. Something that would appeal. This was her forte, turning the negative into the positive. Her fat bank account could attest to that. For a girl who'd left home exceptionally early with nothing but the shirt on her back, she'd done okay.

She took the key out of her purse and let herself in. Darkness prevailed, but always prepared, she again reached into her purse for the small flashlight she kept there. As she flipped it on and moved past the reception area into the even darker open warehouse, the silence settled on her shoulders eerily. She swallowed hard, losing a fraction of her iron-clad control.

The dark was not her friend. It was an old fear,

from childhood, where she'd spent far too much time alone, afraid. Unwanted.

Dammit, not the self-pity again. She was twenty-seven years old. Maudlin thoughts about her past were unacceptable, and she promptly pushed them aside. Her flashlight shimmered, cutting a path across the huge empty place. The beam hardly made a dent in the absolute blackness, and more of her control slipped. Her palms became damp.

Determinedly, she lifted her chin, letting her logic and famed concentration take over. She was a grown-up. Yes, she was alone, but she wasn't leaving until she'd scoped out the place carefully. She needed something to lure her potential client.

She wanted the deal.

She made it three quarters of the way across the place when she came to a door. Stairs, leading down. Good, the offices there would be a good selling point. Swallowing her discomfort around the intense, inky blackness, she bravely wielded her flashlight and went down the stairs, entering another large and even darker room.

A damp, musty smell greeted her.

An unnatural silence beat down, so did a terrible, heavy foreboding. In the strange stillness, Amber's every nerve ending froze, rendering her incapable of movement.

In the distance, she thought she heard a male voice call out, but that couldn't be, she was alone.

Always alone.

Suddenly a sound like savage thunder ripped

through the room, and Amber decided to hell with control. To hell with the deal.

She wanted out.

That's when the earthquake hit.

The unexpected violent pitch and roll of the ground beneath her threw her to the floor, hard. The earth came alive like some monster clawing its way out of hibernation.

Time ceased to exist.

The earth moaned and rocked. As she slid across the cold, concrete floor, her ears rang with the deafening sound. Her skin crawled with horror.

Then she slammed into an unforgiving wall.

Stars exploded into the darkness.

And the last thing Amber heard was her own terrified, piercing scream.

DAX MCCALL LOVED DRIVING. Loved the freedom of the wind ripping through his hair, the scent of autumn as the trees turned. Loved the eye-squinting azure sky.

Hell, he was feeling generous, he simply loved life.

The tune-up he'd done on his truck the night before had it running smoothly, and he took the time to enjoy the way it handled the unpredictable mountain roads of Point Glen.

He couldn't have asked for a better day. Mother Nature loved Southern California, specifically San Diego county, and though it was nearly November, the breeze blew warm. Not a cloud marred the brilliant sky. And thanks to the Santa Ana winds, smog was nonexistent, leaving the air unusually clean and pure.

Sunday. His first day off in weeks. Not that he was complaining, he thought, cranking up the rock 'n' roll blaring from the stereo. He loved his job, and knew he was the best damn fire inspector this county had ever seen. But the hours were ruthless, and ambitious as he was, even he needed brain-rest once in awhile.

The last few fires had really taken their toll. He'd just closed an arson case that had spanned two years and caused five deaths. Sometimes at night Dax would close his eyes and see the charred bodies. Worse, he could still see the expression on the family's faces when he'd questioned them. Horror. Pain. Accusation. Sorrow.

Yeah, he needed a day off. Maybe even a vacation. He thought about the wildfires raging out of control in Montana. He could take some time and go help fight them. Not what most would consider a vacation, but in his heart, Dax was first and foremost a firefighter. When he'd turned investigator, he'd never given up his love of fighting fires. Every chance he got, he went back to it.

A shrill ring shattered the peace. *Damn.* Dax turned down the music and answered his cell phone with all the enthusiasm of a child facing bedtime.

"Better be good," he warned, slowing his truck on the narrow two-lane highway as he came into a hairpin turn.

"Some greeting."

Shelley, the oldest of his five nosy, overbearing, sentimental, affectionate sisters, had only one reason for calling.

"The answer is no," Dax said.

Undeterred, she laughed. "Dax, honey, you don't even know what I want."

"Oh, yes, I do." But he had to smile because he loved her. He loved all his sisters, even if they drove him crazy. "It just involves a teensy, weensy favor, right? Just a teensy, weensy *desperate* favor—for a friend?"

"She's not *desperate*."

Yeah, right. "We've discussed this, remember? No more setting me up." He'd told each of his well-meaning, meddling, older sisters that he refused to go out on any more blind dates.

So he was thirty-two and not married, it didn't bother him any. It wasn't as if he hurt for female companionship. But still, his sisters hounded him with friends. And friends of friends. And sisters of friends of friends.

He'd put his foot down long ago, but in their eyes he was still the baby of the family. A six-foot-two-inch, one-hundred-and-eighty pounder with the physique of a man who'd been a firefighter for nearly ten years before he'd become inspector.

Some baby.

"I've got to go, Shel," he said, cradling the phone between his ear and shoulder as he maneuvered the winding road.

"No, you don't. You just don't want me to bug you. Come on, Dax, your last date looked like a twenty-something Dolly Parton and spoke in that stupid whisper no one could understand."

He felt only mildly defensive. Why dispute the truth? So he was partial to blondes. Buxom blondes. Buxom, bubbly blondes, and last he'd checked, there wasn't a law against that. "Hey, I don't bug you about your dates."

"That's because I'm married!"

"You know what? I've got to go." He simulated the sound of static through his teeth. "Bad connection."

"Where are you?" she shouted, which made him grin and feel guilty at the same time.

"On Route 2, by the old mill." Dax frowned as he slowed. Up ahead was the milling plant and warehouse. Isolated from town by at least ten miles and surrounded by woods, the place served little purpose.

It hadn't been used in years. The land was on his list of dangerous properties, a potential disaster just waiting to happen. It was his job to keep properties such as these vacant of homeless people, mischievous teens and desperate lovers.

A small, sleek sports car was parked in front of it, empty. "Dammit."

"Dax McCall!"

"Sorry." He pulled into the lot. "Gotta go, Shel."

"No, don't you dare hang up on me—"

He disconnected and chuckled. She'd stew over that for at least half an hour before calling him back. Long enough, he decided as he tossed the phone on the passenger seat and got out of the truck, for him to hassle whoever was snooping where they shouldn't.

The door to the building was locked, with no sign of damage or break in, which meant the trespasser had a key.

A real-estate agent.

He knew this with sudden certainty and shook his head in disgust. The bricks were crumbling. Some were missing. The place could collapse with one good gust of wind.

Who could possibly want to buy it?

And why would anyone go wandering around in it? Muttering to himself, he pounded on the door, waiting to face whatever idiot had decided to go into an unsafe building.

No one answered.

Curious now, Dax walked all the way around the building, calling out as he went, but only silence greeted him. Even the woods seemed empty on this unseasonably warm autumn day.

With a resigned sigh, he moved back around to the front, and examined the weak lock. "Juvenile," he decided with disgust for whoever the owners were.

With a pathetic barrier like this, they were asking for trouble. It took him less than thirty seconds to break in. The large door creaked noisily as he thrust it open and peered inside. "Hello?"

Complete darkness and a heavy mustiness told him there was little to no cross ventilation, which probably meant no alternative exit.

It was every bit as bad as he'd thought—a hazardous nightmare.

He propped open the front door with a rock and entered. If no one answered in the next minute, he'd go back to his truck for a flashlight, but he figured by now, whoever had been inside would be more than happy to get out.

"County Fire Inspector," he called loud and clear. "Come out, this place is dangerous."

A door opened on the far side of the warehouse, and he frowned. "Hey—"

The door slammed. Swearing, he ran toward it, yanked it open.

Stairs.

Far below, he saw the flicker of a light and swore again. "Wait!" He stepped into the stairwell, angry at himself now for not stopping to get his own flashlight, because he couldn't see a thing. "Stop!"

Those were the last words he uttered before the quake hit, knocking him to his butt on the top steel stair.

Born and raised in Southern California, Dax had experienced many quakes before. He considered himself seasoned. Still, it was unsettling to be leveled flat without warning, his ears echoing with the roar of the earth as it rocked and rolled beneath him.

The shaking went on and on and on, and he lost his bearings completely. He could see nothing, which disoriented him, and he hated that. Beneath him, the stairs rattled and shook violently. He held onto the rail for all he was worth, not even attempting to stand.

"Don't give," he begged as he clenched onto the steel for dear life. "Just don't give, baby."

At least a six-point-zero, he decided with some detachment, as he waited for the world to right itself again.

But it didn't. He upgraded mentally to a six-point-five.

He heard a roar, then the crash of tumbling bricks, which was a bad thing.

Very bad.

As he ducked his head to his knees, protecting the back of his neck with his hands, heavy debris tumbled down around him.

A new fear gripped him then—the building couldn't withstand the movement. The whole thing was going to go and, in the process, so was he.

Dax prayed fervently for the place, mostly the staircase that he sat clinging to, hoping, hoping, hoping, but with a sick feeling in the pit of his stomach. He knew the ancient building couldn't hold up to this kind of jarring.

It was going to collapse and there were two floors above him.

Dead meat sitting, that's what he was.

A metallic taste filled his mouth and he realized he'd bitten his tongue, hard. Half expecting his life to flash before his eyes, Dax was surprised that all he could think of was his family. His cell phone was back in his truck. They wouldn't know where to find his body, and that would destroy his mother.

His sisters would never be able to set him up again.

Then the bottom dropped out from beneath his world, and he fell.

And fell.

As he did, he heard a scream.

CHAPTER TWO

DAX LANDED HARD, on his already bruised butt.

The hit jarred him senseless for a moment, and the all-consuming dark further confused him. He remembered the destruction of the stairwell he'd been on and knew that meant big trouble when it came to getting out.

He also remembered the scream.

"Hello! Fire inspector," he called out roughly. In the blackness, he quickly rose to his knees, then coughed and gagged on a deep breath of dust and dirt.

Not being able to see, he felt disoriented, but his professional training and innate need to help others quickly cleared his head. *"Hello?"*

"Over here!"

Female. *Hell,* he thought, scrambling as fast as he could over what felt like mountains of brick and steel. The collapsed stairwell, he realized. "I'm coming!" His lungs burned. "Where are you?"

"Here." He heard her choke and sputter on the same dirt he'd inhaled. "Here!" she cried louder, just as he reached out and touched her leg.

"Oh!" Clearly startled, she pulled back.

But Dax was determined, and afraid for her. Had any of the falling debris struck her? Gently but firmly, he closed in, and feeling his way, streaked his hands over her.

She made an unintelligible sound.

"Where are you hurt?" he asked. Without waiting for an answer, he carefully and methodically checked her arms, silently cursing his lack of a flashlight. He ran his hands over her legs, during which he had the thought that even a saint—something he most definitely wasn't—would have recognized what a fine set of legs they were. Long, lean, toned and bare except for a silky pair of stockings.

"Hey, stop that!" Hands slapped at him, and when he got to her hips, she went wild, scooting back and kicking out.

He caught a toe on his chin.

A toe that was covered in a high heel pump, if he wasn't mistaken. And for the second time in so many minutes, he saw stars. "Stop, I won't hurt you," he told her in the same calming, soothing voice he'd used to placate hundreds of victims. No broken bones, thank God.

"Back off then."

"In a minute." He gripped her narrow waist in his big hands. "Are your ribs okay?"

"Yes! Now get your paws off me while I find my damn flashlight." She shifted away from him, and then promptly let out a low, pained gasp at her movement.

Immediately he was there, reaching for her. "Let

me," he demanded quietly, running his hands up her waist, over each individual rib with precision and care. Nothing broken there, except his own breathing because there was something inexplicably erotic about touching a woman he'd never seen. Though he couldn't see her, he sure could feel her, and she was something; all feminine curves, soft skin and sweet, enticing scent.

He felt her cross her arms over her chest, and as a result, the back of his knuckles brushed against the plumped flesh of her breasts.

At the contact, she made a strangled sound, then shoved him. "Not there!"

Her shoulders seemed fine, if a little petite, so did both arms, but he could feel the telltale stickiness on one of her elbows, which he'd missed before. Maybe it had just started bleeding.

Everything else vanished as his training took over. "You've cut yourself." Concern filled him because they were dirty, with no immediate way out, and he had no first-aid kit. Infection was imminent.

"I'm fine."

Her fierce independence made her seem all the more vulnerable, and as all victims seemed to do, she tugged at something deep inside him. So did her cool voice, because in direct contrast to that, he could feel her violent trembling. He ripped a strip of material off his T-shirt and tied it around her arm to protect the cut from more dirt.

She was still shaking.

"You okay?" Damn, he wished he could see her. If

she went into shock, there was little he could do for her, and the helplessness of it all tore at him.

"I just want out of here," she said, slightly less icily then before.

"Are you cold? Let me—" He reached for her, but she shifted away.

"I told you, I'm fine."

It amazed him how calm she sounded. Dax's sisters were all equally loved, but also equally spoiled rotten. They were never quiet, *never* calm. And certainly never in control. If a fingernail broke, if it rained on a new hairstyle, if Brad Pitt got married, the world came to an end.

It wasn't a stretch for Dax to admit that the women he dated—and since women were a weak spot for him, he dated a lot—were much the same.

But this woman in front of him, the one he couldn't see, could only feel, was an enigma to him.

Again, she pushed away.

He heard her struggle to her feet. "Hey, careful," he urged.

"I'm not going to faint."

The disdain in her voice told him what she thought of *that* particular weakness.

"I'm not," she added to his silence. "I had a flashlight. I want it now."

At that queen-to-peasant voice, he had to laugh. "Well, then. By all means, let me help you find it." Stretching out, he felt his way along the floor, painstakingly searching for the light with his fingers. "You're a hell of a cool cucumber, you know."

"It was just an earthquake."

"Yeah well, that was one hell of an earthquake."

"Do you always swear?"

"Yes, but I'll try to control myself." His back to her, he closed his fingers over the flashlight. Though the bulb flickered and was nearly dead, it came on.

Looking at the situation before him, he let out a slow breath and swore again.

Coming up behind him, she made a sound of impatience. "I thought you were going to control yourself— *Oh*." She paused. "This isn't good."

"No." Grim reality settled on his shoulders like a solid weight as he surveyed the situation in the faint light before him. "Not good at all."

The stairway was completely destroyed, lying in useless piles around them. There was no other entry into the basement where they stood, except the hole far above them. On the ground, directly beneath that opening, was a huge mountain of fallen brick and steel.

The pile previously known as the staircase.

There was no way out. They were literally buried alive.

"The entire building…it's gone, isn't it?" she asked softly, still behind him.

Dax thought about lying. It would protect her and his first instinct was always to protect and shelter, at any cost. But he already knew she wasn't a woman to be coddled. "Looks that way."

"We're going to die."

So calm, so matter-of-fact, even when he knew

she had to be terrified. "We still have oxygen," he said positively. "And the flashlight."

That was when the damn light died.

In stunned silence, she drew an audible deep breath.

Reaching behind him, he groped for her hand. Surprisingly, she took it and held on.

"If the quake hadn't slid us across the floor, away from the opening," she said, her voice very sober, very small, "We'd be toast right now."

Burnt toast, Dax thought, gently squeezing her fingers.

"Well, we're not dead yet."

Maybe not, but they would be soon enough. Tons of brick lay on top of the thin ceiling of the basement above their heads. They'd been saved only by the dubious strength of that protection. Dax had no idea how long the floor would hold. He didn't imagine it could withstand the inevitable aftershock.

"Does someone know where you are?" he asked, carefully keeping his growing shock and dismay to himself.

"No. And I dropped my cell." Through their joined hands, he felt her shiver again.

He'd been in some hairy situations before, it was the nature of his job. He was good at saving his own behind, even better at saving others, but he thought maybe his luck had just run out.

Regret and rage threatened to consume him, but he wasn't ready to give up yet. He drew in a ragged breath and nearly gagged on the lingering dust.

"Come on, this is the hallway, there must be more rooms. They'll be far cleaner than this, it'll be easier to breathe." And maybe there would be some sort of steel-lined safe they could crowd into for protection when the ceiling over their head collapsed, assuming they had enough oxygen to wait for rescue.

"There's two offices, a bathroom and a small kitchenette," she intoned. "Furnished." She shrugged, her shoulder bumping against his. "I have the listing in my pocket."

Dax wished the flashlight hadn't gone out, wished that he'd gotten a look at the woman next to him before it had, wished that he'd eaten more for breakfast that morning than a bowl of Double Chocolate Sugary O's.

"We'll be fine." She sounded secure, confident, despite her constant shivers. "We'll just wait to be rescued. Right?"

Dax decided to let her have that little fantasy since he wasn't ready to face the alternative, though he held no illusions—when the weight of the crumbled two stories above them came through the ceiling, they were as good as dead.

Feeling their way through the inky darkness, climbing and struggling, they left the hallway. It wasn't fast or easy, and Dax kept waiting for the woman to falter or complain, or fall apart.

But to his amazement, she never did.

They decided they were in one of the offices, which after a bit of fumbling around, they discovered had a couch, a desk, two chairs and some other unidentifiable equipment. The second office was smaller, and from what they could tell, void of furniture. The kitchenette seemed dangerous, the floor was littered with fallen appliances and a tipped-over refrigerator.

There was no safe place to hide except back in the first office. Like a trooper, the woman stoically kept up with him as they made their way. He couldn't help but wonder at her incredible control, and what had made her that way.

A DISTANT RUMBLING was their only warning, but it was enough for Amber, who reacted without thinking by throwing herself at the stranger who'd become her entire world. Later she'd be mortified by her lack of control, but at the moment control was the *last* thing on her mind.

As the earth once again pitched and rolled beneath their feet, the man snatched her closer and sank with her to the floor.

"Hurry," he demanded, pushing her under what felt like a huge, wooden desk. He crawled in after her.

She had time to think the earth's movement was slight compared to the other quake before he hauled her beneath him, sprawling his big and—*oh my*— very tough body over hers, protecting her head by crushing it to his chest.

Time once again ceased to exist as she closed her eyes and lived through the aftershock. Huddled in the pitch-dark, Amber knew what the man holding her so tightly feared—as she feared—death. It could easily happen, right this second, and she waited breathlessly for the ceiling above them to give and crush them.

Unwilling to die, she held on, reacting instinctively by burrowing closer to the stranger's warmth, his strength. He had both in spades and shared it freely.

After what seemed like years—she'd lost all sense of time—the rocking stopped.

She became aware of how close they were. How big a man he was, how every inch of her was plastered to every inch of him. *A stranger.*

She'd thrown herself at a stranger.

Mortified, she pushed at him. Immediately, he rolled off her and they lay there beneath the desk, separated by inches. Holding their breath.

Nothing crushed them. In fact, the silence was so complete it was nothing short of eerie.

"It held," she whispered.

"Yeah." In the dark he shifted, and she got the feeling he was staring at her. "You're incredible, you know that?"

No one had ever called her such a thing before. "Why?"

"You're so calm. No panic."

"You didn't panic," she pointed out.

"Yeah, but…"

"But I'm a woman?"

"I'm sorry." There was a reluctant smile in his

voice. "But yes, because you're a woman I guess I expected you to wig out over that one."

With hard-won habit and sheer will, she never wigged out. Not Amber Riggs. She had too much control for that. The master himself had taught her the art. Her father had demanded perfection from her, and total submission.

He'd gotten it.

The fact that her cold, hard, exacting military parent could still intrude on her life, especially at a time like this, where every last moment counted, really infuriated her. She shoved the unhappy memories aside.

"I like control," she said, and if her voice was tinged with steely determination, she couldn't help it. She was proud of her cool, sophisticated front. It certainly hadn't come easily. How many times had she been told she mustn't be like the mother she'd never known? The mother who'd been wild and uncontrollable before she'd taken off after Amber's birth?

A slut, her father liked to remind his daughter.

No, Amber must never be like her.

Little chance of that when she'd grown up with no maternal influence to soften her strict, unbending father. Once upon a time, she'd done everything in her power to earn his approval, but it had never come. She'd learned to live without it.

She didn't need his, or *anyone's,* approval.

As a result, her life was quiet, and okay, maybe a bit sterile, but she'd convinced herself that was how she wanted it. She didn't need anyone or anything, and she especially didn't need what she secretly felt unworthy of—*love*.

Instead, she buried herself in the one thing that would never hurt or disappoint her—her work—and she liked it that way.

So what was that stab of regret she felt now, while she lay waiting to die? What was this terrible sadness coursing through her, this certainty that by ignoring all emotion and passion in order to succeed at her work, she'd somehow let life pass her by?

She was single; no husband, no children. Not even a boyfriend or a casual date. A barren woman with a barren life.

What would it be like to have a man waiting for her right now, worrying over her? Loving her with all his heart and soul?

She'd never know now.

Another rumbling came.

Before she could react, the stranger was there, again yanking her close into the heat and safety of his arms. He had big, warm hands and they settled at her back, soothing and protective.

This quake felt much slighter, a huge relief. But it allowed other things to crowd Amber's brain besides fear.

Things like the man she was glued to.

She could feel the fierce pounding of his heart, feel his large hands gently cup her head, feel the tough sinew of his hard body as it surrounded hers. The weirdest sensation flooded her.

Arousal, she realized in shock.

Good Lord, one little emergency and she started acting like her mother!

She couldn't believe it, and promptly blamed the circumstances for her shocking lack of control. But the connection between her and this man felt like ice and fire at once, and it baffled her. *Danger,* she told herself. It was just the danger, the sense of impending death making her feel like this, all liquidy and…well, hot.

"It's okay," he whispered in that incredible voice, the one that made her feel like melted butter.

She couldn't have it, *wouldn't* have it, and yet she couldn't seem to let go of him. A whimper sounded, and she was horrified to realize it was her own.

Needing to be free, she fought him.

"Shh, you're all right," he told her when she struggled against both him and the unaccustomed feelings swimming through her. With frightening ease, he lay her back on the ground, easily subduing her.

Above them came the booming sound of more falling brick, and it was louder, more terrifying than Amber could imagine. The falling debris hit the top of the desk that was protecting them, nearly startling her right out of her own skin.

They were going to die now.

She had to get out. But she couldn't budge, he held her too close, protecting her body with his.

"Don't fight me," he coaxed in her ear. "We've got to stay right here."

"No," she gasped, wrestling, listening to the noise of the building crumbling to dust around them, feeling the heat of him as he held her safe no matter how she fought him.

Didn't he understand? She'd lost it, her prized control was gone, and the greater danger lay right here, in his warm, strong arms. "I need out!" she cried.

"You can't." Regret made his voice harsh, but so did determination as he leaned over her, cuffing her hands over her head, restraining her with his superior strength.

"Listen," he demanded as she silently fought him with everything she had. "Listen to me!" He gave her a little shake. "The building has collapsed on top of us. If you leave the safety of the desk now, when the ceiling of this basement gives…"

Not *if* the ceiling collapses, but *when*. He didn't have to finish his sentence, but God, oh God, she couldn't bear it, this enforced contact between them. She was plastered to him from head to toe and the opaque blackness only added to the sense of intimacy.

"It's stopped," he murmured, relieved, and she felt his cheek brush against hers. "It's over."

She waited with what she considered admirable patience, but he didn't let her go. "Get off me."

"Promise me you won't do something stupid."

Stupid. Oh, that was good. They were going to die when she'd never really even lived. She had nothing to show for her life, nothing except for what would soon be a useless bank account. Now *that* was stupid. "Let me up."

"Not until you promise you won't disturb the balance of things."

Still helplessly stretched out beneath him, she shifted and discovered he had one powerful leg between hers. Every time she moved, the core of her came in contact with the juncture of his thighs.

She'd been too busy trying to get free to pay much attention, but suddenly she realized she wasn't the only one who was affected by their closeness.

He was aroused.

He was actually hard, for *her*. It seemed so absolutely amazing. Surreal.

Later she would blame age-old instincts, but whatever it was, it made her hips arch slightly.

In response, he made a dark sound that shot an arrow of heat straight through her. *This was life,* came the insane thought.

Go for it. Take it.

She moved against him again, tentatively.

He muttered something; a curse, a prayer, she had no idea which, and at the sound, blind desire overcame her. Before she could stifle the urge, she pressed even closer.

"Your name," he demanded, letting go of her hands to slide his down her arms. "I need to know your name."

"Amber."

"Daxton McCall. Dax." His hands came up now to cup her face, and a callused thumb brushed over her lips, so lightly she wasn't sure if she imagined it, but it gave her a jolt of awareness that was almost painful.

Suddenly her world was rocking and she was no longer certain if it was another earthquake or just reaction to the insane sexiness of his voice, his body.

"You're shaking," he whispered.

She couldn't stop.

"Let me warm you." Gently, tenderly, he scooped her closer, running those big, sure hands over her spine to her hips, bringing her tight against his delicious heat…his incredible erection.

It was wrong to sigh over it; so very, very wrong, snuggling up to a man she'd never even seen. A stranger for God's sake.

But for the life of her, she couldn't pull away.

She needed this, desperately. Needed this reaffirmation that they were indeed alive, at least for now.

She was going to live life to the fullest, she promised herself. Every second she had left.

But as a huge thundering crash echoed around them, she couldn't help but scream.

The walls shook, the ceiling shuddered, and they clung together, holding their breath, waiting, waiting, each second an eternity.

No more chances. This was it.

They were going to die.

CHAPTER THREE

TERRIFIED, AMBER CRIED OUT for her stranger, her Dax McCall. She had no idea what she wanted to say, but in that moment, with their world coming apart, it didn't matter.

He understood. "I'm here, right here," he told her, his body close so she couldn't forget.

"It's so loud," she cried, horrified at how weak she sounded.

"You're not alone."

"I'm scared."

"Me, too."

"I need…"

"I know. I do, too. Come here, come closer." And he enclosed her in a tight embrace that was so erotically charged, she could almost forget she lay huddled beneath a desk on cheap flannel carpeting in the basement of a building that had collapsed above them.

Her face was buried in his neck, and because it was so warm, so indelibly male, she left it there, inhaling deeply the very masculine scent of him. "We're going to die," she said against his skin.

She felt him shake his head.

His denial was sweet, but she didn't want to be protected, not from this. "Tell me the truth."

"I don't want to believe it."

"Neither do I." It was unlike her to talk to a stranger, much less cling to one. Even more unlike her to admit to her real feelings on anything. But the words poured from her lips before she could stop them. "I don't want it to end like this. It can't. I've never really lived, not once, it can't be too late!"

He didn't say anything about the loss of her calm, cool sophistication, for which she thought she might be forever grateful. In fact, he didn't say anything at all, he just continued to touch her, maintaining the connection between them.

"Dax, I think—"

"Don't think."

"But there's so much—"

"Don't."

"I can't stop. I can't turn it off."

"You're shaking again." In his voice was a wealth of concern and compassion, two emotions sorely missing in her life. He worried. He didn't even know her, and he worried. Just thinking about it had her eyes misting.

How was it that a stranger could care so much for her in such a short time, when no one else ever had?

That was her own fault, and she knew it. Another regret. She didn't let people in, didn't let people care. Things had to change.

Starting right now. "I want to live."

"You're thinking again."

"I can't stop."

"Let me help."

"Yes." *Anything.*

"Try this…" He angled her head up and met her lips with his.

Far above them, the ceiling groaned and strained under the weight of debris. The ominous, ever-present creaking got louder.

In opposition to Amber's surging, very real fear, Dax's kiss was soft, gentle, sweet.

"Stay with me," he whispered against her lips.

His warm, giving mouth was heaven, such absolute heaven, that she gradually did just as he asked, she stayed with him, lost herself in him, drowning in the very new sensation of desire and passion.

A sound escaped her, a mere whisper of the pleasure starting to thread through her body. He soothed and assured, both with that magical voice and even more magical hands, kissing her again and again, until shyly, eagerly, she opened to him, only to jerk at the resounding thunder of more falling debris.

"Shh, I'm here," he murmured, then dipped his head again.

The shock of his tongue curling around hers was a welcome one, and Amber pressed closer, grateful, desperate for more of the delicious distraction. One of his hands continued to cup her face, stroking her skin, the other drifted down her body, curving over her bottom, squeezing. He rocked her slowly, purposely, against his hips.

But when the ceiling made yet another terrible straining sound, she cringed.

"No, don't listen to that." Now his clever mouth was at her ear, his words sparking little shivers down her spine. "Stay with me, remember?"

As their world crumbled around them, Dax was right there, commanding her attention, drawing her out of her fear. "Listen to the blood pound through your body," he murmured, pressing his lips to her temple. "Listen to the sound of our breathing…do you hear it? Do you?" he urged, willing her to let go of the terror to concentrate on what he was making her feel.

It worked, and when she felt his hot, wet mouth on her skin, she gasped and arched up into him.

"Listen to your body craving mine…."

Oh yes, yes she heard it now, the blood whipping through her system as he tasted her. She heard the sound of his low, rough groan when she writhed against him. Knowing she was causing his harsh, ragged breathing gave her an incredible sense of power. "More," she begged. "Help me forget that we're going to—"

Die, she'd been about to say, but he simply swallowed the word and kissed it away. He kissed her mouth, her face, her throat, all the while using his hands to stoke the fire. Her blouse fell open beneath his hands, and he treated her breasts to the same glorious magic, sucking and nibbling and stroking her nipples until she begged for more.

The rest happened so fast that afterward she could

never fully recall it except as a hazy, sensuous, haunting dream. She tore open his jeans; he shoved them off his hips. He slid his hands up her skirt, groaning when he came to her thigh-high stockings, her one secret luxury. She might have spared a moment for embarrassment, but then he whipped off her panties and slipped his fingers between her thighs, dipping into her wet heat. Touching, stroking, claiming her until she couldn't think of anything but getting more.

Penetration wasn't easy, it had been a pathetically long time for her, but Dax slowed, teasing her aching, swollen flesh with his knowing fingers until she was ready to take him. He was huge, hot and throbbing inside her. Unbearably aroused, Amber tossed her head back, lifted her hips and sobbed as unfamiliar sensations rocketed through her. She was on the very edge, teetering, madly trying to regain her balance, but he didn't allow it.

"Let it happen," he whispered, his fingers teasing and urging and tormenting. "Come for me, Amber. Come for me now."

The pleasure was so intense she couldn't have held back if she'd wanted to. She was wild, completely out of herself, as the orgasm took her.

And took her.

It was endless. Above her, she felt him convulse, heard his hoarse cry, then they fell together, trembling, their hearts pounding violently.

Amber had no idea how much time passed before Dax lifted his head and stroked the damp hair from her face. "You okay?"

She thought about it and smiled. "Yes." Crazy as it seemed, she was definitely okay.

Wrung out by their hollowing, grinding, shattering emotions, they dozed then, still locked in each other's arms.

"ARE YOU TAKEN?" The minute the words fell out of her mouth, Amber winced. *Stupid.* And if she hadn't so neatly cut herself off from socializing all these years, she could have done better. "I mean—"

Besides her, Dax laughed softly. "I know what you mean. And no, I'm not married, I never would have made love to you otherwise."

They'd made love. Good Lord.

And they'd had two more aftershocks. They sat side by side, still beneath the desk. Mortified as Amber was over what they'd done, Dax had refused to let her leave the safety of their meager protection.

"Not that I have anything against the institution of marriage in general," he offered. "But I come from a huge family. Five meddling sisters and two equally meddling parents. Ten nieces and nephews. Tons of diapers and messes and wild family dinners." She felt his mock shudder.

It had always been just her father and herself, so Amber could only imagine the sort of life he described. But family or not, she could understand his need to be alone, uncommitted. She herself was alone most of the time, and greatly preferred it to the alternative. Letting someone in meant letting someone have control over her, which was not an option.

She'd had enough of that to last her a lifetime; first with her father, who'd been almost maniacal in his desire to curb her every impulse, and then she'd repeated the cycle with her ex-fiancé.

She didn't intend to make that mistake again, ever.

"I plan to settle down in another twenty years or so." Dax's voice had a smile in it. "Maybe when I'm forty. Just in time to have a double rocking chair on my porch." Then his amusement faded away. "That's my hope anyway."

If I live.

His unspoken words hung between them. "They'll worry about me," he said after a moment, very softly. "I hate knowing that."

She could hear the deep, abiding love he had for the people he cared about, and wondered what it would be like to know she was unconditionally loved that way.

"How about you?" he asked. "Who do you share your life with? Who's missing you right now, worrying about you?"

She opened her mouth, but had nothing to say.

"What? Too personal?" He let out a little laugh and nudged her. "What could be more personal than what we've already done together? Come on, now. Share."

"No one."

"No one what?"

"There's…no one."

He was quiet for a moment. Probably horrified. "I

have a hard time believing a woman like you has no one in her life," he said finally, very gently.

It shocked her, the way he said "a woman like you." His voice held admiration, attraction, tenderness.

Under different circumstances, she might have laughed. The truth was she'd been a wallflower nearly all her life. Only when she'd struck out on her own, ruthlessly devouring magazines and books on fashion and style, had her appearance changed so that no one could actually *see* that wallflower within her. To the world, she appeared cool, elegant, sophisticated.

Apparently she'd fooled him, too.

"Amber?"

"I think you know I don't have a lover," she said quietly. "Not recently anyway." She ducked her hot cheeks to rest them against her bent knees. "No attachments."

She could feel him studying her. Could feel his curiosity and confusion.

"There's no shame in that." He slid a hand up and down her back.

No, maybe not, she thought wearily. But there was in her memory. "I was engaged once," she admitted. "Several years ago. It didn't work out." She didn't add she'd discovered her fiancé had been handpicked by her father, drawn to her by the promise of promotion. That Roy had used her to further his military career, instead of really loving her as she'd allowed herself to imagine, had been devastating.

So had her father's involvement.

Of course he'd been bitterly disappointed when she'd backed out of the arrangement. She'd failed him, and he'd made that perfectly clear.

Well, dammit, he'd failed her, too.

After that, Amber had hardened herself. Being alone was best. No involvement, no pain. She believed it with all her shut-off heart.

"I'm sorry." Dax reached for her hand, but at the pity she heard in his voice, she flinched away.

"No, don't," he whispered, scooting closer, feeling for her face to make sure she was looking at him. "I'm sorry you've been hurt, but I'm not sorry you're alone now."

She had no idea what to say to that.

"Don't regret what happened here, between us. I don't."

It was difficult to maintain any sort of distance when the man was continually touching her with both that voice and his hands. He was so compassionate, so giving, and he was doing his absolute best to keep her comfortable, all the while filling her with a traitorous sexual awareness.

For the first time in her life, she wondered if she'd judged her mother too harshly. It wasn't a thought that sat well with her.

"Amber?"

That was another thing about him, he refused to let her hide, even from herself. "I won't regret it," she promised, knowing they were going to die anyway. "It would be a waste to regret something so wonderful."

"Yes, it would."

"I don't want to die." She hadn't meant to say it, but there it was.

The words hung between them.

"The ceiling is holding," he said after a moment. "The desk has protected us."

Yes, but they would be crushed soon enough. The ceiling above them was still making groaning noises and no amount of reassurances or placating lies could cover that up. They knew from Dax's careful exploring that one corner of the office had collapsed under tons of dirt and brick. They now had half the space they'd had originally.

Suddenly Dax froze.

"What—"

Dax put his fingers to her mouth. "Shh." He sat rigidly still, poised, listening. "Hear that?"

She tried. "No."

He surged to his feet, banging his head on the desk. He swore ripely, apologized hastily, then crawled out and shouted.

"What are you doing?" Amber demanded, fear clogging her throat. He'd get hurt, something would fall on him.

She'd be alone.

Always alone.

She didn't want to die that way.

"Someone's up there," he told her with a shocked laugh. "They're looking for us. *Listen!*"

Then she heard it, the unmistakable shouts of people.

Joy surged.

She was going to live after all. She was going to get a second chance.

And thanks to Dax McCall, this time around she'd make the most of it.

IT TOOK HOURS to rescue them from the building, but eventually Amber was standing in the asphalt parking lot, blinking like a mole at the fading daylight.

Hard to believe, but they were okay. They were alive. And while they'd been trapped, life had gone on, business as usual.

Well, not quite. Southern California had suffered a six-point-five earthquake.

Amber turned to look at the small crowd of police officers and firefighters surrounding her perfect stranger, and she suffered her own six-point-five tremor.

Dax McCall was tall, lean and built like a runner. No, like a boxer, she amended, all sinewy and tough. *Big*. It was hard to discern the color of his hair, or even the tone of his skin, covered in dust as he was, but to her, he was stunningly, heart wrenchingly gorgeous.

He was her hero, in a world where she'd never had one before.

But that was silly, the stuff movies were made of, and she was mature enough to realize it. He was human, and she had no need for a hero in her life.

Nor for a huge, warm, strong, incredibly sexy man. Still, she stood there, pining after him, allowing herself for one moment to daydream.

I plan to settle down, he'd said. *In another twenty years or so.*

She'd do well to remember that.

Yes, this had been an amazing episode in her life—literally soul-shaking. The way he'd held her, touched her, kissed her, as if she'd been the only woman on earth, was something she'd always remember.

But it was over now, and he wouldn't want to cling to the moment. In fact, he was probably already worrying about how to let her down gently.

That wouldn't be necessary.

Oh, he was kind, gentle, tender. Some woman had certainly taught him right. Probably *many* women. But Amber had no desire to be the flavor of the week, and he had no desire for more. He'd made it abundantly clear that he wasn't into commitments. So really, there was only one thing to do, after she thanked him—cut her losses and leave.

Getting him alone proved difficult. Their rescuers had circled him and were deep in conversation, so she waited. Around her was the eerie silence of a regular day. Trees barely moving, sky clear and bright. Little traffic.

But it wasn't a regular day. Suddenly feeling claustrophobic, more than she had while trapped in the basement, Amber knew she couldn't stay another moment. Vowing to thank him in person later, after a hot shower, a good meal and a very private, very rare, pity party, she got into her car.

Taking control of her emotions and actions felt good. Still, her heart gave a painful lurch as she buckled in. Before Dax had finished giving his report to the police, she was gone, assuring herself she was doing the right thing by leaving.

A part of her, though, a very small part, knew the truth. On the outside, to the world, she was tough as nails and cool as a cucumber. Inside, where she allowed no one, she was one big, soft chicken.

And when she put her foot to the accelerator, it was the chicken who ran.

CHAPTER FOUR

One year later

DAX LED HIS very pregnant sister off the elevator of the medical center and headed toward the obstetrician's office.

Suzette kept tripping over her own two feet, making him sweat with nerves. She was going to do a swan dive on his poor, unborn nephew or niece, he just knew it. "Please," he begged, holding her arm tight, tempted to sweep her in his arms and carry her himself. "Be careful!"

"You'd trip, too, if you couldn't see your feet." But loving being pregnant, she grinned at him. "Don't worry, I won't go into labor on you."

"I want that in writing," he muttered, glancing at her huge, swollen belly. He'd delivered a baby before, during his firefighting days, when the paramedics hadn't arrived in time. It had been miraculous, awe-inspiring...and terrifying.

"Oh relax." Without mercy, Suzette laughed at him. "I feel great."

"Relaxing around you is impossible."

"Really, I'm fine. Except for a contraction every two minutes."

Now *he* tripped, and she laughed again. "I love you, Dax."

She kept smiling at him, with huge, misty eyes, and he immediately slowed, slapping his pockets for a tissue, knowing from past experiences she was going to get all sappy on him and cry. "Dammit, Suzette."

"I'm fine. Really." But she sniffed and blinked her huge, wet eyes. "You're just so sweet. So much a part of my life. And sometimes I can't help but think about how we almost lost you to that earthquake."

Dax started to shrug it off, but she stopped, planted herself and her big belly in front of him, and said, "Don't act like it doesn't matter, don't you dare. If you hadn't been talking to Shelley just before you stopped to check out that building, no one would have known where you were. We never would have found you in time."

Because she was getting herself worked up, and making him very nervous while doing it, Dax tried to soothe her. "It worked out okay—"

"You know darn well it almost didn't! The ceiling of that basement completely collapsed on itself only an hour after they got you and that woman out."

That woman.

It had taken him all year, but Dax had managed to steel himself against the white-hot stab of regret he always felt at the thought of Amber. The pain had finally, *finally,* started to dissipate.

"What if we hadn't gotten to you in time?" Suzette demanded. "You could have *died,* Dax. And you're my favorite brother."

"I'm your *only* brother."

Suzette just shook her head and sniffed again. But he was tired of obsessing about the earthquake, and what had happened between him and Amber. It had invaded his thoughts, his life, his dreams for too long now. It was over. *Over.*

"Those hormones are really something," he said, but he handed her a tissue. "Aren't you tired of crying yet?"

"Nope, it feels good." A big fat tear rolled down her cheek. "Thanks for driving me here."

"Just as long as Alan makes sure to get off for the birth. I am most definitely not available for the coaching job."

He was teasing her and they both knew it. He'd do anything she needed, and for just an instant, for one insane little spurt in time, Dax thought maybe he wouldn't mind being a coach at all.

"Someday this will be you," she said softly, bringing his hand to her belly so that he could feel the wonder of the baby's movement.

"Not in the near future," he said, but he spread his fingers wide, feeling the miracle beneath; moving, growing, *living.*

"It will be," Suzette promised. "Someday, some woman is going to snag you, make you forget why you like being single. Trust me on this."

Without warning, the memory of lying huddled

beneath a desk, waiting to die, holding the frightened but courageous Amber hit him, hard. That day he'd prepared himself for a hysterical, whiny female, but she had surprised him with her inner strength, her quiet resolve to survive.

He'd been drawn to her on a level he couldn't have imagined. Compared to his wonderful but flighty sisters, and the wild bombshells he had an admittedly bad habit of dating, Amber had seemed like a startling breath of fresh air.

He'd wanted, badly, to see her face, and for the first time in his life, it hadn't been to determine if she was as sexy as her voice. He'd wanted to look into her eyes and see for himself if the connection between them was as real as it felt.

In those terror-filled moments, when they'd been so certain the end had come, they'd come together in the dark; desperate and afraid, hungry and needy, joining together to make unforgettable, perfect love, without ever having set eyes on each other.

It had been poignant, amazing...*necessary*. As necessary as breathing.

The image of Amber exploding in his arms wasn't new; it was never far from his mind. What they'd shared had been incredible, as soul-shattering as the earthquake had been, and he couldn't forget it, no matter how hard he tried.

And yet Amber obviously had.

Despite his best efforts to find her, she'd vanished. He'd gotten an all-too-quick glimpse of her that day, and though she'd been nothing like the women he usually found himself attracted to, he'd thought her short, sleek, dark hair and even darker eyes the most beautiful he'd ever seen.

At first he searched so diligently for her because there was every chance he had gotten her pregnant. That he hadn't used a condom was disturbing, he *always* used protection. But then again, neither of them had expected to live through the experience.

By the time Dax tracked her down—not an easy feat when he hadn't even known her last name— she'd been gone. He'd located her office, only to be told she'd taken a leave of absence. She'd subleased her condo.

No forwarding address.

Inexplicably devastated, Dax had gone to help fight the wildfires in Montana. He'd been there a month, during which time his disgruntled secretary messed up his office good, and then took another job.

When he'd gotten back, there were no messages, but by then he hadn't expected any from Amber.

She was long gone.

Clearly, she'd wanted no reminder of that one day they'd shared, which was fine. He had his own life, which consisted of work, women and fun. He hadn't looked back.

Much.

"Let's sign you in," he said to Suzette now, shaking the memories off. "This place is packed."

AMBER WAS LATE. Her alarm hadn't gone off, she'd annoyed a client by running behind, and now she was stuck in traffic.

Definitely, a terminally bad day.

Normally she'd have felt weighed down by all the stress. She'd have fought it with breathing techniques and her famed cool control.

But fighting wasn't necessary, because none of it was important. Her life had forever changed on that fateful day she'd gotten caught in the earthquake, and now all that mattered was Taylor.

She pulled into the medical center knowing if she didn't rush, she'd be late for their three-month pediatric appointment, and she hated that. She was never late, yet here she was racing through the parking lot with baby Taylor in her arms and a huge diaper bag hanging off her shoulder, hitting her with each stride.

If she'd gotten up on time, she chided herself, she wouldn't be rushing now. But she was always so tired lately. It was all the change, she decided. Becoming a mother. Coming back to town after a yearlong…what?

What did one call it when a person ran away from her job, her home, her life?

A *vacation,* she reminded herself firmly. She'd never in her life taken one, certainly she'd been entitled. Just because she'd taken it immediately following the earthquake didn't mean it had anything to do with the choices she'd made.

Neither did one rugged, sexy, unforgettable Dax McCall.

Nope.

God, what a liar she was. The cooing sound stopped her cold. Staring down into her daughter's face, her heart simply tipped on its side.

Baby-blue eyes stared back at her. So had a kissable button nose, two chubby cheeks and the sweetest little mouth.

Love swamped her. Amber had never imagined herself a mother, but Taylor was the greatest thing that had ever happened to her, and looking into that precious face, she had absolutely no choice but to smile.

In response, Taylor let out an ear-splitting squeal and grinned, while cheerfully, uncontrollably waving her arms.

Amber's heart twisted again and she bent, touching her nose to Taylor's. "You are the sweetest baby that ever lived," she whispered fiercely. "I love you."

Taylor drooled, making Amber smile again, though her smile was bittersweet this time. Taylor was her family, her life, her everything. They were alone together.

And together the two of them would be just fine.

That's what Amber repeated to herself as she strode breathlessly to the elevator and hit the button for the second floor. It didn't matter that they were unwanted—Amber by her father, Taylor by hers.

They would survive.

As she waited, she smiled at her daughter and wondered for the thousandth time if Taylor had her daddy's eyes. Were the light, crystal clear baby blues, the kind one could drown in, from Dax?

It still hurt, the not knowing. She'd tried, she reassured herself. The day after the earthquake, after she'd made the rash decision to go to Mexico for an extended vacation that had turned into a yearlong leave of absence, she'd attempted to see Dax.

In spite of her embarrassment at having to face the man she'd thrown herself at, she'd wanted to thank him for saving her life, for she held no illusions. She never would have survived without him, without his quick thinking and razor-sharp instincts, without his warm, safe arms and incredibly soothing voice.

She had no idea where he lived, but knew that as a fire inspector, he had to work out of the main fire house downtown. Somehow she'd summoned her courage to thank him in person, but when she'd gotten there, most of her bravery had faded in the face of reality.

She'd found him all right. He'd been in the break room with one of the firefighters. A woman. And they'd been laughing and teasing and flirting.

She'd prepared herself for anything, anything but that. Standing in the doorway watching, *yearning,* she thought she'd never seen anyone so open, so absolutely full of life.

He was definitely far more man than she was equipped to handle, and with her words of thanks stuck in her throat, she'd turned tail and run. Not exactly mature, but it was done. To make up for her silliness, she'd sent a thank-you card and flowers before she'd left town.

It hadn't been until later, *much* later, that she'd discovered her condition.

Her *pregnant* condition.

The elevator doors of the medical building opened

and Amber got on, straightening her shoulders and hugging Taylor close. To her credit, she had indeed again tried to reach Dax, and at *that* memory, she reddened with embarrassment.

She'd called his office from Mexico, not wanting anything from him, just needing to tell him. She figured she owed him that. He had a right to know.

He'd been in Montana, helping to fight the out-of-control range fires there. She'd left a message with an unsympathetic secretary, explaining where she was and only that she needed to talk to Dax.

He hadn't returned the call.

She understood. He'd moved on.

Yet whatever his faults, he'd once been compassionate and caring to her, and because of that, he needed to hear the truth from her own lips. In person. Though it had been easier to hide all this time, she couldn't continue it.

He had to know about Taylor.

And he would, she promised herself, now that she was back in town—just as soon as she figured out how to do it right.

The elevator doors opened and she entered a huge reception area, filled with women; young and old, sick and healthy, and very pregnant. Most had little children with them. Resigned to a long wait, Amber signed in and stood there, surveying the grumpy crowd, trying to find an empty seat. In her arms, a wide-awake Taylor shifted, stared at all the chaos around her, and let out a happy little gurgle.

"Glad someone's so cheery," Amber said with a

helpless laugh. She dropped the heavy diaper bag to the floor and sighed in relief at the loss of the weight. Another grateful sigh came when she sank into an empty chair. Sitting had never felt so good.

But then, from across the room, a sea of waiting people between them, stood a man. Not just any man, but the one who could stop her heart cold.

Dax McCall.

And, oh God, he was staring right at her. *What should she do?*

All semblance of control flew out the window. So did reasoning. Sure, she could run, but even if her legs were working, running seemed so undignified. She could lie, but that was no good, either. Not only was she horrible at lying, she could never live with herself.

No, she alone had brought on this awkward situation, she would face it. Easier said than done, she thought wildly, still pierced by Dax's unwavering, highly personal stare.

For a second she allowed herself to think— hope—he wouldn't recognize her. After all, the last time he'd seen her, she'd been covered in dirt and debris, battered and afraid, and very unlike herself. And then after that, he'd not returned her call, nor acknowledged her card and flowers.

She should have known better. He recognized her.

Strangely enough, around them life went on. Babies cried, though not Taylor, who was blessedly silent. Parents chatted. Moms-to-be flipped through baby magazines. Medical staff buzzed noisily, going about their rounds and duties.

Amber saw and heard none of it, her gaze held prisoner by Dax's stare. He was exactly as he'd been in her dreams—tall, powerfully built. Unforgettable. He wore snug, faded jeans that fit his athletic physique, and a plaid flannel shirt, open and untucked over a simple white T-shirt.

Plain clothes, not such a plain man.

It didn't help that Amber could remember exactly what lay under those clothes. Though she had never actually seen him in all his naked glory, she'd *felt* him, every single inch, and what magnificent inches they had been. She knew his every muscle intimately, had personally run her hands over those broad shoulders, his wide chest, his flat stomach, those long, tough thighs…and what lay between.

In her mind she was back there, back beneath that desk, hot and panting for him. If she remembered right, and she was horribly certain she did, she'd actually begged him to take her. *Begged.*

Heat flooded her face and she was thankful he couldn't read her mind.

Still, he stood there, strong and silent. Charismatic. Even now, as he remained frozen, there were any number of women in the room shooting him frank glances of admiration.

He didn't appear to notice. In fact, he seemed to notice nothing but her.

Unsure, weak in the knees, Amber smiled feebly and was thankful she'd found a chair. The urge to fling her arms around his neck shocked her, and she decided it was some sort of delayed reaction to what they'd been through last year. After all, there'd been a time, a very brief time, when he'd been her entire world.

He moved toward her, and she held her breath. She saw the exact moment he registered what she was holding—or rather, *whom*.

Hunkering down beside her chair, he gazed with awe and wonder into Taylor's sweet face. "Yours?" he asked.

God, that voice. It should be illegal to combine that mixture of compassion and sexuality. Her pulse beat like a drum as she nodded.

Reverently, he reached out and touched Taylor's pink blanket.

Amber closed her eyes to the sight of him, big and powerful, kneeling by his baby. *His* baby. This couldn't be happening, not like this, God, not like this. How could she still yearn for him, so much that it was a physical ache?

Her heart thundered in her chest, her blood pumping so loudly she could hardly hear herself think.

What to say? How to make this all okay?

How to make him understand?

Dammit, why hadn't she called him again? Yes, his secretary had been rude and aloof, but what if he *hadn't* received the message? How could she have been so irresponsible, just because of her own stupid fears?

"How old is she?"

"Three months. Dax…"

"At least you remembered my name." He let out a tight smile. "I wasn't sure there for a moment."

Shame heated her face, but she didn't let it show. She'd lost her control once around him. She wouldn't do it again. "I've never forgotten."

"You've obviously forgotten some of it, or you would have contacted me."

"That goes both ways."

"Do you really think I didn't try to find you?"

A thrill shot through her, and it was completely inappropriate. "I tried, too." But the feeble excuse faded at his expression. And then at his words.

"Three months," he said slowly. "You said she was three months— But that would make her… Oh my God," he said hoarsely, staring at Taylor. "Oh my God. She's mine."

The pain in his voice was real, very real, and Amber had never known such regret and grief in her life. "Dax."

"How could you not tell me?" he demanded in a hushed, serrated voice. "Did I hurt you that much? Were you that unwilling? Did you need revenge?"

"No." His hurt registered and cut like a knife to her heart. She had no idea what to do, how to make this right.

Where was her easy sophistication now, the distance she needed to pull this off? It deserted her in the face of his utterly honest reaction.

In all her life, she'd never purposely hurt another. She'd never had the power. Her father had always been impenetrable that way. Roy, her ex-fiancé, had been her father's emotional twin, or *non*-emotional. She couldn't have hurt either of them if she'd tried.

There'd been no one else, until Dax. When he hadn't returned her call, she'd figured he was much the same as the other men in her life, but she'd been wrong. Dax wasn't the cold, unfeeling sort, not at all, and she should have known. He was deeply caring and wildly passionate. She imagined he was that way about his work, his playtime, his life, everything.

He'd never hold back, never ruthlessly control himself.

She admired that. Admired it, and feared it.

He didn't move, just stood staring down at his daughter with a combination of awe and fear and devastating sorrow.

Amber couldn't help but notice that he did indeed have the same pale blue eyes as their daughter. His hair, a thick, rich brown, naturally highlighted from the sun, fell recklessly to his collar.

It was the exact shade of Taylor's.

But the physical attributes weren't important, not when compared to the heart-wrenching, awestruck way father and daughter stared at each other.

Amber's chest had tightened at the first sight of Dax, and the fist gripping her heart only tightened with each passing moment. She could hardly stand it.

"What's her name?" he demanded.

"Dax—"

"Her name, Amber."

"Taylor Anne."

"*Last* name."

Amber hesitated, only for a second, but he noticed. His jaw tightened. "It's a simple enough question, I think."

"Her last name is Riggs," she said quietly. "But you're on the birth certificate."

Dax looked at her then, with eyes as cold as ice and filled with fury.

"I have a copy of it for you," she added inanely.

"You're not going to deny it then?"

"No." Her eyes were filled with bright, scalding tears she refused to shed. "She's yours, Dax. That was the one thing I never had any doubts about."

CHAPTER FIVE

"Damn you," he said softly, the hardened expression on his face melting when Taylor drooled and waved two fists in the air. "How could you not have come to me?"

"I called. You weren't in your office."

He swore again, less softly and thrust his hands through his hair. "And you didn't think that maybe this deserved a second call?"

"I left a message."

Those ice-blue eyes pinned her to the spot. "I never would have pegged you as cruel, Amber. Never."

"Oh, Dax. I never meant to be, but I knew how you felt about becoming a father."

He stared at her in disbelief, so much hurt in his gaze she nearly couldn't look at him. "You know nothing about me if you thought I'd appreciate your silence on this," he said quietly.

"I'm sorry." The words were completely inadequate, and she knew it. "Dax, I'm so sorry. I knew I had to call you again. I planned to, but I just got back into town myself and…" And she'd let her fear stand in the way.

"I looked for you." His laugh was short and completely without mirth. "I wanted to see you. You were nowhere to be found."

"I went to Mexico."

"Alone?"

She nodded.

He looked away from her, down into Taylor's face. His eyes warmed and he lifted a finger to stroke it down the baby's face. "What about your family? You didn't go to them?"

Amber thought of her father, and how he'd reacted to the news of her pregnancy. After his shock, he'd recovered quickly, blaming her mother's genes. He'd told Amber she was an embarrassment to him. Worse. And that he didn't want to see her ever again.

She couldn't admit that shame to Dax. "Going to my family wasn't an option."

"No? Well coming to me should have been. You should have told me. I should have been there. For you, for Taylor. For *me*."

"I thought—"

"You had no right to make that decision for me, no matter what you thought." His voice was no more than a whisper, but it was so harsh, she cringed.

"You cheated me," he said. "You cheated *her,* your own daughter."

Amber knew that, God she knew, and she couldn't possibly feel more cruel or guilty. Speaking past the lump of emotion in her throat was impossible.

"Um…Dax?"

At the soft voice behind them, he stiffened, then

drew in an agitated breath before carefully rising to his feet to face the woman who was looking at them, confused.

With clear difficulty, Dax smiled at the beautiful, tall blonde whose stomach seemed ready to pop. "You should be sitting down somewhere," he said, his voice hoarse. "Waiting for your appointment."

"What's the matter?" the woman asked, reaching out for him. "Something's wrong."

"I'm fine," he said.

"No—"

"Suzette."

Something in his voice must have warned her. Now the woman looked Amber over in frank curiosity, and Amber looked right back. She couldn't help herself.

Another pregnancy?

"I'm Suzette," the woman said to her, thrusting out her hand.

Amber stared at it, automatically lifting her own from years of enforced manners, wishing she'd stayed in Mexico, wishing that she and Dax could have had this inevitable confrontation without his "latest" witnessing it, wishing that she was anywhere but here.

"Suzette, this is Amber Riggs," Dax said.

"Oh, are you a friend of Dax?" Suzette asked her.

Amber figured that as a not-so-subtle attempt to figure out the relationship between her and Dax, and she would have liked to crawl in a hole. "Well—" She glanced at Dax.

No help at all, he just looked at her from fathom-less eyes.

Fine. She could handle this. "It's been awhile since we've—"

Dax raised a brow.

"—seen each other," she finished. "A year."

"Well it must be nice to run into each other." Suzette smiled. "And here of all places. How funny."

Hysterical.

Taylor chose that moment to squeal loudly, making her instant hunger known to everyone within hearing distance. Amber tried to soothe her by giving her a pacifier, but she spit it out and turned bright red, a sure sign of an upcoming fit.

"Let me," Dax said, reaching for the baby. His eyes dared Amber to defy him.

She wouldn't, not over this. She handed Taylor over.

At the loss of her mom's arms, Taylor let out an indignant howl.

"What's the matter, sweetheart?" Dax asked, expertly cuddling the baby close.

She's had only me! Amber wanted to say, but at the equal mixture of terror and joy on Dax's face, she restrained herself. "She's hungry. I have formula."

"You aren't...?" Dax jutted his chin out toward her chest. "Breastfeeding?"

"Yes," Amber said quickly, feeling herself go red at his bluntness. To add insult, her body betrayed her by reacting to his nonsexual gaze in a very sexual way. Her tummy fluttered, her nipples hardened. "When we're out, I'd rather give her a bottle."

"Oh." Appeased, Dax looked down at his daughter, his expression so bare and honest and fierce she could hardly stand it.

Suzette jumped when her name was called from the main desk. "Oh, dear. It's time."

"Yeah." Dax nodded toward a man who'd just gotten off the elevator. "Look, there's Alan. You'll have a ride home."

"But—"

"See you," he said, kissing her cheek, nudging her gently away.

The look Suzette shot Dax over her shoulder was filled with questions.

"Have a good one," Dax said, waving, ignoring her silent curiosity. "Talk to you later."

"Yeah. You'd better." With one last glance, Suzette left them to walk toward the man, but that last look Dax received wasn't difficult to read.

She wanted answers.

Amber wondered if she'd get them. "She's pretty," she said inanely. "When is she due?"

"A week or so."

Taylor reached out with a wet fist, and partly by luck, latched onto the front of Dax's T-shirt. There was already a drool stain down the front of him, then she tugged, wrinkling it. Amber winced but Dax simply cupped the back of her little head with his big hand and smiled at her.

Watching them, Amber's heart wrenched. She

didn't want to see how wonderfully perfect the two of them looked together, father and daughter, but there was no missing it. "Shouldn't you be going into the appointment with Suzette?"

"Me?" Dax glanced after Suzette's wobbly figure. "She'll be okay."

Anger vanquished her guilt. "Oh, I see. You don't need to be there for all the hard work, right? Only the fun stuff."

Dax's mouth opened at that, then carefully shut. In spite of the hurt and anger still clearly visible, he let out a little disbelieving laugh. "Tell me you don't think Suzette's baby is *mine*."

Amber lifted her chin, gave him her best intimidation stare.

He didn't even flinch. "My God. You do."

"I don't know what I think."

"Yes, you do. You're just too polite to share it."

She lifted her chin another notch and he shook his head, disgusted. "Suzette's my sister, Amber. Alan is her husband."

It was hard to remain indignant, she realized, when she was an idiot. "Oh."

"Yeah, *oh*." He leaned close, close enough that she caught the scent of him, one hundred percent male. It was so achingly familiar, it would surely haunt her that night.

"*Fun* stuff?" he asked, his brow raised. "Is that what you call it?"

She managed to keep her eyes level with his,

barely, but she couldn't control the blush she felt creeping up her face.

"I have to admit, I find it as 'fun' as the next guy," he said a little thickly, his gaze dropping to her mouth for just an instant. "But as I recall, what we shared was a hell of a lot hotter than just 'fun.' In fact, it was downright scorching."

Though he was right, she swallowed hard. The ball of lust he'd created inside her didn't go down though. "Stop it."

"You headlined my fantasies for weeks," he told her in that same sexy tone. "The way you cried my name, remember? And those sexy little mewling sounds you make when you come—"

"Stop."

The teasing left him instantly and he straightened. "You're right, this is not amusing. Not in the slightest." He shifted Taylor closer, looking like a natural dad. "Let me ease your mind," he said curtly, in direct opposition to the gentle way he surrounded his daughter. "I told you I'm not married. That's still true."

The leap in her heart was ruthlessly ignored.

"And you're right about one thing," he agreed. "I might never have *chosen* to be a father, not yet, but in no way does that mean I won't be the best dad in the world to my baby. I'm a responsible man, Amber, though I have no idea why I'm explaining myself to you, when you obviously didn't care enough to even ask."

"Dax—"

Taylor, tired of waiting, let out another warning cry. She still had a grip on Dax's shirt, and with a kick of her legs, she tugged. Dax grimaced and unsuccessfully attempted to untangle Taylor's fist. "She's got chest hair in that fist," he said, pained.

Good. But Dax's second wince reached her, and with a sigh, she stepped close. "Let me help—"

Their hands touched, his big and rough, hers small and elegant.

The connection was startlingly electric, and given the way Dax went suddenly still, he felt it, too.

They stared at each other stupidly.

Ever since the earthquake, Amber had convinced herself that their undeniable attraction was a direct result of the death threat they'd been under.

Another untruth, it seemed, because there was no threat of death here, and that almost chemical heat between them existed strong as ever.

It was easier to stand and busy herself with loosening Taylor's little fist than to meet Dax's unwavering gaze. Only problem—now she was face-to-face with him, mere inches away, touching his shirt and chest with a familiar intimacy that made thinking difficult.

"Care to share that thought?" he wondered. "The one that's making you blush?"

Her fingers faltered. "No."

"Chicken," he taunted softly.

Her lips tightened, and she might have given him a frosty comment, if she hadn't noticed his breathing wasn't any more steady than hers.

Mercifully, Taylor's name was called from the front desk.

Amber looked up at Dax. He looked right back.

"I need to take her in," she said softly, holding out her hands for the baby.

Dax didn't relinquish her. "I'm coming." His face had hardened into the stubborn expression of a man with a fight on his hands.

But she had no intention of giving him one. She didn't intend to keep Taylor from him, nor did she want to hurt him in any way.

"And then we're going somewhere to settle this," he said firmly.

At that, her good intentions faltered. Memories crowded her, unhappy ones. Always, her father's word had been law. Roy had turned out to be much the same way. All her life, she'd told herself some-day things would be different, and now they were.

No one was the boss of her. Not even the man she'd had a child with. She'd share Taylor with Dax because it was the right thing to do, but she'd *never* let him run her life.

"*Settle* this?" she repeated evenly, as though her heart hadn't settled in her windpipe. Would he try to take Taylor away from her? Would he tell the courts she was an unworthy mother, just as her own mother had been? "What do you mean by that exactly?"

"I mean that this is far from over."

"Yes, but—"

"Taylor," the nurse called again, and without another

word Dax turned, and still holding Taylor, headed toward the waiting nurse, leaving her to follow.

She hated that, mostly because she had never trusted anyone to lead the way for her before, and yet, that very lack of trust had led directly to the trouble she now found herself in.

By THE TIME they got to Amber's condo, Dax's head was spinning. He had so many emotions running through his mind he was amazed he could even speak. He didn't ask, but simply followed Amber inside.

He couldn't take it all in.

He had a baby.

He was a father.

And then there was Amber herself. Her artfully cut, shiny dark hair still came only to her chin. Her even darker eyes were huge in her face, and full of haunting secrets.

But he thought she was the most attractive woman he'd ever been with. He'd always thought so, from that very first day.

Certainly his daughter was the most beautiful baby he'd ever laid eyes on. He'd held her through her doctor's appointment, staring in stunned amazement at her scrawny little limbs and rounded belly, watching enthralled at the way she screwed up her face with fury when the nurse undressed her.

She had a hell of a temper, he'd noted with some amusement, and none of her mother's cool control.

No, his baby girl was all McCall, wearing everything she felt right on her sleeve for the world to see.

And she was his. *His.*

He was a father. He was a father. *Dear God, he was a father.*

Honestly, he didn't know whether to dance or cry, but could have easily done both. "Excuse me," he said, moving past a startled Amber into her living room, and folding his liquidy legs, he carefully set Taylor—still in her carrier—on the couch. He sank down next to her and just stared at her.

"Dax?"

"I'm a father, Amber."

She sighed. "Yes."

The hesitation in her answer reminded him she hadn't come to him. He'd *happened* upon her. The betrayal, even for a woman he didn't really know, cut deep. Dax wasn't perfect, not even close, but he was honest to a fault and expected others to be as well. He'd never have thought Amber capable of this.

"I want to understand," he said, still looking at his baby. "But for the life of me, I can't."

"Understand?"

"Why?" He lifted his head. "How could you not tell me?"

The question, or maybe his face, had her unbuckling Taylor and pulling her into her arms, possessively, protectively, so much so that it was painful to witness.

She actually looked hurt, afraid…and he didn't understand.

He was the wronged party here!

"The reasons don't seem to make much sense now," she admitted, kissing the top of Taylor's head.

"Try me."

"All right." She was in control now, her voice smooth, her gaze steady. "What we had was a fling, Dax. Neither of us wanted more, or would have wanted to drag it out."

Why that infuriated him, he couldn't have said. Maybe because he'd so foolishly looked for her afterward. And then ached for so long at her disappearance. "Speak for yourself."

Her gaze floundered but she remained outwardly calm. "All right. Long after it was over, and a full month into my vacation—"

"Vacation. Don't you mean your Leave-From-Life?"

"—I discovered I was pregnant," she finished without looking at him. "I tried to contact you. You didn't call me back."

"I didn't get your message."

"I'm sorry. I knew I had to try again, but I…" Her jaw tightened. "There are no excuses really. I was wrong. I'm sorry for that, so very sorry." Something haunting flickered across her face. "I was used to being alone, so it seemed rational to do this alone, too."

Dammit, he absolutely didn't want to see that flash of vulnerability, didn't want to be touched by it. With all his being he needed to hold onto his anger.

"You're going to have to get over that," he said, not very kindly. "Being alone."

She said nothing to that, and since she was the queen bee at hiding her emotions, he had no idea what she was thinking. She settled Taylor in a play-pen, where the baby stared happily up at a musical mobile, kicking excitedly.

Dax could have watched that little girl all day long, but at the moment, the show was Amber. Her actions were smooth, and so purposely relaxed that he knew she had to be the exact opposite—strung tight as a drum.

"I like to be alone," she said.

"That's too bad."

She flinched.

And that was where more unwanted conflicting emotions came into play for Dax. He didn't pretend to understand this woman who had tipped his world on its axis, but at the time, he found he couldn't purposely hurt her. "I'm not threatening you," he said gruffly, hating that she clearly thought he was. "You're the mother of my child." Which made his stomach twist. "We need to talk this out, Amber."

"I know." No nervous fluttering for this woman. Standing directly in front of him, her body and hands still, her face guarded, she waited.

Waited for what exactly, he hadn't a clue. Her eyes gave nothing away, but he could have sworn she was expecting him to light into her one way or another. Again, he was struck by her cool beauty. That he knew exactly how much heat and passion lay just beneath that surface didn't help things. "Will you sit?"

"Don't."

"Don't what?"

She didn't move a muscle. "I can't handle the small talk. Just get down to it. You're going to fight me for custody."

It took him a full moment. *"What?"*

"You're going to try to take her away from me, right?"

He stared at her, shocked. She was standing there, cool as a cucumber, waiting for the ax to fall, waiting for him to try to destroy her. "Hold on." He shook his head, trying to clear it. Then he slowly stood to make them even. "Have I at any time in these past few hours said anything, *anything at all,* that could have possibly made you believe I would take Taylor from you?"

"You have to admit, it's something a person in your position would consider."

A headache started, right between his eyes. A tension headache, he realized with surprise. He almost never got tension headaches. "You've been in business too long," he said wearily. "You think with that cutthroat mentality."

She still just waited, making him sigh. Was she really cold? Or was she dying of fear inside? "I have no intention of suing you."

"But?" Her lips curved, but the smile wasn't warm. "I think I hear one at the end of that sentence."

He let out a disparaging sound and massaged his

temples. "But...hell, I don't know. I can't believe I'm here, doing this." Restless, he strode to the playpen.

Taylor turned her attention from the mobile, staring at him with the somberness of an old woman. Bending closer, he smiled at her and suddenly she came to life, wiggling, waving her arms, pumping her little legs for all she was worth, cooing and babbling, doing everything in her three-month-old power to entice him to pick her up.

As if he could have resisted. He scooped her to him, cuddled her close and...nearly passed out. *"Holy smokes."* He wrinkled his nose and held her out at arm's length.

"I need to change her."

"Yeah." But at the dare he found in Amber's eyes, he held onto his stinky daughter. "I can do it." He tucked her close despite the smell and vowed not to inhale. Taylor's head bobbed, not quite steady, and he settled a hand behind her neck, supporting her. She blinked and a long line of drool dripped from her mouth to his shoulder.

Then she gave him a toothless smile.

His heart tightened, and just like that, he fell in love.

Then she opened her mouth and spit up, hitting him full in the chest with a white, foul-smelling liquid that rivaled the scent coming from her diaper.

Amber bit her lip, and he knew damn well it was to hide her laugh. "Would you like some help?" she asked sweetly.

He had no intention of backing off now, even if his eyes were watering. "I can do this."

Obviously pleased with herself, Taylor cooed and smiled wetly.

Dax held his breath and hugged her close. He'd throw his shirt away later. "Let's go, Squirt."

TWO MINUTES INTO IT, Dax was no longer so certain he could handle this fatherhood thing at all. He had ten nieces and nephews, and somehow he'd managed to avoid changing any of them.

Taylor lay flat on her changing table, naked and shiny clean from the sponge bath he'd given her. But for the life of him, he couldn't figure out how to get her to hold still long enough to get the diaper on her. She seemed to have twenty arms and legs, and all of them were doing the bicycle thing at the moment.

Amber appeared in the doorway, an unreadable expression on her face.

Dax wanted to think that the flash of emotion he saw was guilt, regret, sorrow, pick one of the above, but he couldn't be sure.

"Need some help?" she asked.

Yes. "I've got it." He managed to slide the diaper under Taylor's bare tush, only to have her wriggle to her side and kick it free.

"She's a slippery thing," Amber said. "Tenacious, too."

Pride filled him, and before he could remember how furious he still was, he grinned. "Yeah."

Once again he tried to corral her on her back. Taylor grunted and fought him, smiling as she did.

God, she was his. *His.*

All his life he'd been a goof-off, the class clown. And all his life he'd been treated that way. He had to face the fact he'd done his best to live up to that reputation. With older sisters constantly babying him, and women frequently offering themselves, he'd never really thought of himself as particularly...well, family worthy.

Even his job, as serious and important as it was, was really just an extended form of play. He caught bad guys who started fires.

The truth was, he'd never grown up.

The realization wasn't something to be proud of, and suddenly he didn't like his image. He wanted more.

Taylor blew him a bubble.

Putty in her hands, he had to smile, thinking that maybe, just maybe, he'd just been given more.

Oh, he was still hurt at Amber's deception. Angry, too, and a whole bunch of other things he couldn't name at the moment. But he found he could deal with that separately. He wanted this child with all his heart, and he had no intention of letting anything between him and Amber stand in the way of that.

Behind him, he heard Amber shift as she came forward. He could feel her, could feel that unnamed thing that shimmered between them. Glancing at her, he found her watching him as well.

And for a long moment all that was between them

disappeared. He remembered the day they'd spent locked in each other's arms. The heat, the passion, the fear, the need. It had been incredible, and he had to admit, he wouldn't have changed a thing that happened.

Except for maybe Amber's disappearance afterward.

Then he remembered, he was standing there, holding his daughter—his *daughter!*—and that Amber had kept her from him.

And just like that, the moment was gone.

With a strange sense of regret, Dax turned back to the baby and Amber left him alone, without a clue as to what she was thinking.

Nothing new.

Taylor blew him a bubble, and Dax had to let out a laugh. "I don't think she's nearly as charmed with me as you are, sweetheart."

Taylor just drooled.

TAYLOR SLEPT PEACEFULLY, oblivious to the tension around her, her little butt sticking straight up in the air, her fist stuffed in her mouth.

Dax watched her, actually feeling his heart contract. Just looking at her hurt.

It hurt to look at her mother too, he discovered, as he came down the stairs and met Amber's deep, dark, impenetrable gaze.

"Let's get this over with," she said calmly, only her eyes giving away her nerves. "What do you want?"

"Want?" He laughed incredulously. "That's an interesting question."

"Do you have an answer?"

"How about you marry me?"

Her composure slipped on that one, but she regained it quickly enough. "Don't be ridiculous."

"Yes or no, Amber."

"It's simply not possible."

"Sure it is. You just say, 'I do.'"

She stared at him, and incredibly, he found himself wishing she'd come to him months ago. He would have been so thrilled to see her. He would have drawn her close for a hug and probably never let her go.

But marriage? His stomach cramped at the thought. Yet how else to resolve this? He hated the thought of Taylor feeling illegitimate. Hated the thought of being separated from her after he'd just discovered her. "If we were married, then neither of us would have to be away from Taylor. Seems logical to me."

She gave a short, amazed laugh. "Logical."

"More than the alternative anyway. I just found out I have a daughter, Amber. I can't turn my back on her. Or, for some reason, you."

"I'm not an obligation."

"No," he said softly, thinking of the life-altering experience they'd shared. "You're not."

"Dax…"

Again, that thing shimmered between them. Heat. Passion. Need. But it annoyed him, and if he was truthful, it also scared him. "Look, it's simple. Yes or no."

"You're serious," she breathed, then she shook her head. "No." Her shoulders straightened. "I won't marry for anything less than…" She looked down at her hands, which were tightly clenched. She opened them, let them fall to her sides. "I am not going to marry a stranger."

"We stopped being strangers the day of the quake, when we spent hours in each other's arms, terrified, waiting to die."

"I don't usually act like that. I never act like that."

Dax thought it was a shame, but she didn't relent and he let out a sound of frustration. "Look, we're parents. Together. We *can't* be strangers, even if we wanted to be."

"The answer is still no."

"Fine. You don't want to get married." He wouldn't admit his disappointment because he couldn't believe he felt it in the first place. But neither could he ignore the feeling that, despite her calm control, she was frightened of him.

Much as he wanted to hold onto his anger and resentment, it was hard in the face of that.

"I intend to be a father. A good one. I want my daughter. Just as you do. We're adults. We can share."

She nearly sagged with what could only be described as profound relief. "You want to *share* her?"

For some reason that made him mad all over again. Dammit, he wasn't the one who should have to prove his trustworthiness! "Hell, yes, I want to share."

"You're not going to fight for custody?"

"Do I need to?"

His tightly spoken words stabbed through Amber. He stood there looking so certain, so fierce. She hadn't expected this, hadn't expected him to actually want Taylor as much as she did.

But she'd been in business a long time, and what she hadn't learned there, she'd learned from her father. Bottom line, she knew how to win a deal. Start out asking for the moon. Take all if you can. Settle for less only if you have to. "I want Taylor with me."

"Sure." He nodded agreeably. Even sent her a smile that could steal the breath from a nun. "Half the time."

Her stomach twisted. "But—"

"Stop," he said firmly, in that voice of rough velvet. Closing the distance between them, he touched her arms, slid his big, warm hands over her skin. Immediately, heat flooded her. Her body remembered his touch vividly, had craved it nearly every night since that time she'd first experienced it. The sensation of being this close to him again was so overpowering, she had to close her eyes for a moment, or reveal everything she felt.

"Look at me."

Shocked at the command, she did.

"I understand you think we're strangers," he said. "And there's a real fear in that. I'm not going to kid you. This isn't going to be easy, we're going to have to work hard. Together."

Amber tried not to panic at the thought of what getting to know him would entail. Intimacy—and she wasn't thinking of sex, but the other aspects— all of which terrified her.

With surprising gentleness, he slid his fingers up and down her arms. "I have the feeling you think I'm out to hurt you, or trick you. I'm not into games, Amber. You've been hurt before, maybe so much so that you feel you can't trust me…." He paused, studying her when she was unable to maintain eye contact.

"I see," he said quietly. He spoke huskily, as if he cared, and it hurt to hear it because she knew all too well how little she deserved his kindness.

"I'm not like him," he told her, his hands still on her. "The ex-fiancé, or whoever hurt you."

He remembered. She couldn't believe he remembered so much about her.

"I'm not trying to frighten you, or threaten. I'm not going to bully you. But Amber—" He lifted her chin. "That baby is mine, and I plan on being a damn good father. We can do this and make it work. Together. It would be good. But it's *together*. That's the key."

God, that voice. It brought her back to the terrifying magical time she spent with him, a time she could never forget because she'd felt so safe and warm and…wanted.

Unbelievably, she felt wanted now.

"It has to have been hard to do this all alone," he murmured. "She's a little handful. You must be exhausted. Wouldn't some help be nice? From someone with as big a stake as you?"

Amber felt a tiny seed of long-dead hope take root. Was it possible he could forgive her? That maybe he could want *her* as much as he wanted Taylor? That he could grow to love and care for her as well as Taylor, the *real* her, the way no one else ever had?

She allowed herself to think about it. To consider it. To dream.

"We'll make up a schedule," he said, dropping his hands and stepping back. "That's the easiest way, unless you have a better idea."

"A schedule?"

"It's the civil servant in me." He flashed a surprisingly self-deprecating smile. "I like routine."

"I don't understand."

"To divide Taylor between us so there's no problem."

"Divide her," she repeated inanely, her stomach dropping to the ground.

"I don't plan on being a weekend dad, Amber. I'm willing to share, but we do it equally."

Well what did she expect? She'd turned down his marriage proposal. But still, the hope within her died a cruel death. He wanted Taylor, not her mother. Amber lifted her chin, because no matter what he said, she could depend on no one, no one but herself. "Fine. We share."

"Equally."

Oh, God. She was actually going to have to do this, give him Taylor. Her eyes burned, threatened to flood. "I said fine."

"Good."

She needed him gone. "You can start tomorrow. Bring your schedule if you must, but for now, for today, she's mine alone. I don't want to share my day."

Dammit, he looked hurt again. "It doesn't have to be so cut-and-dried."

"Yes, it does."

"Why?"

Because she knew nothing else. "All we're sharing is Taylor. There's nothing else to worry about. Absolutely nothing."

"Are you talking about our attraction?"

"There is no attraction. None. None at all."

His eyes narrowed. "Who are you trying to convince?"

"I'm already convinced."

He took a step toward her and she fought against instinct and stood still.

"So you look at me and feel nothing?" he wondered aloud.

When he took another step, she nearly bolted. Sheer willpower held her there. "That's right."

"You don't remember what happened between us? Hell, what *exploded* between us?"

"This isn't about us—" she stuttered silent when he touched her. "And it's sure not about sex."

"Oh, yes, it is." His voice had lowered, which for

some reason made her tummy tingle, but she could ignore that. What she couldn't ignore was the look in his eyes, the lingering hurt mixed in with a good amount of pride and scorching intensity.

"It's not about what *I* feel," she insisted. "Besides, you can't possibly feel something for me, after what I've done." Her voice was a mere whisper as renewed shame crept up her spine. "I kept her from you, remember?"

"I remember." He touched her face and her eyes nearly closed in pleasure. "You still have to tell me you feel nothing for me," he reminded her.

"I—" She hesitated and saw his eyes flare with triumph. "I don't have to tell you anything." She stood back and crossed her arms over her chest. "Goodbye, Dax."

He stared at her. After a moment, he shook his head and went to the door. "I'll come for Taylor in the morning."

He was leaving. She'd chased him away. Relief, she should feel relief.

She didn't.

And then she was alone, again. Always alone.

CHAPTER SIX

THEY SETTLED INTO a pattern, splitting Taylor between the two of them. Dax would have her on Tuesdays and Thursdays, and every other weekend.

It might have been a perfect arrangement, for any other man.

But as a week passed, and then another, Dax realized it wasn't enough, it would never be enough. He wanted more, he wanted it all.

How did other single fathers do it, share their children with their exes? He didn't know.

Even worse, he actually found himself forgiving Amber. Or if not forgiving completely, at least understanding her. He didn't like it.

Thanks to the luck of his schedule, he'd managed to work only on the days Amber had Taylor. But two weeks after he learned he had a daughter, both work and the baby came on the same day.

It was an experience, to say the least. His family had fallen in love with Taylor, and any of them would have dropped everything to baby-sit, but he wasn't ready to give her up yet.

So baby in tow, he went to his office, confident he could handle it.

Taylor started out the workday fast asleep in her carrier, and everything seemed great. The guys in his office kept poking their heads in to coo over her and Dax kept shooing them out so they wouldn't wake her. But when Taylor's morning nap was over, so was his day.

She cried while he was on the phone to the mayor. She threw up on one of his investigative reports. Then her diaper leaked all over his shirt, causing people to wrinkle their noses when they came too close to him. After a noisy fit over having to drink a bottle with a nipple that infuriated her, Taylor finally, *finally,* blessedly fell back asleep.

By that time, Dax was so exhausted, he fell asleep, too, face down on his desk.

And awoke to his daughter's cries. Picking her up, he pressed her close and expected her to stop crying, as she always did.

No go. In fact, she worked herself up to a furious red, screaming, mass of rage. Dax tried everything; singing like an idiot, dancing like a bigger idiot, and finally begging. Nothing worked, though it amused the staff members who gathered in his doorway to watch.

Taylor was having none of it. Finally, when her screams threatened to bring down the house, he called Amber.

"I've done something to her," he said over Taylor's howl. "I—"

"I'll be right there."

Dax paced while he waited, holding a sobbing

Taylor. When Amber finally appeared, he could have kissed her. "What have I done to her?"

Amber shook her head and took the baby.

Immediately, the baby hiccuped and stopped crying.

The silence was deafening.

Amber continued to soothe her with a wordless murmur, patting her gently on the back. While Dax stared in amazement, Taylor started making loud, smacking noises with her lips, her little hands fisted in Amber's blouse.

She sounded like a starving kitten.

"She can't be hungry," he said in disbelief. "I gave her a bottle. She refused to even look at it."

"Well…" Amber looked everywhere but at him. "The bottle isn't what she wants."

"She doesn't want— Oh. *Oh,*" he said, understanding finally dawning. "She wants breast milk." He laughed, the relief so overwhelming he could hardly stand. "But she's taken formula from me before."

"I told you, she's a bit fickle."

He grinned, now that he could breathe again. "Stubborn as hell, you mean. Gee, I guess she got that from both sides, huh? Here…" Leading Amber to a chair, he backed up a few steps and waited for her to satisfy his obviously starving daughter.

Amber just looked at him.

Taylor, frustrated, turned even redder in the face and let loose with her piercing cries.

"Hurry!" Lord, how could such a small, adorable bundle of baby make so much noise? "Damn, she's got a set of lungs on her."

Amber undid her blouse, then hesitated.

Dax had been staring at Taylor's mottled face, but when Amber didn't make a move, he lifted his gaze.

It caught on the strip of creamy skin she'd revealed from throat to belly. Just like that, his body temperature rose ten degrees.

"I can't do this while you watch, Dax."

It didn't matter if she breast-fed in front of him. Not when he had a good imagination, and it was off and racing now. It didn't take much to picture her peeling the material away from her flesh, exposing one softly rounded breast. The nipple would pucker and tighten, and when Taylor pulled her mouth away, the tip would be wet and swollen.

At the thought, he went weak in the knees. Disgusted with himself, he turned and left the office, going in search of a glass of very cold water.

A cold shower might have been more effective.

No matter how much he didn't want to have feelings for this woman who'd ripped him apart, he did, and that confused him. He wasn't used to being confused where women were concerned.

He could tell himself that this deep attraction was due to Taylor, but that would be a big, fat lie. Already he loved Taylor with all his heart.

But Amber was a separate deal entirely. He'd forgiven her, yes. But he didn't want to forget.

THE NEXT TIME Amber came to the station to pick up the baby, her face was drawn. She was even more quiet and guarded than usual. She offered Dax one unreadable glance and went directly to Taylor, who was lying on a blanket and happily chewing on her own sleeve.

"Hey, baby," she whispered, her face lighting up with the smile Dax had never, not once, seen directed at him.

Taylor wriggled with joy.

"Well, you lived through it," Amber said to Dax over her shoulder.

"What about Taylor?"

"I wasn't concerned." She paused. "You're a good father."

"A compliment, Amber?"

Her spine stiffened. "No, just fact. Taylor can be a lot of work."

"You're not saying my daughter is a handful, are you?"

Amber turned and looked at him, lifting a brow at his teasing tone. Her gaze swept his office, taking in the full wastebasket, the sagging diaper bag, the baby paraphernalia scattered around the room.

And in the corner, at Amber's feet, was the happily babbling, little handful herself.

In her well-fitted power suit, Amber kneeled on the floor and tickled Taylor's tummy. "So how was it, sweetie? Did you have a good time?"

Taylor responded with a big grin and some drool.

"Should have seen her," Dax told her. "She was in high form today. Spit up on the fire chief."

Amber's smile widened as she watched Taylor.

"Did you torture your daddy today, sweetie? Did you? Tell me you did."

What tortured Dax now was Amber herself. She wasn't a tall woman, but she had legs to die for. And with her bent over as she was, he got quite an eyeful, up to midthigh. He wondered if those sheer, silky looking stockings ended at the top of those incredible legs, like the ones she'd been wearing on the day of the earthquake.

Oblivious, Amber leaned even closer to Taylor, nuzzling at the baby's neck. Taylor squealed in delight.

Dax swallowed hard, because while he'd felt every inch of Amber's body that fateful day so long ago, he'd never really *seen* her, and he'd certainly never gotten such a great view of the most mouthwatering, perfectly rounded rear end in town.

"She looks good," Amber said of the baby.

"So do you." The words popped out before he could stop them, but even when Amber whirled in shock and stared at him, he smiled, refusing to take them back.

"That was...inappropriate," she said primly.

"No doubt. It was also the truth."

As if realizing the suggestiveness of her position, she got up carefully, managing to keep her skirt from rising any further. No ungraceful scrambling for this woman, nope she remained cool as ice.

"You were looking at me."

The words were spoken evenly, yet with such surprise, Dax had to laugh. "And is that so hard to believe?"

"Men don't usually look at me that way." She glanced away. "Never, actually."

Odd how she could appear so strong, yet so utterly vulnerable at the same time. "Then they're blind. You're beautiful, Amber."

She searched his gaze, clearly wondering if he was still teasing her.

"Just looking at you makes me think of hot kisses and stolen touches."

She blushed. *Blushed.* So, the cool woman *could* be shaken. "Oh, I'm sorry," he said, anything but. "I'm being inappropriate again, aren't I?"

"You know you are." Tough facade back in place, she walked the room, passed the piles of work on his desk, passed the additional piles that had simply overflowed to the floor. He'd vacuumed before setting Taylor down, so the vacuum cleaner was still in the corner. His coat, which had fallen from the rack, lay crumpled in a heap. His boots were sprawled on the floor, discarded after his last inspection. So was the bag his lunch had come in, from his favorite hamburger joint.

"You're a pig," she said lightly, scooping up his jacket and placing it on a hook.

He wondered at the gesture. Was it because she cared, or because she cared that Taylor was in such a messy room? "Talk to your daughter. She's been a busy girl today."

A small smile crossed her lips. But Dax could see

past the exterior, past that cool defense she wore like a coat. Deep in thought, he stared at her.

"What?" she asked when he came close. She didn't fidget like normal women, so she didn't pat her hair or look herself over for flaws. But her eyes chilled in response to his silent study. "What are you staring at?"

Dax knew how to soothe a woman, but he had the feeling the usual compliments and flirtations wouldn't work with Amber. She was different. Very different. Her dark, gorgeous eyes looked bruised, rimmed with light purple. Her mouth, carefully painted, was tight, pinched. And those shoulders, the ones that seemed to be strong enough to carry the burdens of the entire world, were strained, as if the weight had become too heavy.

"Stop looking at me like that," she demanded.

"Like what?"

"Like…you're hungry, or something."

Oh yeah, he was hungry. For her. How long, he wondered, would it take a man to dig under those walls? To find the real Amber, the one who'd had the guts to have a child by herself, the one he knew would protect that child with everything she had?

"Why are you *still* staring at me?"

Because she looked exhausted. Because she was a puzzle he couldn't put together. Because he couldn't seem to help himself. Backing her to a chair, he applied pressure on her arm until she sat.

"I don't have time to sit." Her voice was weary. "I still have to run to the grocery store, pick up the dry-cleaning and then when I get home, I have a report—" Carefully, she closed her mouth and in a rare gesture of emotion, ran her hands over her eyes. "I have no idea why I'm telling you all of this."

"Because you're too tired. If you weren't, you wouldn't say a word, you'd handle it all. Alone, most likely. But we're a unit now, Amber. You should be able to vent."

"And that means you'll vent, too, I suppose."

"If I need to, yes."

She looked so genuinely unsettled that he wondered what her definition of vent was. "How about I keep Taylor while you do your errands? She's fine here, the guys come in every two seconds just to look at her anyway. She'll be entertained. I'll bring her home to you later."

"I can't take advantage that way."

"Amber." He came from a family of touchers. It seemed perfectly natural for him to lift a hand and touch her cheek. And if he enjoyed the feel of her soft skin so much that he left his fingers there for an instant longer than he'd planned, what did it matter? He was just trying to comfort.

Okay, maybe it was more complicated than that, but he wasn't ready to go there.

And besides, she backed away.

"Why do you do that?" he wondered. "Shy away from touch?"

"I don't like to be touched."

"You did once."

A delicious shade of red colored her face. "I should make it clear to you," she said in that prim voice he was perversely beginning to enjoy. "I'm not being coy here. I acted…wild with you then. I'm not going to do it again."

"Are you thinking wild is a bad thing?"

She looked at him steadily.

"Or that I don't respect you?"

Still, just that look. Damn, she brought new meaning to the word stubborn. "What happened between us was spontaneous, yes," he agreed. "Hot, most definitely. Even wild. But Amber, it was as necessary at that moment as breathing, you have to remember that much."

"It wasn't necessary."

He'd have liked to prove her wrong, right there on the floor of his office. He had no doubt he could do it. She had passion and heat simmering just beneath her surface, all he had to do was set fire to it. The way they kissed, it should only take two seconds.

But he wouldn't, because he didn't like how easily he'd come to forgive her, and he sure as hell didn't like the way he yearned for her, even now. "Even before I knew about Taylor, I wanted to see you again."

"Of course you did. I slept with you after only knowing you an hour."

"Are you talking about when we made love?"

"Sex," she said calmly enough, but the words came out her teeth. "We had sex."

"That's not how I remember it." He smiled wickedly, figuring her imagination could taunt her with exactly what he was remembering. It would serve her right, since he'd been doing nothing *but* remembering.

"I acted cheaply. I don't like thinking about it."

"Cheap?" he asked incredulously, oddly hurt. "That's the *last* thing that comes to my mind when I think of that day." She turned away but he took her arms, forcing her to look at him. "God, Amber, we were terrified. We thought we were going to die. We needed to feel hope. We needed to feel alive, and we did, in each other's arms. How could you have forgotten all that?"

She might have pushed away, but he held her still. "No, listen to me." Somehow it had become critical to him that she not regret what they'd shared. "You didn't betray yourself that day, it just happened. And it was…right. *Very* right, dammit."

Her tortured look faded somewhat. "It gave me Taylor," she said quietly.

"It gave *us* Taylor," he corrected. "And I'll never forget it."

They stared at each other, so close that he could have leaned forward a fraction and kissed her soft, very kissable lips, but he didn't. Much as his body ached for hers, she'd burned him before, and he wasn't interested in getting burned again. "And as for tonight. You're not taking advantage, I offered. I'll even bring dinner."

"Why?"

"You know, all that mistrust is getting really old."

"I'm not mistrustful."

He laughed. "Granted, it's well hidden behind that sophisticated, sleek business front, but it's there."

"Why are you bringing me dinner?"

"See? Right there. Mistrust."

She rolled her eyes.

"I'm bringing dinner because I'll be hungry."

"Oh." She thought about it and started to give him a suspicious look, which she quickly squelched. "I suppose that would be all right."

"Good." He'd have shown up whether she liked it or not. If he knew his little daughter, and he was beginning to know her quite well, he figured Amber hadn't had a hot meal or a decent night's sleep in over three months. That was going to change.

"Go on," he said, pulling her up, nudging her to the door. "We'll see you later." Then he ushered her out before she could gather her wits to resist, which he knew she would have done if she hadn't been dead on her feet.

When she was gone, Dax turned to Taylor, hands on hips, a mock frown on his face. "You've been tiring out your parents," he said, picking her up and holding her close.

Taylor gummed a wet smile.

"It's got to stop. You hear me?"

She let out a sweet little giggle.

Dax kissed her noisily, making her wriggle with delight, which in turn warmed his heart in ways he'd never imagined.

He couldn't fathom being without her.

He was beginning to understand he felt the same way about her mother.

DAX ARRIVED AT Amber's condo at exactly 7:07 p.m. with Taylor in one arm and dinner in the other. Not that Amber had been pacing, watching the clock for the past hour and a half.

She reached for Taylor and squeezed her so tight the baby mewled in protest. Amber couldn't help herself; she'd missed Taylor so much. She kissed the baby's nose and then her face, and then nearly leaped out of her skin at the sexy, unbearably familiar voice behind her.

"I'll take one of those."

Slowly, she turned. "You'll take one of what?"

"A kiss."

Her tummy fluttered. "Hmph."

He grinned, and the butterflies in her stomach took wing. What was it about him? He should have hated her. Or at the very least, still been furious. That he wasn't, and that he looked at her in a way that both confused her and made her...hot, was greatly disturbing.

"Hungry?" he asked, lifting a bag from a local deli.

"It's my father's birthday," she said slowly, her mouth watering at the smell coming from the brown bag. "I was going to call him."

"Call him. See if he'll join us."

He wouldn't, Amber knew that. But she found

she couldn't admit any such thing to Dax. So, as he watched her with that quiet intensity of his, she picked up the phone and dialed the number.

"Hello, Dad," she said calmly when her father answered, as if her heart hadn't leaped into her throat at the sound of his voice after so long. "I wanted to wish you happy birthday."

Her voice was steady. Steady was important, even if she was so nervous she felt as though she might shatter at any moment. "I was also hoping you'd come for dinner and meet your granddaughter."

"Not likely," came the voice that had ruled her childhood. "Not when her mother is a slut."

Dax moved closer, but she held the phone tight to her ear so he couldn't hear. "I'm sorry you're still upset with me, but there's no need for it." She hesitated, then said softly, "I'm not like Mom. Really, I'm not."

"Did you marry that baby's father?"

"M-marry?" She glanced at Dax over her shoulder and found him still looking right at her. "Uh…no." With a carefully blank face, she pointed to the living room, gesturing him away. Anywhere, as long as he was far from her and this conversation.

Dax just settled back and lifted a brow.

With a sound of impatience, Amber covered the phone. "Go," she whispered.

"Maybe *I* should have extended the invite," he murmured. And then he grabbed the phone right out of her hands.

"Give that back!"

"Not yet." He held the phone out of her reach before bringing the receiver to his ear. He had to use his other hand to hold Amber off, but he did so with no problem, slipping one strong, warm arm around her. His forearm banded across her back, his fingers came to just above her rib cage, holding her stronger than a vise.

All she could think was that his fingers were pressed against the curve of her breast. Unbelievably, because she hated being restrained, her nipples tightened. Her breath quickened.

As if he could tell, Dax looked down into her face, his own breath coming a little faster.

"Give me the phone, Dax," she murmured.

His fingers spread wide and brushed the underside of her left breast.

She melted a little. *"Now."*

He shook his head. "Hello," he said politely into the phone, his fingers driving her to distraction. "I'm Daxton McCall, Taylor's father."

Amber groaned. Her father had never approved of her, and this wasn't going to help. He was convinced she led a wild, out-of-control lifestyle, and very likely, this conversation would confirm it.

She shouldn't care that she disappointed him, but she did, and still, to this day, wished she could make everything right, wished that her father missed his own flesh and blood the way she missed having a family.

"I'm taking full responsibility for Taylor," Dax said into the phone. "Any questions?" He continued to smile in that easygoing manner as he ruined her life, but Amber could see there was steel lining that smile and he was not kidding around. Dax was deadly serious and more than a little dangerous looking.

"We'd love you to join us tonight," he said. "Oh, you can't? Then how about you and I meet tomorrow, for lunch. I'm in the inspection office, downtown fire station. Yes. You can express all your anger and disappointment, and you can do it with me. Not Amber. Okay? See you then."

Amber gaped at him as he hung up.

"I hate bullies," he said conversationally.

Too late, Amber remembered she didn't gape as a rule. It was, however, much more of a struggle to control herself than usual. She was discovering that was the norm with Dax. "I can't believe he wants to meet you."

"Well he really wants to punch me in the nose, but he'll settle for a good look at me. I'm going to give it to him."

"He was…nice?"

"Let's say he was polite." He smiled. "Definitely curious."

In less than two minutes Dax had gotten the approval from her father that she'd been fighting for all her life.

It was deflating, depressing and demoralizing, not to mention infuriating.

"Amber?"

She was perfectly aware that her fury was illogical, that she was about to direct it toward the wrong person, but she couldn't help herself. "I want you to go now."

"What?" He looked so stunned she nearly laughed, but this wasn't a laughing matter. *"Why?"*

"I realize you probably don't get a lot of rejections. Consider this a learning experience."

"Amber, listen to me." He took her shoulders in his big hands to see that she did just that. "I can see that you care what he thinks—"

"I don't."

"Of course you do, it's natural." His understanding and compassion were far more than she could take at the moment, but he wouldn't let her move away from him. "I don't want to cause you any grief. That's why I'm going to meet him, to take some of the pressure off of you."

Couldn't he see that just having him in her life was causing grief? Couldn't he see that she needed him to leave, now, before she did something really stupid? Like crying on his broad, capable, oh-so-comfy shoulder? She was alone in this. She *wanted* to be alone in this. "I'm really tired."

"Oh, baby, I know that one." His smile was warm, sweet, caring. And when he slid his fingers over her cheek as if she was the most important person in his world, her throat burned.

"Why are you doing this? Being nice?"

"Because…" He lifted a shoulder. "It's better than harboring resentment. It feels good. Because I want to. Pick one."

"But—"

"Amber, don't you ever get tired of fighting it?"

"It?"

"It." He stroked her jaw with his thumb, then touched the racing pulse at the base of her throat. "This."

"I...don't know what you're talking about."

His gaze took a leisurely sweep over her body, ending at the straining button between her breasts. On either side, her hard, aching nipples pressed against the material of her blouse. He seemed fascinated by the play of his fingers over her collarbone. "Don't you?" he murmured. "Don't deny it, I can see that you do."

With a huff of vexation, she crossed her arms. "I can't help that."

"I'm glad." His smoldering eyes met hers now. "I'm glad you can't control the attraction between the two of us, it's the only way I know I'm reaching you at all."

To hell with control and finesse. To hell with appearances. Screw all of it, she needed him gone, now, before she made a complete fool of herself and tore her clothes off, and then his. She marched to the front door and opened it. "Good night, Dax."

He frowned, though whether at her husky voice or her abruptness, she didn't know.

"Look, it's nothing personal," she assured him. "It's just that I've had enough of men running my life, manipulating me, and deciding what's right for me."

He went very still. "And you think that's what I'm doing?"

"Aren't you? You want me to share Taylor—"

"She's mine, too, Amber. Get it through that pretty, thick head of yours." He cupped her face in his hands, tipping it up to meet his intense gaze. His fingers on her skin made her knees knock together. So did looking at his lips and she wondered, totally inappropriately, if he kissed her now, would she melt as she had a year ago?

Probably.

Definitely.

Which was another reason to get him out of here, quickly. But he wasn't budging, his big body was a stubborn brick wall she couldn't move.

"I hate it that you shy away from me, from the connection between us," he said.

She swallowed at the real glimpse of pain she saw in his eyes. Dammit, did he have to be so sensitive, so open and warm, so…perfect? "I don't feel any particular connection."

He set his hand to the base of her throat, let his fingers once again slide against the skin where her pulse beat wildly. "Liar," he chided softly.

"Good night, Dax."

He stared at her for one long moment, then walked to the door.

A small voice inside her head told her he was right. She *was* a liar. She *wanted* him to stay, *wanted* him to seduce her.

Or maybe *she'd* seduce *him.* It was mortifying to

realize how close she was to letting her hormones run her, just as her mother had.

"You'll dream of me," he said.

She had a feeling he was right, but she shut the door and bolted it. Then she stood there for a moment, touching the door as if it were him.

Her body sizzled. *Sizzled.* A mother wasn't supposed to sizzle! She didn't want this. It would never work, not under these circumstances, not under the *best* of circumstances. Still, she nearly whipped the front door open again.

Instead, she went into the kitchen and ate as if she was still pregnant, refusing to feel guilty for eating a good portion of Dax's food, too.

Later, after she took care of Taylor, she went to bed and tried to forget how fiercely Dax had defended her to her father. Tried to forget how good it had felt, for that one little second, to depend on someone other than herself.

And damn him, just like he'd said, she dreamed of him.

CHAPTER SEVEN

AMBER WOKE UP rumpled, still exhausted and haunted by visions of a starving Dax.

In the light of day she had to laugh at herself. So she'd eaten his dinner. He was a pretty capable guy, certainly he'd managed.

She got out of bed and checked on Taylor, who was still fast asleep. Grateful, she took the baby monitor and headed for the shower. Afterward, warm and steamy and still wet, she caught a glimpse of herself in the mirror. It was rare to spend any time really looking at herself, especially naked, but she looked now.

Somehow, when she hadn't been paying attention, she'd lost most of the baby fat she'd accumulated during her pregnancy. Still, her hips were fuller. Her belly was no longer concave, but softly rounded. And her breasts…they weren't the simple, unobtrusive A-cup they'd always been, but two full sizes larger. Just looking at them made her wonder.

What did Dax think of her body now?

Even as she thought it, she blushed. She knew he saw *something* he liked, because whenever she looked at him unexpectedly, she caught him watching her with a wild, hot intensity that made her hot right back. She tried to pretend she didn't notice, but in the deep of the night she often thought about what they did to each other.

She'd been rude to him last night, inexcusably rude. He had no idea why, couldn't possibly understand how she was letting her past guide her. For most of her childhood, she'd blindly obeyed her father. She'd followed orders, squelched her need for a feminine role model and had done whatever it took to please the man.

Opinions hadn't been encouraged.

As a result, she was naturally inhibited. Being quiet and unobtrusive had been necessary for survival, as had keeping thoughts and emotions to herself. They were habits she'd carried into adulthood.

Now she was fiercely independent, and she liked it that way. Few, if any, had penetrated her protective shell.

Dax had, though, and it was scary stuff.

She dressed, then took Taylor next door to her baby-sitter, Mrs. Chapman. The woman was sixty-five and spry as a woman half her age, even if she spent her days wearing formal velvet dresses and watching soap operas. She loved Taylor with all her heart, which was enough for Amber.

On the drive to Dax's office, Amber practiced her breathing techniques and concentrated hard on calm images, but all she could think about was that one day they'd spent together, so long ago.

He would have done anything to protect her that

day, and so far she'd paid him back by hiding his daughter from him and being as rude and hard to be with as possible. Something had to give, and she wasn't sure it could be her. But she had to try.

She was climbing the steps of the station, her apology on her lips, picturing a miserable and hungry Dax, when he came out.

He had a woman on each arm, and he was smiling—*grinning* actually—looking happy, confident, strikingly handsome and not even remotely miserable.

The bastard. The least he could have done was to look hungry.

The women were smiling, too, also looking happy, confident and strikingly handsome.

Any urge to apologize vaporized.

Wishing she could disappear into a great big black hole, Amber faltered, but of course it was too late to run. She was out in the open, only a few steps below them. Any second, he was going to notice her.

If he ever took his eyes off the other women, that is.

"Oh Dax," simpered the tall, thin, gorgeous blonde on his left. "This has been a long time coming."

"I know. You've been so patient." Dax smiled into her eyes. "Work's been a bear."

"All I want to know is, are you going to make the wait worthwhile?" The redhead on his right lifted a suggestive brow, making promises with her eyes that made Amber roll hers.

"Absolutely," Dax told her, still smiling.

"Good. Because..." The blonde leaned close and whispered something in his ear.

His eyebrows shot straight up.

"No secrets," pouted the redhead, pressing her lush curves against Dax.

He smiled at her, too, his eyes heavy and slumberous.

Amber gritted her teeth. They were almost on top of her now, and he was so busy with bimbette-one and bimbette-two that he hadn't even seen her! *This* was the man she pictured as miserable all night because of her rudeness? *Ha!*

Since she couldn't disappear into thin air, she would have to handle this as she would any uncomfortable situation, with her famed, icy control. "Good morning, Dax," she said, ever so proud of her cool voice. She only hoped he couldn't see the steam coming out of her ears.

"Amber." He stopped short, clearly surprised. "Hello."

Amber didn't want to think about how his smile suddenly warmed, or how this time it reached his eyes. No, she didn't want to think about that, or she'd lose her anger. Anger was good here, anger would get her through. "You look awfully busy this morning."

He dropped his hold on his playmates and looked suddenly panicked. "*Taylor.* There's nothing wrong with her..."

Well darn if that fierce worry in his expression didn't defuse a good part of her temper. "No, Taylor is fine." But since she wouldn't apologize now, she needed another reason for her appearance. Frantically she searched her mind and came up with… nothing. "I was just out for a walk and thought I'd say hello. So…hello." Forcing a smile, she turned away.

"Wait."

She didn't, couldn't.

"Amber?"

She couldn't get away fast enough, and behind her, she heard him swear.

"Amber, wait—"

Then he was there, alone, taking her arm and turning her back to face him. "Just out for a walk?" He shook his head. "Come on, Amber. What's this really about?"

For some idiotic reason, her throat closed. "I told you. I'm just walking."

He shot a doubtful look at her heels. "In those?"

Cool. Calm. That was the ticket. "Are my shoes a problem for you?"

"Not for me." He smiled angelically. "That's a pretty suit."

"Thank you."

"Personally, that short skirt could quickly become a favorite of mine, but it seems a waste to exercise in it."

Dignity, she reminded herself. *Keep it.* "I always walk before work. It's terrific exercise."

His look was long and knowing. "This place is at least twelve miles from your place."

"I'm in excellent shape." She glanced at the

women still waiting for Dax. They had rich curves and fabulous bodies, and she found her temper again. "For a woman who's just had a baby, anyway."

"That you most definitely are." He ran a finger over her perfectly-in-place hair. "You sure look great for someone who's walked so far. Oh, and look at that…" He gestured to her car, parked on the street only fifteen feet away. "How in the world did *that* get here? Don't tell me it's trained to follow you on your morning constitutional."

"Very funny."

He grinned. She should have known better. For whatever reason, there was no controlling herself around him. "Glad I'm such a source of amusement for you. I have to go now."

"Like you did last night?"

Last night. The reason she'd come. "I'll talk to you later." No way was she going to apologize in front of an audience. "When you're not so…busy."

It was as if he could see right through her. "I'm not too busy for you." He reached for her hand. His voice was low so that only she could hear it. Only problem, the exciting, rough timbre of it sent tingles down her spine. "What's the matter, Amber? Can't you tell me?"

It was hard, she discovered, to feel his hands on her. She liked the warmth in them too much. Liked how important she felt. How special.

That she could actually let herself depend on that warmth and strength scared her.

He scared her.

Then she remembered the women. "You visiting with your sisters?" she asked casually, not wanting to publicly misjudge him again, as she had in the medical center.

Was that a flash of guilt that crossed his face as he glanced at them over his shoulder? "Ah…no. Not today."

Okay, then. "Gotta go."

"Wait—"

But she couldn't, she just couldn't.

DAX WATCHED AMBER ESCAPE. His obligation, in the form of four fine legs behind him, burned. Not that Amber would have believed him if he'd told her.

Hell, half of the people he knew wouldn't believe him.

He glanced over his shoulder at the two women. In response, they both waved and giggled. Skin shimmered. Breasts jiggled.

Dax groaned, but the decision was actually easy. He raced after Amber, catching her just as she unlocked her car.

"Amber."

She glared at him.

"Come on, baby—"

She went rigid. "I am most definitely not your *baby*. Check with the two women waiting for you. I'm sure either of them would swoon at the opportunity to be called by such an endearing term."

He had no idea why he found her stiff unyielding attitude so wildly appealing, or why he suddenly felt like grinning. "Just listen to me, that's all I'm asking."

"I'm in a hurry."

Oh yeah, she was in a hurry. But *she'd* come to *him*. And he wanted to know why. "Please?" He risked touching her again, running his fingers up and down her arm. He couldn't seem to help himself, he had to have that connection.

She went completely still. Nothing gave her away, but he just *knew* she responded to his touch. He looked into her inscrutable face and wished she'd show him how she really felt, wished he didn't have to guess. "About the women…"

"Uh-huh."

"I know what you're probably thinking."

"I doubt it." She sighed. "Dax, really. You don't have to explain why you're going on a date, much less why you're doing it in the morning, with *two* women. It's none of my business."

"It's not a date."

The two women, apparently tired of waiting, came down the stairs. The redhead smiled at Amber. "We won him in an auction." She smiled wickedly. "He's ours for the rest of the day."

"It's true." The blonde smiled, almost licking her lips in anticipation. "We can do whatever we want with him, we were promised."

Together, they grinned.

Unbelievably, Dax felt himself blush. "The auction was a long time ago," he said quickly. "And I've been too busy to meet my obligation—" This wasn't going well, he could tell by the ice in Amber's gaze. "It was to raise money for the fire stations on the west side," he added. "All the guys did it."

"But you brought in the most money," the redhead added helpfully.

"Did he now?" Amber asked coolly.

"Uh… Ladies, I'll be with you in just a moment, okay?"

Thank God they took the hint and backed off, giving him and Amber some desperately needed privacy. Only problem, he didn't have a clue as to what to say.

Amber slid on a pair of mirrored sunglasses and got into her car. "Sounds like you're in for quite a day, Dax. I'd say be good, but I already know you will be."

SOMEHOW DAX MANAGED to escape Ginger and Cici's clutches relatively unscathed. It was mid-day by the time he did it, though. Ignoring his stacked messages and overworked secretary, he drove straight to Amber's office.

He couldn't explain his urgency or why, for the first time in the ten years he'd been participating in the bachelor auction fund-raiser, he resented the time he'd spent. All day he'd yearned to be somewhere else.

He'd wanted to be with Taylor. And okay, maybe with Amber, too, but that made no sense. Still, he couldn't get to her office fast enough, couldn't wait to try to soothe her ruffled feathers. And her feathers had most definitely been ruffled, whether she admitted it or not.

Suddenly that thought made him grin, and he loped up the stairs to the building where she worked.

Amber's secretary explained she was in a meeting and couldn't be disturbed. Dax gave her his most charming smile, but she didn't budge. Around him, the office buzzed with new listings, new sales and the general excitement of a place on the move.

Dax waited until the secretary picked up a phone before he simply strode past her desk toward Amber's closed door.

"Hey," the woman called out, "you can't just—"

Dax let himself into Amber's office and carefully shut the door on her secretary's protests.

Amber was behind her desk, a pair of reading glasses perched on her nose, a pencil in her mouth, a phone to her ear. Her eyes were even, her hands steady, her every hair in place. She'd shed the power jacket, but the white blouse she wore was wrinkle-free, prim and proper.

Somewhere beneath that icy control lay the passion he remembered so well. He'd caught a tiny glimpse of it that morning, behind her cool facade. She'd been mad as hell at him, and mad as hell at herself for feeling that emotion in the first place.

Dax grinned again.

At the sight of him, her carefully painted mouth tightened, but that was the only outward sign he received. She didn't rush, and when she was done with her phone call, she slowly set down her pencil, removed her glasses and looked at him. "Back so soon?" Her voice was smooth and very polite. "I would have thought Barbie and Sunshine would keep you tied up for hours."

"Ginger and Cici," he corrected. "And though they were very…persuasive, I managed to escape."

"Hmmm." She bent to her work, but her knuckles went white on the pencil she gripped. "I bet."

"And how was your day?" he inquired conversationally, sitting uninvited on a chair in front of her desk.

"Busy." She glanced at him pointedly. "Still is."

Ah, the cold shoulder. "You probably didn't miss me one little bit, did you?"

"Not one little bit," she agreed.

He couldn't help it, he laughed.

Her eyes chilled several degrees. "If you don't mind…"

"Amber." He controlled himself, but the smile remained. "Admit it, you're jealous as hell."

Aghast, she stared at him. "You've been drinking."

"I don't drink."

"Then you're delusional." She leaned forward. "Just so you know, I never get jealous. Certainly not over a nitwit who enjoys dating brainless—"

"Careful," he said, laughing again. "You might prove my point."

She was still for a long beat. Then regally she rose and pointed an elegant finger at the door. "I think you should leave."

"So you can recapture that famous control?" He rose, too, and came around her desk. "I don't think so. Watching your temper rise is fascinating, Amber. In fact, *everything* about you is fascinating."

She shook her head, her composure slipping enough to show her genuine confusion. "I don't know what you want from me."

"Lots. But I'll start with this." He hauled her into his arms and kissed her. It was a stupid move, uncalculated as it was genuine, but he didn't stop.

She went still as stone, but didn't push him away. Taking that for permission, he dove into her sweet mouth, mating his tongue to hers, giving, urging, pouring everything he had into that kiss until he felt her hands open on his shoulders, then grab fistfuls of his shirt.

"Yeah, now *that's* what I've wanted all damn day," he whispered. "That and this…" He kissed her again, his hands gripping her hips, pulling her closer, then closer still.

With a little murmur of acquiescence that made him even hotter, she wrapped her arms around his neck and kissed him back until he couldn't remember his name, much less his point.

When the kiss ended, he murmured in her ear.

"The women meant nothing to me," he said. "It was an obligation, one I made months ago." Lifting his head, he looked into her eyes. "They paid big bucks. Money that will be well spent." He kissed her again. The helpless sounds of arousal she made were the most erotic he'd ever heard. "Be jealous,

Amber. Wish you could take their place if you want. Kiss me stupid again if it helps. But please, don't be mad at me anymore."

She touched her wet mouth, looking shell-shocked, as if she couldn't believe how she'd lost herself. "I'm not angry," she whispered and sank into her chair. "I need to work now."

She needed to think, he realized, and he would let her because that was how she worked, and he didn't intend to rush her.

Hell, he didn't want to rush himself.

Leaning in close, he gave her one last kiss, pleased to feel her cling to him for just a second.

He was half out of her office when she called him. Turning, he looked at her over his shoulder.

"I wasn't jealous," she told him. "Much." Her mouth curved as she offered him a smile, and Dax felt the weight of the world lift off his shoulders.

CHAPTER EIGHT

THAT NIGHT, ARMS FULL of her briefcase, a diaper bag, dinner and Taylor, Amber let herself into her condo. Her feet were killing her and so was the whirlwind her life had become.

Going back to work had been good for her self-esteem because she was still good at it. She needed the money, too, having depleted her savings over the past year in Mexico. But balancing her wild hours with her newfound motherhood was much tougher than she could have imagined.

Naturally, before she could set a thing down, the phone rang. Dropping her purse and dinner to the counter, she freed up a hand to grab it.

"Let's start all over."

The low, sexy voice liquefied her bones. "Excuse me?"

"I want to start over," Dax said.

Amber settled the phone between her jaw and shoulder, and kicked off her heels. "From where?"

"From the beginning, but I'd settle for the night I brought you dinner. Was it good by the way?"

Amber placed Taylor in her swing. Her jacket hit a chair and relieved of all her weight, she sagged against the counter. "I suppose I should apologize for that. But yes, it was good." She paused. "So was yours."

Dax laughed softly and the sound vibrated through her body, pooling in certain erogenous spots she rarely thought about.

"I like a woman with a healthy appetite."

She thought about the smile she could hear in his voice and wondered if all the women he rescued fell for him. Probably, she admitted.

But she was above such things.

"How was lunch with my father?" she asked, purposely hardening herself. "I never got to ask you."

"Your father is a single-minded, opinionated, walking, talking ego."

"Tell me something I don't know."

"Okay... You care what he thinks of you."

How was it that he went directly to the heart of the matter every time? And how was it that she let him?

"He's also stubborn as hell," he said. "Just like his daughter."

Amber laughed, then shook her head at herself. Distance, she reminded herself. She needed to keep her distance.

Never an easy thing with this man.

She set a sleepy Taylor in motion by gently pushing the swing. "Is this why you called, to list my failings?"

"I grew up with five sisters, I know better than to list a woman's failings. But I could give you a full list of your positive attributes if you'd like. I have a most excellent memory."

Her breath caught. Laughter faded, replaced by a needy emptiness she didn't want to face. "It was a long time ago. It's best forgotten."

"I'll never forget."

Her hand stilled on Taylor's swing. "You think about sex far too much."

"Well I'm red-blooded, aren't I?"

"Yeah." He most definitely was.

"But I've told you, it was far more than just sex. Let me prove it to you."

His voice alone could convince her. She could only be thankful he wasn't here in person to add his smile, his eyes, his incredible hands to the magic.

With a sigh, she set a kettle of water on the stove. She needed tea, her own personal comfort drink. "What did you want, Dax?"

"To talk."

About their kiss? About the fact she'd nearly let it go much further than a kiss? "About?" she asked cautiously.

"Lots of stuff."

Could he really have called just to talk? With her?

"But let's start with your father."

Her stomach clenched. Of course not.

"He'd like to see Taylor sometime. I told him that was entirely up to you."

"I've offered to take her to him before," she said coolly.

"He wasn't ready. He is now."

"I suspect you had a great deal to do with that."

"I thought you'd be happy."

She *should* be, should also be grateful, but instead she only resented the fact that Dax had accomplished overnight what she hadn't been able to do it in a year's time. "I'll think about it," she said, knowing she sounded prim, polite. Difficult.

"Fair enough," he said, accepting her answer so quickly she felt suspicious.

With good reason.

"I have another favor. This one's a toughie."

She'd nearly forgotten to be leery of him! How had he done this to her, gotten her to actually almost *trust* him? "I don't care to be pushed into a decision about seeing my father."

"My favor has nothing to do with your father. I wanted you and Taylor to come with me to a barbecue tomorrow night. At my parents."

She blinked and drew a careful breath as her brain struggled to shift gears. "Why?"

"I don't know, maybe because you're the mother of my child?" He laughed at her silence. "It's not a death sentence. You go, you eat, you smile, you laugh— Wait…it doesn't hurt you to laugh, does it?"

"Sometimes." But she did it anyway as she sat at her table. "I'm sorry. I thought…well, never mind."

"You thought I was going to railroad you into doing something you don't want to do."

Yes.

"For the record," he said, his voice solemn now. "I would never, *never,* do that."

"Never is a long time, Dax."

"Yes."

"What will happen if we disagree about something?"

"What do you mean?"

She bounced up again, stalked the length of her kitchen. "You'll expect me to do things your way."

"Haven't you ever heard of give-and-take?"

"You expect me to believe you'll let me do things my way?"

"Yes! Look, I know I don't hold back much. I have a wide range of emotions, and I'm afraid I have a temper, too." His voice gentled, became disturbingly intimate. "But I'd never hurt you, Amber. It's not a stretch for me to make that promise. It shouldn't be a stretch for *anyone* to make you that promise."

"Yeah well, you'd be surprised."

"I wish we were having this conversation in person. So that I could touch you while I tell you all this."

Heat, the kind he always seemed to cause within her, warmed her from head to toe. "That's… probably not wise."

"When I touch you, you let down that guard. When I kiss you, you let go even more. You let me see the *real* you."

She took a deep breath because suddenly she couldn't seem to get enough air, but the yearning deep inside her didn't fade.

"I like that real you, Amber."

She let out a disparaging sound and sat down again. "I never know what to say to you."

"Say you believe me. That you believe in us."

"There is no us."

As if he heard her panic, he softened his voice even more. "Us as in Taylor's parents."

"That's all."

"That's the most important," he agreed. "For now. You and Taylor, you can depend on me, Amber. That's a promise, and I've never broken one yet."

No one had ever made her a promise and kept it.

"What do you think, Amber? Can I pick you and Taylor up tomorrow night. At six? You'll have a great time."

"Another promise."

"Absolutely."

She swallowed hard, fighting her vulnerability with every ounce of strength she possessed. It helped to glance over and see Taylor sleeping peacefully. Happy and content. "Tomorrow, then," she whispered, and hung up before Dax could question the quiver in her voice.

Drawing in a deep, cleansing breath, Amber beat back her emotions. It was a lifelong habit.

Then she fought her fears the best way she knew how, with food. Lots of it.

THE NEXT NIGHT, at nearly six o'clock, Amber stood in a bra and panties contemplating her closet. She'd been looking at her wardrobe for an embarrassing hour now. "A barbecue," she muttered.

What did one wear to such an event?

Jeans, she decided, with a shrug that would have told anyone watching that she couldn't care less.

But she *did* care, too much. She wanted to look good for a man she hadn't wholly decided to let herself care for.

She slipped into the jeans and stared at herself. They were too tight, thanks to her just-given-birth-three-months-ago body, but she didn't own a larger size.

Fine, so she wouldn't wear jeans. With another shrug, she yanked them off. But her khakis had some sort of stain on them, one that could be directly related to Taylor. Her wool trousers were far too dressy.

Dressy, she could have handled. But this was a family party. Silk and stockings weren't required.

And wasn't that just the problem?

She tossed her wool trousers over her shoulder to join her other discarded clothing on the floor and stood in front of the mirror. "It's not the clothes," she admitted out loud. It was the evening ahead that had her nerves in a riot.

There.

She'd admitted it.

Her bout of anxiety had nothing to do with *where* she was going, it was *who* she was going with.

Dax did this to her, damn him, caused this butterfly dance low in her belly. "And the mess in this room is his fault, too," she decided, looking around at the cyclone she'd wrought. Nearly everything she owned was in a pile on the floor.

The doorbell rang.

She froze. "Oh my God." Galvanized into action, she threw on a denim skirt and shoved her arms into a white button-up, long-sleeved shirt. Last minute panic time was over. She'd have to make do as she was.

Her usually perfectly groomed hair was wild. So were her dark eyes. She had no idea where the flush on her cheeks came from, but it made her look… young. *Too* young.

And the shirt, good Lord. White had not been the wisest choice, only emphasizing her new bra size.

The doorbell rang again and she dashed out of her room, past the second bedroom where Taylor lay sleeping and down the hall.

Her heart was pounding.

No rush, she told herself, and purposely stopped to draw in a deep, calming breath. She was fine.

Just fine.

When she believed it, when she had some semblance of calm, she opened the door.

And immediately lost it again.

Dax was leaning against the jamb, looking shockingly desirable. He wore jeans and a long-sleeved shirt the exact color of his baby blue eyes.

Those eyes smiled into hers as he leaned close, and any semblance of calm flew right out the window. His scent assaulted her; clean, woodsy, and all male. Then her breath backed up in her throat because he was so close she almost—*almost*—tipped toward him.

She wanted a kiss.

Startled, she just looked at him, specifically at that mouth that she knew could drive her crazy. No. No kiss, she decided hastily. She couldn't handle it, not now, not when her control was already long gone.

"Hey," he said, moving even closer, and her heart stumbled. His sleepy, heavy-lidded eyes met hers for one long, silent moment.

Please, was her only, suddenly shocking thought. *Kiss me.*

As if he could hear her, his long lashes lowered over his eyes, his mouth brushed her jaw.

Yes, *yes,* he was going to do it, thank God, for she wanted that with every fiber of her being. Forget control, forget distance, she wanted his kiss. *Now.*

Softly, gently, his lips slid over her cheek, nipped at her throat and then…he straightened away from her. "You're here. I thought maybe you'd changed your mind."

"No." She had to clear her throat. "I'm ready. I… just need to get Taylor."

His grin was more than a little wicked. "You're happy to see me."

She managed a laugh. "Not really."

"Another lie." He tsked. "Santa's going to take you off his list." Then he smiled slow and sure. "You wanted me to kiss you."

"In your dreams."

His laugh was just as wicked as his grin. "Oh, you're most definitely in my dreams."

His eyes were so hot, so sure and knowing, she swallowed hard. "I'll get Taylor."

His gaze dipped down to her mouth, then further still, slowly running over her body in a way that might have, if she'd been a weaker woman, left her legs wobbly.

She locked her knees just in case.

"I've never seen you in anything other than a power suit," he said huskily. "I like the change."

She resisted, barely, the urge to tug at her snug shirt.

He reached for her hand. "You know, I'm beginning to think I'm getting the hang of reading your eyes. They're so expressive they give you away, especially right now."

Could he see then, how uncomfortable she was? How self-conscious?

"You look beautiful, Amber," he said, his gaze directly on hers.

Yes, apparently he could.

"I mean it," he said silkily, and for once, she believed him.

THE MCCALL HOUSE was packed with smiling, laughing, talking people, not to mention barking dogs and a blaring stereo. Halfway up the walk, Amber faltered. If this had been a business gathering, she would have known exactly what to do and how to act.

But this wasn't a work function. This wasn't a required cocktail party or fund-raiser. It was supposed to be fun.

She didn't do fun very well.

She'd counted on using Taylor as a shield, but Dax had the baby secure in his arms, and she looked so content Amber had little choice but to leave her there.

Through the opened gate to the backyard the party looked to be in full swing. Couples danced, kids played, people talked. Everywhere.

Amber just stared at what seemed like a sea of hundreds, all happy and comfortable and having a good time. "Are *all* these people your family?"

"And friends."

"It's…" *Loud,* came to mind, but that seemed rude. Yet she was incapable of coming up with a proper white lie since her stomach was suddenly in her throat. "Different."

"I should tell you now, my family is bossy, nosy and opinionated."

Gee, there was a surprise. "I'm sure I can handle it." But she wasn't sure at all. She had no experience with large families, no experience with families period.

Dax looked at the hand she'd unconsciously placed on her jittery stomach, and placed his own over hers. "They're going to love you, Amber. They're just going to be loud and nosy about it."

The very idea of perfect strangers falling in love with her was as ridiculous as…well, as being at this party.

"They will." He smiled, that special one he seemed to hold in reserve just for her. "Ready?"

"Yes. No. Yes. God. I don't know." It *was* the twenty-first century, but having a child out of wedlock didn't feel like something to be particularly proud of, no matter what the circumstances.

Would they resent her?

Think that she'd trapped Dax on purpose?

Why had she agreed to this?

"I have no idea what's running through that head of yours," Dax said with a low laugh. "But I promise it isn't going to be half as bad as whatever you're thinking."

"Okay." She straightened her shoulders resolutely. "Let's do it."

Laughing again, Dax shook his head. "It's not a firing squad, either. It's going to be fun." A sigh escaped him when none of the tension left her. "Come on, I can see you're not going to relax until we get it over with."

With Taylor snug and happy in one arm, and his other hand firmly holding hers, he drew them into the fray.

They were immediately surrounded.

"Dax! Let me have that baby!" The woman Amber recognized as Suzette pushed her way to the front and took Taylor into her arms. "Oh, she's beautiful!" She turned a smile on Amber. "Nice to see you again, we're so glad you could come. Dax has told us all about you."

Amber shot a look at Dax, wondering what exactly he'd told them about her.

He just lifted a brow and smiled, leaving her clue-
less, which she was quite certain he knew she hated.

"Taylor is such a good baby." Suzette sighed
dreamily. "I can't wait to see mine." She patted her
huge belly. "If he or she ever decides to come on
out! I'm two weeks overdue now." She kissed Taylor's little nose.

Another woman pressed close, looking so much
like Suzette that Amber blinked.

"Hey there, Dax." The woman kissed him, then
leaned over Suzette and kissed Taylor, too. "Hey,
sweetie."

Taylor drooled her pleasure and let out her char-
acteristic squeal, which meant, "I like this! Gimme
more!"

Everyone laughed.

"Give her to me, Suzette," the new woman said.
"She likes me best anyway."

"This is Shelley," Dax informed Amber. "My oldest and most bossy sister."

"Honestly, Dax, you know perfectly well *I'm* the
bossy one." Another blond, beautiful woman pushed
her way through the crowd.

"Amy." Dax grinned and endured her bear hug
and loud smacking kiss right on the mouth. "And
you're right, it's a tie. Amber, this is Amy. The baby
of the clan."

"I'm not the baby, you are!" But she smiled widely
at Taylor, snatched Taylor from Shelley's arms and
reached out an arm to give Amber a brief hug. "Wonderful to meet you, welcome to the family."

Hopelessly awkward and yet unbearably touched at the same time, Amber's heart tied itself into knots. The strange tightness in her chest, the one she associated with Dax, was back. Actually, it hadn't left since she'd first seen him again.

Hormones, she told herself. That's all it was.

"Let me in, let me in!" The woman that pushed her way through this time had definitely been blond before the gray had taken over. She came only to Dax's chest, was twice as wide, and had a face filled with joy and excitement.

She went straight for Taylor. "Let me have that precious little bundle of love! Hand her over to grandma right this instant!"

"That 'precious little bundle' smells to high heaven," Dax warned as Taylor was passed yet again. "She needs to be changed."

"What, like I've never changed a diaper? Yours included."

"Just giving you fair warning, Mom."

"Hey there, precious," she cooed to Taylor, who all but soaked up the attention.

Then Dax's mother turned with an expectant smile to Amber.

"Amber, this is my mother," Dax said. "Emily McCall. And watch out, she's—"

"Happy to meet you," Emily interrupted smoothly. "My goodness, you're lovely! I hope you like meat, you're so thin for just having had a baby! Are you eating enough? *Thomas!*" she yelled, without waiting for an answer. She gestured wildly to the tall, darkly handsome man working the barbecue. "Thomas, get over here and meet the mother of your newest granddaughter. And bring a fully loaded plate!"

"Oh no, I couldn't—" Amber protested, only to be hushed by Emily.

Thomas arrived, carting food and a pleasant smile. "Hello."

Amber held out her hand. Thomas took it, and then gently drew her in for a warm hug. "Welcome," he said, in the same silky rough voice as his son.

He'd hugged her, was all Amber could think. As if she belonged to the family. The casual, easy, genuine affection startled her. She wanted to somehow savor it, and at the same time, wanted to run for the hills. Hard and fast. "Uh…I've got to—"

"Eat," Emily said smoothly, ignoring the panic that surely they all could see. "She's got to eat. And drink, too." She openly eyed Amber's breasts. "You *are* breast-feeding that baby I hope."

Heat raced over Amber's cheeks, but before she could reply, Dax broke in. "Mom. You promised."

"So I meddle," she said, tossing her hands up. "I can't help it, it's my job." Then she smiled so warmly, so openly that Amber never saw it coming. "You need some meat on those bones, girl. Never mind Thomas and Dax, I can't trust them to feed you right. Come with me."

At this, both Thomas and Dax grinned, and Amber couldn't help but imagine her own father, and what his reaction to this little, bossy, demanding, nosy, wonderful woman would be.

One thing she'd always secretly admired about her father was his strength. But at that moment, he would have looked at both Dax and Thomas, at the way they allowed Emily to run their lives, and he'd have instantly labeled them as weak, spineless and insignificant.

And yet nothing could have been further from the truth.

Dax and Thomas were confident, strong-willed men. And she knew exactly how stubborn Dax could be. She suspected his father was the same.

Neither man was weak, not by any means. She was beginning to think maybe it took more fortitude than weakness to allow all members of a family to be equal.

Emily smiled innocently as she continued to railroad Amber with all the subtlety of a bull in a china shop. "Are you drinking a full glass of water every hour?"

"Oh. Well, I—"

"Maybe you're working too hard. Are you managing to get enough sleep? A baby can be so hard on a mother."

"I told you she was nosy and bossy," Dax said over his mother's head.

"Hush you! I told you to scat." Emily kissed Taylor and passed her back to Dax. "So scat!" Then she took Amber's hand. "You come with me now, honey."

Short of being rude, Amber couldn't resist. She

shot a helpless glance over her shoulder at Dax, who just grinned.

No help there.

Then he was swallowed up by the crowd and Amber was left with the petite powerhouse that was Dax's mother.

CHAPTER NINE

AMBER WAS QUIET on the drive home, thinking about the glimpse she'd had into Dax's world.

She'd seen him playful and teasing with his nieces and nephews. Tolerant and protective of his sisters. Loving and warm with his parents.

Then, without warning, he'd cornered her in the foyer against a wall and had kissed her senseless. By the time he'd lifted his head, smiled wickedly and backed away, she'd nearly melted to the floor.

Who was this man, the one who could go from sweet and nurturing, to shatteringly erotic in a nanosecond? It was a sharp reminder of how different they were, for Amber couldn't imagine letting her emotions run her the way Dax did.

Inside her condo, Amber put a sleeping Taylor in her crib, then occupied herself starting a fire in the living room fireplace.

Dax waited until she had the flames flickering before he tugged her up, turning her around to face him. In an easy show of affection, he tucked a strand of hair behind her ear and smiled into her eyes. "Hey."

She tried to move back from him because being in

such proximity always made thinking difficult, but he held her in a gentle grip of steel. "Hey back," she said, trying to look as if being held by such a gorgeous man was an everyday occurrence.

"Talk to me, Amber."

"About?"

"You."

The way he looked at her, the way he spoke...as if she were the most important person in his life.... It took her breath away.

"You and your family," she said inanely. "You're very close."

"Yes. Very." He cocked his head and studied her. "Is that what's bothering you? That my family gets along?"

"You laugh, you fight, you..."

"*Love.* Is that it?"

He understood, she could hear it in his voice. Fearing his pity, she couldn't quite meet his gaze.

"I know your father isn't quite the same as mine," he said carefully.

"Nor was my mother the same as yours."

"You've not said much about her," he murmured, still close, still touching. Always touching.

"There's not much to say. She left when I was born." With long-practiced skill, she shrugged. It no longer mattered. It shouldn't matter.

"She missed raising a pretty wonderful daughter."

"I did fine without her."

His eyes were soft and unusually dark. "Yeah.

You did. But you shouldn't have had to. You should have had her to talk to, to hold you. To love you."

"Love wasn't a huge priority in my household."

"Another shame, but it's not yours." He lifted her face and studied her until she squirmed. "Are you listening, Amber? *Really* listening? I get the idea you somehow think it's your fault your parents are jerks."

"No, not jerks. My father never beat me, or forgot to feed me, or anything like that. He took care of me."

"So he gave you the basics. Big deal. Parenthood is a lot harder than that, and you know it. He failed you. Your mother failed you. Your fiancé failed you, and in a way, I've failed you by not being there when you needed me, when you were having Taylor."

"That was hardly your fault," she reminded him.

"Still, I won't fail you again."

He was deadly serious and more than a little intimidating. "I don't want to be a responsibility to you," she said slowly. "I won't have you come to resent me."

"Trust me," he murmured. "It's much more than that." His thumb brushed over her lower lip and when she shivered, his eyes darkened even more. "So you were alone for most of your life with a man who obviously hadn't a clue how to show his emotions. Do you have any idea how amazing your passion is, in spite of all that?"

She laughed, then stopped short when he didn't smile, just looked at her steadily. "I don't think of myself as particularly...passionate."

"No?" His gaze dropped, ran slowly over every inch of her, leaving a rising heat everywhere it touched. "You should."

"I'd like to think I'm not run by such an emotion."

"Ah, and I am." His lips quirked. "Is that it?"

Dammit, she was amusing him. She pushed at his hand, which was still on her face, but he merely tipped up her chin, his long, warm fingers scorching her skin. "Your father told me what he thought of your mother. How he was always afraid you'd be like her."

"I see. The two of you sat around and discussed me."

"You came up a few times."

When she took a step back, he followed, his big hands tender and gentle as he reached for her. "I'm on to you, you know."

She slapped his hands away and stepped back again. "I haven't a clue what you're talking about."

"You're not like her, Amber, you never could be."

Determined to avoid this, she took one more step and hit the wall. "No I'm not, because I'm so careful." *Usually.* "I've always been, but somehow, with you…" His hands caged her in, her breath backed up in her throat. "Somehow you make me forget to watch myself."

"Really? That's interesting." One of his hands slid down her side now, and since her shirt came to the waistband of her skirt and wasn't tucked in, his fingers slipped under and touched bare skin. "Always so in control." His thumb slid over her belly and she drew in a shaky breath. "And yet not with me. Could you have feelings for me then? Deep ones?" That hand danced around now to her back, and his thumb made a lazy circle very low on her spine, causing a shiver.

The flare of desire in his eyes didn't help. "Dax—"

Those magical fingers played lightly over her tingling flesh. She held her breath when he splayed his big, warm hand over her bottom, pressing her to him so that she could feel his erection.

"You don't want to feel anything for me," he said huskily. "But I feel something for you. Can you feel what I'm feeling, Amber?"

Oh yeah. He was huge, pulsing against her.

"Can you?"

"I…yes." Definitely yes.

"Today scared you."

She stared at him, and he stared back, achingly patient, silently demanding her honesty.

"A little, maybe. All of you. All that passion, all that wild jubilance."

"And all that unpredictability. You don't know what to make of me, do you Amber? Or what to expect?"

"No."

"You hate that."

"Yes." But she looked at his mouth and a part of her burned for it to touch hers, fear be damned, all the while aware of how turned on he was. How turned on *she* was.

"What's between us is a work in progress," he

said. "It can go as you want. You can be in control."
He nudged even closer. "Or not."

"Is there really an 'us'?"

"Yeah," Dax whispered huskily, no longer surprised by that very fact. "There's an *us*." To show her, he took her mouth with his, the promise echoing in his head as he tasted her.

She kissed him back, but then put a shaking hand to his chest. "I'm not ready for this. For you."

Neither was he, no matter what a certain body part was screaming. "No rush."

"Okay. Good." She licked her already wet lips in a self-conscious gesture he was certain she didn't mean to make so damn sexy.

"We could just let this attraction sit in the driver's seat," he said. "And see where it takes us."

"I feel as though I should pull over and ask for directions."

He smiled. "Do we need a map then?"

"I do, yes. I need a plan."

"You can't always plan matters of the heart, I'm learning." He set his forehead to hers. "You're my case in point."

Her dark eyes were liquid and full of unmistakable yearning. He wished, just once, that she would speak of that yearning, instead of fighting it.

Then she closed her eyes.

"No fair hiding." He touched his lips to the corner of her mouth, hovering there, thrilling to her quick intake of breath. "Look at me."

Both her eyes and her mouth opened slightly, and

she leaned toward him, clearly wanting, expecting, needing a kiss. "Dax…"

"Tell me what you want, Amber."

Instead, she shifted closer, dropped her gaze to his lips.

"With words." He smiled wickedly. "It's your plan, you're the one in control, remember?"

"You want me to say it."

She sounded so scandalized he nearly laughed. "Yeah." Softly, in a barely there touch, he kissed the other side of her mouth.

She moaned, and the sound made him hot. "Tell me."

Pleasure sighed out of her when he slid his fingers into her hair, but though she turned into him, pressed her body to his, she remained silent.

He drew back.

She let out an exploding sigh. "Okay! Kiss me, dammit!"

"If you insist," he murmured demurely.

The connection was combustive, instantly sizzling, and there was no way to hold back his low growl of helpless arousal, no way he wanted to.

Already it wasn't enough. The kiss wasn't enough.

Threading his fingers through her silky soft hair, he angled her for a deeper, hotter, wetter kiss. Their bodies swayed together. He could feel her breasts against his chest, her belly flat to his, and when he rocked slowly, melding their hips into a perfect fit so that he could feel the heat between her thighs, he nearly died right there. "If you need a road map to my feelings here," he murmured. "Let me assure you, I want more."

Her breath wasn't any more steady when she met his gaze warily. "How much more?"

He wanted it all. He wanted her to willingly shed that cool, calm control to give him the real Amber beneath. "You know how much I want. Now tell me what *you* want."

She loosened a fist from his hair, then smoothed that hand over his chest, from one side to another, and just that light touch sent his head spinning.

"Words," he said. "Tell me in words."

"I want…" Helplessly, she lifted her head. "You. But I don't know what to do."

"Are we talking about a physical want?"

She nodded.

If it had been any other woman telling him they wanted him, it would have made Dax's evening.

But this wasn't any other woman, it was Amber, and he suddenly wanted far more than her physical want. Swallowing his disappointment, he let out a laugh. "I remember you knowing exactly what to do before."

Her body was taut and quivering as he kissed her this time, telling him plainly what her mouth seemed to be struggling with, and heat roared through his veins. He caressed her slim back, up and down, slowly, fingers spread wide so he could touch as much of her as possible. She did the same, running her hands all over him. Then, slowly, he ended the kiss.

Her eyes were huge on his. "What?"

"I just wanted to make sure you're still in the driver's seat. I know how important that is to you."

He'd been only teasing, but she frowned, seriously considering. "I'm okay. I think." She looked at him. "More."

"Mmm. Aggressive." He stroked his hands down her hips, past her thighs, to the hem of her skirt, then skimmed them back up again, beneath the material now, to…ah, those legs. At the feel of lace, then soft, bare thighs, he groaned.

She squirmed and looked defensive. "They're more comfortable then regular nylons."

"Thank God for comfort."

"And they don't seem to snag like the others—"

"And thriftiness, too."

"They're very practical, you know."

He laughed. "You can't be thinking I don't like them."

"I— You do?"

"I do. Is it okay that they turn me on?" He had to laugh again when she considered.

"Why don't you just enjoy the reaction you're getting from me…?" He slid his hips to hers and lowered his lips to her ear. "Feel what you do to me."

She gripped him tight and nodded.

"More, Amber?"

"Yes, please," she whispered politely, making him crack up again. He'd never in his life laughed while trying to get a woman naked. He liked it. And her. Very much.

"Still so in control…" He continued to stroke her,

determined to shatter her restraint. "Touch me back," he urged.

Her hands slipped beneath his shirt, streaking over his bare back. "Dax—" Her hips undulated against his. "Where's my more?"

That needy, whispery voice nearly brought him to his knees. "Here." His voice was rough. "Skin to skin this time, I want to feel you, all of you."

Apparently in agreement, she tore off his shirt, then sucked in her breath. "You didn't tell me how beautiful *you* are." Her fingertips slid over his chest, her eyes wide with awe.

"Not like you." He had his own ogling to do now as he undid the buttons on her blouse, then slid it down to her elbows. At the sight of her, he let out his own shaky breath, then bent to her. "Oh, baby, not like you." Opening his mouth against her, he scattered hot little nips over her quivering skin. "Amber...you still okay?"

"What?" Dazed, she lifted her head, her arms still trapped by her blouse.

Through the white lace of her bra, her nipples were puckered and begging for attention, which he intended to give. "I asked if you were all right. You didn't want to lose yourself, remember?" Cupping her breasts, he let his thumbs glance over the tips, back and forth as her eyes glazed over. "I don't want to take this further than you want."

"I..." She closed her eyes when he continued that movement with his thumbs, then slid her hands up around his neck, and squeezed him so he could scarcely breath. "I'm fine. Just don't stop."

He might have grinned, but he was having trouble with his breathing. The feel of her in his hands…

"Give me my more, Dax."

Laughing softly he tugged her shirt completely off. Hunger and need pumped through him. It wasn't comforting to realize that he would be only partially sated by making love with her tonight.

The fire was roaring, warm and enticing, and they sank to the thick rug in front of it. He expected some hesitation when he opened his arms, but she came right into them, fitting there as if she belonged forever.

Forever.

What a thought. He'd never believed in forever, at least not for himself. "Still okay?" he asked, running a finger down her body.

She sucked in a breath when he slid off the rest of her clothes, then his. "Yes."

"Just wanted to make sure." He played with her belly button, her hipbone, then her inner thigh, which had her letting that air back out again, through her teeth. When he lingered there, she made that needy little whimper deep in her throat. "You're still in control, right?"

"Dax?"

"Yeah?"

"Shut up."

He grinned, then leaned over her.

The kiss was long, wet, hot and left him aching for more. Levering himself up on his forearms, he cupped her face. "I want you, Amber. Want me back."

She arched up. "Yes."

He felt the wetness between her legs which she spread to accommodate his, but he needed the words. "Tell me."

She licked her dry lips and writhed against him, encouraging him to sink inside her, still saying nothing.

"Tell me." He stroked himself against her and her eyes went opaque.

"I want you, Dax."

He had a second to wish she'd said she *needed* him, but his body was hard and pulsing, poised for entry and aroused beyond the point of no return. When she reared up and hugged him to her, his heart squeezed.

"I have a condom this time," he said hoarsely, and when he finally managed to get it on, he drove them straight to paradise.

AMBER STIRRED FIRST. Her body was a stranger to her, languid and lazy and newly tender in spots she'd almost forgotten about.

Oh, and she was wrapped in warm, solid arms.

It was still dark. Dax lay beside her, his breathing slow and deep and even.

For one weak moment, she let herself sink into him, into the heat and warmth and joy of his big body, enjoying the feeling of being secure and cared for.

In that moment she didn't have to be strong, she didn't have to be in charge, and she reveled in the letting go.

But she didn't fool herself; it couldn't last.

In the end, she had only herself to depend on. No matter how much Dax insisted he wanted to be there for her and Taylor, she could see fear lurking deep in his gaze.

A fear that matched hers.

He'd been so right, she thought, her heart hitching. There was no road map when it came to matters of the heart, no directions to follow.

And God help her, she was hopelessly lost.

CHAPTER TEN

WHEN DAX WOKE UP the next morning, he had an armful of warm, naked woman, a raging erection and a grin on his face.

"I could get used to this," he murmured, turning, tucking Amber beneath him. They were in her bedroom, in her bed. He'd carried her there himself sometime during the middle of the most erotic night of his life.

As her eyes fluttered open, he made his move, swooping down to take her mouth before she could utter a word. A sensuous, sleepy murmur escaped her throat and she rubbed languidly against him, returning his kiss with such heat and passion he groaned.

At the sound, she went perfectly still.

Dax raised his head. "Hey there."

She blinked slowly, looking confused, her usually perfect hair wild and willful.

Because he couldn't help it, he went for that creamy skin at the base of her neck. "Do you have any idea how sexy you are?" he asked.

She lay sprawled and gorgeous, a feast for his eyes. While he nibbled at her neck, his fingers found a velvety nipple that quickly responded to his touch. "Mmmm. You taste better than breakfast."

Her eyes closed again, her head fell back. Her breath came in little pants, quickening when he switched to her other breast. He took his time there, as well, and skimmed a hand down her belly and lower. Finding her deliciously hot, and so wet he moaned, he sank a finger into her. He played in and out of that slippery heat, his eyes crossing with lust when she clamped her legs around his hand, holding him to her.

"I'm not going anywhere," he promised, kissing her lips, her jaw, her ear. He took the sensitive lobe into his mouth and bit gently as his fingers danced over her.

She arched up into his palm, whimpering every time he withdrew. "Yeah," he whispered. "Feels good, doesn't it?"

"Dax?"

"I'm right here, Amber. Always."

Her eyes flew open again. *"Dax?"*

Hadn't they already established that? "Still me." He rose up on an elbow to study her. "Amber, are you awake?"

Again that slow blink. "I had this dream that we…" She licked her lips. "I guess it wasn't a dream."

She was adorable, he decided, slowly shaking his head. And most definitely *not* a morning person. "Not a dream."

She groaned.

"Regrets?"

"I don't feel comfortable with this type of a relationship."

"You felt comfortable enough during the night," he pointed out. "Three times, in fact."

She blushed and looked away. "Five," she muttered.

"Well then…" He grinned. "Why don't we go for an even dozen?" But when he leaned close with wicked intent, she put a hand to his chest.

He sighed and sat up. She had the entire sheet— who knew what had happened to the rest of the bedding—which left him stark naked, but he didn't care. "You still have a problem with us."

She darted him a glance. "When you say 'us' like that, it makes me nervous."

"Join the club."

"You don't look nervous, you look…" She paused, and in an unusually revealing gesture of vulnerability, she bit her lower lip. "You look hungry. As if you could eat me up for breakfast."

"In one bite."

"We're very different," she said softly. "I need time to think."

"No, you need time to control your emotions. To distance yourself from me. It really scares me how easily you can do that."

"And it scares me how much of me you see, how much you understand."

"Yeah, I understand you. Maybe someday you'll understand me back."

Eyes stricken, she opened her mouth, but Taylor chose that moment to cry out.

"She's my alarm clock," Amber said with a shaky laugh. She still held the sheet to her chin, and somehow managed to get out of the bed and keep herself covered. "She'll need to be changed and fed. I'm sorry, Dax."

It was beyond him how she could look as ravaged and luscious as she did, yet so prim and proper at the same time. The heady combination threatened his sanity. "I'm sorry, too."

AMBER SAT IN THE little café across the street from her office, contemplating her day. It could have been a better one.

Yesterday she'd lost a deal when a client had backed out of a sale at the last moment. Harried over that and the ensuing chaos, she'd forgotten to pick up her dry-cleaning, which had left her with nothing to wear but her now slightly too small red suit.

Despite the unseasonably warm weather, she'd been forced to keep the jacket on all day, which only emphasized her new cleavage. But at least it hid the indecently tight blouse and skirt.

The client she'd seen that morning had certainly appreciated her problem. It had taken most of their meeting to assure him she *didn't* combine business and pleasure.

In hopes of improving her mood, she sat with a bowl of frozen yogurt. At least she was finally cooling off. The pleasant buzz of people around lulled

her. She took a huge bite filled with delicious straw-
berries and leaned back with a sigh as it melted down
her parched throat.

"The way you eat that looks positively sinful."

Dax bent over her, his mouth close to her ear, so
that the low, sexy timbre sent shivers racing down
her spine. "Did you know you've got every male customer in this place hard as a rock, just from watching you enjoy that thing?"

"Where's Taylor?" she asked, pleased her voice
sounded so steady. She wasn't about to let him know
he'd made her bones dissolve.

"Mom's spoiling her for us."

Mom's spoiling her for us. So intimate. As if
Amber herself was also a part of his family.

Dax helped himself to the seat next to her, leaned
back and made himself at home. Faded denim
snugged his long, powerful legs, though she had no
idea why she noticed. His T-shirt invited her to Fear
Nothing. "I take it you're off-duty."

He grinned. "Yep. I'm going to take Taylor for a
picnic. Want to come?"

"You're taking a baby on a picnic? She'll eat the
ants and get itchy from the grass and—"

"Amber." He laughed. "I want to take *you* on a
picnic. I'm shamelessly using our daughter as an excuse."

"Oh." Another huge bite of frozen yogurt helped
her stall, but she stopped when she realized Dax's
gaze was riveted to her mouth. His body seemed
tense, his muscles tight beneath his shirt. And oh

Lord, she'd have to be totally naive to miss the bulge behind the button fly of his Levi's.

"Take some mercy on me, Amber," he said with a groan. "Either stop eating that thing as though you were in the throes of an orgasm or toss it. You're killing me."

"Hmm."

"Was that an apology?"

"I refuse to apologize because you can't keep your mind out of your pants." Gathering her briefcase, purse and yogurt—she wasn't about to give that up for him!—she rose. "I'm going back to work."

"Amber. Come on, wait up—"

When she kept going, she heard him swear behind her, heard the scrape of his chair as he came to his feet.

She moved faster.

They didn't speak as she practically ran across the street and into her building, but when she entered her office and tried to shut the door behind her, she was stymied by a one-hundred-and-eighty pound block wall.

Half in, half out, with the door nearly cutting off his nose, he grinned down at her. "You're nuts about me, I can tell."

She groaned and backed away from the door. "I'm only letting you in because I can't stand the sight of blood. That, and my secretary, Nancy, is watching." She plopped into her chair and glared at him.

He shut the door behind him, then set a lean hip on the corner of her desk. "Let me see," he said,

reaching for her spoon. "If it's as good as it looks...
hmmm." His tongue darted out to catch a drop. "Oh
yeah. It is."

So rattled by the sight of his wet tongue sliding
over his own lips, Amber lost every thought in her
head. Her hands loosened with the loss of blood flow
to her brain, and the small bit of frozen yogurt still
left in the cup spilled out...right down the front of
her jacket.

Dax was there in a flash, laughing, slipping her
jacket off her shoulders.

"No, don't," she gasped, gripping the edges of her
jacket, pressing it to her too-tight blouse. "I want it
on—"

"Hurry," he urged, tugging the jacket from her
shoulders, leaving her exposed in nothing but the
blouse she didn't want anyone to see. "Before it gets
on your—" Abruptly, Dax stopped talking.

Stopped breathing.

He couldn't help himself, she was incredible. Yes,
he'd already seen her, seen everything. He'd touched
and licked and kissed every inch of her, but that
didn't stop his heart from constricting and certain
other parts of his anatomy from standing at attention
at the sight of her straining against the tight confines
of her white silk blouse.

"I wanted that on," she grumbled, crossing her
arms over her chest.

He hardly heard her, could hardly think, but he
had to touch.

Her face remained cool, impassive as he slid his

fingers over her, but at the base of her neck, her pulse drummed wildly, giving her away.

"I'm sorry," he whispered, watching her nipples harden, pressing for freedom against the fabric. "But you're so beautiful, you stun me."

"We agreed we're too different for this," Amber said, not quite steadily, tightening her arms in front of her.

All it did was emphasize her glorious body, and the breasts she seemed embarrassed of. "No, *you* agreed."

She gave him a hot look.

It was filled with such frustration, he had to smile. "Okay, we agreed that you think *you* need space in order to protect your emotions from me."

"I don't think it, I know it."

And so did he. Dammit, so did he. "I shouldn't have come." He shoved his fingers through his hair and backed away.

"I'm sorry."

"For which?" At the door, he spun around. "For driving me crazy, or for driving me crazy slowly?"

That comment had anger flashing in her eyes. "I'm sorry you're upset that you're not getting your way."

"What's my way? Do you even know?"

"You want to have a…a fling."

That stopped him cold and he stalked back toward her. "Why don't you just marry me, dammit, and settle once and for all what I really want."

CHAPTER ELEVEN

AMBER GAWKED AT HIM and, in truth, Dax couldn't blame her. He was shocked, too. After that first time when he'd so foolishly asked her to marry him, he'd vowed not to think about it again.

But he knew now how he felt about being a father to Taylor. He wanted to do it right. Part-time wasn't right, not in his opinion.

He also knew how he felt about Amber, knew it was permanent, not some passing phase.

He knew this, just as he knew he'd been using her resistance to fuel his own, using it to mask his own fear of commitment.

But that was cowardly. The deep emotions he had for Amber were here to stay, and he would face them.

He had to convince her to do the same.

"Did you just…" She gazed at him helplessly, her head going back in forth in an automatic denial that had his jaw so tight he could barely breathe. "Did you…"

"Yes. For the second time. And I have to tell you, that frightened, trapped-doe look is not quite the response I was hoping for."

The look disappeared instantly as she veiled her thoughts from him.

"I told you before," she said slowly. "It's unnecessary. Nothing's changed."

"That's not an answer," he said grimly. "An answer would be 'yes, I'll make your wildest fantasies come true,' or 'no, let me rip out your heart.'"

"You're being impossible."

"Yes," he snapped. "We've already established that I'm wildly emotional, temperamental and overly sensitive. That I can't control any of that. I'm also, apparently, impossible. But I want to marry you. I want to be a family. So answer the damn question."

He couldn't have handled this any worse, and he knew it. Thanks to his own stupidity, he'd backed her into a corner with no way out. But he wouldn't withdraw the question, not when he'd put his pride on the line.

In control now, Amber didn't even blink.

"It's that tough, huh?"

"It's not as though we've had the most conventional of relationships," she told him in a tone that said she expected him to be reasonable.

He wasn't in the mood for reasonable. "Of course this relationship hasn't been normal, not from the very beginning! We met under extraordinary circumstances, for God's sake, and we've been through things other people haven't." He lifted his hands helplessly. "Nothing's been the same since that earthquake, and nothing's been the same since I met you." Dropping his hands, he shook his head. "I held you when I thought we were going to die, Amber, and yes, that was a long time ago, and yes, now everything's different. I see things differently, I feel differently." He reached for her, touched her pale face. "I have never regretted what happened. You have to know, you and Taylor are the best things that ever happened to me."

She turned away and scrubbed at the yogurt stain with a napkin. Though the stain didn't come off, she slipped the jacket back on anyway. Buttoning it, her back to him, she softly said, "You scare me."

"Does it help to know you scare me, too?"

"Actually, 'scare' isn't a strong enough word," she clarified. "*Terrify* works better."

He came up behind her, torturing himself with the feel of her spine and curved bottom against his chest and groin.

At the contact, her fingers fumbled on her buttons.

Reaching around her, he brushed her hands away and took over the task. "It's not like you to be so fidgety."

"I'm nervous. Marriage proposals do that to me."

Surrounding her as he was, he could hear her every breath, could smell her sweet, sexy scent. Felt her small tremors. Wildly protective emotions rose in him, powerful and suddenly certain. "Amber…" His arms folded around her. His mouth found its way to her ear and was heading toward her jaw when she straightened.

"I'm having enough trouble keeping my thoughts together," she said shakily, facing him, pressing her hands to her heart. "If I let you kiss me now, I don't know what will happen."

"Really?" That pleased him. "What *could* happen?"

"You know very well what."

"I want to hear you say it."

She rolled her eyes. "You know all you have to do is look at me and my thoughts scatter. I certainly can't concentrate when you put your mouth on me. I can hardly breathe."

His smile spread a bit. "Maybe you concentrate too much."

"Yes, well, it's a bad habit of mine."

"Are you ever going to answer the question?"

She drew a deep breath. "I know it's rude, but I need some air."

"You need to think."

"Yes."

Well-versed in this particular play, he followed her out, but she was stopped by Nancy at the front desk and handed a stack of messages that made her sigh.

Dax watched while she flipped through them with quick impatience. And saw her, really saw her—the weary eyes, the slight bruises beneath them, the tension in her body.

She was truly exhausted.

Nancy added a pile of files that needed immediate attention. On top of that, she placed a virtual mountain of correspondence, all of which required review and a signature.

It had to be at least a week's worth of work.

Amber took everything stoically, she even managed a smile for her employee, but Dax saw right through her.

"Put it in your office and let's go," he said quietly.

Nancy held up a finger before Amber could move. "The Garrisons. They want to see that property again."

"Terrific," Amber muttered.

"Today."

"They've seen it five times this week."

"I know. But they want to see it again and they want to see it with you."

Amber drew in a slow, purposeful breath, and Dax wondered how it was that only *he* saw her growing exhaustion. He knew how hard she worked, knew how much time Taylor demanded, and added it all up.

It equaled a breakdown for Amber.

"Call them then," she said wearily. "Tell them I'll pick them up at—"

"Tell them they can see the damn property by themselves," Dax interjected. He took the stack of work from Amber's arms. "You've done enough today. You're taking off."

Both Amber and Nancy stared at him.

"Ms. Riggs is leaving for the day," he announced for anyone listening. "She won't be back until morning."

"I will most definitely be back today," Amber said, her eyes on Dax. "I just need some air."

"You're going to get your air." Dax smiled his most charming smile. "But you won't be back today."

Taking her hand in a grip of steel, he tugged her from the office.

"Dax…would you stop!" Her heels clicked noisily as she raced along beside him. "I have important business to attend to."

"You most certainly do," he assured her, ruthlessly tugging her along. "We were in the middle of something."

"I know, but I can't just leave, not now—"

"Your air," he reminded her. "You needed to get out so fast you couldn't answer my question. Remember?"

Her lips tightened, but she remained silent until they exited the building.

It was a glorious Southern California day. The sky was a deep, brilliant blue and scattered across it were little puffs of white clouds.

A picture-perfect scene.

Now if only the woman next to him could slow down enough to enjoy it.

Instead, she spun on her heels away from him and started walking.

Dax spared a moment to admire her stride. "I'm coming with you," he called.

"Like I could stop you."

He moved to keep up with her. She was pale, but never faltered. The slight wind tossed her hair, played with the hem of her skirt. Dax avoided thinking by concentrating on traffic. He avoided touching Amber by keeping his hands in his pockets.

Three blocks later, they came to a park. All green

and woodsy, it had a series of trails and welcoming benches. A perfect place to ask a woman—for the third time—to marry him.

A perfect place for his future to be decided.

They were hidden from the street by trees. The sounds of birds singing drowned out any traffic they might have heard. They were alone, isolated, surrounded by beauty.

"Well," he said after a moment.

"Well."

They stared at each other stupidly, and Dax wondered if she could possibly be as attracted, as confused, as totally, irreversibly in love as he was.

Then he saw the unmistakable signs—redrimmed eyes and damp lashes.

Dammit.

"I've thought about…you know," she said, her voice a bit ragged.

"You mean about spending the rest of your life with me?" he asked gently. "Is that why you're crying?"

She looked away. "It's been hard being a single parent. No family support, few friends. Both are my fault, but it's fact." Then she turned back to him. "Having you in my life, taking responsibility for helping with Taylor, it's been a real gift."

"But?"

"But I can't accept your offer. It's generous, kind and almost overwhelmingly irresistible, but as I told you before, I can't do it."

"Mind if I ask why?"

"It's obvious neither of us were meant for marriage."

"I don't believe that," he said softly. "And I don't believe *you* believe it. Don't chicken out here, Amber. Don't hide, not from me. Tell me the truth. I deserve that much."

"You know the truth. I'm not marriage material, and you…you like women too much to give it all up just because we have a baby."

"First of all, I stopped looking at other women the moment you came into my life."

"Which time?"

"Both," he told her grimly.

"I understand getting married is a logical solution to the unexpected unit we've become." She hugged herself. "We have a baby. We both love her with all our hearts. We're willing to share her, but the truth is, neither of us really want to be separated from her. Getting married would solve that."

"Yes," he agreed, sliding closer. "It would also solve another, deeper problem."

"Which is?"

"I want you."

"You—" She closed her eyes. "You just had me recently. A few times as a matter of fact."

The memory, as well as her tone, made him smile. "I want more than sex," he clarified. Because the admission was a new one for him, and scary, his humor vanished. "I've never said this before about anyone else, but sex with you isn't enough. I want to spend nights together. I want to *be* together. I know we started out in a whirlwind, that we've done everything backward, but let's fix it."

"Marriage won't do that, Dax."

"Why are you so resistant?"

"Because…because, dammit, it's not enough for me!" She blushed and closed her eyes. "I'm sorry. I know this sounds stupid, but to me a marriage should be about…about love. I've never thought of myself in those terms, but deep in my heart, if I'm going to do it, that's what I want."

"Love."

"That's right."

"Well that's convenient, since I happen to be madly in love with you."

"What?" She flew to her feet and stared at him as if she'd just discovered he was an alien. "What did you just say?"

He stood, too, and when she would have turned away, he took her shoulders in his hands. She trembled. That made two of them. "I think you heard me just fine."

"I've…I've never heard those words before." Her voice was a mere whisper. She licked her lips. "I'd like to hear them again."

His heart threatened to burst out of his chest. "I love you."

"You can't."

"Why not? You're perfectly lovable."

Her mouth was open, her eyes wild. Her hand went to her chest. "Oh God. Now I can't breathe."

"Good. Neither can I." He resisted the urge to

laugh because he wasn't kidding. He really couldn't breathe. "I've never said those words to a woman before, Amber."

They stared at each other.

"You're mistaken," she decided tremulously. "You have to be."

"No."

"You have no idea. I don't let people in, I'm not—"

"Amber." It was so easy, so right to touch her, he thought, as his thumb gently stroked her jaw. His fingers slipped into her hair. "I've loved you from that very first day."

"But I don't know how to love you back."

"You could practice."

Moisture gathered in her beautiful eyes and she shook her head back and forth.

"Practice with me, Amber," he whispered, his heart raw.

Her eyes were huge. "I'm not ready. I need time."

"How much?"

"I don't know!"

Because she was still shaking, he gathered her stiff body close. "I'm sorry," she whispered against his chest, but her hands snaked around his neck and for a moment, she clung.

He stroked her back and tamped down any regrets. "Don't worry. It so happens, time is in plentiful supply."

And strange as it seemed, given she'd turned him down yet again, Dax felt an inkling of hope for their future.

CHAPTER TWELVE

THAT NIGHT, DAX lay in his bed staring at the ceiling wondering how long it would take for sleep to claim him when the phone rang.

Given how his heart picked up speed, he knew who it would be. "Hello?"

"Did you mean it?"

Amber. Unsure and unhappy. "I meant every one of those three little words," he assured her grimly.

"Another promise?"

"Another promise."

There was a long silence, and he knew she was very busy thinking.

"Have I broken one to you yet, Amber?"

"No," she said slowly, but she sounded slightly reassured. "I have to go."

His heart twisted, a feeling he was beginning to associate with her. "Good night, Amber," he whispered.

DAX FOUND AMBER at what he now knew to be her favorite lunch spot. He grinned at her bowl of strawberry yogurt. "Are you going to let me watch you eat that?"

She stopped licking her spoon and eyed him over the bowl with an interesting mix of pleasure and wariness. The wariness he expected because it had been four days since he'd sought her out.

The pleasure was a nice surprise.

"No," she finally said.

Ignoring that, because whether she wanted to admit it or not, she was crazy about him, he swiveled a chair around and straddled it. Leaning forward, he took in her cool, sedate, navy blue suit. "I don't suppose I can convince you to spill again so that you could lose the uptight clothes."

Surprising him, she laughed. "Actually, I thought of you this morning when I put this on."

"Yeah?" For some reason, that gave him ridiculous pleasure. So did the thought of her standing, fresh out of a shower, naked, thinking of him.

Her voice was low. "I thought of it as my armor."

"Against?"

She played with the yogurt now. "Sometimes you give me a certain look and it makes me feel…funny."

He gave her one of those looks now and the air sizzled between them.

"That's the one," she said a bit shakily, pointing at him with her spoon. "That's it right there."

"Do you feel funny now?"

"A little, yeah."

"Me, too." He heard the rough arousal in his voice and couldn't stop himself. "And it has nothing to do with the clothes you wear." He leaned close. "You could put on real armor and it wouldn't matter one damn bit."

Her eyes closed briefly, and he knew he didn't mistake that quick flash of helpless desire on her face before she carefully masked it and rose. "I have work."

He touched her arm, stilled her. "You can believe in me, Amber. Believe in yourself enough to see it."

"I'm trying, Dax. Whatever you think of me, I want you to know that."

He rose, too, and skimmed his fingers over her cheek. "I know you've had no one to trust with yourself before, but I promise you, I'm different."

And then, because they were in the crowded café, and because neither of them were quite steady, he stepped back. "Think about it."

AMBER WANTED TO DO nothing but think about it. As she entered her office, her mind whirled. She moved toward her desk and the mountain of work waiting for her.

Halfway there, the earth rumbled beneath her feet. For a second she allowed herself to believe it was her overly active imagination.

It wasn't. The earthquake was short and quick, and absolutely terrifying.

There had been many this year, and she remembered each and every one of them because they'd brought on a heart-stopping panic she couldn't control.

A normal reaction for someone who'd been

through what she had, she assured herself, gripping her desk, prepared to dive under it if necessary.

"It's okay," she said out loud as she waited, tense and frozen. "Just an aftershock." She knew they could occur for years after a main quake. The knowledge didn't help. Many people in the area had been terrorized by the aftershocks, not just her. It was normal.

Normal.

She told herself all of this, repeatedly, but she still forgot to breathe and her chest hurt. Her vision spotted.

And though it was over long before she even fully registered it, she remained there, rigid, heart drumming, palms damp, shaking like a leaf.

The door to her office opened and shut, and suddenly Dax was standing there, saying her name in that deep, wonderful voice.

"I came the second I felt it," he said. "I was still on the street. I thought— I didn't know how you would feel— Dammit, I hate those things!" he exclaimed, taking her arms in his strong, reassuring hands. "Are you all right?"

"Certainly." But she clung to his big, welcoming body. Just for a moment, she told herself. She'd allow herself to lean on him for just a moment. "I'm fine."

"Don't." With a gentleness that was so tender, so sweet it hurt, he curled a strand of her hair behind her ear. "Don't fake being strong for me."

"It was just an aftershock. Hardly even big enough to register on the scale."

"It registered on my scale," came his gruff reply, and for the first time she heard his breathlessness, felt the quiver in his own muscles, and realized he felt the fear, too.

She gave herself permission to hold him for another moment.

"It's okay," he whispered, gathering her tighter, absorbing her weight with ease. "We're okay."

"Taylor," she said, lifting her head. Urgency overcame her. "I want to call—"

"We will. Soon as I can remember my mother's phone number. We'll go get her together, okay? Amber, just hold onto me for a second."

We'll go get her.

We'll.

Together.

For some reason, the words softened her as nothing else could have and she let out a lungful of air, burying her face in the wonderful spot of his neck that seemed meant for her. "Don't be afraid," she told him. "I have a big, tough desk. It'll hold."

He laughed, as she had meant for him to, and somehow that softened her even more so that her arms wrapped even tighter around him.

"We're both shaking like leaves," he muttered, sinking with her to the floor. "I really hate earthquakes."

"Just for the record here," she wondered. "Who's comforting who?"

"I'm not sure, just don't let go."

She didn't. They sat huddled on the floor in each

other's arms like two little children. Her legs were entwined with his, her skirt high on her thighs. His hands were on her back, slowly running up and down in a reassuring gesture that hadn't been anything but sincerely comforting, until his hands slipped beneath her jacket to the silk of her blouse.

The embrace shifted, became charged with erotic awareness, and Amber lifted her head to stare at him, into his warm eyes, then at his mouth, the one she suddenly wanted on hers. The shattering, shocking truth was, she wanted that more than she wanted her own next breath.

Dax groaned and closed his eyes. "Don't look at me like that, it's dangerous to my health."

For the life of her, she couldn't remember why she'd wanted to hold him at arm's length, couldn't remember why she was trying so hard to resist this magnetic pull she felt whenever she was with him.

Hell, she was starting to have that pull even when she *wasn't* with him.

Her arms were already around his neck, it took little movement to have her fingers fisted in his hair so that she could tug him closer, then closer still so that their mouths were a fraction of an inch apart.

"Amber." The sound of her name on his lips, spoken in that husky voice, made her heart tip on its side.

She closed the distance between them, let her eyes drift closed. Her lips parted and she felt his warm breath mingle with hers.

Her office door opened.

"Oh, excuse me," came Nancy's shocked voice.

Professionalism kept her from gawking, though Amber was certain she wanted to. After all, how often did she see her boss sprawled on the floor in a man's arms?

"I'm sorry," Nancy murmured.

Amber groaned when the door shut. She pushed away from Dax.

He let out a frustrated sigh. "I'm betting from the look on your face that what just happened is worse than the aftershock."

"I've worked hard to make sure everyone here respects me and the work I do. And in a matter of seconds, I've just ruined that image."

"Well that's pure bull."

Amber stared at him. "That's easy for you to say. You're a man, working in a man's world. You're not judged by your appearance, or who you sleep with."

"Neither are you."

"It's different here. It's highly competitive. One nasty rumor and I could be ruined."

"I see. And being caught in my arms equals a nasty rumor. Flattering."

She winced at his unusually chilly voice. "I didn't mean to insult you."

"That's the hard part, because I know it."

THAT NIGHT WHEN DAX brought Taylor home to Amber, he made no attempt to draw her into conversation. He didn't even come in, but stood at the doorway, silently and solemnly holding Taylor close for a long moment. Arms tight around the chubby little baby, he closed his eyes and hugged her tight.

Then he lifted her high, smiled at her squeal of delight and kissed her goodbye. "I love you, baby," he whispered, and his smile was a heart-wrenching mixture of sweetness and sorrow.

All that emotion both shocked and humbled Amber to her toes. "Do you want to come in?"

He shook his head, and as if to prove his point, remained on the step as she took the diaper bag from him. He was careful not to touch her. Though she had no right to feel that way, it hurt.

She knew he was going to work. She'd seen the news. There was a fire raging in a downtown apartment building. It was filled with hundreds of trapped, terrified people, and though he rarely fought the actual fires these days, he would be on the scene. His job required it.

But she knew his distant attitude had nothing to do with that fire and everything to do with her. "Be careful tonight."

"Always." With one last, loving touch to Taylor's chubby cheek, he turned away.

"Dax."

Slowly he turned, but she didn't know what to say, how to reach him. How to make him understand.

How could she, when she didn't understand herself? "Nothing," she whispered, and then he was gone.

AMBER DID HER BEST to keep her mind occupied for the rest of the long evening. She bathed Taylor, then read her stories, even though the baby was far more interested in chewing on the pages than listening to the words.

She even tried to do some of her own work. Nothing satisfied her and her mind drifted.

To Dax.

Desperate to distract herself, she flipped on the television, then stood riveted in horror. The downtown fire was live on all the local channels.

The flames weren't contained. Even worse, there were still people trapped on the higher levels. The city had put out the desperate call for help to neighboring counties, and though that help was on the way, for many it would be too late.

She knew Dax would never stand on the sidelines. He'd be there, in the thick of that heat, fighting for those people's lives.

Glued to the screen, she lost track of time, chewing on her nails as she hadn't done since she was a child. When the roof of the building collapsed, she leaped to her feet, then kneeled before the television, her heart in her throat.

Three firefighters were reported missing.

She waited and waited, but they didn't give any more information, not the identities of the men or their conditions, not even after the fire was contained and then, eventually, extinguished.

No longer able to stand the not knowing, Amber turned to the phone, just as it rang.

"Honey, it's Emily McCall."

"Oh, thank goodness. Do you think you could watch Taylor for me? I have to go down."

"Oh, Amber, listen—"

"I have to go, I have to know—"

"I know, I know. But he's okay. He's not hurt. That's why I'm calling."

The relief was so overwhelming, Amber couldn't breathe. "You're sure?"

"Thomas drove down there when this mess first started, he just called me."

Dax was okay.

Amber's limbs started to shake in reaction and she collapsed onto the couch.

Emily's voice was thick with tears. "I worry about him so much. I can hear in your voice you worried, too."

"Yes. He— We— I…" She blew out a breath and tried again. "It was awful, the not knowing. I tried to imagine… Taylor needs him."

"Of course she does. What about her mother?"

"I need him, too," she said, meaning every word. "So much."

"He's my life," Emily said simply. "And so is your daughter. I'm so thankful we're all together."

The guilt that stabbed at Amber wasn't new. She felt as though she had stolen Taylor's first three months from Dax and his family and now, only a few short weeks later, couldn't imagine how she had done it.

Or why.

Her reasons for wanting to be alone hadn't made sense for hours now.

"Why don't you bring me that sweet little baby?" Emily suggested. "Then you can decide what to do."

"About what?"

Emily's voice was hushed, as if she kept a huge secret. "Well, I shouldn't say anything." This spoken in the hopeful tone of someone who wanted to be pressed.

"Please."

"Well, you know I pride myself on letting my children lead their own lives. I don't mean to be nosy."

If she hadn't been in such shock, Amber might have laughed. It was common knowledge among Dax's family exactly how wonderfully, purposely nosy Emily could be.

"But as long as you're asking," she said slyly. "I was hoping maybe *you* had something to tell *me*. That maybe you and Dax were going to…oh, I don't know. Get married?"

Oh Lord. "Mrs. McCall—"

"Oh, no, you don't," Emily interrupted with a laugh. "Let's not go backward here. You called me Emily at the party."

"Okay. Emily—"

"Or you could just go ahead and get used to calling me Mom."

Amber's emotions were in such a tailspin, she had no control left with which to handle this situation. "I'm sorry," she managed. "But as far as wedding bells, I don't have anything to tell."

"He hasn't asked you to marry him?" Emily's disappointment sang through the line. "That boy! I taught him better than that—"

"No, no, it's not…" How to explain that *she* had screwed everything up? That there was every chance Dax no longer wanted her? "It's not his fault."

"You don't want him?"

"This is very complicated. I can't seem to think straight."

"Of course you can't! Where's my head, pressing you to talk to me before you're ready. Maybe you haven't even decided if you like me—"

Now Amber did laugh. Emily McCall could wear down a saint. "I like you, very much," she assured the older woman. "It's just that—"

"That you don't think of me as your family yet." Emily sniffed, clearly insulted. "I understand."

"You know that's not true."

"No, it's okay, you don't owe me anything."

"Emily, please. I think you're an amazing woman."

"You do?" Pleasure quickly replaced hurt. "Really?"

"Yes." It had never been easy for Amber to share herself, but for some reason, the words came now. "I think the way you love your family is beautiful."

"It's no more than any mother would do."

Maybe it was the late hour or the emotions of the day, but suddenly it was easy for Amber to admit the truth. "Not any mother."

"Not yours?"

Emily's sympathy and pity didn't frighten her as she thought it would. "Definitely not mine. But I used to dream about it, and if I could have drawn my mother the way I wanted her to be, she would have been just like you."

"Oh darling, now you're really going to make me cry."

"Don't you dare." Amber laughed through her own impending tears. "You'll get *me* started. And after what we've been through this evening, I may never stop."

"Dax is careful, you know. He's the best at what he does."

He was the best at everything he set his mind to. His work. Fatherhood. She could only imagine what a husband he'd make. The warm glow that came from that thought no longer surprised her.

"I imagine you have a lot on your mind," Emily said. "Especially with the thought of babies and marriage and all the like."

"I thought you didn't want to be nosy."

"Oh, you." But Emily had the good grace to laugh at herself. "You already have my number. Just like all my children." Her voice went stern and demanding. "Now bring me Taylor. You go to my boy."

IN THE END, Amber didn't drop off Taylor, figuring Dax would want to see her. He seemed to thrive on any opportunity to do so.

Plus she needed Taylor to hold, needed to feel that small, warm bundle of life against her, reminding her that no matter what happened with Dax, she mattered to someone.

Dax had given her a key to his house, insisting he didn't want her waiting for him outside if he was ever late when they were supposed to meet. Amber had felt uncomfortable with that, had assumed she would never use it, but it came in handy now.

Less than one minute after she arrived, Dax pulled into the driveway, setting her nerves to leaping. Head down, shoulders tense, he opened the front door and stepped inside. As if he sensed her, he stilled and slowly raised his head to reveal a weary, hollow face.

When he saw her his eyes warmed. So did Amber's heart.

CHAPTER THIRTEEN

"Hey." Dax acknowledged her, but he didn't move into the room.

Amber's nervousness tripled. Was he bothered by the fact that she'd let herself in? Was he sorry he'd given her his key?

Why didn't he say something, *anything?* "I hope you don't mind," she found herself saying awkwardly.

With an audible sigh, he kicked off his shoes.

"I...used the key you gave me."

He dropped his jacket where he stood and the leather hit the floor with a thud.

"Taylor's here, too." She felt stupid and intrusive, but a search of his expression told her nothing. A first. "Your mom offered to baby-sit, but I thought you'd want to see her."

He rolled his head on his neck, winced and then sighed again.

"If you're too tired, I'll just..."

He spoke then, though the words were muffled by the sweatshirt he was pulling off over his head. "I'm never too tired for Taylor." He tossed the sweatshirt aside, his words in direct opposition to the exhaustion on his face. "Or you, for that matter."

"Because I could just scoop her up and leave...."

He leaned back against the wall, arms crossed. "Didn't you just get here?"

"Yes."

His face was bleak, his eyes red-rimmed, and his big, tough body so weary she imagined he was standing on his feet by sheer force of will. "I saw everything on the news," she said. She watched as he dumped out the contents of his pockets into a small bowl on the low table in the entry.

His silence was killing her.

"I couldn't tear myself away from the television," she added.

He nodded and rubbed his eyes, but still didn't speak. Her heart was racing so fast she didn't know what to do.

"When the roof collapsed—" she drew a shaky breath "—and those firefighters fell through the gaping hole..."

He flinched and her heart ached at the stark pain she saw so clearly in his eyes. "Oh, Dax."

He hadn't stepped toward her, hadn't really looked at her, not once. He hadn't made one move that told her how he felt about her being there. "Would you rather I go?"

"Actually, I'm hoping you're going to tell me the real reason you're here."

"I...I thought...I just wanted to be."

He came toward her, his face still bleak and grim,

but now there was something new in his gaze. He stopped a mere foot away from her. "I've never known you to stutter."

"I don't. N-n-not—" Ruthlessly she bit her tongue. "Not usually anyway." Frustrated, she reached up to shove back a loose strand of hair at the exact same moment his fingers came up to tuck it behind her ear. His hand slid over hers and he brought those joined hands to his chest. "You've been biting your nails. A new habit?"

"Another one that I've not had for years."

"What's the matter? I've never seen you so unsettled."

"Unsettled. I guess that's what you'd call worrying myself sick." All her pent-up fear spewed out. "I went through hell tonight, watching the news."

"It's my job."

"I know. *I know!* That's not what I'm saying."

"What *are* you saying?"

"That I worry, okay? I don't want to, but I do."

He let out a long breath and all the tension suddenly draining out of him, immediately replaced by a new, different sort of tension. *"Yes,"* he whispered, his eyes glittering with emotion. "Yes, *that's* what I wanted to hear."

"I suppose then, that you'd love to know I couldn't even breathe, thinking that you'd be hurt. Or worse!"

His other hand slid up her spine, around to cup her face. His thumb brushed over her lower lip before his fingers sank into her hair, holding her head still.

Closing that last gap between them, he nudged her up against his body. "Yeah. I would love to know that."

She flattened her hands against his chest and had to tip her head back to look into his eyes. "Is that ego talking?"

"No. It's not even remotely related to anything in my brain." He smoothed his hand over hers, holding it close to his chest. "It's right here, where pride has no place. And if you think you should be ashamed about worrying for me, think again. Not when I do nothing *but* think about you, worry about you, want you. It feels incredible to know you're capable of doing the same."

Had she been so selfish to keep that from him? "I care about you, Dax. So much it hurts."

For the first time that night, his eyes heated, his mouth softened. He closed his eyes and with an aching tenderness, rubbed his jaw to hers, drawing her so tight to him she could feel his every breath.

Then he pulled her even closer, burying his face in her neck. "We lost twenty-two people tonight. Six of them children. One was a baby girl, the same age as Taylor."

Shock reverberated through her and she hugged him as tight as she could. "I'm so sorry."

"I had to tell her mother—" He swallowed hard. "I kept seeing Taylor, kept imagining how I'd feel if I had to face you, tell you that— *God*."

Envisioning the scene, Amber felt his anguish as her own. "You did everything you could, all of you did everything you could to save them."

He made a wordless sound of grief that tore at her. In her arms was the strongest, toughest, most heroic man she'd ever met, and she didn't know what to do for him. She wanted to take his pain away, wanted to hold him close so that nothing could hurt him ever again. She had no idea how long they stood there, rocking slowly, absorbing each other's heat and strength, when Taylor cried out.

"I'll get her," Dax said. "I...I need her."

Amber followed him to the room he'd set up for Taylor. It had been his office before, so the crib was between a leather sofa and an oak desk. Both were now covered with stuffed animals, toys and freshly laundered baby clothes. The place was a comfortable, cozy mess.

Taylor had fallen asleep again, on her tummy as usual, her padded bottom sticking up in the air, her fist in her mouth.

Dax stood by the crib, his hand on Taylor's back, a look of combined sorrow and joy on his face, so poignant it hurt to look at him. But that wasn't a good enough reason to turn away.

For the first time in her life, Amber reached out and made the first move. It was difficult, but only until she touched him. At the contact with his warm, hard body it was the most natural thing in the world to slip her hands around his waist and hug him from behind. "She's okay, Dax."

He nodded and turned, gathering her close. The exhaustion was still there in his expression, but some of the bleak despair seemed to have lifted. That it was herself and Taylor doing that for him gave her a warm burst of something so thrilling, so breathtaking, so wild and fierce, it terrified her.

It was *hope*.

Was it real? Could it last?

Dax leaned past her, stroked a gentle hand down Taylor's back and with an achingly tender expression, bent and kissed his baby, murmuring something Amber couldn't hear.

Straightening, he looked deep into Amber's eyes as a slow, unbearably sad smile crossed his mouth.

Then he left the room.

Confused, she followed him as he padded down the hallway to his own bedroom.

He didn't turn on the light, but she made out his silhouette as he tugged off his shirt and let it fall. His shoulders slumped as he stood there in the middle of the room, still and silent.

"Dax?"

"I'm fine," he said, emotionlessly. "You don't have to stay."

The only light in the room came from the pale moon shining through the window, so she couldn't see his expression. She didn't have to in order to know he felt empty to the core. "You want me to go?"

A harsh laugh escaped him. "No. But I know you're still afraid of all this, and I'm just vulnerable enough tonight to beg."

"I can't help the fear, Dax," she said carefully. "It's all a part of it for me. But I can tell you what I feel for you is different than anything I've ever felt before."

She felt his surprise.

She closed her eyes for a moment and pressed her fingertips to them while she drew in a deep breath. "I won't deny what's between us, but I feel like I'm on an emotional roller coaster."

"I understand that you like to keep your emotions in check. Hell, you've had to in order to survive, but Amber..." He lifted his broad shoulders helplessly. "I can't do the same."

In the dark his silhouette seemed larger than life, more vital, more full of passion and hope than she could ever be, and never had she felt the lack in herself so much as she did in that moment. "I know," she whispered.

"I won't ever hurt you," he said quietly. "I've told you that. But I can't temper myself, hide my emotions. No matter how much I want you, I can't change. Not even for you."

He was close enough now that she could see him more clearly. The contours of his bare chest were delineated by the faint moon's glow. He was powerful, and he was beautiful.

And he could be hers.

All she had to do was believe it.

He turned away and sank down onto his huge bed. With a little groan, he flopped on his back and covered his face with one arm.

Exhaustion had clearly claimed him.

Was it too late to tell him? Could she find both the courage and the words? "Dax?"

He let out an answering grunt, but didn't budge.

She moved close, until her knees bumped the mattress. She lifted one to the bed and bent over him, gently setting a hand on his bare chest.

At the unexpected heat of him, she nearly pulled back, but the sensation of skin to skin felt so good, she set her other hand on him as well. Then closed her eyes to savor it.

Suddenly his hands came up, tugged her down. Gasping in surprise, she fell over him.

"If you're going to lean over me, staring as I sleep," he muttered, "then at least get down here and keep me company while you're doing it."

Those were the last words he spoke. He drew her close, tucked himself around her, then immediately fell into a deep, exhausted slumber.

He was warm and safe and strong. There was no way to resist snuggling in even closer.

Then she, too, fell asleep.

SHE DREAMED THEY made love…she could feel him, all of him, skin to skin, burning her, healing her, making her body hum.

She dreamed of his hands skimming over her body, shedding her clothes. The picture was so vivid she could feel the calluses on his fingertips when he touched her bare flesh with such terrifying tenderness it made her weep and press closer.

She dreamed she touched him, too, and under her hands the muscles of his big, tough body quivered. In his eyes she saw need and ecstasy and anguish and oh…

This was no dream.

"You're awake." Indecision and sweet resignation swam in his eyes.

They'd already established she wasn't a morning person, nothing had changed. Then she realized it wasn't morning yet. She blinked in confusion because she was wrapped around him like a blanket.

"I woke up like this," he murmured. "We must have gravitated toward each other in our dreams."

He expected her to walk away. She could hear it in his voice. He thought she'd made a decision about him, about her life, and that decision didn't involve him.

He thought wrong.

"Touch me, Dax."

The strain on his face nearly broke her heart. "I am."

"More."

"It won't change anything," he said tightly. "We'll still be fundamentally at odds, wanting different things, and—"

She shifted closer to that intriguing, throbbing heat pressing between her legs. "Mmm." She grabbed his hands from her hips and slid them over her body. To her waist, her ribs, her breasts.

"Amber." He groaned. "You feel incredible, but—"

"You talk too much." She kissed him softly, then not so softly, drawing him in deeper, and he let out a tortured sigh, deepening the kiss himself. As if he could read her mind, her dream, her need, he caressed her, worshipped her body and set her senses on fire.

"My clothes," she managed as his mouth dipped and nipped over her collarbone, trailing to a breast. His tongue circled her bare nipple, and she arched closer. "Where did my clothes go?" She moaned when his hot, pulsing erection nudged at her wet center. *"Where did yours go?"*

"We must have shed them in the night."

He rose above her, swirling that inventive, greedy tongue over her other breast, teasing the nipple until she nearly cried.

When she tried to lift up her legs and draw him inside her, he evaded her, slipping down her body. She felt his warm breath high on the inside of her thigh. Equal parts thrill and fear coursed through her. "Um...Dax?"

"Shh. You talk too much." His tongue swirled over her. Then his teeth, and when he sucked her into his mouth, he made her wild, frantic. Shameless. And as the orgasm tore through her, he took her to heights she'd never even imagined.

Unbelievably, he would have rolled away then, but she managed to open her eyes and saw his vulnerability, and understood he appreciated hers.

He wouldn't take advantage of her.

She felt the resolute, unmistakable connection of their hearts and souls, and knew he never could. She reversed their positions, holding him in place as she slowly and torturously experimented on his body with her mouth.

When he tossed back his head, his face tight in a mask of agonized pleasure, she lifted her mouth off of him and licked her lips.

He moaned.

"Am I doing all right?" she whispered.

"You're doing better than all right," he managed in a strangled voice. "And if you stop now, there's every chance I'm going to die on the spot."

Empowered, she gave him a wicked grin before resuming.

In less than two minutes, she had him clawing at the sheets, shaking, begging for release. The thrill of that was such a rush she nearly came from just watching him.

"Love me," she whispered.

"I do." His eyes squeezed shut, hiding himself from her. "Amber—"

"Condom?"

She saw him hesitate, and desperate for the feel of him thick and throbbing inside her, she reared up and opened his nightstand herself.

He made a rough sound, reached past her and grabbed a foil packet. With a new boldness, she took it and attempted to put the thing on, but it wasn't nearly as easy as it seemed it should be. "It's not big enough," she said, surprised when he let out a groaning laugh.

"Amber, stop. This isn't—"

Before he could deny her, she drew his face down to hers, arching her hips as she kissed him, forcing his decision.

A low groan came from deep in his throat, and he barely managed to get the condom on before he thrust into her, hard and deep. "I'm sorry." His voice was as rough and ragged as his breathing. But he held her hips and thrust again.

She wanted to tell him not to be sorry, that this was what she wanted, but all she could do was cry out with the pleasure of him inside her. She tossed back her head and gave him everything she had, and as she did, her heart opened, rejoiced, and in return, received.

When it was over, when she lay limp and exhausted in his arms, their bodies still connected and pulsing with the passion and love they'd shared, she smiled for the first time in too long as she drifted back off into sleep.

Dax held Amber in his arms long afterward, listening to her soft, deep breathing, watching her relaxed face. Though he relished the sight of her sprawled against him, though he soaked in each and every lush curve and all the feminine roundness that so turned him on, he almost wished she'd put on some clothes, because even the feel of her creamy, soft skin against his made him want her again.

He had the feeling he would always want her.

The yearning for her spread within him and he pulled her even closer, needing to take what he could before she woke all the way up this time, and remembered she wasn't ready.

It took every bit of restraint he had to keep from

kissing her awake, to keep from trying to convince her that what they shared was so incredibly right.

How could she not know?

Or maybe that was it. She *did* know, and the reality was too frightening.

Her body certainly hadn't had any such reservations. She'd given all of herself, holding nothing back. The way she'd held him, stroked him, the way she'd looked at him, had spoken clearly of her heart's desires.

His own heart raced in remembered response.

He'd never, in all his thirty-two years, been touched the way she'd touched him. She wasn't experienced, no one with that much wonder and awe in her eyes at the simplest of his kisses could be experienced, but she had a surprisingly sensuous, earthy streak and was such a quick study that he got hard just remembering.

He enjoyed everything about her; the easy intelligence in her eyes, her sweet, warm laughter, the wonderful way she mothered Taylor.

Leaving her would be the hardest thing he'd ever had to do, but there was no choice. He was in love with her. Hopelessly, irrevocably in love. It was his first time, but he knew himself, knew that he'd do everything in his power to insure this went his way. He would seduce, cajole and convince her—whatever it took—that they belonged together.

He would probably eventually succeed.

But it would be no good unless Amber decided for herself that they belonged together. No good because he'd never know if it was the path she would have chosen for herself.

In her sleep, she frowned and whimpered, and the sound went through him like a knife. "Shh," he whispered, soothing her with his hands and voice. "I've got you."

Immediately she stilled. The frown faded. So did much of her tension. Her soft, warm breath tickled the skin of his neck. Her feet were snuggled against his, soaking up their warmth and her hands rested trustingly against his chest. Even their hearts beat in unison, he could feel the rhythm echoing through him.

He missed her already, and though he needed to get some sleep, he didn't want to close his eyes, didn't want to miss a minute of this.

God, it hurt, the letting go, but in the end, he could do little else.

AMBER AWOKE TO THE sound of Taylor's cooing in the next room. It was a happy sound and she smiled.

Until she realized she was in Dax's warm, welcoming bed. Alone. She stretched, looking for him, and at the sight of a note on his pillow, her heart stopped.

Dear Amber,
I had to get back to work.
  I'll be busy for several days, maybe more, before I can get another day off. Please, if you

can, let my parents have my days with Taylor.
They love her and will take care of her.

> You can trust them, Amber.

Love, Dax

You can trust them. He apparently thought she
didn't know that, and had to be told.

Her own fault, she admitted, closing her eyes.
She'd done a good job of letting him think that she
was incapable of trust, period.

With a soft groan, she lay back and listened to
Taylor's joyous babbling. It should have felt right to
wake up in his bed, it *would* have felt right, if he'd
been there.

She'd let him think what they shared was purely
physical, let him assume the problems between
them were insurmountable. She'd hurt him, and that
knowledge was an anguish she'd have to face.

And somehow fix.

CHAPTER FOURTEEN

SHE WAS A COWARD. Not an easy admission, but Amber wouldn't shy away from the truth.

Somewhere along the road, she'd accepted that Dax really did love her. It was a miracle, and it still made her marvel, but she accepted it.

She also accepted that she felt the same.

But she hadn't told him, and that was inexcusable. The words had fairly screamed from her heart last night and she'd kept them to herself. Selfish and afraid, she'd held them near and dear, where they could do little good.

He deserved to know.

It wasn't exactly complimentary that it had taken her so long to really *get* it, but she could face that, too. She'd been hiding. She'd kept herself from living her life to its fullest because she was afraid.

That was going to change.

Last night had been a turning point for her, and if she was being honest, she also had to admit her transformation hadn't started last night. It had begun a year before in a dark, dirty basement where she'd faced her mortality.

She'd changed.

She'd learned love didn't have to hurt, that she could indeed trust someone other than herself. Dax needed to know that, too, and he needed to be thanked for teaching her that lesson, but before she could even begin to do that, she had to make him understand how much he meant to her.

But he wasn't home, and he wasn't returning her calls. It might have taken her too long, but she'd found the depth of her true feelings for him and she wouldn't give up. She could do this, she could fight for what she wanted.

And what she wanted was Dax McCall in her life, in her home, in her heart.

Forever.

Since Dax had made himself so thoroughly scarce and unavailable, Amber was forced to start with something else. Something she'd been wanting to do for awhile.

It required only a trip to the county recorder's office.

She gave Taylor Dax's last name.

They both deserved that, father and daughter, and she wanted Taylor to be a McCall. She thought Dax wanted that, too, and doing it felt right, very right.

There was something else she wanted to do, and while she waited to talk to Dax, she went for that as well. It was tough, and meant swallowing a lot of pride, but it was for Taylor.

Her father answered the phone in his usual gruff,

booming voice, and when he heard Amber, he became all the more gruff. "What do you want?"

As she had all of her life, Amber went on the defensive, and strove to cover that with icy coolness. "You told Dax you wanted to see your granddaughter. Was that true?"

"Yes." He cleared his throat, a sign of unease. But her father was never uneasy.

Could he be as nervous as she?

There was a time in Amber's life when she would have been agonizing over this, wishing he would show just the slightest interest, give her one little word of encouragement.

Suddenly—or maybe not so suddenly at all—it didn't matter. She ached for his presence in her life, solely for Taylor's sake now.

Yes, she still wanted a father who approved of her and what she'd done with her life. But she'd learned she was fine without that approval. Better than fine. "Have you changed your mind?"

"Actually, it was more than that."

"I don't understand," she said slowly.

His voice was harsh. Gruff as ever. Irritated. "Can't a man see his only daughter, as well?"

"Me?"

"You hard of hearing, Amber?"

There was no softening in his tough attitude. There came no words of apology or any request for forgiveness. She understood she'd never get that, but it didn't stop her sudden smile. "No, of course not."

Amazement gave way to a tentative peace. "You can see us whenever it suits you."

"Well, it suits me."

It suited her, too, and after he'd hung up, Amber reflected on her life, where it was going, and she smiled again.

DAX KNEELED IN THE destruction and ash of the burned-out apartment building, taking notes. His investigation was in full swing.

But he was no closer to finding the arsonist now than he had been four days ago. Swearing to himself, he stared down at his pad, but he couldn't see a single word. He'd worked himself to near exhaustion.

He'd had to.

The arsonist, whoever he was, was now wanted for more than starting the fire. He would have to be accountable for all the destruction he'd caused, and for the waste of human life.

Murder.

Finding him or her would depend on Dax and how good his investigation was. But damn, it was hard to keep his head straight when his heart hurt. He truly hadn't expected to fall in love, it just hadn't been part of his grand plan. But it was done, there was nothing he could do about it, except go on with his life.

He'd been at work so long his eyes were grainy. The fierce pounding in his head was probably due to lack of food; he couldn't remember when he'd last had a meal. But if he slowed down enough to eat, then his brain would kick in again and he'd be back to ground zero, mooning pathetically over a woman he couldn't have and missing the daughter he wanted to hug with all his heart.

Disgusted with himself, he lurched to his feet. He was doing no good here. He drove to his office, where he intended to read and reread all the reports until he could figure out what he was missing. Then he'd go to his mom's and hold his daughter for awhile.

His office looked like a disaster zone, which was defeating. The desk was piled high with files and other reports, many of which had fallen to the floor, next to a bag of diapers.

For the first time in his career, he stood at the doorway, thinking about the job he loved with all his heart and felt…overwhelmed.

And hungry, damn hungry.

It wasn't a stretch to use that hunger as an excuse to make his way to the kitchen.

There was always food in a fire station, wasn't there? It felt good to be able to count on something, he thought in a rare moment of self-pity. But while there was food in the refrigerator, none of it was prepared.

He went into the connecting room, the "great room," the men called it because of its size. There was a big screen television on its last legs, several couches—all of which had seen better days—a scarred but functional dining room set, and their pride and joy—a pool table.

"Hey!" he called out. "Who's cooking lunch?"

The two on-duty men watching soap operas didn't budge.

The two playing pool kept up their game. Through the open window he could plainly see two more men standing outside where they'd just finished washing their rigs.

No one answered, or so much as glanced his way.

Dax wasn't insulted, he knew all too well why he was being ignored. They had a tacit agreement. It wasn't necessarily a fair one, but it was simple.

He who got hungry first, cooked.

The last one to eat cleaned up.

Most people thought firefighters ate so fast because they were always trying to keep one step ahead of the fire bell. Not true.

They just didn't want to do dishes.

"So nobody's hungry," he said dryly.

Nobody moved.

Of course not. If they answered in the affirmative, then they'd have to cook. If they said no, then they couldn't eat whatever he cooked.

It was tricky, and if he'd been in a more generous mood, he'd have better appreciated the humor. But he had no humor left. "Damn," he muttered and turned back to the kitchen. The laughter that broke out behind him made him swear even more colorfully.

But he cracked the refrigerator open again. He'd lost fair and square.

A nap might have better suited him than preparing spaghetti sauce for the entire gang, but he was stubborn as well as hungry. Cranking up the radio on the counter, he chopped up a green pepper and tried to stay in the moment.

Tried to stay out of his past.

Tried to stay out of the part of his brain that hurt.

The loud, hard, pulsing rock blaring from the radio helped. So did all the food he popped into his mouth instead of into the pot.

But he kept coming back to one thing…Amber had asked him for more time, for some space. It was all she'd ever asked of him.

And he hadn't given it.

The selfishness of that, the pure greed of it, had him stopping in his tracks, a forgotten knife in one hand, a mushroom in the other.

When had he become so rigid, so unyielding?

Disgusted with himself, he chopped more vegetables with a vengeance, nearly slicing off a finger.

He *would* give her what she wanted, and while it was all fresh in his mind, he yanked his cell phone out of his pocket and dialed her number to tell her so.

When he got her message, he hung up, frustrated. Fine. She could have her damn time. But he wouldn't let her go. *Couldn't* let her go.

His ears played a cruel trick on him then. He thought he could hear her voice. To block it out, he cranked up the volume on the radio.

He could still hear her.

Another vicious crank of the dial helped, barely. His ears rang. The floor vibrated with the beat. The windows rattled.

In unison, he heard the guys bellow for him to

lower the volume, but he ignored them and had to smile at the irony.

He could still hear her.

One last touch to the radio and he had the volume maxed out.

Ahh, he thought…peace. *Finally.* Maybe now he could get some damn food into his gnawing gut.

Satisfied, he grabbed a tomato and froze.

She was standing there, or at least he was dreaming that she was. Rubbing his eyes ruthlessly, he blinked the gritty exhaustion away and looked again.

She was still there in the doorway of the kitchen, hands braced on the jamb on either side of her as she looked at him with an unreadable expression on her face.

His heart stopped, then kicked in again with a painfully slow thudding. The clothes she wore were unlike her, softer, more feminine, and incredibly, unwittingly sexy. He couldn't tear his gaze away. The long, flowing, flowery dress was tight in the bodice and flared gently at her hips before falling nearly to her ankles. There was a row of tiny, dainty buttons down the front, starting at the mouthwatering spot just between her full breasts.

She'd never looked so lovely.

God, he wished she was his.

CHAPTER FIFTEEN

DAX TOLD HIMSELF to cool it. She was probably here
to go over something about Taylor, and he wondered
how he would live through all the *time* he'd vowed
to give her.

She sent him a tentative smile and raised her eyebrows at the music.

With a flick of his wrist, he turned off the radio.
The silence was nearly as deafening as the music had
been. "Taylor—?" he asked.

"She's fine," Amber said quickly. "She's with
your mom."

He nodded, then said gruffly, "I miss her."

She clasped her hands together, but other than
that, remained perfectly still. "I know. I...wanted
to talk to you."

Great. How was he going to keep from grabbing
her and holding on tight? He realized he still held
the knife and a tomato, and he set them both down,
wiping his hands on a towel because he had to keep
them busy. "I'm making lunch."

A smile flickered across her firm, unpainted
mouth. Had he ever seen her without lipstick? Yes,
he remembered with a violent reaction in his lower

body. She'd been sleeping in his bed at the time, a satisfied, cat-in-cream smile on those naked lips.

"I didn't realize you could cook," she said. "Or that you'd..." She trailed off, her voice steady enough, but he could see the telltale sign of a blush creeping up her cheeks.

Interesting. She didn't seem so in control now. "Or that I'd what?"

She lifted a shoulder. "Look so good doing it."

Unfortunately, sweet as that admission was, it only made his ache more pronounced.

The awkward silence settled again and Amber took a step toward him. "I'm sorry to intrude, but I haven't been able to reach you."

"Yeah. About that..."

"Don't be sorry," she said quickly. "I know you've been busy."

Which wasn't exactly the reason he hadn't called or gone by to see her. "Yes, I've been busy," he said carefully, stepping around the counter to face her. "But I've also been a jerk. I should have gotten back to you, but frankly, I was too busy being selfish."

"Selfish?" She laughed at that. "You? I doubt that, Dax."

"I promised not to push, I promised to be patient, and I couldn't do either. I can do better. I can give you your time and space."

"Dax—"

"But I can't let you go. You should know that up front."

"It's okay—"

"No, dammit, it's not."

"Dax—"

"Let me finish. For the first time in my life I broke a promise and I'm sorry for that, so sorry."

"Oh, Dax." Misery crossed her face. "Don't apologize, that's not what I came here for. I wanted to tell you…" She looked at her feet for a long moment before lifting her head again. "I have come to a conclusion," she said in a businesslike tone.

He swallowed. "That sounds bad."

"No." The sophistication fled. "It's just so much harder to tell you than I imagined, and truthfully, I imagined it being pretty tough."

His heart sank. "You can tell me anything, Amber. You know that."

Clearly filled with pent-up energy, she slowly walked the room. "You've been in my head a long time now, Dax."

"Uh…okay." *That was good, right?*

Her back to him, she studied the wall, which was covered in pictures. The guys had been pinning up photos ever since the station first opened ten years before. There were families, girlfriends, boyfriends, kids…an entire ten years' worth of living.

What did she see? he wondered. *What did she feel?* He wished he knew.

"I know it seems silly," she said to the wall. "To tell you that I can't stop thinking of you."

"I understand perfectly."

She turned to him then. "It's really quite maddening."

He nodded. Definitely maddening.

"You're different, you know. Different from anyone I've ever known."

"Is that different good, or different bad?"

She smiled a full-blown smile that took his breath. "I learned things from you. I learned I didn't have to be strong all the time, that I *could* lean on someone else once in awhile. I can be independent, Dax, and still let someone in."

"Someone?"

She laughed. *Laughed.* "You, silly. I let *you* in."

While he stood there with his mouth open, staring stupidly, she came toward him, smile still in place, her gaze tentative. "I learned to trust you. To let you trust me." Her warm, loving eyes touched him first, then her hands when she stepped close enough to set them on his chest. "And I realized something else, and this is the biggie…" Those clever hands slid up his chest and cupped his face. "I was afraid. I knew and understood that. What I didn't know, or understand, Dax, was *your* fear."

She curled her fingers in his hair, holding him when he might have stepped back and denied her. "The truth is Daxton McCall, despite your bravado and tough words, you're every bit as scared as I am."

Behind them, the swinging door to the kitchen opened as two of the firefighters stuck their heads in.

"Not that we're admitting anything," one said. "But we're looking for food— *Oh.* Excuse me." He straightened with a new, more charming smile when he saw Amber. "I didn't realize we had company."

"*You* don't," Dax said, his eyes still on Amber. "Get out."

"But how about lunch?" asked the other one, shoving his buddy aside and sniffing theatrically. "Something smells good." He winked at Amber. "Or is that you?"

Dax growled at them, and they both quickly backed out.

Amber looked appalled. "Dax! That's no way to treat—"

"Say it again," he demanded, reaching for her, giving her a little shake. He didn't know whether to allow this glimmer of hope within him, and the not knowing was killing him. "Say it!"

"That you obviously need some etiquette classes, or that you're a chicken?"

He grated his teeth. "The chicken part."

"Oh, I think you heard me." Dropping her hands from him, she sashayed away to the counter, and picked up his knife. She hacked at a tomato. "You really changed things for me." Her words were a tad uneven, but her hands were a blur as she demolished the tomato. "You taught me so much about how I could feel for people, about how people could feel for me…"

He came around behind her, sliding his hands along her expressive arms to hold them still. In the interest of both their fingers, he gently set down the knife. "I can't dispute the chicken part," he admitted. Wrapping his arms around her, he held her tight, buried his face in her neck. God, he loved her so much.

He turned her to face him. "It's true, I used your resistance to reinforce my own. I don't know what I expected would happen between us, but it certainly wasn't for me to fall so deep."

Her eyes filled and she opened her mouth, but he softly set a finger to her lips. "Yes, the thought of a future with just one woman terrified me more than anything I'd ever faced, but I knew there was no other woman for me, *anywhere,* and there never would be again."

"Oh, Dax." A tear spilled over and he gently swiped it off with his thumb.

"I fell in love with you, Amber," he said huskily. "And I fell good and hard. That was the easy part. The hard part came later, when I realized you didn't feel the same way, and that you might never feel the same. I'm sorry I hurt you, I never meant to."

"I know."

Because he could, he pulled her close and wondered what was going to happen.

"I called my father," she said. "I'm going to see him. For Taylor." She lifted her head from his chest and stroked his jaw as she looked deep into his eyes. "I also changed Taylor's last name, officially, to Mc-Call. I thought that was important."

His heart swelled, but before he could even attempt to tell her how much it meant to him, she dropped her hands from him. "That's part of why I came here today. I wanted you to know what I had done."

That was it? Hello. Let me drive you crazy. See ya?

Her smile wobbled and she carefully stepped back from him. "Well…" She whirled and walked quickly to the door while his heart died a thousand deaths.

Then, before she turned the handle, she hesitated.

Killing him.

"Aren't you even going to try and stop me?" She whirled around to look at him. "You realize I have no idea what I'm doing! I could really use some help here."

His heart leaped into his throat, but before he could say a word, she lifted a hand. "No, wait. Don't help me. That's not right. I'm the one who has to do this, not you."

"Amber…" Had he missed something? "Honey, are you making any sense?"

She drew a deep breath. "Dammit, Dax, I love you, too." Her smile shook badly. "How's that for sense?"

Stunned, all he could do was nod. "It's good."

"I guess I'll have to prove it to you." She swung open the double doors of the kitchen and cleared her throat.

Six curious men turned their heads.

"Listen up everyone…" She looked at Dax over her shoulder. "I love Dax McCall."

Wild cheers, lewd whistles and a chorus of cat-calls greeted this announcement. Amber grinned. "Did everyone get that?"

More cheers.

She slammed the doors on them and turned back to Dax, who was still standing there, mouth open, heart pounding, love and shock singing through his veins.

"I meant it," she said quietly, once again clasping her hands together. Her smile was still very shaky and her eyes suspiciously wet. "I really meant it. Now I dare you to be more trusting, to lay more on the line than that!"

Oh, he was up for the challenge, yes he was. With his own shaky smile, he stalked past her and yanked open the kitchen doors. "Okay another announcement…I'm forsaking bachelorhood—"

Loud groans greeted that announcement, which made him laugh. "I'm getting something better, trust me."

Someone called out something about getting lucky every single night with the same woman and Dax grinned. "That, too, but more importantly, I'm going to marry Amber, and spend every single day of the rest of my life a very happy man."

Next to him, Amber gasped. *"Marry?"*

He hauled her close. "Love conquers all, we know that. We belong together. Say you'll marry me, Amber. Say you'll give me forever."

In tune to the renewed catcalls, laughter and cheers of congratulations, Amber laughed and went up on tiptoe to kiss him. In soft agreement, she said, "Yes, I'll give you forever."

* * * * *

EXPOSED: MISBEHAVING WITH THE MAGNATE

USA TODAY Bestselling Author

Kelly Hunter

Dear Reader,

There's something satisfying about aiming for the stars and failing (wait for it...), and then picking up, dusting off, setting jaw and aiming for those stars again. It takes a certain wilfulness and courage, the ability to learn from mistakes. Sometimes it takes time to gather the strength to try again. For Gabrielle Alexander the time has come to head back to France to confront childhood dreams and disappointments, and childhood sweetheart Luc Duvalier. What happens after that is cause for much champagne.

There's a companion story to this one from Harlequin Presents called *Revealed: A Prince and a Pregnancy*. It follows the romance between Simone Duvalier and Rafael Alexander, so if you like Gabrielle and Luc's story, perhaps you'll pick it up.

I love hearing from readers and you can find me online at www.kellyhunter.net or www.kellyhunter.co.

Happy reading,

Kelly

CHAPTER ONE

'BREATHE IN, BREATHE OUT,' muttered Gabrielle Alexander as she stood and stared at the daunting wooden door that led to the servants' quarters of Chateau des Caverness. She knew this door, knew the feel of it beneath her palm and the haughty hollow sound the brass knocker made when it connected with the wood. Gabrielle had been sixteen when she'd last walked through this door; sixteen and shattered at the thought of leaving everything she knew and loved behind. Such turbulent times, thought Gabrielle with a wry smile for the girl she'd once been. How she'd pleaded with her mother to be allowed to stay; Lord, how she'd begged and argued and finally wept. But the people she'd loved had not loved her. Josien Alexander had shipped her daughter off to Australia with a heart as hard and as cold as an arctic iceberg.

All because of a kiss.

'It wasn't even a good kiss,' muttered Gabrielle as she stared at the door and dug deep for the courage to put her hand to the knocker and make it do its thing. Seven years had passed; Gabrielle knew a lot more about kissing these days. She knew the feel of hot sweet kisses on her lips. Ragged greedy kisses on her skin. 'It was a very ordinary kiss.'

Liar, said a little inner voice that would not remain silent.

'A practice kiss. A practically meaningless kiss.'

Big fat liar.

'So shoot me,' she murmured to that little voice inside her. 'You remember it your way and I'll remember it mine.' She grasped the knocker and lifted it. 'Better still, let's not remember it at all.'

But that was harder done than said. Not here in this place, with the scent of summer grapes all around her and the warmth of the sun beating down on her shoulders. Not with her heart swollen and heavy with the knowledge that this place, this chateau, this fragrant idyllic corner of France's Champagne district was the only place that had ever felt like home and that for seven long years she'd stayed away from it.

All because of a kiss.

Taking hold of the brass ring, Gabrielle lifted it and brought it down hard against the wooden door. Boom. Nothing quite like a dreaded sound from her childhood to get her blood pumping and the hairs on her arms standing to attention. Boom. Once more with feeling. Boom boom and *boom.*

But the door did not open. No footsteps echoed along the dark and narrow hallway Gabrielle knew was behind that door. She turned from her mother's quarters to stare across the courtyard at the chateau proper. She *really* didn't want to go knocking on any of those doors.

Josien had pneumonia; that was what Simone Duvalier, childhood playmate and current mistress of Caverness, had said in her phone message. What if Josien was too ill to get out of bed? What if she tried to answer the door and collapsed on the way?

Muttering a prayer to a God she barely believed in, Gabrielle dug in her handbag until her fingers closed around the key she sought. Smooth and cold, it both beckoned and repelled. She had no right to unlock this door—this wasn't her home any more. Caution pleaded with her not to slide the key in the lock but caution never had been Gabrielle's strong point.

Wilful, her mother had called her on more than one occasion.

Headstrong.

Fool.

The key turned easily, smoothly, and with a click and a slight nudge on her part the door swung open. *'Maman?'* Gabrielle stepped tentatively inside the darkened hallway. *'Maman?'* A flash of red caught her eye—red where there'd never been red before. A blinking row of little red lights and a no-nonsense square panel, the kind that signalled state-of-the-art alarm systems that summoned large men with flat top buzz cuts and firearms to the door. *'Maman?'*

And then the cacophony began. No discreet beeping for this alarm system, it was air-raid-klaxon loud and could doubtless be heard for miles. Uh oh. Gabrielle ran towards the blinking lights and wrenched the casing open, staring in dismay at a keyboard containing both letters and numbers. She punched in her birth date. The ear splitting noise continued. She keyed in Rafael's name and date of birth next, but Josien was clearly not the sentimental type. She tried entering the year that Chateau des Caverness had been built, the name and year of its most successful champagne vintage, the number of ancient Linden trees lining the sides of the lane leading up to the chateau, but the alarm just kept on screaming. She started pressing buttons at random. 'Shiste. *Merde*. Bugger!'

'Nice to hear you're still multilingual,' said a midnight-smooth voice from close behind her and Gabrielle closed her eyes and tried to stop her already racing heart from doubling its tempo yet again. She knew that voice, the deep delicious timbre of it. A Champagne voice, a voice of Rheims, it was there in the lilt and the texture of the words. A voice that conjured up forbidden thoughts and heated yearnings. She'd heard it in her dreams for years.

'Oh, hello, Luc.' If he could do deadpan, so could she. Gabrielle turned slowly and there he stood, looking every inch the head of a Champagne dynasty in his tailored grey trousers and crisp white business shirt. Gabrielle could have spent a lot longer staring at Luc Duvalier and cataloguing the changes time had wrought in him but circumstances and a healthy respect for her eardrums dictated moving right along. 'Long time no see. I don't suppose you could help me turn this thing off?'

He brushed past her, long, strong fingers moving swiftly over the panel. *'Cinq six six deux quatre cinq un.'*

The alarm cut out abruptly and silence cut in. A loud, ringing kind of silence.

'Merci,' she said finally.

'You're welcome.' Lucien Duvalier's perfectly sculpted lips tightened. 'What are you doing here, Gabrielle?'

'I lived here once, remember?'

'Not for the past seven years, you haven't.'

'True.' Now that quiet had been restored, Gabrielle could look her fill. She studied the tall, dark-haired, dark-eyed man standing before her, trying for detachment and failing miserably. Luc had been twenty-two when she'd last seen him and even then the promise of tightly leashed power and outrageous sexuality had hovered about him like a velvet cloak. Night, the household staff had called him. And Rafael, Luc's childhood partner in crime, with his fair hair and his teasing blue eyes, had been Day.

'Sorry about setting the alarm off,' she said with an awkward shrug. 'I should have known better than to use the key.'

Luc said nothing. He never had been one for small talk. But it was all she could manage. Taking a deep and steadying breath, Gabrielle tried again. 'You're looking well, Lucien.'

When he still made no reply Gabrielle looked past him, across the courtyard towards the chateau tucked snugly into the terraced hillside. 'Caverness is looking well too. Cared for. Prosperous. I heard about your father's death a few years back.' She didn't feel inclined to say any more on the subject. Had she wanted to lie through her teeth she could have added something about being sorry to hear of old man Duvalier's demise. 'Guess that makes you king of the castle now,' she added recklessly. She met his dark burning gaze without flinching. 'Should I kneel?'

'You've changed,' he said abruptly.

She certainly hoped so.

'You're harder.'

'Thank you.'

'More beautiful.'

'My thanks again.' Gabrielle held back a sigh. If Luc wanted to categorise the changes in her, she might as well show him the big ones. She wasn't a gangly sixteen-year-old on the cusp of womanhood any more. And Luc wasn't the centre of her life. 'Look at us,' she chided lightly. 'Childhood playmates and here I've greeted you with less warmth than one would greet a stranger. Three kisses, isn't it? One for each cheek and then a spare?' She moved closer and brushed his left cheek with her lips, breathing in the subtle pine scent that clung to his skin and trying very hard not to let it wrap around her and squeeze. 'One.' She pulled back and made for his other cheek, never mind that he stood as if turned to stone. 'Two,' she whispered and let her lips linger a fraction longer this time.

'Back off, angel.' Luc's voice was nothing more than a dark and dangerous rumble as his fingers came up to caress her jaw before sliding around to the base of her neck. 'For your own sake if not for mine.'

A warning. One she would do well to heed. Not that she did. A frisson of awareness slid down her spine and she closed her eyes the better to diffuse it. So he could still make her body ache for his touch. Nothing to worry about. She was older now. Wiser. She knew better than to lose her heart to the head of the House of Duvalier. Not that a few more iron clad reasons to ensure she kept her distance from this man wouldn't come in handy. 'Are you married these days, Luc?'

'No.'

'Celibate?'

'No.'

'Are you sure?' She brushed his ear lobe with her lips. 'You seem a little…uptight. It's just an innocent greeting.'

The fingers at the base of her neck tightened. 'You're not innocent.'

'You noticed.' She pulled back smoothly, dislodging his hand with a shrug as she stepped away and shot him a careless smile for good measure. 'You always were observant. Perhaps two kisses *are* greeting enough for you, after all. Shall we take a rain check on the third?'

'Why are you here, Gabrielle?'

Here in this place where no one wanted her. Luc couldn't have made the implication clearer if he'd painted it on a sign and hung it on the door. 'Simone phoned and left a message. She said my mother had been ill. She said…' Gabrielle hesitated, unwilling to reveal any more weakness to this man. 'She said that Josien had been calling for her angels.' Whether Josien had been calling for her children, who'd been named after two of the winged entities, was anyone's guess. Rafe thought not. Rafael thought Gabrielle's decision to travel halfway across the world on the strength of a fevered plea a colossal mistake but even so… Even if Josien refused to see her…

Some mistakes were unavoidable.

Gabrielle attempted a nonchalant shrug. 'So here I am.'

'Does Josien *know* of your expected arrival?' asked Luc quietly.

'I—' Nervously, Gabrielle fiddled with the cuff of her stylish cream jacket. 'No.'

Luc's gaze grew hooded and Gabrielle thought she saw a flash of something that looked a lot like sympathy in their depths. 'You always were too impetuous for your own good,' he murmured. 'I gather your brother declined to accompany you?'

'Rafe's busy,' she said guardedly. 'As I'm sure you must be. Luc, if you could just tell me where to find my mother…'

'Come,' he said, turning abruptly and heading for the door. 'Josien is staying in one of the suites in the west wing until she recovers more fully. A nurse attends her. Doctor's orders. It was that or the hospital.'

Pulling the door closed behind them, and pocket-

this was the path she'd chosen to
it she would, no matter what B
thought, or *anyone* thought
see her mother.

Some mistakes we
'Would you lik
Luc quietly.
'No.' Luc's
her. Some
again,
with
b

calling for her children at all? What then?

The nurse who met them in the sitting room of the suite was a grizzle-faced man in his mid fifties whom Luc introduced as Hans. Hans had a firm handshake, a steady gaze, and a warm smile for Gabrielle.

'Stubbornest patient I've ever had,' he said. 'She's just taken her medication so you've about five minutes before she begins to get drowsy. Not that she won't fight the sleep. She always does.' Hans gestured towards yet another closed door. 'She's in there.'

'Thank you.' Gabrielle's nerves were at breaking point and her body felt weary beyond belief, courtesy of the twenty-three-hour flight from Sydney, but

ollow and follow
afe thought, or Luc
Gabrielle had come to

e unavoidable.
me to accompany you?' asked

offer of support scraped at her, shamed
numiliations were best kept private. Then
maybe this meeting *would* go more smoothly
a third party present. With Luc present, Ga-
rielle amended with brutal honesty, so that Josien
could *see* that, as far as Luc was concerned, the mistakes of the past had been paid for. And they had
been paid for, hadn't they? Surely they'd been paid
for? 'Yes.'

Luc's lips curved ever so slightly. 'Which is it?'
Gabrielle's gaze met his and skittered away. 'Yes.'
'Four minutes,' said Hans dryly.
'Thanks.' Steeling herself, Gabrielle reached for
the handle to yet another closed door and headed inside. It was warmer in here. Darker too, for the afternoon light had to pry its way through two layers of
gauze curtain material before finding entry. A large
four poster bed dominated the space so that the figure tucked beneath the fluffy white bedcovers looked
tiny in comparison. Seven years ago, Josien Alexander's hair had been as black as a raven's wing and
had fallen almost to her waist. Now it was streaked
with silver and cut to sit just beneath her chin but
she was still the most beautiful woman Gabrielle

had ever seen. Josien's eyes—those startling violet blue eyes that had always watched and judged but never smiled—were closed, and Gabrielle was grateful for the reprieve. She needed that moment to bind her emotions tight.

'Josien,' said Luc gently. '*Pardonnez-moi* for the lateness of the hour but you have a visitor.'

Josien turned her head and slowly, slowly, she opened her eyes, focussing first on Luc, and then on Gabrielle standing awkwardly beside him. With a swiftly indrawn breath, Josien closed her eyes and turned away.

Gabrielle felt the sting of bitter tears welling in her own eyes but she blinked them away, and made herself speak even though her words would come out ragged and choked. 'Hello, *Maman*.'

'You shouldn't have come.' Josien kept her face averted.

'So people keep telling me.' Luc's face, when Gabrielle glanced his way, was as hard and unyielding as the stones from which the chateau had been built. 'I hear you've been unwell.'

'*Ce ne'est rien,*' said Josien. 'It's nothing.'

It didn't look like nothing. Luc had been right. Her mother looked frail. 'I brought you a gift.' Gabrielle reached into her bag for the album of photos she'd put together so painstakingly. Rafe would kill her if he knew how many photos of him she'd included in the mix, but he didn't know and she wasn't about to tell him. 'I thought you might like to know what Rafe and I have been doing these past seven years.

We bought a broken vineyard, *Maman*, and brought it back to life. We've done so well. Rafe's a brilliant businessman. You should be proud of him.'

Josien said nothing and Gabrielle felt her lips tighten. So what if Rafael had eventually gone as far away from Josien and this place as he could get? That was what people did when raised on a diet of scathing criticism interspersed with icy indifference. Rafe had never deserved any of the treatment Josien had dealt him. He really hadn't. 'I'll leave it here on the end of the bed in case you want to look at it some time.'

'Take it and go.'

Yeah, well. That was what you got when you believed in tooth fairies, happily ever after, and mothers who actually cared. 'I've taken a room in the village, *Maman*. I'll be in the area these next few weeks. I know you're tired right now but maybe when you're feeling better you could give me a call. Here.' She fished a business card from her handbag. 'I'll leave you my number.' Gabrielle's words were met with more silence. Gabrielle bit her lip—praying for one pain to subdue another, but Josien's rejection had cut too deep. She should never have come here. She should have listened to Rafe and to Luc instead of listening to her heart. 'So...' Gabrielle felt the world sway, and then Luc's hand was beneath her elbow, fragile purchase against the darkness threatening to engulf her.

'Jet lag,' murmured Luc. It wasn't jet lag causing her to sway and they both knew it, but he afforded her the courtesy of an excuse for her body's reaction and Gabrielle seized it.

'Yes. It's been a long day.'

'Wait for me outside,' he said as he gently shepherded her towards the door. 'It's about to get longer.'

LUC WAITED UNTIL the door clicked closed behind Gabrielle before turning to the woman in the bed. Josien Alexander was an enchantingly beautiful woman and always had been. Coolly unfathomable, she ran the housekeeping staff at the chateau with an iron fist and no second chances. She'd raised her children the same way. Luc had bowed to Josien's will all those years ago because he'd seen the sense in sending Gabrielle away, but he saw no sense in Josien's actions now. All he saw was pain.

Josien's eyes were still closed as Luc strode back towards the bed but he didn't need her eyes, only her ears. 'My father told me of our duty to you before he died,' he said grimly. 'I've done my utmost to honour it. I've tried my damnedest to make allowances for your behaviour, Josien, but, so help me, if you don't make time for your daughter while she's here you can pack your bags and leave this place the minute your health allows it. Do you hear me, Josien?'

Josien nodded, tears tracking noiselessly down her cheeks, and Luc struggled to contain his frustration and his fury. 'You've never been able to see it, have you? No matter how badly you wound them or how hard you try to push them away...you just don't get it.' He looked at the photo album and his roiling emotions coalesced into a tight ball of anger directed squarely at the woman in the bed, no matter how fragile or beautiful she was. 'You've never been able to see how much your children love you.'

LUC CAUGHT UP with Gabrielle halfway along the hallway. He needed a drink. The thorn he'd never quite managed to extricate from his side looked as if she needed one too. 'In here,' he told her, and ushered her into the library that doubled on occasion as his formal office space, usually when he entertained clients and wanted to impress. 'Where are you staying?' he asked as he headed for the bar, reached for the brandy and poured generously.

'In the village,' she replied, careful not to let her fingers brush his as she took the half full glass from his outstretched hand and downed it in a single gulp. 'Thanks.' Her gaze went to the label on the bottle and her eyes widened. 'What…? For heaven's sake, Luc! This stuff has to be at least a hundred years old and expensive enough to make even you wince. You might *warn* a person before you handed it to them. I could try *tasting* it next time.'

'Where in the village?' He poured her another shot. She could taste it now.

'I took a room above the old flour mill.'

'I'll have someone collect your bags,' he told her curtly and downed his own brandy before setting the glass back on the counter somewhat more forcefully than necessary. Gabrielle flinched at the sound. She looked jittery, strung out. She looked like he felt. 'You can stay here,' he told her. 'There's room enough.'

But Gabrielle shook her head. 'I can't,' she said with a stubborn tilt to her chin that he remembered of old. 'You heard her.' Gabrielle smiled bitterly and swirled the brandy in her glass. 'She doesn't want me here.'

'When last I checked,' he said, his voice deceptively mild, 'Luc, not Josien, was master of Caverness. There's room for you here. There's no need for you to stay in the village. Simone, I'm sure, will be glad of your company.'

'And you?' Gabrielle lowered the glass from her lips, and pinned him with a grey-eyed gaze that held more than a hint of pain. 'Will you be glad of my company too? There was a time when you couldn't wait for me to leave.'

'You were *sixteen*, Gabrielle. And if you don't know the reason behind my encouraging you to finish growing up elsewhere then you're not nearly as smart as I thought you were. One more week and I'd have had you naked beneath me. In your bed or mine or halfway up the stairs, I wouldn't have cared,' he said bluntly. 'And neither would you.'

He'd surprised her. Shocked her. He could see it in her eyes. 'Well, then…glad we cleared that up.' She took another sip of her brandy and set her glass carefully on the bench, as if even that small motion took up all of her control. 'I suppose I should thank you.'

But she didn't.

'I lost my virginity to a handsome Australian farm

boy when I was nineteen,' she said in a low, ragged voice. 'He was charming, and funny, and he made my pulse race and my body ache for more of him. He was everything a girl could wish for when it came to her first time, and it still wasn't enough.' Gabrielle headed for the door. Luc stood rooted to the spot. 'I'll be staying at the old flour mill for the next three weeks. If you could send word to me if my mother's condition changes, I'd be very grateful.'

'Why wasn't it enough?' Luc's throat felt tight, the words came out raspy, but he had to know. 'Gabrielle, why did he disappoint you?'

He didn't think she was going to answer, but then she turned as she reached the door and speared him with a glance that held more than its share of self-mockery. 'I really don't know. Maybe he just wasn't you.'

Luc waited until she'd shut the door behind her before he let his curses fly. He was a man who took pride in his self control. He'd worked hard for it; fought against his deepest nature to secure it. Only one woman had ever made him lose it. The results had been disastrous for all concerned. Josien had been hysterical, his father aghast, and Gabrielle... innocent, trusting Gabrielle had been exiled.

She'd lost her virginity to a handsome Australian.

Fury roared through him as he picked up his glass and flung it at the fireplace, his temper only marginally appeased when the glass exploded in a burst of glittering crystal shards.

CHAPTER TWO

'YOU SHOULDN'T HAVE said that.' Gabrielle had a habit of talking to herself whenever she felt stressed. She'd been talking to herself ever since she'd set foot back in France. Her footsteps made a crunching sound as she hurried across the gravel courtyard towards her hire car, every step taking her further away from Caverness and the people in it. She needed to leave before she broke down completely. She needed to leave this place *now*.

Gabrielle made it back to the village without mishap. She drove on the correct side of the road and didn't lose her way. She even observed the speed limit. And when she got to the old mill house she locked herself inside her room before finally giving in to weariness and sinking back on the bed with her forearm across her eyes, as if by blocking her sight she could block out the memory of her conversation with Lucien. 'You should *not* have said that.'

It had been seven years since she'd last seen Luc. Seven years of complete indifference on his part. No phone calls, no letters, no contact. Not once. A sixteen-year-old girl had deduced from Luc's actions that he'd simply been playing with her when he'd kissed her all those years ago. That the housekeeper's daughter had meant nothing to him.

Not once, not *once*, had it ever occurred to her that Luc had been trying to protect her from a relationship she'd been nowhere near ready for.

Still wasn't ready for if her recent reaction to him was anything to go by.

So she had money behind her now, and self-esteem, and a good deal more to offer a man on an intellectual level. That still didn't equip her to deal with the likes of Luc Duvalier. Luc, whose brooding black gaze could make her forget every ounce of self-preservation she'd ever learned.

How many minutes in his company had it taken her to test the strength of her physical reaction to him? Two minutes, or had it been three? How long had it taken her to lay herself bare for him? Telling him that her first lover had been a disappointment to her. Gabrielle groaned and rolled over onto her side, burying her head in a pillow and pulling the blue chenille bedspread around her for comfort. What kind of woman told a man that?

A woman who'd never quite forgotten the ecstasy and the agony of a single stolen kiss, said a voice that would not be silenced.

A woman who'd known all along that no one at Caverness would bid her welcome and mean it.

A fool.

LUC DIDN'T USUALLY wait impatiently for his sister to return home from her work, but this day he did, seeking Simone out in the kitchen, never mind the box of fresh fruit and vegetables in her arms or the fact that she hadn't yet managed to put the box down.

'*Bonjour*, brother of mine,' she said cheerfully. 'I come bearing good food and even better news. The sales figures are finally in and we,' she said, setting the bags on the counter with a flourish, 'had a *very* good quarter.'

'Congratulations,' he said, but something in his voice must have alerted Simone to his turmoil for she turned sharply, set the box down on the bench, and took her time looking him over.

'Something's wrong,' she said warily. 'What is it?'

'Josien had a visitor this afternoon.'

'Who?'

'Gabrielle.'

Luc watched his sister's face light up with wry resignation. Simone and Gabrielle had been close as children. Closer than sisters, never mind the huge gap in social standing between them. 'Gaby is here?' asked Simone. 'Here as in here at the chateau? Where?'

'Here as in staying in the village, and before you start in on my manners, yes, I offered her a room, which she declined. Dammit, Simone! Why didn't you warn me that you'd sent for her? And why the hell didn't you tell Josien?'

Simone's expression grew guarded. 'I left a message on Gaby's answering machine saying her mother was ill. That's all I did. What was there to tell?'

'You knew she'd come,' muttered Luc darkly.

'I thought she'd call first.'

'Well, she didn't.'

'So what happened?' asked Simone warily.

Luc gave it to his sister straight. 'Josien wouldn't talk to her. Wouldn't even look at her.'

A barrage of swear words followed his announcement, none of them becoming to a lady. 'So then what happened?' demanded Simone. 'Did *you* make Gabrielle feel welcome?'

'Sort of.'

'Sort of? For heaven's sake, Luc, you're a grown man! Would it have killed you to behave like one?'

'I did behave like one,' he said grimly.

Simone halted, midway between the fridge and the counter. 'Oh, hell,' she said. 'You still want her.'

Luc didn't deny it. What he didn't reveal to his sister was just how intense his desire for Gabrielle had been. He'd barely been able to control it. And he needed to. 'Gabrielle needs a friend right now, Simone, and it can't be me,' he said gruffly. 'I don't want to do wrong by her again.'

Simone's gaze softened. 'Dear heart,' she said. 'The way I remember it, you've never done Gaby wrong. Others have—most certainly they have. But not you.'

'You're a little biased,' he said.

Simone smiled. 'Only a little.'

'She's staying at the old mill house,' he offered next and exhaled his relief as his sister upended a wicker basket full of oranges onto the counter and hastily started refilling it with a variety of foodstuffs from the refrigerator. 'You're going after her?'

'Of course I'm going after her,' said Simone. 'Isn't that what you want? Somebody has to make her feel welcome.'

GABRIELLE WOKE TO the sound of vigorous pounding on her door. She sat up with a groan, slung her legs over the side of the bed, and pushed the heavy fall of dark curls from her face before checking her wristwatch for the time. Eight p.m. French time and the early hours of the morning by Australian reckoning. She'd slept for almost three hours. Now she'd never get back to sleep for the night. 'Who is it?'

'Simone,' said yet another voice from her past, albeit a voice currently heavy with impatience. Gabrielle went to the door and unlocked it gingerly before swinging it open. She didn't know if she could cope with any more blasts from the past today. Between them, Luc and Josien had proved quite sufficient. She stared for a moment at the elegant raven-haired beauty in the navy-blue suit, trying to reconcile the image of cool sophistication standing before her with the hoyden that had been Simone. And then she saw the magnum of champagne in the woman's left hand and the basket full of delicacies at her feet and knew that the hoyden was alive and well beneath those daunting designer clothes.

'Look at you, sleepyhead,' said Simone, and Gabrielle found herself enclosed in a warm and perfumed embrace. 'I couldn't believe it when Luc told

me you'd come home. Why didn't you call me? I'd
have picked you up from the airport. I'd have made
all the arrangements. Oh, look at you!' Tears gathered in Simone's expressive brown eyes. 'I always
knew you'd grow to be even more beautiful than
your mother. It was always there. In your eyes; and
in your heart.' Simone pulled back. 'Luc told me
what happened with Josien, Gaby. I could *strangle*
her. Josien *did* call for you, I swear she did. I thought
she wanted to make amends. I'd have never left that
message for you otherwise. Never.'

'I know,' said Gabrielle. 'I knew my welcome
would probably be somewhat…cool. But I came
anyway. You must think I'm crazy.'

'No,' said Simone gently. 'Not crazy. Hopeful.
I made us a picnic,' she said, stepping back to the
door to retrieve her basket. 'And I don't care where
we eat it.' She hefted the magnum up to eye level to
reveal the label. 'The day you left I stole two bottles
of our oldest and finest and hid them in the caves. I
swore on my sainted mother's grave that the day you
returned we would drink one of them. Of course, I
never expected you to stay away so *long*. What kept
you?'

Gabrielle felt her lips curve, she couldn't help it.
Finally, a welcome without restraint. 'I was busy
growing up and carving out a life for myself in Australia,' she said dryly. 'And I want to know what
you're saving the second bottle for.'

'You'll see,' said Simone. 'About this picnic…
Shall we eat it here on the bed or shall we dine some-

where where we can see the clouds? We could head for our old picnic spot.'

'So we could.' Gabrielle eyed Simone's attire sceptically. 'You look every bit the successful businesswoman you always vowed you'd be, but are you sure you'll be able to walk up the track in those shoes without breaking your neck?'

Simone looked down at her stiletto-clad feet and frowned. 'You're right. I really hadn't thought this through. Luc shoved me out of the house so fast I forgot to change clothes.' She stared at the small double bed, then cast her eye around the poky little room. 'I lied. I do care where we eat and this isn't the place. We'll have to go back to Caverness so I can change clothes.'

'No,' said Gabrielle hastily. 'No way. I'm sorry, Simone. I'll meet you up at our picnic spot if you like, but I've had enough of Caverness for one day.' If Gabrielle went back to the chateau right now she'd only start throwing things again. Namely herself. At Luc.

'It's just a house,' said Simone, and, at Gabrielle's level stare, 'Okay, a castle. A very big castle.'

'No.'

'I'll smuggle you in and smuggle you out,' said Simone. 'Just like the old days. No one will ever know.'

'Luc would know.' He'd always known.

'All right then,' said Simone. 'Let's approach this like rational, sensible, intelligent women. I'll just borrow your clothes and get changed here.'

'I like it,' said Gabrielle. 'But I'm warning you I shopped for clothes in Singapore on the way over and had to sit on my suitcases to get them to shut. There's wreckage within those cases that I'm not sure you're ready for. There's chaos in there that I'm not sure *I'm* ready for.'

'Unleash it,' said Simone, and released the champagne cork quietly and without spilling a drop of the precious liquid. 'I live for chaos.' Setting the magnum on the bedside table, Simone began to rummage through the basket at her feet. 'I could have sworn I put some champagne flutes in here somewhere. Special picnic ones.'

'Plastic ones?' said Gabrielle.

'Don't be ridiculous,' said Simone. 'Heathen. Where have you been *living* these past seven years? Ah, here they are.' She brandished them aloft with a flourish. 'Not plastic. Polish crystal. Perfectly shaped, beautifully balanced, and as delicately made as petals on a rose. *Plastic* champagne flutes,' muttered Simone with a shudder as she filled the two glasses and handed one to Gabrielle. 'God help us and welcome home.'

THEY ATE ATOP the highest hill in the area, surrounded by grapevines and with the rooftops of the chateau spread out below them, and, in the distance, the rooftops and church spires of the village.

'What will you do while you're here?' asked Simone after the last crumbs of cheese had been nibbled and the last sliver of pâté had been devoured. 'Luc said you planned to stay in the area for a few weeks.'

Gabrielle nodded. 'I came here on business as well as to see *Maman*. Rafe and I make wine these days.'

'Oh?' said Simone, her voice a little too offhand to actually *be* offhand. 'What kind of wine?'

'Cabernet sauvignon, mostly, and some cabernet merlot. For the high end of the market and worth every cent. We're looking to extend our export opportunities into Europe and set up a distribution arm. It makes sense to look for premises in the place we know best.'

'Rafael wishes to return?' said Simone.

'No. Not Rafe. Just me.'

'Oh.'

'Don't sound so disappointed.' Gabrielle slid Simone a sideways glance.

'I'm not disappointed,' said Simone with a toss of her head. 'Not at all. I'm just…curious. What kind of operations base are you looking for? Business premises or residential property?'

'Both.'

'With or without land attached?'

'Depends on the land,' said Gabrielle. 'Why?'

'The old Hammerschmidt vineyard is on the market,' said Simone. 'The vines are in a dreadful state, the winemaking equipment is fifty years out of date, and the house needs a lot of attention, but the cellars are good and the location is excellent. Luc's been looking into acquiring it.'

'Really?' said Gabrielle dryly. 'And you're telling me this why?'

'Because it would probably suit your purposes.'

'If it did I'd be in direct competition for the property with Luc.'

'Really?' said Simone airily. 'Could be fun.'

'For whom?' said Gabrielle. 'Seriously, Simone, I appreciate your help but where's your sense of family duty? Your loyalty to Luc and to your family business? There was a time you put loyalty to family before your own happiness. Where did *that* Simone go?'

Simone's expression grew shuttered. 'That Simone grew up to regret not holding tight to her happiness with both hands. I'm older now. Wiser.'

'Trickier,' murmured Gabrielle.

'That too.' Simone sipped at her champagne and stared at the valley spread out before her, half of which she owned. 'So how is he?' she said tentatively. 'Rafael.'

'Driven,' said Gabrielle with a wry twist of her lips.

'Is he happy?'

'I really don't know.'

'Is he married?'

'No.' Gabrielle took pity on her childhood friend and gave her the information she sought. 'He's had a few relationships over the years. Less than he could have had. Nothing he ever put before his work.' Gabrielle sipped at her champagne. 'He's building an empire,' she said softly. 'Proving his worth, over and over, to a mother who never loved him, an heiress who wouldn't believe in him, and a best friend who didn't support him.'

'That's not a fair call, Gabrielle.' Simone's voice was low and tight. 'It wasn't like that.'

'I know,' said Gabrielle. 'And on an intellectual level, Rafe would agree with you. He knows Luc's hands were tied when it came to setting up in business with him. He's quite capable of admitting that you and he were far too young to be thinking about marriage, let alone eloping to Australia. He *says* he works like a dog because he enjoys it. But if you ask me—and you did—the real reason he works so hard is that the ghosts from his childhood won't let him stop.'

'I think I need more wine,' said Simone.

Gabrielle held out her own champagne flute as Simone reached for the bottle. 'Hit me.'

'Don't tempt me,' muttered Simone as she refilled Gabrielle's glass and then her own. 'We probably shouldn't talk about brothers, you and me.'

'No, we probably shouldn't.' Gabrielle smiled faintly. 'By the way, I saw yours again today. I really thought I'd be able to handle it. Handle *him*. I couldn't.'

'I'm not surprised,' said Simone. 'I've yet to meet a woman who can. A word of advice, Gaby, from my heart to yours. Luc changed after you left. He grew up, grew tough, and got guarded. He's not an easy man to know. Not an easy man to love. Believe me, plenty have tried.'

'Is that a warning?'

'More a plea to be careful,' said Simone. 'You used to be able to turn Luc's head with a glance and I doubt you've lost the knack. Getting him to lay down his heart is a different matter altogether. Just…be careful.'

Gabrielle played with the blades of grass beneath her fingertips. 'I didn't come back for him, Simone. I don't even know if I still want him. I haven't forgotten what came of wanting him before.'

'Neither has he,' murmured Simone. 'My advice was for if you were still interested in him. If you're not, then maybe all you need do is talk with him about what happened all those years ago and see if you can both put it behind you. Maybe that's the way to handle this.'

'You mean be civilised,' said Gabrielle. 'Me and Luc.'

Simone's lips twitched. 'Yes.'

'Civilised sounds wonderful,' said Gabrielle wistfully. 'Except for the dredging up the past bit. You don't suppose there's a way of being all civilised and restrained without bringing up the past at all?'

'Well, you could try,' said Simone thoughtfully. 'Why don't you come over to Caverness tomorrow afternoon and take a wander through the gardens with me? You could stay for a meal. Try again with Josien if you've a mind to, although I don't fully recommend it. You could attempt a civil discussion with Luc. See if you can find common ground that isn't rooted in the past. Ask his opinion on setting up a distribution arm here for your Australian reds. Make him feel useful. Men like that.'

'Then what?' said Gabrielle somewhat sceptically.

'Then you mention your fiancé.'

'I don't have a fiancé.'

'Not sure you need to mention that.' Simone started grinning and it wasn't because of the bubbles. 'All right, forget the non-existent fiancé. Set the boundaries for your relationship with Luc some other way—but set them nonetheless. Maybe Luc will follow your lead.'

'And if he doesn't?'

'Run,' said Simone, and kept right on grinning. 'Damn, I've missed you. Here's to hilltop reunions, restraint when dealing with troublesome men, and laying to rest the ghosts of our past.'

'Hear hear,' said Gabrielle and lifted her near-empty not-plastic champagne flute to her lips. Where had all the champagne gone? 'Restraint, you said?'

'Civilised restraint,' amended Simone. 'Nothing to it. More champagne?'

Gabrielle hesitated. 'Didn't you just fill my glass?'

'They're very little glasses,' said Simone sneakily. 'May I remind you we're talking Chateau Caverness 1955 here? This isn't just any old champagne.'

Indeed it wasn't. 'All right,' said Gabrielle, and reached for the magnum with what she thought was a great deal of restraint, never mind Simone's descent into helpless laughter. 'Maybe just one.'

CHAPTER THREE

AT FIVE PM the following afternoon, after an evening of laughter with Simone followed by half a day of sleep, Gabrielle drove, yet again, through the entrance to Chateau des Caverness and parked her car in the gravel courtyard next to the servants' quarters. Ignoring the door to her childhood completely, she switched on her mobile and found the number Simone had keyed into the phone last night.

'Where are you?' she said when Simone answered the phone.

'In the orchard, waiting for you,' said Simone. 'And if you've waited until now to tell me you're not coming I'm going to be very *very* annoyed.'

'I'm here,' said Gabrielle. 'I just didn't want to walk through three acres of garden looking for you, that's all. I'm not exactly wearing sensible shoes.'

'Colour me intrigued,' said Simone. 'I thought you'd be wearing something restrained.'

'I am wearing something restrained,' said Gabrielle. Her square-necked knee-length plum-coloured sundress was very restrained. She'd even plaited her wayward hair and woven it into a heavy bun on top of her head, princess style, and secured it with a thousand pins. She'd followed up with the application of very subtle, very expensive, make-up and only the merest dash of her favourite perfume. She was a walking, talking picture of stylish restraint. 'Except for the shoes.'

The leather sandals with their delicate straps and flimsy heel were an exercise in idiocy. Idiocy being the word that summed up Gabrielle's thoughts on accepting Simone's invitation to tour the gardens and stay for dinner afterwards. Civilised restraint was all well and good in theory. Putting it into practice was hard.

'Take your shoes off, then, and come around the front way on the grass,' suggested Simone.

'That's not exactly civilised,' said Gabrielle. 'It's a little unrestrained.'

'Do it anyway,' said Simone with a snicker. 'Get all that wild abandon out of your system now so that when you happen across Luc there'll be none left for him.'

'You're making a surprising amount of sense,' muttered Gabrielle.

'I always do,' said Simone as Gabrielle reached the stone wall, slipped off her shoes, and stepped through the archway and into the formal front gardens. There'd been a box-hedge maze in here years ago. A maze that had towered high over her head and had provided endless hours of play for all the children of Caverness; her and Simone as well as Rafael and Luc. To Gabrielle's delight, the maze was still there, although these days it didn't tower over her but stood chest high so that a person could see the summer gazebo at its centre.

'You kept the maze,' she said into the phone.

'I kept the maze,' said Simone. 'You want to do this tour by phone or are you actually planning to converse face to face?'

'Picky picky,' murmured Gabrielle. 'I brought a few things for the dinner table. I'll put them on the terrace on the way round. See you soon.'

Sandals in one hand, goody bag in the other, Gabrielle skirted the maze and headed through the formal statuette garden towards the grand entrance to the chateau. Gabrielle's footsteps slowed when she saw that the terrace was already in use, but then she squared her shoulders and continued on her path. The grey stone steps were cool and hard beneath her feet after the softness and warmth of the summer grass, but she would not linger long, and she did not put her shoes on. 'Good afternoon, *Maman*, Hans,' she said to the seated pair. Gabrielle glanced warily at the third person to complete the tableau. Luc wasn't sitting and didn't look as if he had been sitting with the others. He looked as if he'd been simply passing by and had merely stopped for a word. 'Luc.'

Hans greeted her cheerfully. Josien's greeting was far more subdued but it *was* a greeting and Gabrielle felt pathetically grateful for it. Luc said nothing.

'I'm just on my way to meet up with Simone,' said Gabrielle, feeling intrusive and out of place. 'She's determined to give me a tour of the gardens.'

Josien's gaze flickered over Gabrielle, taking

in her attire and her hair and the sandals hanging loosely from her fingertips, and Gabrielle smothered the impulse to check herself over for dirt and stains. Yes, Gabrielle wanted to reconnect with her mother, but not if it meant becoming Josien's whipping girl again. This was who she was, the woman she'd grown up to be, and if Josien wasn't satisfied with her appearance or her behaviour then so be it. Gabrielle took a deep breath, set her shopping bag on the wire table beside her mother, and stood a little straighter. Luc still hadn't said a word. Okay, so their last meeting had been a little…tense, at times, and maybe he didn't want her here any more than Josien did, but would it have killed him to say hello? How was she supposed to act civilised if he wouldn't even afford her that small courtesy?

'Simone took the gardens in hand a few years back,' said Luc into an increasingly awkward silence. 'She's been focussing on the old orchard area of late. Most of the trees have gone to make way for roses. But not all.'

Gabrielle tucked an escapee strand of hair behind her ear with nervous fingers. Finally, a conversation. She could do conversation. Sort of. 'It sounds lovely.' She delved into her grocery bag and withdrew a posy of violets, their delicate scent filling the air as she set them carefully on the table. 'For you, *Maman*. I had planned to leave them with Hans, but seeing as you're here…' Gabrielle turned to go before Josien could reject them to her face.

'Thank you.' Josien's reply came to her on the

breeze, thready and formal but a reply nonetheless. Gabrielle looked back at her mother and Josien held her gaze but only for a moment before she looked away, her hands folded tightly in her lap. Luc looked stern. Hans was eyeing Josien curiously. With a heavy, deliberate tread Hans rose from his chair, crossed to the table and picked up the posy. 'My mother used to like violets too,' he said in his big gruff voice as he thrust them into Josien's hand. 'Pretty little things.'

Gabrielle didn't stick around to see the result. With the fear of rejection rising up inside her like a tidal wave, she fled.

LUC CAUGHT UP with Gabrielle towards the bottom of the stairs leading down into the formal knot garden. 'Mind if I join you?' he said.

'No.' She glanced at him warily.

'You left your bag on the table,' he said next. 'I didn't know if you meant to or not. I left it there.'

She hadn't meant to. But there was no going back for it now. 'I'll get it later.' When Josien had gone. What had Simone suggested by way of civilised discussion again? Gabrielle couldn't remember. Her brain was too busy trying to deny the raw sexual appeal of the man striding alongside her.

Yesterday Luc had been wearing working attire—a suit befitting the head of the House of Duvalier. Today his clothes ran to casual. A blue shirt with a boldly embossed stripe running through it—it was shaped to accentuate the breadth of his shoulders and had tiny tortoiseshell buttons all the way down the front. The size of those buttons was more in keeping with the size of a woman's fingers than a man's and made Gabrielle's fingers dance with wanting to free them from their buttonholes. She ordered those wayward fingers still and dragged her gaze away from his chest and those buttons and concentrated on the rest of him.

Big mistake.

Luc's trousers and work-roughened boots were more suited to the fields than to the boardroom, but they didn't look out of place on him, not one little bit. All they did was give his inherent sexuality a dangerously earthy edge.

Luc could do mindless, earthy abandon just as easily as Gabrielle could. She knew it for a fact.

'How do you like living in Australia?' he asked her as they started walking through the formal French garden with its neatly clipped hedges. It was a question any acquaintance might ask her, new or old. A civilised question. A question that took her thoughts in a different direction altogether from the place they'd been headed.

Thank goodness.

'I like it fine,' she said and summoned a smile. 'Australia's a beautiful country. There's opportunity there. Less of a class system.' Her smile turned rueful. 'I wasn't the housekeeper's daughter once I reached Australia, I was the sophisticated French girl with the Australian father and a brother who'd just bought a beat-up old winery and renamed it Angels

Landing. I could be whoever and whatever I wanted to be. I could be me. It was very liberating.'

'I can imagine,' murmured Luc with a swift white smile. 'Did you run wild?'

'Oddly enough, no.' Gabrielle swung her arm as they walked, setting her sandals to swinging like a lazy pendulum. 'Once there was nothing to rebel against I stopped rebelling.'

'I bet Rafe was relieved.'

'Maybe,' said Gabrielle. 'And maybe he always knew that as soon as I'd broken free of this place I would find my way.'

'You sound as if you hated it here,' said Luc.

'I didn't.' Gabrielle shook her head and looked around her at the chateau and the grounds surrounding it. 'I don't. How can you hate something so beautiful? No, it was my place in the grand scheme of things here that I hated. It wasn't that I necessarily wanted to own Caverness, you understand.' She didn't want Luc to think that. 'I just didn't want Caverness to own me.'

'I understand.' Luc's eyes had darkened. 'How do you feel about coming back here?'

'Conflicted,' said Gabrielle with brutal honesty. 'Part of me feels like I've come home. The rest of me's desperate to get away. I know there's no place for me here, Luc. Not in Josien's mind and probably not in yours or Simone's either, although you're both being very kind.'

'You're wrong,' said Luc. 'There's room for you here, Gabrielle. Always.'

'We'll see.'

'Gabrielle, if ever you need my help with anything, *ask*,' Luc said carefully. 'You'll get it.'

'Why?'

'You were driven from your home because of me.'

'The way I remember it,' said Gabrielle with a swift sideways glance for his stern profile, 'there were two of us in that grotto that night. Besides, I may have lost one home but I soon found another and found myself in the process. I know I fought against leaving here initially, Luc.' Gabrielle winced at the memory of the scene she'd caused—the pleading and the tears, the utter desolation that had enveloped her and that everyone, Luc included, had been witness to. 'But it helped me to grow up.' Grow up strong.

'And your estrangement from your mother?'

'Would probably have happened anyway,' said Gabrielle with a shrug. 'Lose the guilt, Luc. It doesn't suit you.'

Luc's eyes flashed fire. 'Careful, Gabrielle.'

'Much better,' she murmured. 'All that buttoned-down fire. That's very you.'

All that buttoned-down fire came roaring to the surface as Luc caught her by the arm and drew her into the secluded shadow of the chateau walls. He stood there, glaring at her in silence as he let the awareness between them build. And build. 'Why do you *do* that?' he said at last. 'You push and you push and then you push me some more. I warn you, but you never seem to *listen*.'

'I'm listening now,' she said through suddenly

dry lips, and took a step backwards only to come up against solid stone wall. 'I'm listening very intently.'

'Good, because I'm choosing my words carefully. Do you remember how it was when I lost control with you, Gabrielle? Do you? Is that what you want from me?'

'No.'

Yes, said a little voice that would not be silenced.

'No,' she said more firmly. 'I want us to be civil with one another. That's all.'

'Civil,' he said mirthlessly. 'Around you?'

'Yes.'

'God help me.'

'You could at least *try*,' she said darkly. 'You can't even greet me properly.'

'Have you ever stopped to wonder *why*?' he grated.

She hadn't. All she'd seen was the lack of what he bestowed on others so naturally.

'Just remember, this was your idea, not mine,' he muttered, his voice a dark delicious rumble as he set his palms to the stone wall either side of her and bent his head to hers. 'You want my greeting, here it is. *Bonjour*, Gabrielle.' She felt the fleeting warmth of his lips against her cheek and then his lips were gone. The heat in her cheek started to spread. Probably best to ignore it. She pulled back ever so slightly to find him staring down at her, his expression thunderous. 'See?' she said tentatively. 'That wasn't so bad.'

'I haven't finished yet,' he murmured, and set his lips to her other cheek. He started higher on her cheekbone this time, and lingered longer, tracing a meandering path along her cheek to her mouth where he very discreetly, very deliberately, wet the corner of her mouth with his tongue.

Gabrielle gasped, she couldn't help it, as an answering burn started low in her stomach.

'Say *"Bonjour, Lucien",*' he whispered, his lips barely leaving hers. Say *"Comment ça va?"* and try to stop your body from aching because you want to feel more of me. Clench your hands into fists all you like, angel, but sooner or later someone's going to figure out that you're not angry, you're just aroused. Under normal circumstances there'd be people around us, watching us, waiting to see what takes place between us. Do you really want them to see what happens next, Gabrielle? Do you?'

'No,' she whispered. 'This isn't going to be civilised, is it?'

Luc smiled briefly. 'No.' And brushed his lips against hers with the lightest pressure, the faintest whisper of heat, but it was enough to make Gabrielle close her eyes and tilt her head the better to receive more of him. He settled his lips against hers more firmly and his hand came up to cup her face, cool fingers on heated cheeks before he slid his thumb to her jawbone and his fingers into her hair. His mouth moved over hers, still civilised, but only just. This wasn't a simple kiss of greeting, nothing like it. There was a question in this kiss. And for Gabrielle there had only ever been one answer. With a shuddering sigh, Gabrielle opened her mouth and let him in.

Luc knew that kissing Gabrielle was a mistake; he'd always known. She held nothing back, she never had, as she opened for him and spun them into oblivion, the kiss sliding from barely contained to outrageously wanton in a heartbeat. Her taste assaulted his senses, rich and heady, like the finest of wine. Her scent was one he would never tire of, not if he lived to be a hundred, and as for her touch... He wanted her hands on him more than he wanted to breathe.

'Touch me,' he murmured, between more of those greedy, soul-shattering kisses. 'For pity's sake, Gabrielle, touch me.'

With a ragged little noise, half sob, half plea, Gabrielle dropped her sandals, wound her arms around his neck and did as she was told.

The rain came suddenly, hitting hard, dousing them both with cool and stinging droplets. Gabrielle broke their kiss and gasped, flinching away, her arm coming up to protect her face from the spray. Luc blinked and shook his head before he too raised his hand to ward off the unexpected assault that didn't appear to be coming from overhead. 'What the hell..?'

'Sorry.' Simone's voice came to him as if from a great distance, never mind that she stood only a few feet away with a hose in her hand and an angelic expression on her face. 'I turned the tap on and the water pressure just whipped that hose right out of my hands and sprayed everything in sight. I simply couldn't control it.' Simone's level gaze pinned them both. 'You know how it is.'

Gabrielle blushed a fetching shade of pink.

Luc wiped the water from his face with his sleeve and rammed his hands in his pockets to stop them from reaching for Gabrielle again. 'Next time we meet in public I'm saying hello and that's *it*,' he told Gabrielle grimly.

'Good idea,' she murmured as she knelt down to pick up her sandals, the action putting her at eye level with certain parts of his anatomy still straining for attention. Luc looked away fast, clenching his jaw as he fixed his gaze upon the stone wall straight in front of him and kept it there.

'And then I'm heading for the other side of the room,' he told no one in particular, his gaze still firmly fixed on the wall. 'Possibly the other side of the earth.'

'It's called Australia,' said Simone dryly. 'And it certainly worked for the pair of you last time. More water?'

'No,' he said quickly.

'I'm good too.' Gabrielle popped into Luc's frame of view with the speed of a rain-drenched weed. She smiled brightly and shook out the droplets of water from her dress for good measure. 'So where were we?'

'About to take a tour of the gardens?' said Simone with the lift of an elegant eyebrow. 'Are you planning on joining us, brother?'

Not if he could possibly help it.

'Leave me alone with this woman and you're a dead man,' murmured Gabrielle.

'She'll get you alone sooner or later,' argued Luc. 'Why delay the inevitable?'

'Nothing's inevitable. Except maybe you and I needing to get that out of our system.' Gabrielle swept past him. 'At least it's done now. Finished. Lesson learned. No need for a repeat. Are you listening?'

'Intently,' he said dryly. 'You seriously believe we can just carry on being all civilised after that?'

'Absolutely.' Chin high, she headed for the nearest garden path and started to lead the way up it. 'I'm an extremely civilised person.'

'I noticed that,' said Simone, with a heartily amused grin as she sent Luc a wink and followed in Gabrielle's wake. 'So much fuss over such an ordinary little kiss. Really, Luc. Take Gabrielle's lead and forget all about it. Put all that pesky kissing business far, far behind you. There are far more important things to consider on a day like today.'

'Like what?' What could be more important than contemplating the loss of one's control and quite possibly one's mind? And when he might conceivably have the opportunity to lose them again?

'Gardens,' said Simone firmly. 'Gardens are far more important than kisses—wouldn't you agree, Gabrielle?'

Gabrielle did agree. Heartily.

Women.

CHAPTER FOUR

DINNER THAT EVENING would have been both pleasant and relaxing, thought Gabrielle with a heartfelt glare in Simone's direction—if Luc hadn't decided to join them. She vaguely remembered ordering Luc not to leave her alone with his sister. She dimly recalled mentioning red-wine and hearing Simone talk of preparing a meal to accompany a red wine experience, but nowhere during the conversations that had taken place did she recall either her or Simone actually issuing Luc a dinner invitation. Not that he needed one, she decided glumly. Caverness being his home, and all.

It was just that, now that she had her wits about her, sharing a cosy home-cooked meal with Simone and Luc didn't seem like a very good idea at all. If she had any sense at all, she would stay as far away from Luc as she possibly could, the reason being that if he wasn't in sight she wouldn't want and if she didn't want she wouldn't touch. If she never touched, she would not take—and she would not lose herself in the process. Simple.

Problem solved.

The more immediate problem being how to make

her exit without insulting her hosts. Simone would understand, surely.

'This civilised dinner thing—it really isn't working for me,' she said as Simone scooped stuffing mixture into the duck and plugged the hole shut with a parboiled and well-skewered orange.

'I'm pretty sure it's not working for the duck either,' murmured Simone, 'but do you see me stopping?' Simone swiftly began to squeeze the juice from two more oranges. 'It's your own fault. You shouldn't have mentioned that you'd brought two of Rafael's wines along. You should have known there'd be no getting rid of Luc after that.'

'My fault?' spluttered Gabrielle. '*My* fault? Who was it that promised him roast duck in citrus?' Or, in this particular case, citrus in roast duck. Duck had been Luc's favourite dish as a boy, and if the light in his eyes at its mention was anything to go by it was still a firm favourite. 'You deliberately planned to prepare something he couldn't resist.'

'Of course I did.' Simone was unrepentant. 'It's all part of the be-civil-to-Luc plan that we put together last night, remember? The fact that you couldn't manage to make that plan *stick* for more than two minutes in each other's company is hardly my fault.'

The fact that Simone was *right* was hardly reassuring.

'If you run out on this meal I'm going to be very displeased,' said Simone, fixing her with a stern glare. 'You can leave when the meal is over, not before.'

In which case it was time to move this meal along, decided Gabrielle as she surveyed the restaurant sized cooking bench currently strewn with ingredients. 'How can I help? Give me something to do.'

'Open the wine,' said Simone with a grin. 'That might help.'

'Luc's opening the wine.' Gabrielle slid a sideways glance to where he stood on the far side of the kitchen. 'Correction, he's examining the label at the moment.' Gabrielle felt a flutter of apprehension. The branding and labelling of the wine was her department, her work, and she took a great deal of pride in it. The Angels Landing label with its winged angel graphic and elegant raised text had won numerous industry awards in Australia but Australia wasn't France. Would her work find favour with Luc?

He looked up and caught her gaze. 'Bold,' he said.

'So's the wine.' Gabrielle tried to stop feeling protective of the product but to no avail. Years of work and a great deal of heart had gone into the making and presentation of that wine—she could never be blasé about people's reaction to it.

As winemakers themselves, Luc and Simone would understand.

'Go,' said Simone, nodding towards Luc and the wine, and Gabrielle headed swiftly across the kitchen, making sure to stay on the opposite side of the table to Luc.

'You wish to talk me through the tasting?' said Luc.

'If you'd like me to?' She'd tried for nonchalance,

but if the tilt to Luc's lips was any indication she hadn't quite nailed it.

'I would,' he said with admirable formality. *'Merci.'* His smile widened. 'You always were good at selling wines to customers. Do you remember when you and Simone took over cellar door sales the afternoon Marciel fell ill? How many cases of our oldest and most expensive vintage did you sell? Twenty-eight?'

'Twenty-nine,' said Gabrielle. 'And we had a definite cuteness advantage over Marciel.' Marciel had been grey, grizzled, and formidable. She and Simone had been grubby, pinafored, and seven and nine years old respectively. Simone had been lauded for her efforts. Gabrielle felt her smile begin to falter as the memory returned in full. Gabrielle had been beaten for overstepping her boundaries.

With a horsewhip.

Rafe had gone ballistic when he'd seen the welts on her back and legs. He'd been thirteen and her champion but there'd been no protecting her from Josien. Not back then. Not until later, when Rafe's size, his strength, and his own icy fury at Josien's punishments had compelled Josien to think twice before meting them out.

'What is it?' asked Luc, his deep delicious voice reaching into her and dragging her back to the present. He always had been able to read her. It had been one of the best things about their friendship as children, and one of the dangers of being with him as she'd grown older and her crush on him had intensified. 'Gabrielle? What's wrong?'

'Nothing,' she said, deliberately letting go of unhappy memories and pasting on a smile. As children she and Rafe had been extremely adept at hiding Josien's cruelties from the world and she had no mind to expose them now. Some might call that weak, some might call her complicit in her own punishment, but to Gabrielle's way of thinking the word that should be used in those types of situations was *survivor*. She and Rafael were survivors both. And quietly, rightfully, proud of it. 'That one's our most mature wine,' she said, indicating the bottle in Luc's hand. 'Having said that, it's still only five years old. Rafe wanted to give it another year before releasing it, but economics got in the way. We needed the cash flow,' she said. 'This wine is one year younger and we've only bottled a small amount of it. Most of the vintage is still in barrels,' she said indicating the bottle on the counter. 'They're both beautifully balanced wines, don't get me wrong, but the younger one's my favourite. It's my favourite out of all the wines we've produced to date.'

'Why red wine?' asked Luc. 'Why didn't Rafe stick with what he knew? He took with him a lot of knowledge about the making of sparkling wine.'

Indeed he had. Both Luc and Rafe had learned a great deal from old man Duvalier about the making of champagne. Luc had been a skilled practitioner even then. In contrast, Rafe had been inclined to experiment. Most of Rafe's experiments had failed but sometimes…sometimes his wild combinations had garnered even old man Duvalier's praise. 'I don't know why he went for the reds, in all honesty,' said Gabrielle. 'He'd just bought the vineyard when I arrived on his doorstep. As far as I can gather he saw that old winery and fell in love. The vines in the ground were red varieties so red was the wine he made.'

'Why the Angels Landing name?' asked Luc.

'Because it fit,' said Gabrielle with a tiny half smile. Because Angels Tears hadn't exactly cut muster as an uplifting name for a new beginning. No need to mention that she'd labelled Rafe's first bottling of a barrel of private stock Angels Tears, or that it was the best of Rafe's reds by far. It wasn't for public consumption, not the name and not the wine. 'Open them.' Never mind that they wouldn't get through both, Luc would want to compare vintages.

'What made you go for corks instead of a screw top?' asked Luc as he obliged.

'Tradition,' said Gabrielle. 'Rafe knows exactly which market he's targeting and they don't do screw tops. Yet.'

Bottles opened and wine breathing, Luc took his time collecting glassware from the cupboard while Gabrielle watched him with a combination of exasperation, lust, and a growing knot of trepidation. Luc's opinion of the wine mattered to her. If he didn't like it she was going to be crushed.

'Colour's good,' murmured Luc after pouring three tasting serves from the first bottle.

'Yes.' The colour was superb. She waited for Luc to pick up his glass and willed herself not to fidget. 'Simone, do you want some?'

Simone's face was a study in contradiction as she headed almost reluctantly towards them. 'I'd feel a lot better about this if I could separate the maker from his wine,' she muttered.

'I'd feel a lot better if we could just get this over with,' countered Gabrielle. 'Just try some and be done with it. Say hmm, quite nice, very interesting, and put me out of my misery.'

But that wasn't the way wine tasting worked at Chateau des Caverness.

'Bouquet's a little…' began Luc with his nose to the glass.

'A little what?' asked Gabrielle anxiously.

'Interesting,' said Luc. Was he smirking? She couldn't see his mouth for the wine glass but his eyes were definitely laughing at her.

'Nice berry notes,' said Simone.

'Apricot as well,' said Luc. 'Unusual. Hmm.'

'For heaven's sake, Luc, will you get to the "quite nice" part?' muttered Gabrielle.

Luc smiled, briefly, and his eyes took on a rakish gleam. 'Patience, angel,' he murmured. 'Wine tasting's a civilised business. I thought you knew that. Being such a civilised and restrained person yourself and all.'

She usually was. Around anyone but him. 'Luc,' she said with what she considered a great deal of restraint, 'don't make me hurt you.' Gabrielle took

a calming breath and turned her attention to the ir-
regular streaks running through the marble bench-
top—like little rivers and estuaries they meandered
and widened, separated and petered out. She wished
her awareness of this man would peter out too, but
the more time she spent in Luc's company, the stronger it grew. She wanted to know what he thought of
her wine. She wanted to know what he thought of
their recent kiss. And heaven help her but she wanted
to kiss him again. What would happen if she and
Luc did embark on an affair? A steamy, searing,
no-holds-barred exercise in raunch? Would that be
enough to get him out of her system? Would it leave
her sated and ready to move on or would spending
time in Luc's embrace spoil her for all other men?

She really didn't like the sound of that last option
at all. No. No, thank you. No.

'What are you thinking?' murmured Luc.

Gabrielle glanced up and sent him a careful smile.
'Nothing that concerns you.' She waited some more
while the ever so civilised head of the House of Duvalier faffed about with his wine. 'Well?' she said
impatiently. 'Can we skip to the civilised part now?'

'Well, I like it,' said Simone. 'It's a big-bodied and
very bold wine with a depth and smoothness that be-
lies its age.' Simone smiled briefly and took another
sip. 'I don't know what it is about these Australian
wines…there's always such richness of *flavour*.'

'Rafe thinks it's a reflection of the youth of the
wine industry there,' said Gabrielle. 'Everyone's still

experimenting. There hasn't been time to develop a whole lot of ritual or subtlety.'

'There's subtlety here,' said Luc, tasting the wine and lifting his glass to once more study the colour.

'You think so?' Gabrielle let her pleasure at his words seep through her. 'I think so too. Try the other bottle.'

Luc tasted the second one and his smile turned wry. 'The last one had some excellent qualities embedded in it,' he said. 'This one's brilliant.'

Simone sighed. Gabrielle beamed.

'What kind of distribution are you aiming for?' asked Luc, his eyes sharp and his words all business. Gabrielle hadn't seen this side of him before. She liked it. Liked that he took her expansion plans seriously.

'The exclusive kind,' she said. 'We're not looking to inundate the market. We just want to establish a presence here.'

'What do you need?'

'Storage, for starters.'

'In the caves?'

'Preferably, yes.'

'You'll pay premium price for that.'

'I know.' Gabrielle sighed. 'And, realistically speaking, underground storage may not be feasible hereabouts. I'm looking into all the options on offer.'

'What else do you need?'

'A marketing development strategy, a workable entry-level price point, and an on-ground sales force.'

'Who do you have in place for those?'

'Me.' Luc would have had an entire team working on it, but she didn't have those kinds of resources. She waited for him to say that it couldn't be done, she waited for his lips to curve in an indulgent smile as he humoured the bit player, but he didn't do either of those things.

'Busy times, these next few weeks,' he said.

'Yes.'

'Let me know if you need an introduction to some of the major distributors in the area,' he said next. 'I'll set something up for you. A tasting, perhaps. You could use the facilities already in place at Caverness. That might work.'

Gabrielle tried to keep her mouth closed, never mind that it wanted to drop open. A Chateau des Caverness wine-tasting session was an experience savoured by even the most jaded industry stalwarts and it wasn't just because of the quality of the product. Stepping into the cellars behind the chateau was like stepping into history. There were caverns filled with vintage champagne. Tiny grottos with tea light candles sitting in scooped-out hollows in the walls. Pyramids of bottled wine stacked in carved-out triangles in those same cave walls. Rough-hewn tables set ready for impromptu wine tasting. Narrow passageways flanked by rusty iron gates, cave paintings that dated back centuries, and always the cool grey rock beneath the fingertips. Sensual and seductive, the caves of Caverness existed to woo the senses of *extremely* discerning buyers.

'Of course, if I'm going to put the House of Duvalier's reputation on the line I'll need to know a little more about your production schedule and what sized contracts you're capable of fulfilling.'

Luc the businessman.

And what on earth was the businesswoman Gabrielle going to say in reply? Luc's offer was a generous one and completely unexpected—the patronage of the House of Duvalier would go a long way towards securing orders from exactly the type of buyers she and Rafael hoped to target. She *should* be jumping all over the idea.

She wasn't.

Rafe wouldn't like it. He wouldn't want that kind of connection to Simone. For her part, Gabrielle didn't particularly want to do business with Luc. Her feelings for Luc were complicated enough. Tying the growth of one's business to the goodwill of a man she'd just been contemplating having a passionate and potentially short-lived affair with didn't seem like a particularly sensible idea.

'You can talk to me about that,' she said guardedly. 'Better still, why don't I talk to Rafe and get back to you? You might not need to know about production schedules and estimates of vintage sizes at all.'

'You don't think he'd go for the idea?' asked Luc.

'I don't know what he'd think,' said Gabrielle. 'Rafe's not one for accepting charity. Or for becoming indebted to people.' She was back to choosing her words carefully. 'It's a generous offer, Lucien, and I thank you for it. But I just don't know if we can accept it.' She smiled a little wryly. 'Your father would turn in his grave.'

'My father, for all his good points—and, yes, he did have some—was an extremely short-sighted man. He should have backed Rafe when he had the chance.'

But he hadn't. The words lay there in the silence, all the more potent for remaining unsaid.

'I'll phone Rafe and put the notion to him,' said Luc. And at Gabrielle's open-mouthed astonishment, 'What?'

'You don't think a mediator might come in handy?' said Gabrielle. 'I mean, you haven't spoken to him in seven years and now all of a sudden this?'

'What makes you think I haven't phoned him in seven years?' asked Luc curiously.

'I, ah… Have you?'

'Many times,' he said, and at Gabrielle's continued shock, 'Which bit surprises you most? That Rafe and I have kept in contact or that you didn't know about it?'

'Both,' she admitted baldly. Rafael had been so disillusioned when he'd left for Australia. Gabrielle hadn't thought he'd kept in contact with *anyone* from Caverness. Not Lucien, not Josien, and certainly not Simone. 'What do you talk about?'

This time it was Luc's turn to look wary. 'Everything but sisters.'

As far as exquisite food and fabulous surroundings were concerned, the meal was a resounding success.

By mutual, unspoken agreement they'd stripped the conversation of anything remotely concerning the past once they'd settled down to eat, concentrating instead on the present and the future. Simone expanded on her plans for the garden. Luc spoke of the experimental champagne varieties he hoped to trial once he acquired more land. They spoke of the changes that had taken place in the village over the last few years. The new priest, the newly formed men's choir. The opera diva who'd purchased a crumbling chateau for a song and had kept the local tradesmen in work for years in her effort to restore it to its former glory. Her pockets were deep, according to Lucien. Her youthful face was a testimony to the marvels of modern surgical techniques, according to Simone. She'd had widowed heads of dynastic champagne houses falling over their feet to court her.

She'd just silenced gossiping tongues completely by marrying a local widowed thatcher some ten years her junior, who came complete with thinning hair, three little ones in tow, not two euros to his name, and a heart—according to the villagers in the know—of pure gold.

'But doesn't that make her outcast amongst the upper echelons of society here?' asked Gabrielle, fascinated. 'And what do *his* friends think of *her*? Where do they fit?'

'According to them, together,' said Simone. 'The village is slowly coming to terms with it.'

Gabrielle grinned. 'Good for them.'

'The villagers or the happy couple?' asked Luc dryly.

'Both.'

'The village is changing,' said Simone. 'There's new blood in it, a younger generation with fewer ties to the old ways. It's not as class conscious.'

Gabrielle eyed Simone curiously. 'I'm not saying you're wrong,' she said. 'But, Simone, every door has always been open to you. How do you know it's not as class conscious? People knew who I was the minute I stepped in the village. Knew I was Josien's daughter and judged me accordingly. I didn't think much had changed at all.'

'How did they judge you?' asked Luc, his eyes sharp.

'When I asked for a room I was offered the smallest and cheapest. Servant class all the way,' she said with a tight smile. 'I was too tired to argue.'

Luc's lips tightened. 'Stay here, then.'

Gabrielle shook her head. 'I was not too tired to argue today. I've moved into a bigger suite with its own bathroom facilities. Madame very curtly implied that this was doubtless a luxury I wasn't used to and asked for the entire three weeks' payment in advance. In cash.'

'Old bat,' said Simone. 'I never did like that woman. What did you do?'

'I gave her a week's worth and told her I'd keep an eye out for something more spacious.'

'Caverness is spacious,' said Luc darkly. 'Very spacious.'

'To buy,' said Gabrielle.

'Wish I'd been there to see the look on her face when you said you were looking to buy,' said Simone.

'You wish to *buy* property hereabouts?' barked Luc.

'It's your lucky day,' murmured Gabrielle to Simone. 'You get to witness the look on Luc's face instead. It's equally incredulous.'

'It's not incredulous,' snapped Luc, shutting his astonishment down fast. 'You took me by surprise, that's all. Given your conflicted feelings about returning to these parts I'd have thought acquiring property here a reckless move.'

Rafe thought the same. Not that Gabrielle felt inclined to mention it. 'I guess we'll all just have to wait and see,' she said.

'Have you looked at the old Hammerschmidt place yet, like I told you to?' asked Simone.

'Not yet.'

'This isn't incredulity on my face,' said Luc tightly. 'No, wait. Yes, it is. But it's not for you or your possible ability to afford such a purchase,' he told Gabrielle before turning to glare at his sister. 'It's for *her*.'

'Don't you look all snarly at me,' said Simone. 'You want the land but don't know what to do with the rest of it. Gabrielle needs storage and distribution facilities and somewhere to live. Hmm, let me think.' Simone put her fingers to her temples and closed her eyes. 'I'm sensing a mutually beneficial solution here.'

'No,' said Luc.

'No,' echoed Gabrielle. 'Not going to happen, Simone. Luc's not looking for a partnership arrangement and neither am I.'

'Just a suggestion,' murmured Simone.

'Yes, well, it's not one of your better ones,' said Gabrielle with dark amusement. 'You could always telephone Rafael and suggest *you* buy the vineyard in partnership with *him*,' she suggested sweetly. 'You've doubtless kept in regular contact with him all these years as well.'

'Wrong,' said Simone. 'I'm as much of a stranger to the let's-part-as-friends concept as you are. Can we change the subject now?'

'With pleasure,' said Luc and reached for his wine.

CHAPTER FIVE

GABRIELLE DID NOT linger over after-dinner coffee.
She drank the brew down hot and black, helped Simone and Luc sort the kitchen, gathered her scattered
belongings together on the kitchen bench and excused herself to make use of the powder room before
she left for the village.

Gabrielle did not need to be told where the nearest bathroom was. It was along the great hallway,
turn right, past the stairs, first door on the right. She
didn't notice Josien standing at the bottom of the
stairs until she drew level with her. So still, thought
Gabrielle with more than a flicker of apprehension.
So still and silent, like a statue—a cold and beautiful
marble statue. *'Maman.'* Had Josien been waiting for
her? Hans had informed them earlier that Josien had
retired to her suite. According to Simone, that was
Josien's usual practice and in no way connected to
Gabrielle's presence at the dinner table. Forget her,
Simone had directed, and Gabrielle had for the most
part succeeded in doing just that. 'I— Hi.' She tried
a tentative smile. 'Did you wish to see me?'

'I suppose you think you're one of them now,'

said Josien bleakly. 'Socialising with them, inviting yourself to dine with them.'

Gabrielle felt her smile falter.

'You never did know your place.'

'On the contrary, *Maman*, you never let me forget it.' Gabrielle drew herself upright, determined not to be Josien's whipping girl—not this time. Not ever again. 'But you are right in one respect. I'm no longer bound by your version of where I belong. This time *I* decide where I fit into the fabric of society here, not you. And if I want to have a meal with my childhood friends, I will.'

'He'll never marry you, you know.' Her mother's beautiful face was so at odds with the ugliness of her words. 'You're not in his league.'

Gabrielle could think of only one man her mother could be talking about. 'Maybe I don't want to marry him, *Maman*. Have you ever considered that possibility?'

'Then why did you come back? Flaunting your precious vineyard and your fancy clothes. Do you really think a little bit of wealth will make the slightest difference to a man like Lucien? You're still the housekeeper's daughter, Gabrielle.'

'You underestimate me, *Maman*. You always have. And just for the record, I didn't come back for Lucien, I came back for you. That was a mistake. I see that now.'

'Where did Rafael get the money to buy the vineyard?' asked Josien, her abrupt change of topic causing Gabrielle to blink in her effort to keep up with the conversation, if you could call it that. 'Who staked him?'

'Harrison,' said Gabrielle. The father she'd only ever exchanged birthday and Christmas cards with until she'd joined Rafe in exile. The one who lived in Australia. The man whose name both Gabrielle and Rafael bore. 'Harrison Alexander. Remember him? The man you married? The man whose children you had? Rafe looked him up. You were wrong about him not wanting us, *Maman*. He did want us.'

'Harrison staked him?' Josien's voice trembled slightly. 'But why?'

'Maybe that's what fathers *do*,' said Gabrielle wearily. She really didn't want to talk with Josien any more. Not about this. Not about anything. 'Why can't you just accept that Rafael finally found someone who believed in him, *Maman*? Why must you taint everything with sourness and disbelief?'

Josien stayed silent.

'I'm going to the washroom,' Gabrielle told her mother. 'And then I'm heading back to the village. Don't feel you have to wait around for me to leave. I know my own way out.'

Josien turned, her chin high and that exquisite face thrown into perfect relief. Gabrielle knew that face. Loved it. Despaired of it.

'He always was soft, Harrison.' Josien's words came to her as a whisper; Gabrielle wasn't even sure her mother had meant for her to hear them. 'Too soft for the likes of me. I should never have married him but I was desperate, you see. Desperate to escape this place, desperate to be someone I wasn't, and Harrison was in love with me, in love with my face. He didn't see what was underneath until it was too late. I never let him see.' Josien turned to stare at Gabrielle and the desolation in her eyes almost swallowed Gabrielle whole. 'Harrison Alexander may be your father, Gabrielle, but he's not Rafael's.' She turned and began her ascent up the stairs, leaning heavily on the handrail for support. 'And he knows it.'

'No,' whispered Gabrielle. Caring and supportive, Harrison had always been there for her and Rafael these past seven years. They would never have achieved what they'd achieved without his unwavering support and encouragement. 'I don't believe you.' And when her mother continued wordlessly, regally, up the stairs, leaving Gabrielle staring up at her from below with white-knuckled fists and hot and prickling eyes, 'You're lying!'

LUC DUVALIER WAS a success story by anyone's standards. He had it all. Wealth. Health. Family. And youth. He was twenty-nine. He ran a Champagne dynasty that was the envy of his peers, brokered multimillion-euro deals with monotonous regularity, and had a reputation for being relaxed and in control no matter what the situation.

He'd never worked harder at being relaxed and in control than he'd worked tonight. He'd succeeded though. Gabrielle had eventually settled down and he'd almost managed to forget the kiss they'd shared earlier, aided somewhat by Simone's expertise as a hostess and the delivery of his favourite food. All he had to do now was see Gabrielle to her car without forfeiting the tentative trust he'd built with her over the past few hours and the evening would be, by anyone's standards, a resounding success. Civilised even, though he was loath to bandy the word about too soon.

Simone had disappeared, to put the garbage out, even though Luc had offered to do it.

'This is the part where you show Gabrielle that you can be trusted alone with her at the end of an evening,' Simone had told him in a deceptively gentle voice. 'I have faith in you,' she'd added, only this time her voice had held an underlying hint of steel that he'd recognised of old. He wasn't the only Duvalier around here who liked things neat and tidy and right.

And then Gabrielle walked back into the kitchen white-faced, and eyes bright with what looked a lot like unshed tears. She tried on a smile but it was a dismal effort and one she soon abandoned. 'Time to go,' she murmured and collected her belongings from the table with trembling hands. 'Where's Simone?'

'Outside. She'll be back soon.'

Gabrielle moved jerkily towards the kitchen door. 'I'll catch her on my way out. Thank you, Lucien, for the pleasant evening.' She hesitated, before reluctantly holding out her hand as if expecting him to shake it. He didn't touch her, he didn't dare.

'What's wrong?' he said curtly.

'Nothing.' She withdrew her hand, clutching at her handbag as if it held crown jewels.

'I won't touch you, if that's what's bothering you,' he said. 'I can be civil around you, Gabrielle. I have been.'

'I know.' She looked stricken. Correction, even more stricken, if that was possible. 'I've enjoyed your company, Lucien. I really have. As for our kiss, well…I enjoyed that too,' she said baldly. 'Possibly a little too much. I'm all for ignoring it and hoping the impulse to kiss you some more will go away.'

'It's been seven years, Gabrielle,' he said grimly. 'And it hasn't gone away.'

'Or we could stay away from one another. Cut and run,' she said with another smile that didn't reach her eyes. 'I'm all in favour of that particular approach. It's tried and true. Proven.'

'We could explore it,' he said. Another option, and one he wanted on the table. 'You and me. And this. You're not sixteen any more, Gabrielle. And I'm not honour-bound to stay away from you. There's nothing stopping us from exploring the attraction between us.'

'No.' Her eyes darkened. Pain flashed through them again. What the hell was wrong with her? 'No, I suppose not.'

'So I'll call you,' he said. 'About setting up that wine tasting.'

'Yes.'

'Or you call me. Tomorrow some time. About meeting for dinner again soon.'

'Yes.'

Unease settled over him. She was telling him what he wanted to hear. Telling him whatever he wanted to hear in order to get away from him, unless he missed his guess. While her eyes telegraphed panic and no small measure of pain. 'Gabrielle, what's wrong? What happened between here and the powder room?'

'Nothing. Really, Luc. It's nothing. You've been a gentleman all evening.' She found a brilliant smile from somewhere and pasted it on her lips. 'A rakish and charming gentleman and I've thoroughly enjoyed you. I'm just not ready to risk a goodnight kiss with you without a garden hose handy, that's all.'

He let her walk to the door on that remark, let her turn the handle and turn her head and glance at him through eyes that told him that there was something else going on here. Something he didn't understand. But he let her go, let her take refuge in humour. If she wouldn't confide in him there was nothing else he could do.

'Goodnight, Gabrielle,' he murmured wryly. 'Sweet dreams, and just for the record... I'm not ready to risk kissing you goodnight at all.'

LUC WAITED UNTIL he heard Simone's voice and Gabrielle's answering murmur before heading for the main hall and the powder room, scanning the tops of the sideboards and flower stands along the way for something, anything, that would have caused Gabrielle to become upset. He stood at the bottom of the grand staircase, and looked around again, puzzled.

There was nothing here, nothing he could see that would have caused such a reaction from Gabrielle. Household trinkets. Vases. A painting of an ancestor or ten. That was all. He looked towards the top of the staircase thoughtfully. Had she gone upstairs?

Had someone else come down?

The only other two people staying in the chateau were Hans and Josien and they'd both retired for the evening long ago. Hadn't they?

He stood there, listening for the sound of Gabrielle's car engine starting, listening to the crunch of car tyres on loose courtyard gravel as she manoeuvred the vehicle carefully through the archway and accelerated down the drive. The kitchen door thudded shut and the sound of rapid footsteps on floorboards met his ears as he stood there in the hallway, in the half-light of a nearby lamp. That would be Simone.

No footsteps sounded overhead. No sound came from upstairs at all…except… He heard it then, a creak, slow and careful, and following on from it the soft metal click that went with the closing of a door.

GABRIELLE FRETTED HER way through the following day. The memory of Luc's most recent kiss tugged at her senses and the thought of his offer of dinner, not to mention his offer to let her use the caves of Caverness for a wine tasting for the Angels Landing reds, echoed through her brain. She needed to pay attention to such things. It was important to know where she was heading with regards to Luc for he was a force no sensible woman ignored, but Luc wasn't the only man on her mind today. Rafe had been on her mind too. Rafe, and everything else that went with Josien's declaration that Harrison wasn't his father. For the first time in her life, Gabrielle dreaded the thought of phoning her brother. Her stomach churned whenever she passed by the phone, eating away at her, making her feel ill. She hadn't asked for this secret. She wished to hell she didn't have to keep it. Rafe was her rock, the one constant in her life, and she hated to think that by keeping this information from him, she was betraying him.

But she hated the thought of damaging the relationship Rafe had with Harrison more.

Gabrielle cursed and slammed the door hard on thoughts of fathers who weren't fathers and the things she now knew that Rafael did not.

Poisonous words designed to destroy a relationship between father and son.

Weight-ridden words designed to build a chasm between sister and brother.

Cruel, loveless words from a mother who did not deserve the title.

Words she was not inclined to share with anyone. Not with Luc when he'd asked her what was wrong, and definitely not with Rafael. No, better to forget she'd ever heard those particular words and speak to Rafe of other matters altogether. Matters that would bring their own ghosts of the past along for the ride, and for once in her life she did not dread their reappearance. There were worse ghosts to fear and always had been.

She just hadn't known of them.

Who? Who could be Rafe's father? Not Phillipe Duvalier. Heaven help all of them and especially Rafe and Simone, but, please God, not him. There had been a slight partiality for Rafe on Phillipe's part. He'd encouraged Rafe's friendship with Luc. He'd made a creditable attempt at training Rafe in the business of winemaking once Rafe had shown an interest. He'd shown Rafe kindness, at times, but the kindness of a father? No.

Rafe didn't resemble the Duvaliers in looks. There was nothing of Josien's looks about him either, except perhaps in the perfection of facial features, albeit a more strongly hewn version. Rafe had Harrison's colouring. Fair hair and blue eyes. Bluer than Harrison's. Bluer and deeper.

Who if not Phillipe Duvalier?

Who if not Harrison?

'Doesn't matter,' Gabrielle told herself fiercely. 'Don't care.' And following swiftly on the heels of that declaration, *'How I hate her.'*

Such an unbridled, uncivilised emotion, hate, but this time, *this* time, she refused to push it away. With another heartfelt curse, she reached for the phone.

Rafe had a habit of barking out his name into the phone and following up with a brusque hello. This time was no exception.

'Is now a good time to call?' she asked him.

'Gabrielle?' Warmth crept into his voice like sunshine seeping through clouds on a stormy day. 'It's about time you called. I've just been speaking to Luc.'

Ah. 'So you know about his offer?'

'Yes.'

'And?'

'You know my feelings on getting involved with the Duvaliers, Gabrielle. On any level—no matter how small.'

'I thought I did,' she countered tartly. 'That was before Luc informed me that you and he had stayed in contact. What was that all about?'

'You,' said Rafael curtly. 'The first time he called you were still on the plane to Australia. He wanted to check that I was meeting you. One thing Luc doesn't lack is a sense of responsibility. He wanted me to call him once you'd arrived safely. He wanted to know how you were every now and then. I saw no harm in telling him.'

'You told him I was a weeping, self-pitying wreck?' Gabrielle closed her eyes in mortification. 'Gee, thanks.'

'I told him you were fine,' said Rafe dryly. 'You know I'd never betray you.'

Gabrielle closed her eyes and rubbed at her forehead. Not game to speak for fear of the words on her tongue.

'How's Josien?' asked Rafe. 'Did she want to see you?'

'She'll live.' This she could talk about, never mind

that there was no keeping the bitterness from her voice. 'And, no, she did not.'

Rafe didn't say I told you so. He didn't need to. 'You okay with that?' he asked gently.

'Which bit?' she said savagely, and let loose a black humoured chuckle of her own when Rafe laughed. 'Truly, Rafe, I'm fine.'

'Fine as in you're a weeping, self-pitying wreck, or fine as in fine?'

'Fine as in I've finally learned my lesson and I'm moving on,' Gabrielle told him vehemently. 'Josien can't hurt me any more. I won't let her.'

'I like it,' said Rafe. 'There's something in your voice that makes me believe it.' His voice wrapped around her, familiar and comforting. 'Sometimes you've just got to let people go, Gabrielle. For your own sake.'

'I know.' Gabrielle took a deep and shuddering breath. *Don't go there*, a little voice whispered. *Don't even visit that place where fathers aren't fathers and Rafe is only half yours. Don't dwell there.* 'I've been looking at distribution options hereabouts,' she said in a stronger voice. 'Looking hard. It's not easy, Rafe. It's a closed system and I don't have the family name, the contacts or the leverage to open any doors. Luc's offer to let us hold a wine tasting for distributors at Caverness is a generous one and will open those doors. It could make a big difference to our entry point into the market. If there was no personal element to consider I'd be jumping all over his offer. It's exactly the kind of upmarket opportunity we need to start this ball rolling.'

Rafe said nothing.

'I haven't said yes,' said Gabrielle. 'I knew Luc's offer wouldn't sit particularly well with you. I don't know that I'd feel all that comfortable doing business with him either. But I'd like you to consider it. As I'm doing.'

'I don't want his help.' Her brother's voice hardened. 'I do not want our business becoming entwined with that of the House of Duvalier.'

'Not even if it benefits us more than it benefits them?'

'Especially if it appears to benefit us more than it benefits them. They're not the most successful family-run champagne dynasty in France because of sheer dumb luck, Gabrielle. Luc's offering us this deal because he's after something.'

'Atonement?' suggested Gabrielle.

'You,' said Rafael bluntly. 'You're a grown woman, Gabrielle, and I know you can handle yourself. I just don't know if you can handle Luc. There's wildness in him underneath all that iron control. Always has been, always will be, and you've always called to it. He's always shielded you from it. Over and over I've watched him, Gabrielle. He was always so careful and controlled around you, always protecting you.'

'Protecting me from what?'

'Himself,' said Rafe.

'So he has a wild streak that he never indulges.

So what? He'll be careful, I'll be careful, and we'll both be fine,' she said lightly. 'Have a little faith and don't let concern for me colour your decision. If the answer's still no once you've thought about it some more, so be it. I just want you to give it due consideration.'

'I can't,' he said gruffly. 'I know it makes good business sense, Gabrielle. But I can't do it.'

Gabrielle bit her lip and nodded, never mind that he couldn't see her. 'All right. That's all I needed to know.' Time to move on. 'I'm emailing you the details of an old vineyard that's for sale a few miles from Caverness. The old Hammerschmidt place— do you remember it?'

'The abandoned one?'

'You do remember it,' she said. 'I think it has potential.'

'To buy or to lease?'

'To buy.'

'So you still want to go back there to live? Even with Josien the way she is?'

'Yes,' said Gabrielle firmly. 'Josien has nothing to do with my decision to return. I love it here, Rafe. I know you and Angels Landing will always be there for me, but Australia doesn't call to me the way it calls to you. It never has and it never will. I don't want you to think I'm abandoning you—I would never abandon you. I want you in my life. I need you in it. You know that, don't you?'

'Here comes the but,' said Rafe gruffly.

'No buts,' she said, deliberately striving for light-

ness. 'I want our wines to sell well over here. I want
to stay and work hard and make that happen, but
most of all, behind it all…' she closed her eyes and let
her heart speak for her '…I just want to come home.'

CHAPTER SIX

'YOU'VE BEEN AVOIDING ME,' said Luc as he eased himself into the vacant wicker chair opposite Gabrielle.

Gabrielle looked up at him and tried to persuade her heart that he was just another charming rake of a man, no different from any other man and certainly no finer. She was sitting in a pavement café, a strong and sweet black coffee at her elbow and a folder containing potential properties for purchase spread out in front of her. A week had passed since she'd dined at Caverness. A long, frustrating week filled with a lot of hard work and no significant visible or calculable gain. Whatsoever.

'Why?' he said next, lounging back in his chair, a brooding, elegant presence as he surveyed her through bold black eyes.

'Maybe I've been working,' she said as she closed the folder and sat back in her chair, glad of the dark sunglasses that covered her eyes and to some extent hid the heat in her cheeks. 'Maybe I haven't given you a second thought.'

'Maybe you haven't,' he said with a charming grin. 'And that would be depressing, considering how often I think of you.' He toyed with the menu, tossed it aside. 'I've arranged to tour the Hammerschmidt vineyard. I want to take a closer look at the soils and the vines. Would you care to join me?'

'To what end?' she said warily. Gabrielle did want to look over the old vineyard before it went to auction. She didn't necessarily think it was a good idea to do so with Luc. 'You're not really suggesting we do as Simone suggests and form a partnership, are you? Because I can't see it working for us.'

'Neither can I. Never mix business with pleasure, angel. And I do plan to pursue the pleasure angle.'

'So why look at this place together, then?'

'Because it would give us both an advantage over other bidders come auction day. They're asking twenty-two million euros for the property, Gabrielle. I can only see about thirteen million in assets that are of use to me. I want your opinion on its worth to someone with different plans for it.'

'So…this would be like a business meeting for us, as opposed to something more social?'

'Definitely,' said Luc. 'Although I'm not opposed to pleasure coming afterwards. I'm not opposed to sorting the pleasure element of the day out *now* so that we know where we stand on that particular subject. Have dinner with me.'

'Why?'

'Because you want to?' he offered.

'No, what I want to do is get a distribution network for our wines in place.'

Luc's eyes sharpened. 'All you have to do is ask.'

'If only it were that simple,' she murmured. 'I've spoken to Rafe about your offer to hold a wine tasting for us at Caverness.'

'I've spoken to him about that too,' said Luc. 'He didn't refuse. I took that as a good sign.'

'He didn't say yes,' Gabrielle felt obliged to point out. 'I think I can safely say that he's not likely to say yes any time in the near future. Just my sisterly opinion.' Backed by a definitive no. 'He's a little concerned about what might be in it for you.'

'I'm wounded by his cynicism,' said Luc. 'I'm also the tiniest bit impressed by it. My father always used to consider cynicism the mark of a clever businessman. What exactly does Rafe think I'm after?'

'Me,' she said dryly.

'Ah.'

'Is he wrong?'

Luc shrugged and his midnight eyes gleamed. 'I can't deny it—the thought of having you has crossed my mind. It's a very pleasurable thought. But my motives for helping you get your wines in front of the right people are a little more straightforward than that.' Luc's eyes lost that lazy gleam and shadows moved into place. 'My hands were tied all those years ago when Rafe asked for support. I wanted to go into partnership with him, offer him the House of Duvalier's backing. Phillipe did not. My father forced an ultimatum upon me. Rafe or Caverness. I chose Caverness.'

'Bastard,' muttered Gabrielle.

Luc smiled grimly. 'Me or my father?'

'Your father.'

'To him, it was just good business. Why risk a reputation that had been generations in the making on an unknown? Why provide his only son with the distraction of another business to build when he needed me here?'

'So you're defending your father?'

'To some extent, yes. Rafe and I put him in an awkward position, Gabrielle. Seen through older, wiser eyes Phillipe did not deliberately set out to crush Rafael's dreams. We put a proposal to him which he refused. He made a business decision. A safe one. I do not steer as safe a course as my father, Gabrielle, but make no mistake, my offer is not based on sentiment alone. Yes, part of me simply wants to do for Rafael what I could not do before. The other part of me believes that offering patronage to the Angels Landing wines is simply good business. The wines are brilliant. The House of Duvalier's reputation will be enhanced because of the association and it's a market we don't currently cater to. If buyers wanted to source Angels Landing wines through the House of Duvalier, I would take my cut as a distributor.'

She believed him.

'And then there's you,' he said with a sigh that sounded more frustrated than lovelorn. 'I like to think of my attraction to you as a different problem altogether. I'm attracted to you and don't see why I should deny it. Our kiss in the garden suggests you're not exactly indifferent to me. The solution seems fairly straightforward.'

'You want me to become the *comte's* convenient mistress?'

'I'm not a *comte*,' he said. 'All I have is the castle.'

'All right, the billionaire's preferred plaything, then.'

'I'm not a billionaire either. Yet.' His lazy smile warned her it was on his to-do list. 'No, I want you to become my outrageously beautiful, independently wealthy lover.'

'Isn't that the same option?'

'No, you might have noticed that the wording's a little different.'

'They're just words, Luc. The outcome's the same.'

'It's an attitude thing.' He looked at her, his smile crookedly charming. 'So what do you say?'

To an affair with the likes of Luc Duvalier? 'I say it's dangerous. For both of us.'

Luc's eyes gleamed. 'There is that.'

'Not to mention insane,' she pointed out.

'Quite possibly. Was that a yes?'

She really didn't know what to say. She'd wanted to come back to the village a sophisticated, self assured, successful woman, and Luc was treating her exactly like one. No need to mention what a fake she felt. 'So how do we start this thing? If I were to agree to it. Which I haven't.' Yet.

'We start with dinner. Tonight. No expectations beyond a pleasant evening with fine food, fine wine and good company. And we see what happens.'

'I don't know,' she said, reaching for her coffee. 'It seems a little…'

'Straightforward?' he suggested. 'Civilised?'

'For us, yes,' she murmured. 'Where would we eat? Somewhere public or in private?'

'Somewhere public,' he said firmly. 'The restaurant I'm thinking of is a fine one—excellent food, small premises, and always busy. A man might take his lover there if he was trying to keep his hands off her.'

'Shall I meet you there?' she said.

'I will, of course, collect you,' he said, playing the autocrat and playing it well. *'Shall I meet you there,'* he murmured in disbelief. 'What kind of question is that?'

'Says the new-generation Frenchman,' she countered. 'Liberated, egalitarian, non-sexist…'

'Helpful, attentive, chivalrous…' he added with a reckless smile. 'And very beddable.'

He was that.

'All right,' she said. 'I'll give you the day—and tonight—to prove that a civilised and pleasurable and manageable affair wouldn't be beyond us. If you can prove this to my satisfaction, I'll make love with you. If this gets out of hand, however…'

'Yes?' he said silkily. 'What do you suggest?'

She leaned forward, elbows on the table. Luc

leaned forward too. 'Well, I don't know about you,' she murmured, 'but I'm a clever, outrageously beautiful, independently wealthy woman. I plan to run.'

THE REAL ESTATE agent was not waiting for them when they pulled up at the gate to the Hammerschmidt Vineyard an hour later. Gabrielle glanced at Luc suspiciously, her suspicions turning to resignation as he cut the engine of the rumbling Audi and produced a massive set of keys from the centre console of the car. 'He was tied up with another sale when I saw him this morning,' said Luc. 'He said he might be running a little late.'

'So we wait for him?' said Gabrielle.

'No,' said Luc. Clearly, the master of Caverness waited for no man. 'We start without him.'

THE HAMMERSCHMIDT VINEYARD comprised two hundred acres of prime grape-growing countryside of which less than half had been developed, underground storage caves, a few hundred wooden winemaking barrels in dreadful repair, old fashioned winemaking equipment, and a large two-storey house built in the Napoleonic style. The Hammerschmidts had played at winemaking for years, according to Luc, bankrolled by a seemingly endless supply of family money gained from the business of banking, which, rumour had it, they were extremely good at. They were not, according to Luc, particularly good at making champagne.

'So there's no reputation to be bought,' she said wryly.

'None whatsoever,' said Luc. 'The Hammerschmidt name is most definitely a liability. If you bought it, you'd rename it.'

'So what would you call it?'

'I think Folly' he said. 'Because whoever buys it is definitely going to be half mad.'

'Angels Curse?' she said. 'No, too dark. Angels Falling?' Gabrielle frowned. 'Possibly a little bit downbeat. Angels Wings? Angels Flying? There. That one could work. Nice tie-in to the core business. Kind of uplifting.' She stared out over the old vineyard. 'Because, boy, does this need lifting up.'

'If ever you're looking for marketing work, call me,' said Luc. 'I would love to let you and Simone loose on a House of Duvalier campaign.'

'So much blind faith,' said Gabrielle airily, but her head ballooned from the compliment, putting a spring in her step and a smile on her lips. 'So how long has this place been on the market?'

'Six months,' said Luc. 'But it's been vacant ten years or more. The vermin have taken up residence, along with the pests. It's a mess.'

According to Luc, the people hereabouts were more than ready to see someone who knew what they were doing take over the vineyard.

That someone being him.

If she were a neighbour she'd be all for the House of Duvalier coming in here with their money, knowledge, reputation, and the wherewithal to set this place to rights too.

The house took Gabrielle completely by surprise. Simone had called it a wreck. It wasn't.

'It's beautiful,' she said in wonder.

'It's a façade,' said Luc. 'Wait until you step inside. The house is uninhabitable.' Luc punctuated his words with the turn of the door key in the lock before putting the shoulder of his immaculate suit to the door and shoving hard. The door gave way but not by much. There seemed to be a build-up of garden debris behind it, garden debris that rustled even as Gabrielle stepped back and leaned down to peer into the pile from a safe distance away. Australia had taught her the value of being wary of those things that rustled in the undergrowth. Things that rustled in the undergrowth in Australia had a habit of being dangerous, if not lethal.

A narrow black nose appeared, followed by the sweetest little face imaginable, dominated by liquid brown eyes and surrounded by needle-sharp spines. With sleepy dignity the hedgehog made its way to the front door and peered outside before turning and ambling back down the darkened corridor. The garden debris rustled again and a miniature version of the first hedgehog followed.

'Well, maybe not *completely* uninhabitable,' said Gabrielle and grinned when Luc gave her one of those looks that suggested she was being ridiculous.

'After you,' he said, the epitome of good manners.

Gabrielle looked at her shoes, then looked at the hedgehog nest. 'Are you sure you wouldn't like to carry me over the threshold? Because, by all means, feel free.'

'That would involve touching you,' said Luc, 'and we both know that's never a good idea.'

'I'm curious,' said Gabrielle as she carefully picked her way through the hedgehog house. 'How do you plan to conduct this civilised affair without ever actually touching me?'

'I didn't say I *wouldn't* be touching you,' he said. 'I have touching plans. But the time between that first touch and being, for want of a better description, all over you, won't be very long. I'm pacing myself. Waiting for the right moment.' Gabrielle stepped on something slippery and wobbled alarmingly before putting her hand to the wall to steady herself. Luc put one of his hands to her waist.

She stepped away quickly. Luc let go fast, as if he'd been burnt.

'That wasn't it,' he murmured. 'A civilised man would not make love to a woman in a ruined *manoir.*'

'How very thoughtful of you.'

'I know,' he said. 'The things I have planned very definitely require a bed.'

Gabrielle closed her eyes and suppressed a needy whimper. If he kept talking in that low liquid voice about the things he might require from a lover, she for one wouldn't be needing a bed. 'What kind of things?' she whispered helplessly.

'Wicked things.' His voice rumbled through her.

'Wanton things.' She bit her lip as her breasts responded to the caress in his words, tightening, peaking, aching for his touch.

'Stop,' she begged. 'Lucien, please. Not here.' When she opened her eyes he was staring down at her, his grin rueful and his eyes dark with need.

'Stopping is something we won't be doing, I guarantee it. I'm seriously considering laying in a week's worth of supplies beforehand.'

Only a week's worth? Gabrielle had seven years' worth of longing for this man to ride out. It was going to take longer than a week.

'We, ah, should probably try and keep interruptions to a minimum,' she said.

Luc's smile had more than a hint of the devil in it. 'I like your forethought.'

'Clear the decks of any pressing items of business,' she continued.

'You are so right,' he murmured. 'Shall we get on with the tour?'

Oh, yeah. This tour.

It didn't take more than half a dozen steps down the hallway for Gabrielle to concede that Luc hadn't been exaggerating when he'd said that the inside of the house was a disaster. There was mould on the ceilings, dampness seeping up through the walls, leaks in the roof, and window drapes that should have been burned a hundred years ago if only to prevent the onset of plague. Ivy clawed at once glorious French windows, seeking purchase and finding it in the window cracks and joints. The ground floor

flooring was a dull and pitted marble, the upper sto-
rey floorboards felt spongy in places where the rot
had taken hold. The stairs were unsafe, the elabo-
rate wrought-iron balustrade rickety, and as for the
kitchen... The state of the kitchen was enough to
make anyone who took pride in the preparing of food
weep with despair.

'Maybe after a good clean...' she said, and winced
at Luc's steady glance that told her he wasn't even
going to dignify her comment with a reply. 'Okay,
so it needs work,' she muttered.

'No, it needs bulldozing.'

'But the façade...' That beautiful Napoleonic
façade.

'All right, hold the bulldozer, but it still needs
gutting. The façade you're so enamoured of needs
extensive and expensive restoration and the inside
of the house needs rebuilding. Am I wrong? Because—' he spread his arms wide to encompass the
large upstairs room they were currently standing in
'—I don't think I'm wrong.'

'You're right,' she said. 'You're absolutely right.
It's just...' The rooms were so splendidly propor-
tioned, with their high ceilings and their tall French
windows. With the heavy drapes gone the natural
lighting within the house would be superb. The view
from this window alone made Gabrielle sigh with
pleasure and Luc sigh with something else entirely.

'It needs a lot of work, Gabrielle, and deep, deep
pockets,' he warned.

'I know,' she said with another wistful sigh.

'There's really not a lot to recommend it, is there? Except for the hedgehogs—the hedgehogs were cute.' The distinct odour of mice and other vermin hinted that the hedgehogs weren't the only inhabitants of Hammerschmidt Manoir. 'On the bright side, the state of the house should bring the value of the property down considerably. I think even a builder would think twice about taking on a project house like this one. Whoever buys this place will be after the land— like you. The house is a liability.'

'Does that mean you're not interested in the property?'

Gabrielle shot him a lightning grin. 'I didn't say that. I still want to see the winemaking equipment and the storage caves.'

Like the house, the winemaking and storage areas were without power. Luckily for them, Luc had a torch.

'Boy scout,' she said.

'Not ever, and well you know it,' he countered. He'd run wild as a boy, they all had; the chateau and the land surrounding it had encouraged children that way. But he had grown up with the caves of Caverness at his back, hence the torch. He probably had spare batteries and quite possibly another torch tucked away somewhere on his most spectacular person. Not that Gabrielle felt inclined to examine him and find out.

Luc's 'no casual touching' rule suited her fine. Just, her fingers twitched, fine.

'How far into the caves do you want to go?' he

asked, flicking torchlight around the entrance tunnel once he'd shifted the rusting wrought-iron gate aside.

'Not far.' The well-lit and equally well-mapped caves of Caverness were one thing, a maze of abandoned underground tunnels was quite another. 'After you.'

'Ladies first,' he murmured.

'You are such a gentleman.' Swiping the torch from Luc's unresisting fingers Gabrielle lifted her chin high and started into the darkness, with Luc a few steps behind her, chuckling softly.

'So…' he said as she shone the torchlight high. 'Still scared of bats?'

'No,' she said loftily. 'I've outgrown that particular fear.' Mind you, it never hurt to send a prayer of silent thanks that there were no bats hanging from the roof of this particular grotto. At least, none in torch range. She swung the thready beam of light downwards fast; it was probably best not to know.

Gabrielle shivered as they moved further into the tunnel and the temperature plummeted. Luc was wearing a suit. Gabrielle wore a thin cotton blouse.

'Cold?' murmured Luc silkily.

'Not at all.'

'So if you're not scared and you're not cold, why is the torch trembling?'

Ah. That. 'Probably a fault in the wiring.' Something rustled beneath her feet and Gabrielle lost all pretence of bravery as she shot one hand out to grasp hold of Luc by his shirtfront and pointed the torch towards her feet with the other. 'What was that?'

'Me choking on my shirt collar?' he suggested dryly.

Oh. She released her grip and smoothed his shirt back in place for good measure, but she did not step away. 'Stay close.'

'I am close.'

He also had another torch in his pocket, which he withdrew and switched on, adding its glow to the light coming from her own, sweeping it back and forth along the floor of the cave.

'Whatever it was, it's gone,' he said, and with a wider sweep of his torch, 'This isn't a bad storage area, Gabrielle. Look, it's high, dry, good sized, and it smells well ventilated. Add a solid door rather than the wrought-iron gate at the entrance and install some lighting and you'd have good temperature control in here year round.'

'Are there any more caverns like this?'

Luc the intrepid stepped forward, Gabrielle followed, making sure she stayed within arm's length and only bumping into him twice. She kept one hand on his back after that, and to hell with not touching him until they were ready to make love for a week. That particular rule only applied outside underground caves potentially crawling with rats and harbouring bats.

The Hammerschmidt grottos boasted three more vast caverns, each one larger than the last. Storage enough for ten years' worth of Angels Landing harvests, decided Gabrielle, with the potential to excavate deeper underground as needed. With very little effort the caves could be made useable and very easily rentable.

'Seen enough?' murmured Luc.

She had. The caves were an asset—no question. They could talk their merits to death later, but for now the cold had seeped into her bones, she was shivering uncontrollably, and warmth and sunshine were high on her list of priorities.

'Hold this,' said Luc and thrust his torch into the hand at his back. The next minute a jacket fell around her shoulders, warm from the wearing and bearing the unmistakable scent of Luc. He took back the torch and took her hand and headed back the way they'd come in.

Once outside he stood her in the sun and stared down at her broodingly. 'You never did have any sense when it came to the caves,' he said gruffly. 'Warmer now?'

'M-much,' she managed.

'You want me to warm you?'

'N-not unless you're free all n-next week, n-no.'

'So can I have my jacket back?'

'Over m-my dead body.' Which could be a possibility if he attempted to take his jacket from her. She glared at him and tucked her arms in the sleeves for good measure, this time suppressing a shiver of pure delight as Luc's warmth wrapped around her. 'Exercise,' she said. 'Exercise will warm me up. Let's take a look at the vines.'

'You want to walk them or run them?' he said with the tilt of his lips. They'd run the fields as children, she, Luc, and Rafael. Rafe had always given her twenty rows' head start. Luc had been known to give her thirty and still catch her at the finish line.

'I'd rather walk,' she said and suited actions to words. Luc fell into step beside her, keeping a careful distance between them, a distance he hadn't enforced in the caves.

'Are you trying to keep your hands off me, Luc?'

'Not trying,' he murmured. 'I *am* keeping my hands off you.' He glanced skywards as if for heavenly support. 'I can't believe you haven't noticed.'

Gabrielle grinned and then stopped abruptly as they came upon the first row of vines. The grapes, unpruned, uncared for, and full of disease, were a disaster. The thorny, rambling monsters planted at the end of each row of vines looked vaguely familiar but they didn't look like grapes. 'Are these…roses?'

'Got it in one,' said Luc dryly.

She looked along the rows of wire that supposedly supported the vines and currently supported Rosacea's finest. 'But who in their right mind would plant rambling roses amongst the vines?'

'No one,' he said darkly.

'Pretty though.'

He looked at her as if she'd grown another head. Gabrielle sniggered. 'What would you do with these vines?'

'Rip them out and replant.'

'And the trellis?' The wood and wire framework had to be at least a hundred years old.

'That would go too.'

'Expensive,' she murmured.

'Very.'

'You'd be better off starting from scratch.'

'Don't tempt me,' he said. 'The land is perfectly sloped for the sun on the grapes and it's close to Caverness. They're big pluses.'

'Yes, but do they match the big drawbacks?'

'I haven't decided yet.'

Neither had Gabrielle. 'It could have been so good,' she said.

'Let the hedgehog be a warning to you,' he countered, with a crooked grin that warmed her the way his coat had. 'Let's talk about it some more over lunch.'

'Lunch where?'

'I know a place you'll like,' he said. 'It's in the hills.' And when she hesitated. 'It's only lunch, Gabrielle. Save your hesitation for dinner.'

Well, when he put it like that...

'VERY NICE,' SAID GABRIELLE as they were seated at an outdoor table of an elegant hotel café nestled into the hills of Champagne. Minutes later a pitcher of iced water had joined the party, accompanied by a chilled glass of white wine for Gabrielle and a foaming brown beer for Luc. The café was famed for its selection of sour dark breads and cheeses as well

as for the views of the countryside from its hillside
terrace. A cheese and pâté platter would be joining
them directly. Luc had ordered it. Gabrielle's mouth
watered at the thought of it but she turned her attention to her surroundings until it turned up.

'The view from the hill behind Caverness is better,' she commented idly. 'Ever thought of putting a
café up there?'

'No.'

'Because it wouldn't be economically viable?'

'No, because I like the hilltop as it is.'

'So you're not always all about business?'

Crinkles framed Luc's eyes. A smile lurked nearby.
'Never have been.'

'And yet the House of Duvalier thrives under your
rule.'

'I never said I wasn't good at what I do, Gabrielle. I am.'

'If you hadn't inherited the family dynasty what
would you have done?' she asked curiously.

'You mean after the fighter pilot phase and the
medicines-sans-frontiers phase had ended?'

'Yes,' she said with the tilt of her lips. 'After you'd
finished with those particular adventures.' Luc's
dreams always had been adventurous, even when
they'd been children. Not for him boring games like
cowboys and Indians. No, when they'd played make
believe they'd been World War Two resistance fight-
ers smuggling refugees to safety or World War One
aces trying to outmanoeuvre the Red Baron, with

Rafael the Baron and Simone and Gabrielle Luc's wingmen. 'We never did catch that Red Baron, did we?'

If Luc had trouble keeping up with the conversation he didn't let it show. 'Simone caught him once.'

'Only because Rafe let her.'

'No, she bested him. I saw it all. Rafe only pretended that he'd let her catch him. Even a twelve year old has his pride. But she out-thought him, fair and square.' Luc sounded more than a little proud of his sister and so he should be. As a youth Rafe had had more evasive manoeuvres up his sleeve than many a world leader. He still did.

'If you ask me, Rafe fell a little bit in love with her that day,' said Luc with a wry smile. 'And whenever Simone surprised him after that, or shielded you from Josien's wrath, he fell in love with her that little bit more. He's loyal, Rafe. To you. Even to Josien, in his way. He'd have worked his heart out for Simone had she gone to Australia with him.'

'Then how come you didn't say that seven years ago?' muttered Gabrielle. She didn't mean to sound accusing. She didn't want to argue with Luc about Simone and Rafe's disastrous relationship, but her words were sharper than she'd intended.

'You think I didn't?'

'I think you made like Switzerland and tried to be neutral.'

'What if I did?' he said mildly, but his eyes were guarded. 'Simone was eighteen and born to a life of luxury. Rafe was twenty-two, penniless, and about to move halfway across the world on a whim. He had nothing to offer her but love and a determination to succeed that bordered on obsessive. I care for Rafe like a brother but that doesn't mean I'm blind to his faults. I'm not blind to Simone's either. Would you have had me say that I thought Simone too demanding and immature to lead the life Rafe wanted her to lead? Would you have had me accuse Rafe of being too driven to succeed to be able to afford a wife at that time? You supported Rafe, Gabrielle, and I was glad of it. But you only saw the romance, not the enormity of what Rafe asked of my sister.'

'He asked her to *believe* in him,' she said heatedly. 'Is that so wrong?'

'He asked her to forgo her family and her inheritance for him, Gabrielle. There was no middle ground with Rafe. No compromise. He was leaving and Simone could either go with him or it was over.'

'You don't know what it was like for Rafe here,' said Gabrielle raggedly. 'Josien's hatred for him was like a cancer, eating away at every plan and hope he ever entertained. If Rafe hadn't left here when he did, Josien would have destroyed him. He *couldn't* stay.'

Luc's eyes had darkened, whether with temper or with sorrow she couldn't fathom. 'I know,' he said simply. 'And Simone could not leave. Can't you see that?'

She could. She did. And she hated seeing it laid out so clearly, every fault line and crevasse exposed. 'I don't even know how we came to be arguing about this,' she muttered. 'It's just...I see Simone so care-ful with her questions about my life in Australia, with her feelings still so raw, even after all these years. I see Rafe who can't even bring himself to speak her name, and all I want to do is make their pain go away.'

'You can't,' said Luc gently. 'Only they can do that, and only when they're ready. It's the way of love, and of life.'

'When did you get so wise?' she asked, shooting him a half-hearted glare.

'I've always been wise,' he countered. 'You just never noticed.'

A tiny smile escaped her. 'I was probably too busy noticing other things about you. Sixteen-year-old girls don't necessarily look for wisdom in a beau.'

'No?' He looked intrigued. 'What did you look for?'

'Beauty,' she said. 'Which you had in spades. Mystery, which you had as well, never mind that I'd known you all my life. Danger, which I could al-ways sense in you but never saw in action. Sexuality. I trust I'm not the only woman to ever tell you that you have that one covered. And weakness. I looked for that too.'

'And did you find any?'

'You were chivalrous. Protective to a fault and I played on that. Used it to make you notice me. I called it weakness back then and I planned my se-duction of you around it.'

'Brat,' he said without heat.

'I know,' she admitted readily enough. 'And foolish with it. I would not necessarily call a man's protective streak a weakness *now*.'

'No?' The cheese platter came and Luc thanked the waiter in acknowledgement. 'What would you call it?'

To a woman who could have done with a whole lot more love and protection as a child? She perused the cheeses. 'Practically irresistible.'

His smile came slow and sweet, with only a hint of the sexual wattage she knew Luc was capable of. Such charming restraint. Such exemplary behaviour. He'd promised her as much, she'd demanded nothing less of him. The problem was that deep down inside she didn't want Luc the civil and well-behaved suitor. No, she wanted the other Luc. The one who could not, and would not, be tamed. She knew he was in there. And, as dangerous as that Luc was to her well-being, that small reckless voice inside her wanted him to come out and play.

'You're looking very thoughtful,' he murmured.

'Am I?' She was feeling very wanton. 'I'm just rethinking my plans for the afternoon. I've a couple of tasks to see to before dinner.'

'I'll return you to the village after we've finished up here,' he told her. 'Will that give you enough time to see to them?'

'I think so.' She'd never preplanned wanton behaviour before but surely it wouldn't take more than a couple of hours.

Luc turned the wattage up on that lazy smile. 'Have I been manageable enough for you this morning?'

'Yes, indeed. Your meekness and self-restraint have been a wonder to behold.'

'I know.' His smile was anything but meek and Gabrielle gloried in it. 'Are we still on for dinner?'

'Yes.' Madness notwithstanding, she'd made her decision. She would join Luc for dinner and dress to please a man and see if she could put a dint in all that iron self-control. 'Yes, we are.'

'I'VE FORMULATED A PLAN,' Gabrielle told Simone later that afternoon over a glass of wine at Simone's favourite café.

'What kind of plan?' asked Simone, looking sunspelled and feline-lazy.

'A plan for exploring my physical attraction to Luc. I'm figuring to encourage that particular aspect of our relationship along somewhat. Get it over and done with, so to speak, so that I can stop *thinking* about it so much and get back to concentrating on my work.'

Simone turned her head and looked at Gabrielle from over the rim of her sunglasses. 'Hnh,' she said finally.

'The thing is, I'm a little nervous about heading out to dinner with a man whose mind I intend to mess with.'

'So you should be,' said Simone.

'Looking for a little support here,' murmured Gabrielle. 'Possibly a little help. I need to know what a woman should do when she wants to drive a man insane with lust.'

'She should *not* ask the man's sister how to go about it,' said Simone dryly. 'There are some things a sister simply can't, or won't, help you with.'

'You're right. My apologies. That was thoughtless of me.' Gabrielle drummed her fingers on the café table top. 'Suppose I were to ask you for more generic advice about heading out to dinner with a man I wanted to seduce. Advice not targeted towards any one individual in particular. Would you have any suggestions on how to go about it then?'

'But of course,' said Simone. 'That's a different request altogether.'

'Excellent. So where does one begin?'

'You'll need a dress.'

'I have a dress.'

'I never doubted it for a moment,' said Simone. 'You'll also need a coat to go over this dress. The reveal is very important.'

True, so very true. 'When would you say was the best time for this reveal to happen?'

'Somewhere public. Somewhere where many eyes will be drawn to you. I'm very fond of making a man feel possessive. Of course, I should warn you that if we were talking about Lucien I would encourage you to skip that step altogether. He's always been possessive of you and needs no further encouragement in that direction.'

'What about a bunch of little reveals throughout

the evening, just to keep his attention? A wrist here, a hint of perfume there.'

'Perfect.'

'Then what?'

'Banter.'

'Sexual?'

'Sophisticated.' Simone shook her head. 'I swear, Australia has had an unforgivable influence on you. Where's your sense of subtlety?'

'Okay, sophisticated and subtly sexual banter.'

'No, no, no!' said Simone. 'A woman intent on driving a man mad with lust does not talk of sex at all! All she need do is imagine the sex.'

'I'm not sure that particular piece of advice is going to work for me.' Imagining sex with Luc tended to fry her brain. Attempting sophisticated non-sexual banter while frying her brain could prove quite a stretch.

'No one said this was going to be *easy*,' said Simone dryly. 'Seduction is an art, and like any form of art it requires commitment, constant practice, and skill.'

'Okay, I'll use my imagination. Then what?'

'Pheromones,' said Simone sagely. 'Do not underestimate them.'

'Pheromones. Right. Good to know. I'm not even going to ask you how you know this stuff. Anything else?'

'Yes. Seduction isn't a game so never, ever treat it as one. Seduction is war.'

'War,' echoed Gabrielle. 'Not an art form?'

'So much to learn,' said Simone on a pitying sigh. 'So little time.'

'I'm a little uncomfortable with seduction as war,' argued Gabrielle. 'Couldn't seduction be a duel instead?'

'All right, seduction is a duel,' said Simone with an airy wave of her hand. 'You'll be wanting the points on the blades removed next.'

'I *do* want them removed,' she said earnestly. 'I don't want to hurt anyone, Simone. Especially not the person I intend to seduce. That's not part of the plan.'

'I'm relieved to hear it, all things considered, but the fact remains that I've just armed you with a blade. The traditional use of any blade is to force the acquisition of something that would not otherwise be freely given. The traditional response to such a weapon is surrender, but not always. Sometimes the wielder of the blade gets more than they bargained for.'

Gabrielle contemplated Simone's words. 'I'll be careful,' she said finally.

'I hope so.' Simone studied her pensively. 'I started out in this conversation feeling protective of Luc. Now I'm sitting here wondering how on earth I'm going to protect *you*. You're out of your depth, Gabrielle. Luc knows how to fascinate women. I believe he knows obsession. He's felt the sting of it before. For you. I doubt he'll play at seduction with a blunted blade the way you intend to. Are you *really* ready for this?'

Gabrielle gave the question the attention it deserved. 'I'll be *very* careful,' she said finally.

Simone sighed heavily. 'I hope you know what you're doing, Gabrielle, because I don't want to lose you again.' She looked broodingly at her near-empty wine glass. 'Either of you.'

LUCIEN DRESSED CAREFULLY for his dinner date that evening. Not a suit, no, a suit was too formal, but a pair of suede trousers and a favoured casual shirt, soft to the touch and tailored to his physique. His watch had an antique gold face and a brown leather band and was also one of his favourites. A person had to know watches to know that it was Cartier. The cufflinks with the Duvalier crest he was undecided about. On the one hand, this was who he was. On the other hand, Gabrielle's relationship with Caverness and the House of Duvalier was somewhat stormy.

He needed advice. Female advice.

'What do you think?' he asked when he cornered Simone in the television room. He held up the cufflinks. 'Yes or no?'

'More information required,' said Simone. 'Where are you going?'

'Out for a meal. A casual, informal, getting to know you meal.'

'With a woman?'

'Yes.'

'A woman you wish to impress?'

'Not exactly *impress*,' he said. 'This woman

knows me already. She's probably not all that impressable.'

'Don't wear them, then,' said Simone. 'Give the House of Duvalier the night off. That is, unless you'd rather wear them and feel secure in the knowledge that your shirt won't be coming off in a hurry.'

'My shirt isn't going to come off at all,' said Luc darkly, and set to threading the cufflinks through his cuffs. 'Tonight isn't about seduction. Tonight is all about showing restraint.'

'Pardon?' said Simone.

An incredulous pardon if ever he'd heard one. 'Restraint,' he said again.

'Hnh,' said Simone, but by the time he looked up from fastening his cuffs she'd turned back to her book. Luc sighed at her impressively short attention span and decidedly unsisterly concern for his needs.

'So, let's say I did want to make sure that the evening was a pleasant non-sexual one for all concerned. What do I do?'

Simone lowered her book with a sigh. 'What do you usually do?'

'Pleasantly non-sexual isn't exactly in my repertoire,' he confided. 'Hence the need for advice.'

'Is Gabrielle the woman you're intending to have this pleasantly platonic evening with?'

'Possibly,' said Luc. 'Probably. Although there's no need for your advice to be specifically tailored to Gabrielle. Generic advice will do. You never know when a few pleasant platonics will come in handy.'

'You have no idea how underprepared I am for this conversation,' said Simone darkly.

'Well, if you don't know, just say so,' he began, but stopped when she held up her hand.

'I'm thinking…' she said. 'Just give me a moment.'

He gave her two. 'Well?'

'Well…since you asked so nicely and waited so patiently for me to collect my thoughts, I'll share a few ideas I have on the subject.'

'Appreciated,' he said.

Amusement slid through Simone's gleaming gaze. 'I recommend ignoring outright any moves laden with subtly sexual overtones.'

'Ignore them,' said Luc with a puzzled frown. 'As in…*ignore* them? Really?'

'Completely,' said Simone. 'Act as if they never happened. If a woman greets you in a dress designed to destroy a man, smile in an easy and open fashion, comment on the suitability of the weather, and ask her if she likes puppies.'

'Puppies?' echoed Luc.

'Puppies,' she said firmly. 'Not kittens. Stay away from the kitten talk—you never know where that one might lead. Keep the conversation grounded. Nothing too sophisticated. Something casual and feel-good without being threatening. Puppies are perfect.' She eyed him speculatively. 'It's a pity you didn't come to me earlier with this. I could have arranged for you to borrow one.'

Borrow a puppy? Four bounding legs, sweeping

tail, floppy ears, liquid eyes, and a wet, inquisitive nose? His sister had gone insane. 'Thank you, but no.'

'You also need to do a little something with your hair.'

'My hair? What's wrong with my hair?'

'Well, it's falling all over your face and needs cutting for starters, but apart from that a woman's going to take one look at it and want to run her fingers through it. Tie it back. Like a soccer star or a scorpion king. Trust me, your features won't suffer for it.'

'*What?*' He really wasn't keeping up with the gist of this conversation at all.

'I'll lend you a black leather band. Very manly.'

'Won't pulling my hair back make a woman want to rearrange it?' Luc didn't know a lot about how a man's hair affected a woman's fingers but he knew enough about his own reaction to a woman's tresses to know that whenever they put it up, he rarely rested until he'd taken every last pin and hairband *out*.

'Not at all,' said Simone blithely. 'Where's your coat?'

'Do I need a coat?'

'But of course you need a coat. A coat makes you look solid and dependable. You should keep it on. You should probably make your companion keep hers on too. Just a nice platonic dinner between two people wearing coats and talking puppies. Not a lot to get excited about there.'

No, thought Luc with the first faint stirrings of unease. There wasn't. 'Anything else?'

'Isn't that enough?'

She was probably right. 'Well, thanks for the advice.'

'You know me.' Simone favoured him with a sisterly smile. 'Always happy to help.'

CHAPTER SEVEN

LUC'S DINNER DATE with Gabrielle started well. He wore a coat. She met him at the door to her apartment and, lo, she happened to be wearing a coat also. A severe black leather three-quarter-length, double-breasted coat cinched tightly at the waist with a wide black belt. Her black leather purse had a severe Prada look about it, and her hair had been scraped off her face into a no-nonsense schoolmarm bun with not a wayward tendril in sight. Luc's fingers began to itch, but he shoved them in his coat pocket and thought of puppies. He stepped back to let her by as she shut the door and brushed past him towards the narrow garden path. He glanced downwards to make sure she was minding her step on the uneven cobbles and all coherent thought fled. Gabrielle's shoes were black like the rest of her attire, but there the resemblance to the rest of her attire ended. The elegant four-inch stilettos owed nothing to practicality, severity, or plainness. These shoes had one purpose and one purpose only.

To bring a man to his knees.

'St Bernards,' he muttered.

'What?'

'Puppies. St Bernard puppies. I saw some today. I'm thinking of getting one.'

'You?' she said sceptically. 'And a puppy.'

'Yes.'

'At Caverness.'

'Yes.'

'Josien will be pleased,' said Gabrielle dryly.

'For company,' he said, suddenly inspired. 'He could sit at my feet on those long winter nights, in front of the fire while I...' While he what?

'Rest?' supplied Gabrielle.

'Yes, rest, and maybe do a spot of reading. The Napoleonic Wars, The Battle of Waterloo, that sort of thing.' Did that sound platonic and non-sexual enough? 'The Joy of Shoes.'

'The what?'

'The Joy of Choux. It's about pastry. You haven't read it?' Pastry... Puppies... Whatever. He figured they were interchangeable.

Gabrielle sent him a very steady stare. 'Have you been drinking?'

'Not yet.' Although those shoes could doubtless drive a man to it.

'And what happened to your hair?'

'What do you mean?' He narrowly resisted putting his hand to his recently curtailed locks.

'Where is it?'

As far as he *knew*, the hair that usually fell around his face was currently tied high on the back of his head, Soccer Striker or Scorpion King style. Not that he was either. 'Simone tells me it takes a man of pure courage to wear his hair like this.'

'I'm sure she did,' murmured Gabrielle. 'Did she tell you it takes a man of outstanding beauty to carry it off?'

She hadn't.

'Fortunately, you've got that one covered as well,' she said next with somewhat grudging appreciation. 'Tell her I approve. My fantasy life may never be the same.'

Was that sexual innuendo? It could have been. Luc decided to ignore it anyway, just to be on the safe side. They'd been doing so well. Right up until her shoes and his hair.

'Tell you what,' he offered. 'You take your hair down and I'll do the same with mine.'

'Have you any idea how long it took the hair-dresser to put my hair *up*?' said Gabrielle eyeing him narrowly.

'Two minutes?' Not according to the look on her face. 'Five minutes?' His fingers really itched. 'Okay, ten. But I swear I could turn it loose for you in no time at all.'

'Luc…' She raised a stern yet delightfully elegant hand in his direction. 'Don't touch.'

'Good idea.' *Good* idea. He was in desperate need of more platonic conversation. 'You know, a puppy would have a field day with your shoes.'

Gabrielle looked down at her shoes and did that thing women did with their bodies when trying on clothes, or in this case shoes. The tiny turns and twists while they studied the item in question from every conceivable angle. 'What's wrong with my shoes?'

Oh, nothing a black lace corset and matching panties wouldn't fix. 'All those skinny little straps. All that space in between.' Crimson toenails. He'd never before paid particular attention to the colour of a woman's toenails but he seemed to be spending a great deal of time studying these ones. 'They seem a bit insubstantial, that's all.'

'Not for a restaurant, surely,' she countered sweetly as she straightened and smoothed her coat back into place with similarly crimson-tipped hands. 'It's not as if we're going to be mountain climbing.' Her smile was just this side of wicked. 'A man like you will be no doubt thinking of saving that particular joy for your mountain-loving puppy.'

She swept past him with another blinding smile and her chin held high, the rest of her swathed in punishment black. A waft of something floral and French teased at his nostrils, one of the newer, younger fragrances that snuck up on a man and wrapped around him when he least expected it. Or maybe that was just Gabrielle.

They made it to the car, to the restaurant, to the door of the restaurant without catastrophe. They stepped inside and warmth and the aroma of good food chased away the elusive scent of the woman at his side. The restaurant wasn't a large one, it seated thirty perhaps, but Luc knew from experience that every table would be filled before the night was through and that it wasn't unusual for the wait staff to book both early and late sittings for the same table space.

The room was small and narrow, a red leather bench seat ran the length of one wall, allowing closely placed tables for two or four to slot in next. Plain cushioned restaurant chairs had been placed on the other side of the tables. A narrow pathway down the middle of the room served as the food highway, and a scattering of slightly more private tables graced the other side of the room. The bar stood to the back of the room, the kitchen was situated behind that. A coat rack stood by the door. Gabrielle hesitated and her hands went to the belt at her waist.

'It's warm in here,' she murmured.

Yes, it was. Luc's hands went automatically to her shoulders to help with the removal of her coat before he remembered Simone's suggestion about keeping coats on. 'It'll be cooler by the window,' he said. 'You don't want to take a seat and see if you're more comfortable with your coat on?'

'No.' But she looked undecided. 'No one else is wearing their coats in here.'

True. The coat rack was currently groaning beneath the weight of discarded outerwear. One of Gabrielle's shoulders appeared, and then another. Two shoulders and an expanse of smooth and creamy skin. Luc swallowed hard. What *was* she almost wearing?

Something strapless, obviously. Strapless and crimson—a deep blood-wine red—Gabrielle's dress clung lovingly to every perfect inch of her hourglass figure and finished somewhere around mid-thigh.

'Rottweilers,' he whimpered.

'What about them?' Gabrielle turned and slanted him a look through eyes that knew only too well the effect such a dress was likely to have on a man.

'Could be useful protection for the chateau,' he said, dragging his gaze away from the curve of her neck and the pins in her hair before restless fingers got the better of him. He parked her coat on the rack and followed it up with his own.

'Mmm,' said Gabrielle. 'They could keep your St Bernard company.'

Luc didn't even attempt an answer. He was too busy staring down the myriad admiring glances coming Gabrielle's way. 'I swear, if I'd known what you were wearing before we left your apartment we wouldn't have been going anywhere,' he muttered darkly, scowling at a local brewery owner who'd shown the bad sense to stare at Gabrielle in open appreciation. The man nodded to him in recognition, his grin widening. Luc put his hand to the small of Gabrielle's back. Mine, said the gesture, and he didn't care who knew it. 'Shall we be seated or would you care for a drink at the bar first?'

Gabrielle looked at the barstools while Luc pondered the elasticity of that perfectly fitted dress. Clearly there would be no sitting on a barstool for Gabrielle. Not unless she wanted to be dragged from the restaurant and plastered against the wall of the nearest dark alleyway while he slaked his thirst and made sure those endless legs were wrapped around him. They might make it to the alleyway, he thought grimly. If they were lucky.

'A table, I think,' she said with a smile.

'*Good* call.' He was a man on the edge, and everyone in the restaurant but Gabrielle seemed to know it. The people he knew smiled and nodded and looked away fast, as if sensing the unpredictability of his next move.

The elderly, slightly built dark-haired waiter headed their way fast as well. There was a ripple in the fabric of the atmosphere of his room and he wanted it smoothed.

'Monsieur Duvalier, always a pleasure. A table by the window for yourself and the *mademoiselle*?' The waiter was eyeing Gabrielle with a careful smile and a forehead full of frownlines. 'Mademoiselle Gabrielle?'

'Paolo?'

'*Oui!*' Paolo beamed. 'You remembered.'

'Of course I remembered.' Gabrielle's smile was conspiratorial. 'Saturdays, Sundays, and Mondays. The bread run. You delivered the baguettes from a basket on your pushbike.'

'I tried.' Paolo glanced at Luc. 'Not that I ever made it to the kitchen door. Always her mother would send her tearing down the laneway to meet me. I missed you once you left, *chica*. There was no one left to save my poor legs the climb.'

Gabrielle smiled. 'Do you still have the bread run?'

'But no. The bread run bought this business. My

son, he became a chef and does the cooking, and *his* sons work as kitchen hands. This old man is content to wait tables. With good word of mouth and excellent patronage, old Paolo's family prospers.'

'Bravo,' said Gabrielle softly as Paolo seated them at a table by the window and disappeared, returning shortly thereafter with a jug of iced water, a tiny bowl of olives dipped in herb oil and a basket of fresh and crusty bread.

'It is fortunate you chose this evening to dine with us,' Paolo told Luc as he draped first Gabrielle's napkin across her lap and then Luc's across his. 'A case of the 1976 Saracenne Reserve Brut arrived this morning and has spent the entire day being lovingly lowered in temperature to exactly four degrees. Of course, I had to promise my firstborn great-grandson in order to take delivery of this miracle of champagnery, but I'm confident it will be worth it. Can I tempt you with a bottle?'

'What say you?' Luc asked Gabrielle. 'Shall we devote the evening to marvelling at the competition?'

'I think we should.'

Paolo rattled off the daily specials before indicating the blackboard menu on the wall and leaving them alone to make their selections.

Gabrielle sat back, and looked around Paolo's restaurant with wide approving eyes.

She smiled and that relaxed Luc. The murmur of contented voices and the aroma of good cooking soothed the beast inside him. The flickering candlelight settled him. The breaking of bread redirected

Luc's hunger enough that he could look at Gabrielle without his body screaming for release. She'd turned off the courtesan for the moment and only the real Gabrielle shone through. The one who approved of an old bread vendor aiming high and reaching his goals. The one who'd treated Paolo with the same courtesy and respect one would afford a statesman and had probably never treated him any differently.

Luc had known many beautiful women but he'd never known one with less awareness of her beauty than Gabrielle. Granted, she'd been surrounded by remarkable good looks, what with Rafe for a brother and Josien for a mother, but she'd never seemed to find beauty within herself, never mind that her resemblance to her mother was remarkable.

She didn't see it, thought Luc as he sat back the better to study her face in the candlelight. She just didn't see it.

'What?' she asked him warily. 'I hope you didn't mind me talking to Paolo. He always had a kind word for me. Always.'

'I don't mind you talking to Paolo.'

'Then what is it?'

'Nothing.'

'I'm not seeing nothing.'

Funny that. Because she was probably blind enough. He wondered where a compliment might fit into the grand scheme of things. Simone hadn't said anything about limiting compliments. Besides, he'd done a great deal of talking about puppies already. He was fresh out of pup talk. 'You're beautiful.'

GABRIELLE HADN'T KNOWN exactly how much she'd missed France until she sat in Paolo's tiny crowded restaurant on a Saturday night with Luc. Lulled into relaxation by champagne neither she nor Luc could find fault with, she sat back and set about getting to know the man Luc had become.

He was a sensualist—it showed in the pleasure he took from his food and his surroundings. An intimidating man, she thought, studying his face in the candlelight and finding no softness there. The softness was in her memories of him as a child. They might have called him Night but he hadn't been all brooding and restless darkness. He'd been her knight at times—champion of the underdog. Where had his restlessness gone? she wondered. The recklessness she remembered? Did he still dream of conquering new frontiers or had the challenges that came with being the head of the House of Duvalier been enough for him?

No, they hadn't, she realised with blinding clarity. That was what his fascination with the Hammerschmidt vineyard was all about. He didn't need a crumbling manoir surrounded by a couple of hundred acres of worthless grapevines, no matter how closely located to Caverness they were. He needed a challenge. Beneath all that seemingly effortlessly acquired wealth and charm, a panther paced the cage. Bound by birthright. Fettered by society's expectations. He'd been as trapped by Caverness as she'd been.

He was still trapped. Pacing. Pacing.

That was what drew her to this man so completely.

The bone-deep knowledge that when it came to making love with him the panther would escape his cage and be exactly what he was meant to be. As dark as night. As fierce as the devil. And free.

She wanted to be alone with him, wanted it with a fierce and urgent intensity.

He looked at her and he knew her thoughts. No words required.

Never underestimate the power of pheromones.

'How's the food?' she asked.

'Excellent. Yours?'

'Mmm. Exquisite.'

'How am I doing so far?' he murmured. 'Civilised enough for you?' His words held a dark and dangerous edge that made her shudder in anticipation.

'Yes.'

'Ready to bed me now?'

'Yes.' Her body felt boneless, languorous, as the panther rattled the cage.

'Right now and to hell with coffee and dessert?'

'Yes.'

Paolo materialised beside them as if drawn there by the force of Luc's will alone.

'Are you sure?' murmured Luc. Gabrielle nodded. Luc's eyes didn't leave her face. 'Paolo, we'd like the bill.'

Paolo looked at their half-eaten meals and the still half-full bottle of precious champagne. 'But is there something wrong?' Luc smiled tightly and a look passed between them. 'Ah,' said the old man. '*Bon appétit*. I will put a regular cork in the Saracenne so you may take it with you.'

'*Non*, Paolo. Take it to the kitchen and do with it what you will. The meal was outstanding, as always. My compliments to you and your family.'

Gabrielle was never sure how she managed to stand and to walk to the door of the restaurant as if everything were not bathed in the colour of desire. She got her coat on with Luc's help and watched with eyes that followed every movement of his long, strong fingers as he did up her buttons and cinched her belt tight.

He reached for her the moment they were seated in the relative privacy of the car, his fingers in her hair, expertly seeking and removing pins as his lips slanted over hers and demanded she open for him. He groaned when she did, the raw and needy groan of a man pushed to his limits as his tongue began a fiercely sensual invasion, stripping her of everything but the need to respond. Her hands went to his hair, she wanted it free, and it took her less than two seconds to achieve that particular goal. Her hair came down more slowly—the hairdresser had been thorough—but when it finally tumbled down around her shoulders and over the lapels of her coat Luc groaned again as the intensity of his kiss ratcheted up another notch. Gabrielle wrenched her lips from his and pushed him away with an unsteady hand.

'Drive,' she ordered raggedly.

'Where?'

'Anywhere.' Although… 'Maybe not Caverness.'

Her courage did not extend to flaunting her intimacy with Luc in Josien's face—not because of what her mother might think of her, but because Gabrielle feared that somehow, heaven only knew how, Josien would turn her feelings for Luc into something ugly. 'My room.'

'Caverness is my home, Gabrielle.' His voice was as ragged and strained as hers. 'Sooner or later I will want you there.' But he drove towards the old mill and said no more as they exited the Audi and strode towards the front door. 'I aim to stay the night.'

'I aim to let you.'

Conversation complete.

They met no one on the way to Gabrielle's room. She preceded Luc inside, he locked the door behind him, and she made one last desperate attempt at being civil as she turned to face him and lifted her chin. 'Drink?'

'No.' He shrugged off his coat and tossed it over a chair before coming to stand in front of her, not touching her, not yet. But his eyes promised her every wild thing she wanted of him this night. Everything and more. 'I want you.'

Her hands went to the buckle on her coat and then to the buttons. Moments later a cloud of black leather landed at her feet. She smiled and arched an eyebrow in wordless challenge. 'Which bits?'

'All of them.' A smile crossed his lips, a smile no sensible woman would turn her back on, but she did just that and swept her hair to one side and glanced at him over her shoulder.

'The clasp on my necklace is a little stiff.' Her gaze slid down that lithe and intimidating body and her smile grew the tiniest bit smug. He was ready for her. 'Would you mind? I'd hate to break it.'

His fingers brushed the back of her neck and the necklace came loose in her hand. Luc slid his hands to her shoulders then, his palms warm, cupping the curve of them before he slowly trailed his fingers down her arms. 'You could start with the back of my neck,' she offered. His lips on the bare and sensitive curve of her shoulder.

'I could,' he murmured.

But he didn't.

He started with the zip that ran down the back of her dress, lowering it slowly, smoothly, before walking around her, studying her the way an art aficionado might study a Da Vinci. 'What's underneath?' he said, his voice a husky purr.

'Oh, nothing much.' She wasn't going to step out of her dress for him. If he wanted her undressed he could do it himself. 'I've often wondered what would have happened all those years ago,' she murmured, 'if we hadn't been interrupted. You were sitting on an old wooden table, I believe. As for me...' Her eyes caught Luc's and held. 'I was sitting on you.'

'I'm warning you, Gabrielle. If you want a re-enactment, this is going to get out of control fast.'

'Maybe.' Maybe that was exactly what she wanted. 'There's a table here.'

'There's a *bed* here,' he countered darkly.

Yes, there was. 'Maybe if you sat on the edge of it…'

'Maybe if you let me kiss you…'

That was what he'd said to her last time, too. She stepped forward and offered him her lips, the lightest touch.

'More,' he whispered, and she was catapulted back to the caves of Caverness and she was sixteen and trembling with equal parts terror and lust as she offered Luc more and spun them into madness.

They were on the bed before she knew it, Luc sitting on it with Gabrielle wrapped around him, her knees either side of him, while he devoured her mouth, one hand in her wild tumble of hair and the other on her derrière, urging her closer to his straining hardness. Last time he'd done that, her innocence had left her gasping in shock at his boldness. This time she gasped at the outrageous size of him, the thickness and heat that went on, and on.

Her dress was no barrier to hands as sure as Luc's. His hands were on the rounded globes of her buttocks in an instant, sliding over the silk of her panties as he surged against her. With a ragged moan Gabrielle put her hands to his face as she'd done once before and poured all that she was into a meeting of mouths.

'Would we have managed to take our clothes off, do you think?' she murmured against his lips.

'No,' he whispered as his fingers slid beneath the edge of her panties. 'Maybe some of them. Maybe if I could have got them off you without having to let you go.'

'How?'

The sibilant hiss of shredding silk gave her an answer she approved of wholeheartedly. She doubted that she would have been bold enough to reach for his belt at sixteen, but she reached for it now in her haste for skin against skin. His zipper went next and then his briefs. She glanced down, measuring him with her eyes, willing her body not to want so badly, willing herself to relax and to wait. 'I'd have been a little nervous right about now. Back then.' Hell, she was a little nervous *now*.

His eyes had darkened, there was fury there, carefully banked. 'I'd have taken care of you.' There was bite in his words. 'I'd not have disappointed you.' Long dark lashes shaded his eyes as he bent his head and set his lips to her collarbone, used his teeth on her there to nip and his tongue to caress. 'Why didn't you wait?'

Ah. There. There was the bite. But she wasn't entirely to blame for bestowing her virginity elsewhere. 'Why didn't you ask me to?' She craved his mouth on her breasts and had no hesitation about twining her hands in his hair and dragging his head there none too gently. Her dress fell away, and she whimpered her satisfaction as she closed her eyes and let sensation ride her, rule her, as her tightly budded nipple made contact with the heat of his tongue and the hardness of teeth.

Lucien could be savage, when he wanted to be. He was savage now, closing his lips over her and suckling hard, darkly pleased by her wild keening cry and the convulsive arch of her body. This wasn't about sex; sex was about bodies. This was possession, and he wanted her soul.

He drew her back on the bed to lay atop him and she went with him willingly, better for her because of his size, better for him because he had access to all of her. Another tremor ripped through her as he suckled her other breast, and with another whimper she settled herself against his length and rocked against him, her body already swollen and slick with need. Her dress had bunched around her waist, and she still wore her shoes but apart from that she was naked. He craved skin on skin, all of her up against every last bit of him. Her dress slid over her head easily; her shoes were harder to get her out of but he managed.

'Shirt,' he muttered, right before her lips claimed his. She undid all of two buttons before haste and frustration got the better of her. Fisting her hands in his shirt, she wrenched it apart. Buttons flew and Luc's breath left his body with a whoosh as she began to trace the curve of muscle over rib, of nipple over muscle. 'Now,' he muttered, with the last of his control. 'Gabrielle, I need to be inside you *now*.' He'd waited so long already. Foreplay and patience were not an option.

'Just so you know,' she muttered as she took him in hand and guided him slowly into her centre. 'I don't want you civilised and gentle. I just want you.'

And just like that, she released the panther from his cage.

He filled her in an instant, rolling her onto her back, fighting for supremacy over her and control of himself as he eased out of her and slid back home. Over and over, while her body destroyed his with greedy hands and a reckless mouth that drove him insane. 'No.' He had to keep control, he had to. He could not lose himself to this.

'More,' she whispered as he eased up on one elbow and splayed his other hand across the softness of her belly and found her centre with his thumb. This time the rhythm he set up was twofold in its intensity and she responded as if he'd taken a whip to her. Straining, clinging, screaming.

He watched her eyes go blind as she crested the peak. He felt convulsions rack her body as she came for him, over and over; she came for him hard.

Then and only then did he allow himself his own release.

GABRIELLE LAY QUIETLY in the aftermath of Luc's possession, her body not yet recovered enough to do more than breathe, and her mind not functional enough to assess the situation.

'What was that?' she asked finally.

'Overdue,' he said darkly. 'At least, that's what I'm hoping the reason for that particular madness was.' A shudder ripped through him and he twitched inside her, still filling her completely. 'Long, long overdue.'

'Okay.' She pondered the secrets of the universe for a while. Deliberated on what the goddess of lust would have thought of that little display. 'Felt a little intense,' she said next. 'Is that, ah, normal? For you?'

'Yes.'

'Oh.'

'No,' he admitted gruffly.

'Me either. Good though,' she added and lapsed back into contemplation. 'If that sort of uncontrollable edge thing works for you.'

'Yes.' He rolled onto his back but he did not pull out of her or away from her. He took her with him. He still had his shirt half on, his trousers mostly on. She wasn't wearing a stitch.

'Does it?' She hoped her voice wasn't telegraphing the anxiousness she felt. 'I mean… It could take some getting used to if you're not used to it. If you're a person who likes being in control of things… I mean.'

'Gabrielle?' His hand came up to cradle her skull and his lips brushed her forehead. 'Shut up.'

Shutting up. Shutting right up. Excellent suggestion. 'Luc?'

'What?' His voice sounded long suffering.

'Can we do it again?' The twitch of his body seemed to suggest he could.

'Yes.'

'Soon?'

'Yes.'

'Luc?'

'What?'

She shifted to settle astride him, her hands on his bare chest and her thoughts a little grave. 'I know

I still have to figure out how to remove the bulk of your clothes without giving up my position of dominance here, but do you think that this time you could be naked too?'

SHE GOT HIM NAKED. She got him sweaty. She got his hands fisted above his head as he poured his release into her and cried out her name.

But she could not, until that very last moment, make him surrender himself to her completely.

CHAPTER EIGHT

THE STONE-FACED miller's wife lasted all of ten minutes after Luc left the following morning before rap-
ping on the door and informing Gabrielle that the
room had been re-let and that she would need to find
accommodation elsewhere. Today. Oh, and she had
thirty minutes to pack.

This time, Gabrielle took a three-month lease on a
fully furnished apartment situated on a leafy square
in the expensive part of town.

If anyone tried to kick her out of this place for
being lover to a single man of good standing, she'd
damn well go out and buy a house. No one was going
to belittle the rapture she'd found in Luc's arms.

No one.

SIMONE, BLESS HER, did not even try. She came round
for coffee at Gabrielle's new abode, her smile warm
and her treatment of Gabrielle exactly the same. A
little confrontation, a lot of teasing, and always the
underlying warmth of a sister of the heart. She did
not repeat her warning of yesterday. Now that the
deed with Luc had been done, Simone accepted it

with the ease of one well used to accommodating life's little inconsistencies.

'Nice,' said Simone after looking through the apartment. 'But why the sudden change? I thought you had a few more days before your time at the old mill was up?'

'I needed something with a little more room,' said Gabrielle. 'And I needed it now.'

'She threw you out, didn't she?' Simone's gaze was very direct.

'Yes.'

'Because Luc stayed over?'

'Not in so many words, but yes. I think so.'

'Does Luc know?'

'No, and I'd appreciate it if you didn't mention it to him. I needed more space so I moved. End of story.'

'It's a good story, don't get me wrong,' said Simone. 'Let's just pray Luc never hears the other one.'

'Amen,' said Gabrielle.

'So, who won the war?' asked Simone next.

'Not me and stop prying. We are not having this conversation.'

'Just trying to keep up with the situation to hand,' said Simone. And with an impish grin. 'You don't look like a casualty of war.'

'I'm not.' Not yet, at any rate. 'And I really can't talk to you about this, Simone. It's too new. I don't even understand what's going on myself yet.'

'So who will you talk to about it?' asked Simone. 'Will you tell Rafe?'

'Not yet.'

'Because it's too new or because you know he won't like it?'

Gabrielle smiled wryly. 'Both.'

'Will you tell Josien?'

'No,' she said, her smile fading fast. 'That door is closed to me, Simone, and I'm done with standing on one side of it like a needy child waiting for it to open. There's nothing for me there.' Nothing but pain. 'Nothing there for Rafael either.'

'Gabrielle—' Simone's expression grew sombre. '*Maman* died so long ago I can hardly remember her, but I never envied you yours. I know she made childhood difficult for you. I wish things could have been different for you. For you and Rafe both.'

'Me too.'

'I know she used to hit you.' Simone hesitated, not quite managing to meet Gabrielle's gaze. 'I saw her once. Not smacking you. Not scolding you for whatever it was she thought you'd done wrong. She was beating you. Hurting you.' Simone shook her head as if to deny the memory of it. 'I ran for my father but by the time we returned you were gone. My father said he'd talk to Josien but talking isn't doing, so I went and found Rafael and told him what I'd seen. I'll never forget the look on his face, Gaby. The helpless fury in his eyes. The pain and the fear. He was twelve and you were six and I knew at once that this wasn't the first time she'd hurt you. We ran back to the chateau and Rafe told me to go inside, and that he would find you and take care of you, and I went inside because I was scared. Gabrielle, I'm so sorry I never did anything. Not then. Not later, when Rafe would treat you with such care and tenderness that I knew in my heart she had taken to you again.' Simone looked tortured. 'Did he find you?'

'Always,' said Gabrielle with a tiny smile. 'Always.' She covered Simone's hands with her own and willed Simone to look at her. 'You were a child too, Simone. You did what you could. Your father did what he could—he made Josien seek counselling for her anger and her rage and it helped. It helped a lot. Besides, you forget that I was no angel. Sometimes I deserved to be punished.'

'Not like that,' said Simone fiercely. 'Never like that, and not later either when she came at you with words rather than whips. Don't let her hurt you again, Gaby. Don't you listen to her when she tells you that what you've found with my brother is wrong. Don't let anyone tell you that!'

'I won't.' But the weight of Simone's words settled heavily on Gabrielle's mind. Reminding her, as if she needed reminding, that not everyone would see her relationship with Luc in a positive light. Josien would disapprove. Rafe, with his uncomfortable history with Simone, would wish she'd chosen differently. And then there was the yawning social and economic gulf between a man of Luc's standing and a woman like herself. Gabrielle tried to feel worthy of Luc but she was desperately vulnerable to the judgement of others. She was a product of her childhood, of Josien's beliefs about class and about status, and those lessons learned early were not so easily disregarded. There was truth in them, and sense in them, no matter how much she wished otherwise. 'I'm feeling morose.'

'Likewise,' said Simone. 'You have no idea how I worried for you as a child.'

Gabrielle turned away, carefully, casually. 'Did Luc know?'

'That Josien used to beat you? No,' said Simone faintly. 'He suspected, but no one ever confirmed his suspicions. Not Rafe. Not you. And certainly not me. Rafe was so very level-headed about it, you see? Whereas Luc…' Simone shook her head again, more memories denied. 'Luc would not have kept a level head at all. So we protected you, as best we could. We shielded Luc from the ugliness you endured at your mother's hands, and I prayed to God every night that I was doing the right thing.'

'From where I'm standing, you did exactly the right thing. Look at me, Simone, and tell me what you see. Am I damaged? Am I fearful or abusive? Do I look upon love and the giving of it as a weakness or a curse? No. I think I turned out just fine. I think all of the children of Caverness turned out fine. The occasional minor flaw here and there, maybe…' She thought of Rafe's compulsion to succeed. Of the fierce need the children of Caverness had to protect each other, even now, so many years later. 'Probably. But who doesn't have those? I'm fine. And you…' Gabrielle smiled and reached for Simone's hand, seeking strength in touch and finding it. 'Such a valiant and tender heart. It's no surprise that my brother cannot forget you. The surprise is that he's stayed away from you this long.'

'Well, when you put it that way,' said Simone with a choked laugh, 'you're absolutely right. The man's a fool and I'm a goddess. I could grow quite fond of this perspective.'

'Keep it,' said Gabrielle with a squeeze of her hand. 'Embrace it.'

'Maybe I will,' said Simone. 'Mind you, I'm still going to need chocolate in order to get over all this soul-baring and childhood trauma.'

'Chocolate would help,' agreed Gabrielle thoughtfully. 'Belgian?'

'Oh, Gaby.' Simone's laughter came more freely this time. 'Is there any other kind?'

TWO DAYS AND two Luc-filled nights later, and midway through their rapidly developing morning ritual of showering and having breakfast together before getting on with their respective workloads, Luc confronted her about her reluctance to dine with him that evening at Caverness. It was a conversation Gabrielle had seen coming. It wasn't one she particularly wanted to have.

'I'm not ashamed that we're lovers, Gabrielle,' he said, his expression tightly controlled as he pulled a clean shirt from his overnight bag and shoved his arms through the sleeves. 'Why are you?'

'I'm not,' she said defensively, a damp towel wrapped securely around her as she rummaged through the wardrobe for something to wear. 'I'm just uncomfortable about going to Caverness with Josien there, that's all.' There, she'd said it.

'She can hardly bring herself to even acknowledge you, Gabrielle,' said Luc bluntly. 'What makes you think she'll give a damn?'

'She probably won't,' muttered Gabrielle, shielding her distress from Luc behind an open cupboard door. 'But it'd be like handing her a weapon, and I do know what she does with those.'

And then Luc's hands were on her shoulders, gently turning her around to face him. 'I won't let her hurt you,' he said quietly.

'Luc…' Gabrielle tried to think of a way to convey her fears without provoking the warrior in him. 'This isn't your fight, it's mine and I just don't want to set her off again.'

'I'll stop her,' said Luc. 'Trust me.'

But in this she could not. 'You know what she said to me last time?' she said with the bracing of her shoulders and the clenching of her heart. 'She said that Harrison wasn't Rafe's father.'

Luc stilled, every inch of his big body radiating tension. 'Did she tell you who was?'

'No.' Gabrielle's lips twisted. 'My guess is she's saving that little snippet for the moment where it will do the most damage. How can I look at her after that, Luc? How can I look at her and not hate her?' Luc stared at her in silence, his expression guarded but not surprised. It was his lack of surprise, the swift calculation behind his gaze before he offered up a response, that caused her to step back swiftly, away from his touch. 'You know.' Her hands shook, everything shook. 'You know who Rafe's father is.'

Luc inclined his head warily.

'Who?' Gabrielle clenched her arms tightly around her middle. 'Lucien, who?' Dear God, not Phillipe. That would make Rafe half-brother to Lucien, half-brother to Simone, and that would destroy him. Him and Simone both. She shook her head. 'No. No, it *can't* be.' She couldn't hold Luc's gaze. 'Not Phillipe.'

'It's not Phillipe,' said Luc immediately. 'God, no! Is that what you thought?'

'I didn't know what to think! She gave me half the story, Luc. The only man I've ever known who was able to reason with Josien was your father. The only man ever to put up with her moods was your father! What was I supposed to think?'

'It wasn't Phillipe,' said Luc. 'Gabrielle, no! Rafe's father was a guest here at Caverness. A friend of my father's who came to stay for the summer the year your mother turned sixteen. A man well used to taking what he wanted. A prince.'

'He *raped* her? This *prince* amongst men?'

'No.' Luc smiled grimly. 'Your mother fell in love with him. And he with her, at least for a little while. Until she fell pregnant. He would not marry her, Gabrielle. He could not. His marriage had already been arranged.'

'To a princess, no doubt.'

'That bit I don't know.'

Gabrielle's initial fury that Luc had known all along what she didn't was gone, washed away in the relief that Phillipe was not Rafael's father. But cold, hard anger remained and found a target in Luc. 'So how do you know what you do know? Why you and no one else?'

'My father told me before he died. He felt responsible for Josien's circumstances to some extent. Responsible for Rafael's upbringing, and yours too for that matter. He had assured the prince that Josien and her child would always have a home at Caverness. He wanted to make sure I would not renege on his words.'

'He did *what*?'

'He did what he could,' said Luc. 'Surely you can see that? My father wasn't always right. He wasn't often there, for that matter. But he was honourable, and he did what he could to improve your mother's lot.'

'I—' Gabrielle stared at him, barely taking in the words. 'Oh, damn.' It explained so much about her mother's attitude and her actions, her biases and her rage. Why Josien had never had any time or love for Rafael. Why Gabrielle had been shipped off so rapidly after Josien had found her and Luc together. 'So it's true. You have no idea how badly I didn't want it to be true.' What was she supposed to *do* with this information? 'Does Rafe know?'

'I've never told him,' said Luc.

Then he didn't know. Rafael thought Harrison Alexander was his father. 'Does Simone know?'

'No. At least, I think not. Again, I've never told her,' said Luc gruffly. 'I've never told anyone, Gabrielle. Until now.'

'Thank you.' With her arms still tightly clasped around her waist, Gabrielle tried a smile but couldn't keep it on her face. Rafael was only her half-brother and the bastard son of some lousy prince who'd once had a penchant for seducing sixteen-year-old girls. Rafe would love that. 'What do I tell him?' she whispered. 'What do I tell Rafe?'

'If you want my advice, nothing,' said Luc. 'This isn't your secret to tell, Gabrielle. This is between Josien and Rafe.'

'So why did she go and tell *me*?'

Luc sighed heavily. 'My guess is that you were right. She wanted to wound you, and what better way than by trying to take away from you the one person who's always been there for you? She wants you gone, Gabrielle. You threaten her. You always have.'

'I threaten nothing!'

'She sees herself in you: a class-locked woman about to take up with a wealthy man who'll doubtless discard you after the fascination fades. She sees no other course for you.'

'She's wrong,' said Gabrielle in a low and shaking voice. 'I have *many* options open to me.'

'Happens I think so too,' murmured Luc. 'She can't win this battle, Gabrielle. She can't take Rafe away from you and she can't make me stay away from you either. Not this time. Not unless you let her.

Come to Caverness with me tonight. Stay for dinner. Stay the night. Fight her. Don't you dare let her win.'

'I won't.' She was not like her mother. She refused to be. 'I'll come to Caverness with you.' While the fear of not being strong enough to withstand yet another of Josien's vicious assaults wrapped around her like a suffocating and blinding fog.

'And you'll stay the night in my bed?'

'Yes.'

Luc crossed to her and took her in his arms and she let him, absorbing his strength and his certainty. She would need it for the night ahead. He smiled his encouragement and his lips brushed hers. A promise wrapped in a kiss. 'That's my girl.'

THE EVENING STARTED WELL as far as Luc was concerned. Josien was resting in her rooms and did not require visitors. Hans saw to Josien's meal. Luc saw to everyone else's. Simone saw Gabrielle's unease and tried to put it to rest with easy talk about nothing much, and Gabrielle tried to settle and follow Simone's lead; she really gave it a solid shot.

But she jumped six feet when Luc settled down to watch television beside her, and she did not snuggle up beside him as had become her habit. Gabrielle did not look out of place to Luc's eyes, but he could tell from looking into her eyes that she was finding the entire experience acutely uncomfortable.

Behind the mask of self-assured lover lay the heart of the housekeeper's daughter and she saw no place for herself here, and Luc could think of no other way to ease her anxiety than to take her to his room and within their lovemaking make the world around them disappear, at least for a little while.

Simone yawned loudly after the end of her favourite show, pleading tiredness before swooping down to give Gabrielle a kiss on each cheek before doing the same to Luc. 'Come with me into Epernay in the morning if you feel like it,' she offered to Gabrielle. 'I'll show you what I do. Lucien, may I see you for a moment?'

Luc followed his sister into the hallway, wary for no reason he could fully comprehend other than he thought he was in trouble and he couldn't figure out why.

'What are you *doing*?' she said when she judged them far enough away that Gabrielle could not hear their words.

'What do you mean?'

'Gabrielle's wound so tight you could snap her with a glance.'

'Yes, thank you. I had noticed.'

'Well, *do* something.'

'Do what? Tell her to stop feeling like she doesn't belong here? It doesn't work that way, Simone. Gabrielle has to fight that particular battle herself.'

'It'd help if you got rid of Josien,' muttered Simone. 'She's a good housekeeper, Lucien, but can't you see that this won't work? You can't have the housekeeper's estranged daughter in your life as your mistress and expect *anyone* to feel comfortable. If you want Gabrielle in your life—and clearly you do—Josien and her intolerance will have to find a place out of it.'

Luc shoved a hand through his hair, cursing the promise he'd made to a dying old man. 'Josien stays,' he said curtly.

'But *why*? You don't like her, Luc. You tolerate her. We both do. As for Gabrielle…Gabrielle's afraid of her and with good cause. Can't you see that it's time we let her go?'

'Josien stays,' he said tightly. 'I promised Phillipe she would always have a home here.'

'Why would he demand such a promise of you?' Simone's eyes grew even more troubled. 'I know he acted like the king of the damn castle at times, but Josien's not an indentured serf and it's not our duty to look after her for the rest of her life, or ours. Give her a job in one of our other offices if you must. Send her to Paris, make her a House of Duvalier sales rep and watch her slay the competition. Ask her if she's ever considered doing something other than keeping house at Caverness and, if she has, make it happen for her. I don't care what it takes, Lucien, just get her *away* from here. Because this thing you have with Gabrielle won't work until you do.'

'She's right,' said a voice from the shadows. Josien's voice. Luc turned and there she stood in the doorway to the library, looking tragically beautiful and disturbingly frail. Hans stood behind her, a silent, watchful presence.

Simone groaned, but then she rallied. Luc watched as Simone's eyes grew hard and completely without mercy, harder than he'd ever seen them. '*Have* you ever considered doing something else for a living, Josien?' Woman to woman and smothered in ice. Luc's gaze met Hans's, the older man lifted his hands in surrender. Not buying in. But Luc had to. Simone had left him no choice.

'There is an opening in the Paris office for a sales rep,' he offered carefully. 'We also have an apartment there that you could use until you found your feet.' He wasn't reneging on his father's promise. Surely he wasn't. 'You could go to Paris once you're more fully recovered and take a look at both the accommodation and the position on offer.'

'I could drive you.' Hans stepped forward and offered his arm to Josien with a gentle smile. 'Make sure you did not overtax yourself. I've never seen Paris in the springtime. Have you?'

Josien stared at Hans, her eyes wide and uncertain, and then she did something that Luc had never seen her do. She blushed. 'No,' she said quietly. 'I have not.'

'So, you're interested?' said Simone, her eyes still flinty, every inch the autocratic mistress of the house. A mistress who'd had more than enough of this particular employee's presence. 'You'll look at taking a position elsewhere?'

'Yes,' said Josien.

Luc returned to the lounge room with a lighter step than when he'd left it. Gabrielle wasn't on the sofa where he'd left her. She was pacing the room restlessly, every movement of that lithe and lovely body poised as if to run.

'No,' he said.

'You haven't even heard what I'm going to say.'

'No, it would not be better if you left. It would be infinitely worse. So stay.' He shot her a knowing stare. 'How am I doing so far?'

'So-so,' she said grudgingly.

'So will you stay?'

A tiny smile lifted her lips. 'I'll need incentive.'

'I'll be sure to provide it.'

'A little privacy…'

'My room is very private. So private it's positively remote. Matter of fact I'm heading there now.'

'What else is in this room of yours?'

'A bed,' he said. 'Good mattress. Four posts. You'll like it.'

Her smile grew a little more sure but her eyes stayed uncertain. 'I don't know why I'm so worried about being here with you like this. I just am. It was different at my place. More neutral and less complicated, whereas when we come here…' She shrugged awkwardly. 'All the stuff that's happened between us in the past comes crashing on in. It's not just you and me any more—it's Simone and Rafe and Josien as well, and how what we're doing affects them.'

'I know.' He took her in his arms. 'Has anyone ever told you that you think too much?'

'No.'

'Well, you do. Fortunately, I have a solution. Come to bed with me. Now. I guarantee I can turn your mind to something that doesn't require any thought at all.'

Her smile turned wry, but she hooked her arms around his neck and brushed her lips across his. 'Has anyone ever told you that you have an extremely one track mind?'

'No, but I am aware of it,' he countered with a grin.

It took them for ever to reach Luc's bedroom. He needed to kiss her halfway up the stairs and again at the top of them. Two steps later he cornered her against the wall, just past the gilt-edged mirror, and laid waste to her hairpins before ravishing her neck. His knees almost buckled when he pushed her up against doorway to his study and she wrapped her legs around his waist and dragged his mouth to her breast. He managed to get the door closed behind them, managed to carry her to the big brown leather sofa and deposit her on it before his hunger got the better of him and he pushed her skirt waistwards and, kneeling, set his lips to the soft and creamy skin of her inner thighs.

'You'll let me know if there's anything else bothering you, won't you?' he muttered as he wrapped his hands around her buttocks, dragged her closer, and set himself the task of reaching his final destination some time this decade.

Gabrielle whimpered and twined her hands in his hair, muscles quivering and her eyes dark with desire as she stared down at him. 'Yes, I'll let you know.'

'Like if you'd rather watch something else on television.'

'Okay.'

He brushed the inside of her knee with his lips. 'Or if you'd rather have something else for dinner.'

Her hands tightened in his hair. 'Yes. Yes, I'll let you know.' She sounded distracted. She *was* distracted.

He dragged his lips along her inner thigh. 'What kind of toothpaste do you use?' he murmured, and grazed her skin with his teeth.

'Oh, hell,' she muttered.

'Not sure I know that one but I'll do my best. You know me.' Very deliberately he brushed his knuckles over her panties, sliding his lips a little closer to his goal when she whimpered again and opened her thighs wider for him. 'I like to fix things.'

'Luc…' She strained against him, already lost to sensation, already at the mercy of her body's response to him. He loved that about her, that she could give herself over to him so completely during lovemaking. Loved it, and feared it because one day, some day, he would follow her, and once he did that would be it for him. There would be no other women—no other love for him—but Gabrielle.

He feared losing himself to her.

He feared he could become utterly obsessed with her.

He feared he already was.

'Luc, please!'

'Tell me what you want.'

'You. I want you.'

'Where?' His teeth scraped the edge of her panties.

'Everywhere.'

'Hold on,' he murmured and, pushing her panties aside, set his mouth to her in earnest.

She held on for less than a minute before her first climax overtook her. He freed himself and plunged inside her moments after that, holding on, holding on so very tightly to his control as he drove her to climax again, and again, until finally his screams joined her own.

LUC SEEMED A LITTLE withdrawn at breakfast the following morning, at least as far as Gabrielle was concerned. They'd spent most of the night in each other's arms, making love or making war, Gabrielle never quite knew which one it was—all she knew was that when it was over her body was boneless and her mind was blissfully blank.

Whatever was running through Luc's mind at those times was a mystery to her.

For all his teasing words in the lead up to their lovemaking, Luc never had much to say in the aftermath. He held her, that was all. He held her close and kept his thoughts to himself.

Simone had left for work not long ago, obviously having realized Gabrielle wasn't going to be ready in time to go with her. Josien and Hans were nowhere to be seen. She and Luc were here alone. She should have been relaxed. *Luc* should have been relaxed.

He wasn't.

'I'm sensing a little discomfort here,' she said as he attempted to disappear inside the morning paper. 'Have I overstayed my welcome?'

He lowered the paper carefully, a picture of elegance and control. 'No.'

'Then talk to me.'

'About what?'

'*Anything*. Something. Tell me what your plans are for the day and I'll tell you mine. Ask me what I thought of our lovemaking last night. Tell me what you thought of it.'

'I thought…' He set the paper down completely, ran his hands through his hair and looked towards the window. 'I thought that if our lovemaking had been any more perfect I'd have died from need of you,' he said quietly. 'I thought, when I thought at all, that a man would have to be mad not to want to wake up to you every day, and I wondered what the hell I'd do when next I didn't.' His gaze cut back to hers, guarded and strangely angry. 'Is that enough of my thoughts for you, Gabrielle? Do you want more?'

'I, ah, no.' There seemed to be plenty to be going on with there. 'So we, ah, take a lot of pleasure in being with each other. This is a good thing.' She tried a tentative smile. 'Isn't it?'

He stared at her broodingly. 'So what did *you* think of last night?'

'I thought…' She had the insane urge to be utterly truthful, to lay herself bare with her words as well as her body. 'I thought that if I gave any more of myself to you there'd be nothing left for me.' She met his gaze head-on. 'Does that help any?'

'Not in the slightest,' he said gruffly, and, leaning across the table, captured her lips with his. 'What are your plans for the day?'

'I'm inspecting some wine storage facilities at one of the vineyards first up, then I have a meeting with a distributor in Epernay who's interested enough in the Angels Landing reds to give me twenty minutes of his time—this is, by the way, a major coup. And then I'm meeting with the Hammerschmidt vineyard estate agent to get some chemical use history and soil and water test information, and quiz him about whether there are any restoration restrictions on the house.'

'You do know you could get all the Hammerschmidt information directly from me and save yourself that particular part of your day?' he murmured.

'Yes, but then the agent would not know who I was and that might prove a problem if I want to bid for the property at auction,' she whispered back amidst kisses.

'And do you?'

'I do. Rafe, on the other hand, needs a little more convincing.'

'It's a big investment, Gabrielle, and the place has a lot of drawbacks.'

'Do you plan to bid on it?'

'Up to a point,' he said, and moved his lips to the curve of her jaw. 'The purchase needs to be an economically smart move for the House of Duvalier.

As soon as the price goes above twenty million, the bidding is over for me.'

'Just like that?' she said.

'Yes.' His mouth continued to wreak havoc with the nerves beneath her ear. 'Just like that. If your calculations stack up better than mine and you're prepared to pay more, it's yours. No hard feelings.'

Gabrielle closed her eyes, wound her hands in his hair, and tried to continue the conversation without whimpering. 'I'm not sure my calculations are going to get me above that price. For us, there's also the thought that a twenty-million-euro outlay will buy us a lot more vineyard in Australia than it will over here. That's Rafe's argument.'

'It's a good one,' said Luc.

'I knew you'd say that.' She was in his lap, he was on the chair, and her body was telling her she wanted this man again.

'Unless you have it in mind to try and get the land rezoned so you can subdivide and sell off part of it, that old vineyard is a lot more land than you need, Gabrielle. A lot more *hassle* than you need.' His hands were on the buttons of her shirt. Hers were on his.

'You know, you sound just like him.' Gabrielle eyed him suspiciously. 'Have you and Rafe been communing by bat phone again?'

'No.' Luc shook his head and his hands stilled. 'I like what you and your brother have built with the Angels Landing wines, Gabrielle. I respect your plans to expand into the European market. But from a purely business perspective there are other ways to achieve the same result. You'd be far better off hooking into someone else's storage and distribution facilities for a while and building your brand before committing to such a large outlay.'

'I know,' she said. It felt good to talk this over with Luc, even if they were potentially vying for the same piece of land. 'I guess I just liked the old place. Nothing to do with business, I know, but it had a nice feel about it. It felt right.' She set her hands to Luc's bare chest and shuddered at the pleasure the contact afforded her. 'Try running that one past Rafe.'

'If you did purchase Hammerschmidt would Rafe return and make it a viable vineyard?'

'Rafe won't return,' said Gabrielle. 'Not to live. He'd definitely want it viable but he loves Australia. He's accepted there. Harrison—' Gabrielle took a deep breath '—Rafe's father gives him a lot of support. Harrison owns grazing property rather than vineyards but he's thrilled by Rafe's progress. He takes an interest. He holds a stake in the business. They get along well.'

'Would Harrison consider a move to Hammerschmidt to oversee the vineyard's renewal?'

Gabrielle hadn't considered that option before. 'He might, but again he has his own properties to run. There's really only me. I've worked alongside Rafe for seven years, Luc. You don't think I could bring that old vineyard back to life?'

'Could you?'

'Yes. With guidance I dare say I could. Although

probably not as quickly as you could. I'd have to do it in stages. Buying the place would clean us out. There'd be very little money left for renovation.'

'You'd live in the house?'

'I'd reclaim some of the house, to start with, so I could live in it. As for the rest…I really don't know what I'd do with the rest.'

'You're not alone there,' he said wryly. 'I haven't quite figured out what use the house would be to me either. Perhaps for Simone…perhaps we need to consider who would live where if one of us ever married.'

Gabrielle's hands stilled along with the rest of her body. He felt her sudden tension, damned if he didn't. 'Is that likely in the near future?'

'I don't know,' he murmured, lifting his gaze from her body to her face, his eyes intent and his face carefully composed. 'Is it?'

'What do you mean?' Gabrielle shied away from the notion that Luc was considering her for marriage. She didn't want the role or the duties that went with it. She only wanted Luc. 'Are you asking me if I would want to live here as your wife?'

'Would you?' he said quietly. 'Could you be comfortable living here as my wife?'

With Josien as housekeeper? With the pressure to fit into the upper echelons of society here? She, the lowly housekeeper's daughter? 'No,' she said raggedly. 'Not without a lot of adjustments that I'm not sure I have the ability to make. I can be your lover, Lucien. But I wouldn't make you a good wife.'

'Why not? Because you don't want to be or because you think others wouldn't like it?' He didn't sound angry, more curious.

'It's complicated,' she said.

'Not that complicated,' he countered. 'You know the chateau and you know the House of Duvalier business.'

'From the point of view of a child,' she reminded him. 'The child of a servant.'

'Employee,' he said curtly. 'Josien's an employee. Yes, she retreated to Caverness with two young children in tow when her marriage to Harrison didn't work out. Yes, she took on the role of housekeeper, but even then I wonder if she didn't play the part to spite her prince more than anything else. She knows more about society protocols and the smooth running of a chateau than any princess I know. She's been offered more domestic management positions than I can count. Men have tried to court her—rich and poor and titled as well. She owns three apartments that I know of—a small one here in the village and two luxury apartments in Epernay. Josien's an independently wealthy woman in her own right, Gabrielle. She could step into any part of society whenever she wanted to, just like that,' he said with the click of his fingers. 'And so could you.'

'But…' Gabrielle reeled beneath the barrage of information contained in Luc's statement '…why does she stay?'

'Because it suits her,' said Luc with a shrug. 'When it no longer suits her I dare say she'll move on. I've offered Josien a sales position in the Paris office, Gabrielle. I offered it to her last night, with Simone's encouragement. Simone thought—*we* thought—you might be more comfortable around here with Josien gone.'

'Oh.' Gabrielle put the heels of her hands to her eyes, grateful for the darkness, that small reprieve from the bombardment of information that her brain would have to process. Not sight, not right now. Not colour or the wary look on Luc's face as he told her what he and Simone had done. 'You fired her? Because of me?'

'Not fired her. Encouraged her to consider the many options open to a woman of her abilities. And, yes, because of you. She hurts you, Gabrielle. And I won't have it. Not in my house.'

'Oh, Luc.'

'I did warn her,' he said. 'Look at me, Gabrielle. Tell me I'm not a fool for thinking you'd be more comfortable here without Josien around.'

She lowered her hands to his shoulders and raised her gaze to his. 'You're not a fool,' she said. 'Part of me's horrified that you're encouraging Josien to move on because of me. Part of me thinks this could have been avoided altogether if only I'd stayed away from Caverness and from you. I could have stayed away from Caverness, and happily,' she confessed. 'I don't know that I could have stayed away from you.'

'Stay with me again tonight,' he murmured. 'Come over after you finish your work. We can go

out to dinner. We can go anywhere you like. Just…
be with me.'

'I can do that,' she said as his hand came up to
cradle her head.

'Humour me,' he said when next he broke their
kiss.

'What do you think I'm doing?' He kissed her
again and need roared through her. Would this hunger
for him never ease?

'Make love with me,' he whispered, and proceeded to show her exactly how he liked that done.

ANOTHER WEEK PASSED. A week in which Gabrielle
worked hard on putting a fledgling distribution
network together that might support her admittedly
crazy plans for purchasing the Hammerschmidt vineyard. Rafe had Angels Landing, Luc had Caverness,
Simone had…many things she could call her own although Gabrielle couldn't think of anything specific.
Even Josien owned residential property. Gabrielle
wanted a place to call home too. Not Angels Landing, not Caverness, somewhere else. A place that
beckoned to her, somewhere she could fill with new
memories and her own belongings. A place where a
woman could stare out a window and smile and plan
and dream big dreams.

Somewhere like Hammerschmidt.

The auction was tomorrow. She could almost justify, on paper, a purchase bid slightly higher than
Luc's. All she had to do was convince Rafe that it
was a good idea.

Damn, but she hated making late night pleading phone calls. And tonight she intended to make not one, but two.

It was mid-morning in Australia and Rafe was working. He sounded good humoured. He'd been working in amongst his barrels of wine, he told her. An activity that never failed to lift his spirits.

'Did you get the latest figures I sent you?' she said.

'I got them.'

'Did you go over them?'

'Yes.'

'What do you think?'

'I think you want to bid on the Hammerschmidt place,' he said dryly. 'And I still think it's unnecessary.'

'From a business perspective, maybe. Probably. I know it's risky, Rafe, but if we got it at the right price it would be a good investment. A good base for European operations. I'd like to bid for it.'

'You've fallen in love with it,' said Rafe heavily.

'Yes.'

'Do you know if anyone else is interested in it?' said Rafe.

'I know that Luc plans to bid for it.'

Silence at that, and then a heavy sigh. 'He'll have more money to throw at it, Gabrielle. You *know* this.'

'I know. We've talked about it a bit. There's no animosity between Luc and me on this, Rafe. We've looked at the place together, talked about what whoever buys it might do with it. A lot of the ideas I sent you about the phased redevelopment of the property came from Luc.'

'Remind me again why he's helping you if he plans to bid for the property himself,' said Rafael curtly.

'Because he wants to,' replied Gabrielle defensively. 'He likes running the different scenarios. I think he sees it as a challenge.'

'Would Luc redevelop the vineyard in stages too?'

'No, he'd do it all at once.'

'Gabrielle…' Rafe paused as if he wasn't quite sure what he wanted to ask. 'Just how much time have you been spending with Luc?'

'A bit.' Gabrielle grimaced and shut her eyes tight. She never had been any good at lying. 'A lot.'

'Are you sleeping with him?'

'We don't really sleep all that much.'

Silence at that and another heavy sigh. 'So you're sleeping with him, planning to bid against him tomorrow for a property you both want, and presumably you intend to continue sleeping with him after that?'

'Yes,' she said warily. 'Something wrong with that?'

Rafe snorted. 'I guess not.' And with concern rippling through his voice, 'You're playing with fire, Gabrielle.'

'I know,' she said in a small voice. 'Luc's told me his stop bid.' She breathed in deep, gathered her courage, and gave it to him straight. 'It's twenty million. Can we afford to pay more than twenty million?'

More silence. Gabrielle pictured her brother pacing away his frustration, his blue eyes razor sharp and his golden hair glinting in the half light of the cellars. 'I ran your business plan past Harrison,' said Rafe. Rafe didn't sound happy, he sounded resigned. 'We can afford the twenty million but only just. Not without risking Angels Landing, and not without Harrison taking a stake in it. I want you on the phone to me when the bidding commences.'

'You'll be asleep.'

'Trust me,' he said grimly. 'I'll be awake for this. I want your promise that when I say stop, you'll stop.'

'I promise,' she said.

'No matter who's bidding,' he said. 'No matter how close you think they are to their limit price.'

'Got it.'

'No matter how much you want this vineyard.'

'I promise,' she said again. 'On my soul, Rafe. I promise to stop bidding the moment you give the word.'

'All right,' he said. 'On your soul and mine, let's try and bring this one home.'

GABRIELLE'S NEXT PHONE CALL was to Lucien. He'd gone to his Paris offices for the day. He sounded tired and somewhat tetchy. She didn't know if he was home yet, but he hadn't called her and he hadn't come over.

'I'm in my office at Caverness,' he said when she

got hold of him. 'And I have your mother and Hans with me.'

Oh. 'Are you on speaker phone?'

'No.' Just a general warning that he wouldn't be talking to her freely, then.

'So if I started talking dirty to you...'

'You would definitely live to regret it.'

'Are you coming over later?' she asked him.

'It'll be late,' he said. 'I've work to finish up first.'

'I don't mind late.'

'You could always come here,' he said quietly. With her mother and Hans sitting beside him and doubtless listening to every word he uttered.

'I—I'd rather not. Not tonight.' While a little voice inside her berated her for being a coward.

'Your place, then,' he said as if it didn't matter. It was the same conversation they had every night, albeit phrased a little differently. His place or hers, as long as he could sleep with her and wake to her. 'Your mother has some news.'

'Am I going to like this news?'

'Here, I'll put her on.'

'No! Luc—' Too late. 'Hello?'

'*Bonjour* Gabrielle.'

'*Maman,*' she said carefully. And waited.

'Luc's been telling me of your plans to stay in the area.'

'Oh.' Had he?

'And of your plans for the old Hammerschmidt vineyard should your bid tomorrow be successful.'

'Oh.'

'I just wanted to wish you luck,' said Josien. She sounded as if she meant it. 'And to let you know that Hans has accepted a permanent position with an elderly widow in the south of France. She's frail and in need of care.' There was a long pause. 'She's in need of a housekeeper too. Perhaps the position will be filled by the time I'm ready to return to work, perhaps I won't be interested in taking on another housekeeping position, I'm really not sure of my plans just yet but the fact remains that Hans has invited me to go there with him and I've accepted his offer.'

'Oh.' Gabrielle didn't quite know which bombshell she should respond to first. That Josien was leaving Duvalier employ or that she and Hans had decided to move on together. 'I wish you every happiness,' she said finally. 'Whatever you decide to do.'

'I—thank you,' said Josien quietly. 'I would like—if you wouldn't mind—I would like to see you tomorrow morning before the auction. I moved out of the chateau proper and back into my own quarters yesterday. So it would mean that you would come there. For breakfast perhaps, or a mid-morning coffee? Shall we say ten o clock?'

Clamping down hard on her fear of all the hurtful things Josien might have to say to her, Gabrielle said yes.

LUC CAME TO HER later that evening, looking weary and stern, and ever so slightly dishevelled. But his eyes lit up when he saw that she'd prepared a supper for him and he wasted no time in devouring it and then reaching for her. He made love to her lazily, expertly bringing her to orgasm before surrendering to his own. These past two weeks of being with him every night had taken some of the urgency away from their lovemaking but none of the passion and sensuality. Luc could make her yearn for him, soar for him, weep for just that little bit more of him.

Even when he held her and kissed her as if the world could crumble around them before he'd ever let her go.

'Luc, may I ask you a question?' she said, propping herself up beside him and letting her eyes feast on the tumbled beauty of the man in her bed.

'Of course,' he murmured, smiling at her with sleepy eyes.

'Why are you always so careful of me when we make love?'

Not the kind of question he'd been expecting. Wariness crept into his eyes as the sleepiness left them. Not the kind of question he looked as if he wanted to answer. 'You'd rather I wasn't?'

'Maybe,' she murmured. 'Maybe I simply want to know why you refuse to let passion rule you completely when you're with me. I worry that you think I wouldn't be able to cope with whatever lies beneath all that iron control. The thing is, I would cope. I'd probably die of ecstasy if you ever truly let abandon take hold of you while you were taking hold of me. So all I'm saying…what I mean to say…is that there's no need to hold back on my account.'

Luc's arm didn't move from its place around her

shoulder but she felt the withdrawal of the other pieces of him he *did* share with her clear down to her soul.

'You hold back too, Gabrielle,' he said gruffly.

'I do not!' she said indignantly. 'You get all of me.'

'Maybe in this,' he said reluctantly. 'Maybe you give everything when it comes to making love, but in so many other ways you hold back.'

'Name one!'

'You won't accept my offer to help you launch your wines,' he said curtly. 'You refuse to accept help from the House of Duvalier, even though it would be of benefit to you.'

'Because of Rafe,' she said hotly. 'I know it makes sense to take you up on your offer, but the bottom line is that Rafe doesn't want to. It's his business too, Lucien, and I will not go against him on this.'

'But you will continue to push for his agreement to purchase a vineyard he doesn't want in a place he never intends to return to? How does that work? How does that benefit the business you built together?' Luc caught her gaze and held it. 'Why haven't you and I sat down together and sorted out a partnership bid on the Hammerschmidt block, Gabrielle? Have you even mentioned that as an option to Rafe? Have you contemplated cutting Rafe out of this purchase altogether and bringing me into it? No. You don't want to blur the lines of business between us either. Nothing to do with Rafe. *You* don't want it.'

'Neither do you!' she shot at him. 'You said so

yourself. Never mix business with pleasure, you said.'

'And I have since had time to reconsider those words. I *want* to mix business and pleasure, Gabrielle. I want you in every part of my life, but I already know what you'll say to that. No, Luc, I couldn't possibly live at Caverness. No, Luc, I won't consider going into business with you. No, Luc, I don't want to be your wife. You don't *want* all of me, Gabrielle, it's as simple as that. You only want the part of me that suits you.' He drew away from her then to sit on the edge of the bed with his back to her. 'And then you turn around and wonder why I hold that last tiny piece of me back.'

'No,' she whispered. 'No, it's not like that.'

'Then marry me,' he said raggedly, still not turning to face her. 'Buy Hammerschmidt with me tomorrow. Commit to me. All of me.'

'It's too soon,' she protested.

'Not for me,' he said and began to gather up his clothes. 'I'm heading home. I need an early night.'

'Luc!' She scrambled upright and snatched for the bed sheet to cover her nakedness. 'Luc, please…' He turned and looked at her, just looked at her, and the rawness of his pain nearly brought her to her knees. 'Stay. We can work something out. Some sort of compromise. A way of doing business together. A time line for…commitment. Something.'

But he shook his head. 'I can't deal with you in half measures, Gabrielle. I can't be civilised and reasonable around you. It's all or nothing. Always has been.' His smile was bittersweet as he reached for the door handle. 'We talked before about what we would do if our affair got out of hand. Well, it is out of hand, Gabrielle. It was never *in* hand, not for me. This is the part where you run.'

CHAPTER NINE

GABRIELLE DIDN'T RUN. She slept fretfully instead and woke late the following morning. She rolled on her back and stared at the ceiling, wondering in all seriousness whether she needed to get up at all. If she denied the morning, she could probably attempt to deny what had happened last night as well. Just close her eyes and snuggle into the sheets with the scent of Luc all around her and pretend that he was still in her bed and that any minute he would wake and reach for her as he'd done every other morning for the past week.

Only he wasn't there.

Gabrielle closed her eyes, her mind awash with muddled images and pleading words. Marry Luc. Don't marry him. Buy the vineyard. Risk the business. Don't buy the vineyard. Take Luc up on his offer to buy the vineyard together. Restore it together. Live in it together. The list of options went on and on. Make love. Make war. Make Luc see that saying wait didn't mean that she was saying no to any of his offers. Go to Caverness this morning. Take her suitcase with her. Find Luc. Phone him. Just close her eyes, hope for the best, and *love* him.

Above all, tell him she loved him.

She glanced at the bedside clock and groaned. It was after nine. Wasn't there something else she was supposed to be doing this morning besides obsess over her relationship with Luc?

Heaven help her—Josien.

She'd promised to visit her mother.

Get up, said the little voice inside her. *Get up and go and see her, or are you too cowardly to do that too?*

'Yes,' said Gabrielle to the latter accusation. She felt fragile and weepy and too cowardly by far to go another round with Josien.

Maybe you could talk to her, said the little voice. *Tell her about Luc. Ask her advice.*

'No.' Dear Lord, when had she *ever* taken Josien's advice? When had her mother ever given her advice worth following? No. Far better if she wanted advice to talk to Simone. Simone would understand her fear of all the steps involved in committing to Luc. All the tangled little threads. Simone *knew* what it was like to be asked to take an irrevocable step into a world she hadn't been raised to.

Simone knew what it felt like to refuse to take such a step.

Only Gabrielle hadn't refused. Had she? Gabrielle groaned and flung the sheet aside.

She needed to shower and get dressed and gulp down coffee and decide whether to go to the auction or not, and whether she would go and see her mother or not. She needed to get *up* and get going.

Damned if she was going to run.

A COMPOSED AND REGAL Josien opened her door when Gabrielle knocked on it at a quarter past ten that morning. Josien didn't have anything to say as they walked down the corridor towards the kitchen. Gabrielle didn't have anything to say either. Wariness ruled Gabrielle's thoughts. She didn't know why her mother wanted to see her and she didn't particularly care. Unless it had something to do with Josien deciding to reveal to Rafe that some anonymous prince was his father. If that were the case, Gabrielle cared a lot.

Hans was making coffee in the kitchen when they arrived. Gabrielle took it in her stride and told him how she liked her coffee when he asked her, and let him fuss over her as he saw her seated at the small wooden kitchen table. He had croissants for her and a selection of jams, a selection of bread rolls too, still warm from the baking.

'Josien walked into the village for them this morning,' said Hans with a conspiratorial glance in Gabrielle's direction. 'She needed something to do while she waited for your arrival. Something besides fret that you wouldn't turn up, that is. Sit,' said Hans to Josien. 'She's here now. *Talk* to her. Tell her all those things you told me.'

Josien sat. But she didn't seem to know how to begin.

'When do you leave for your new position?' Gabrielle asked Hans, more to fill the awkward silence than actually wanting to know.

'Next week,' said Hans with a lightning glance at Josien. 'We've been offered the caretaker's cottage at the entrance to the estate to live in. It needs work. A lot of work. But I'm confident it will be quite comfortable by the time Josien and I have finished with it.'

'It sounds exciting.' Gabrielle smiled faintly at his enthusiasm. Another man in need of a challenge. He had a big enough one on his hands with her mother, but then, looking into Hans's wise and compassionate eyes, she suspected he already knew that.

It seemed amazing to Gabrielle that Josien had chosen a gentle man to be with. A caring man. All the things Josien was not. Maybe he could soften her. Maybe he could succeed where no one else had. She hoped so. 'A bold new beginning.' She remembered her own terror at leaving Caverness at sixteen, and the unexpected benefits that had flowed from her departure. She remembered what she'd been back then, and where she stood now. 'I thoroughly recommend it.'

Josien turned towards the bench and fumbled with some papers. 'I'm planning on liquidising some of my assets,' she said in a low strained voice. 'The Duvalier family has been good to me over the years. I have a nest egg.'

Gabrielle smiled politely. 'It sounds like you have

your plans well in hand.' Some people did. Gabrielle was not one of them, however. Not today, at any rate.

Josien glanced at Hans, took a deep breath, and spoke again. 'I don't know how much money you'll need to buy Hammerschmidt but there's money here if you need it. One and a half million euros. If it would help.'

Gabrielle blinked and set her coffee mug down on the table with a clatter.

'I know what it's like to want to bring your own monetary value to the table of a wealthy man,' continued Josien. 'To want to be seen as worthy.'

'Oh, *Maman*.' Every criticism Josien had ever laid on her came crowding into her brain. One by one, Gabrielle pushed them away until only the blindingly obvious remained. 'You just don't get it, do you? I don't have to prove myself to Luc in that manner. He doesn't care for my wealth or lack of it. He never has. All he sees is me.' She met her mother's gaze squarely. 'That's the way love should be. Isn't it?'

'I thought…' said Josien brokenly. 'I thought I was helping.'

'I know,' murmured Gabrielle, close to tears. 'I'm so sorry, *Maman*. You and I, we never get it right. I never think I'm good enough for you. You never seem to see the real me, only what others might think of me. I want the vineyard for *me*, *Maman*. Not to impress Luc. Not because I want to build an empire. I just want to stay here and work hard and love Luc, and be me. That's all I'm trying to do.'

'The money's there,' said her mother. 'If you need it.'

Gabrielle smiled and blinked away the sting in her eyes even as she shook her head in despair. 'Thank you.'

CHAPTER TEN

LUCIEN WOKE THE MORNING of the auction with his control stretched thin and his temper dangerously close to erupting. He didn't know where he'd gone wrong with Gabrielle last night, only that one minute she'd been accusing him of not giving enough and the next minute he'd been heading for the door. There'd been heated discussion about giving and taking. There'd been an ultimatum in there too, one he never should have delivered. That was the problem with ultimatums. They delivered it all.

Or nothing.

Simone wasn't about when he stalked into the kitchen and set the coffee maker to making coffee. He'd need to advertise for another housekeeper soon. Not live in, as Josien had been, but someone from the village who would come and go as needed. Two people, perhaps, who would share the load between them and call in extra help when needed. Simone often railed against the maintenance that was such a necessary part of the upkeep of Caverness. Heating it in winter, airing it in summer, chasing away the damp and making sure it shone. For all its elegance and grace, Chateau des Caverness asked a great deal of the people who cared for it. Gabrielle knew that. She was right to be wary of it. Who the hell lived in a castle this day and age anyhow? Why did he need to? Maybe, with Simone's agreement, they could turn the chateau into their head office—centralise the House of Duvalier's management operations here, open part of it to the public, keep just one wing of it available for family, and go and live elsewhere.

A place where the ancestral wealth didn't stare down at a person from every portrait and tapestry. A place where a woman not comfortable with the trappings of old money would feel more at home.

Luc smiled humourlessly. Finally a reason for buying the Hammerschmidt Manoir that made sense. He and Gabrielle could have made a comfortable home of it. Oh, it was still a little grand, still a home that would require maintenance, but it would have been theirs. Not his, but theirs, and together they could have stamped their mark on it.

Except that Gabrielle had not been enamoured of that suggestion either.

Auction day today. He'd told Simone he'd meet her there.

It was the last place he wanted to be.

He'd made his bid last night. His bid for Gabrielle's heart.

And he'd lost.

GABRIELLE WAS RUNNING LATE. She'd returned to her rented apartment before heading for the auction and had lingered there too long. Wiping benches that hadn't needed wiping, changing clothes that hadn't needed changing. Anything to keep from confronting the real issue—what to do about Luc. Gabrielle believed what she'd said to her mother. Luc cared nothing for her station in life or lack of it. He cared for her. Enough to offer up everything he could by way of helping her get established here. Enough to make her his lover. Enough to want to marry her.

Enough.

There were no parking spaces out the front of the elegant hotel in Epernay where the estate agents were holding the auction. Gabrielle finally found a parking spot two streets away, and running slightly late became running alarmingly late. An auctioneer's assistant met her at the door, his smile relieved as he signed her in and allocated her a bidding number. He ran through the deposit requirements should her bid be successful and Gabrielle nodded dutifully and looked around for the one face she hoped to see above all others.

But she couldn't see it.

She'd gone to the chateau directly after visiting with her mother.

Luc hadn't been there either.

Not that she had the foggiest idea what to say to him when she *did* find him. It would depend on what she saw in his eyes. On what kind of opening he was prepared to give her. She scanned the crowd again, spotted Simone, and headed towards her. Where the hell was he?

Luc strode into the auction room with moments to spare, nodding to the auctioneer's assistant who hurriedly greeted him and pointed him to where Simone sat waiting, third row from the front, with an empty chair on either side of her. He'd thought maybe Gabrielle would be sitting with Simone but she wasn't. He spotted her on the far side of the room, standing with her back to the crowd as she stared out the window, her profile pensive and her arms wrapped around the waist of her sleek black business suit.

'Where have you *been*?' asked Simone as he took the seat beside her. 'The auctioneers have been waiting for you to arrive for the last ten minutes. They almost started without you. I almost started without you. Gabrielle's been looking for you too. She was hoping to speak with you before the auction, but then she went over towards the window to try and get better reception on her phone. That or to spare my tender feelings,' said Simone, the lightness of her words at odds with the shadows in her eyes. 'I think she's calling Rafe now. She's already spent the last ten minutes trying to call you.'

He'd neglected to recharge his phone last night. Just one more thing amongst the many things he should have done differently last night. 'Did she say what she wanted to speak to me about?'

'No.' Simone settled back in her chair as the auctioneer began his spiel. 'Too late, brother. You'll have to speak with her afterwards. Looks like we're away.'

GABRIELLE TURNED, STARTLED, when the auctioneer cleared his throat and began to speak in that penetrating, staccato way auctioneers had of speaking. Deliberately fast, deliberately trying to force urgency into a situation that called for cool deliberation. Deliberately encouraging the reckless decision.

She hadn't been here in this crowded and claustrophobic auction room. She'd been a million miles away, sleepy and sated and snuggled up in Luc's arms. Reliving last night's lovemaking. Rewriting it. Omitting her stupid statement about Luc holding back. Instead she'd closed her eyes and breathed Luc in and then she'd slept and woken in his arms. No questions, no arguments, no tension. No this.

It was time to phone Rafe. She did so hurriedly, scanning the room as the auctioneer continued his spiel. Luc had arrived, finally, and taken his place beside Simone. Dark eyed and radiating tension, he looked dangerously out of patience with the world in general and probably her in particular. He looked her way with a question in his eyes and her heart began to pound. He didn't ignore her. He didn't cut her down with a glance. He wasn't smiling—there wasn't a lot to smile about—but the way was not closed to her; he'd given her that much and for now it was enough. Rafe picked up his phone and Gabrielle spoke quickly and quietly into hers. 'It's me. I'm at the auction.'

'Where are we up to?' he said, his voice calm and reassuring, an anchor in an ocean of uncertainty.

'They're describing the property. I'm looking at

a slideshow of it now.' A very beautiful, well-put-together slideshow showing all of the benefits and none of the drawbacks of the property. 'Rafe?' she said tentatively, knowing full well that now was not the time to say what she had to say. 'He asked me to marry him.'

Rafe cursed in rapid dialect French. The language of his childhood, a language he rarely used these days unless his patience was being severely tested. 'And?' he said tightly.

'The auctioneer just asked for someone to start the bidding at eighteen million.'

'Let someone else open the bidding,' said Rafe, 'and tell me what you said to Luc.'

'I said I needed more time. Luc said he didn't. He offered to buy Hammerschmidt in partnership with me.'

Rafe swore again and Gabrielle held the phone a little further away from her ear as she waited tensely for him to stop. 'Did you agree?' asked Rafe finally.

'No. They have a starting bid of sixteen million.'

'Luc's bid?'

'No.'

'What do you want to do, Gabrielle?'

'Cry,' she said faintly.

'Not an option, angel,' said Rafe. 'What's the bid?'

'Eighteen.'

'Luc's bid?'

'No.'

The bidding continued, slowing to increments of two hundred thousand. The auctioneer spoke again and Gabrielle relayed his words. 'Nineteen and on the market.'

'If you want it,' murmured Rafe, 'I suggest you bid.'

Gabrielle nodded. 'Nineteen-two,' she said into the phone.

'Whose bid?'

'Mine.'

'You mean ours,' said Rafe.

'I don't know what I mean,' she muttered, perilously close to tears—optional or not. 'Nineteen-six.'

'Whose bid?'

Gabrielle's gaze met Luc's. 'Mine.'

'LUCIEN, WHAT ARE you doing?' asked Simone.

'Nothing.'

'Yes, I gathered that,' she said with the patience one might afford a dimwit. 'Aren't you meant to be bidding?'

'Yes.' But not against Gabrielle. He simply couldn't bring himself to do it. If Gabrielle wanted the old vineyard, he would not stand in her way. 'I asked her to marry me.'

'Really?' Simone lost all pretence of not being particularly interested in the unfolding events. 'Fast work. I know you have history, but still… Very fast work.'

'I love her.'

'Yes, I gathered that,' she said dryly.

'I asked her to consider buying this place together.'

'Good idea,' she murmured, graciously neglecting to remind him that she had been the one to suggest that particular notion in the first place.

'She said no,' he said grimly. 'To both.'

'Ah,' said Simone delicately. And then, with the mysterious way she occasionally had of reading his mind, 'Maybe you rushed her. Maybe that was what she wanted to talk to you about. Maybe she's had time to think your offers over and she's changed her mind. Women do change their minds on these things, you know.' She eyed Gabrielle narrowly. 'I can't believe she didn't *tell* me.'

'Glare at her later,' said Luc. 'Don't distract her while she's bidding.'

'*Me* glare at her? Look at you! You look like you want to shove a poker through someone and roast them over hot coals. Smile at her, for heaven's sake. No, not like you plan to eat her. For goodness' sake Luc, where are your *manners*? Show a little control.'

'Gabrielle happens to think I have plenty of control,' he said, and tried not to think of a naked Gabrielle tied to a pole. 'She'd prefer I lost a little more of it at times.'

'Brave woman,' said Simone. 'Dangerous move. I did warn her, but she never listens. She never has, when it comes to you.' Simone slid him a curious glance. 'Are you planning on giving her what she wants?'

'Yes.'

Simone sat back in her chair and smiled widely at the world, resting her elbows on the armrests as

KELLY HUNTER 391

she crossed her legs and set her sandal to swinging. 'It's amazing what people will bid when they want something bad enough,' she said cheerfully. 'God, I love auctions.'

'THERE'S A NEW BIDDER,' said Gabrielle into the phone. 'A woman.' Gabrielle nodded as the auctioneer glanced questioningly at her. She nodded a second time and waited. 'Twenty million,' she said, feeling faint. 'Not ours.'

'What's Luc doing?' asked Rafe.

'Watching me.'

'Yes or no question, Gabrielle. Could you be happy at Hammerschmidt without Luc in your life?'

'No.'

'Stop bidding,' said Rafe.

'I THINK GABRIELLE'S reached her limit,' said Simone, sitting up a little straighter and losing the smile. Luc thought so too. Gabrielle was speaking rapidly into the phone, her brow furrowed. She'd already shaken her head at the auctioneer to signify no. The auctioneer was merely giving Gabrielle and whoever was on the other end of the phone with her—and that would be Rafe—time to confer. Gabrielle shook her head again. Another no. The woman bidding against Gabrielle began to look smug. But not for long.

'New bidder,' said the auctioneer. 'Gentleman at the back. Thank you, sir. Your bid at twenty million two hundred thousand.'

Simone swivelled in her seat to see who'd joined the bidding. So did Luc.

'Isn't that Daddy's old school friend?' said Simone. 'The prince?'

'Yes. Only he's not a prince these days. He's a king.'

'I didn't know he had an interest in vineyards'

'It comes and it goes,' said Luc grimly. What the hell was His Royal Highness Etienne de Morsay doing here? Why now? Why this vineyard? Luc didn't believe in coincidences. He didn't believe in fairy tales either. Etienne wasn't here to make amends. He was here because he wanted to keep Rafael from gaining a foothold back into Europe. What other reason would he have for bidding?

'THERE'S ANOTHER NEW BIDDER,' said Gabrielle, frowning into the phone as she stared at the man at the back of the room and tried to remember where she'd seen him before. Nicely built for an older man. Broad shouldered, well clothed—the man carried the unmistakable veneer of old and distinguished wealth. 'I feel like I should know who he is, but I don't.'

And then the distinguished-looking gentleman turned his head to look directly at her with eyes as blue as a clear summer sky, and then she knew.

If she hadn't been leaning against the window she'd have stumbled. As it was she struggled for breath as she tried to make sense of the why of it. What on earth was Rafael's real father doing bidding on Hammerschmidt? Surely it couldn't be a coincidence. Could it?

And then her gaze whipped around the crowd as the auctioneer announced yet another new bidder.

Luc.

'Luc just bid against him,' she whispered into the phone.

'What price?' asked Rafe.

'Twenty-one.'

The prince with Rafael's eyes bid again. Luc topped him. The prince bid again. And again, while she stared at this man, this prince, this monster, and watched him shatter any last hope she had of ever calling Hammerschmidt home. 'It's twenty-four five now.'

'Give Luc my congratulations,' said Rafe.

'It's not his bid.'

'No, but the final bid will be.'

'What makes you think he'll succeed?' Gabrielle winced as the bidding went up again, too high for comfort or for common sense. 'What the hell is he *doing*? He's way past his stop price. This is insane!'

'That's Luc for you,' said Rafe, grim amusement laying heavy on his voice. 'He never could see straight when you were around. You might want to consider marrying him, angel. He's buying this place for you.'

'Er, Luc?' Simone's voice came as if from a great distance. 'About our limit price…'

'What about it?'

'We've passed it.'

He was aware of that. 'Gabrielle wants the vineyard,' he muttered. 'And that bastard can't have it.'

'Oh. Well, then,' muttered Simone and settled back in her chair with a very feminine smile of satisfaction. 'That's different.'

CHAPTER ELEVEN

LUC WATCHED, HIS BODY tense as he waited for all the players in this room to make their moves. The auctioneer and his crew were seeing people out. The auctioneer had shaken Luc's hand briefly, smiled broadly, and excused himself to make sure that all the other plump pigeons in the room knew what else he had coming up for sale. The auctioneer would get to Luc later, when Luc was ready. The wily auctioneer had no fear that the House of Duvalier would renege on the purchase.

Simone was mingling—graciously accepting congratulations on the purchase and cleverly disseminating the information that, yes, the vineyard would be renovated and returned to the proper growing of champagne grapes and that, yes, indeed, there would be work available and that people could drop their résumés off at Caverness, particularly if they were skilled local workers—saying all the things Luc should be saying and wasn't.

Luc had more important issues to deal with.

Gabrielle stood over by the window, looking hesitant and wary as she finished her phone call and slipped her mobile into her handbag. Her eyes were on Etienne but then she dragged her gaze away from the older man and, with a squaring of delicate shoulders, she turned to look at Luc. Her lips tilted but her eyes stayed sombre as she started towards him. Luc stood and waited, while blood thundered through his veins and he tried not to feel like a schoolboy caught doing something stupid for the sake of trying to impress a girl.

Or protect a girl.

'Congratulations,' she said when she reached him, and held out her hand for him to shake as she kissed him lightly on the cheek.

'Gabrielle,' he muttered, nothing more than a warning as every muscle in his body tightened at her nearness.

'Relax,' she whispered as her lips brushed his other cheek. 'You're only getting two kisses from me on account of this being a public place. Then I'm going to berate you for paying so much for that stupid vineyard.'

Luc barely resisted grabbing her by the waist and dragging her against him. 'It's not going to make the slightest bit of difference. I'm still going to want you just as much as if you *had* kissed me again,' he said gruffly. 'Possibly more.'

'Something to remember for future reference,' she said and stepped away from him with a smile that slid straight through him. 'I need to talk to you.'

And he with her. But not here. There were far too many people watching them. One in particular. 'Later.'

'Now. Luc, I have my suitcases in the car and I find myself in need of a place to stay.' Her words were crisp but he felt her anxiety as if it were his own. 'I was hoping to stay with you at Caverness.'

'I'll make space in my cupboard,' he said gently. If he wasn't mistaken she was attempting to address some of the issues that had plagued them last night. Awkward in a room full of people, but she attempted it nonetheless. 'For your clothes.'

She still looked anxious. As if she wasn't quite sure he understood what she was saying. 'I have a lot of clothes.'

'Caverness has a lot of cupboards,' he countered.

'Luc, I need to talk to you,' she murmured. 'When can that happen?'

'I'll be tied up here for a little while longer.'

'An hour?'

'Longer,' he said. 'Why don't you head back to the chateau with Simone and get settled? I'll deal with whatever needs dealing with here—' his eyes flickered to Etienne '—and I'll find you there.'

'It's a big castle,' she said. 'I'm thinking we should specify a time and place.'

She was absolutely right. 'Seven o clock?'

'Seven it is,' she said. 'Shall I dress for dinner?'

'No. You should eat beforehand. Food should not be a priority.' Fair warning.

'Where shall I meet you?' she asked. 'Or would you prefer to collect me? You being a thoroughly liberated Frenchman and all.' She smiled then, a wicked little smile just for him. 'You may collect me from your bedroom.'

'I'll meet you.' Luc smiled as he leaned closer and brushed her ear with his lips. A taste of her, and a promise to keep. 'At seven o clock, behind Caverness,' he murmured. 'In the caves.' Etienne was heading their way. 'Go. Get out of here.'

But it was too late.

'Lucien,' said Etienne, with the hint of a smile. 'Not exactly a bargain.'

'Satisfying though,' said Luc, without the slightest hint of friendliness.

Etienne shrugged. 'It amused me to see just how high you would bid, but then if the property had fallen to me I'd probably have had a great deal of explaining to do to the treasury and that's never pleasant,' he said. 'It occurred to me, seeing you with the young lady here, that we might have been bidding with exactly the same purpose in mind.'

'I doubt it,' said Luc, but Etienne had turned his attention to Gabrielle. 'Well bid, *mademoiselle*. I strongly suspect you have more good sense than either of us. Etienne De Morsay at your service.'

'His Royal Highness, King Etienne De Morsay,' added Luc grimly. 'An old friend of my father's.'

Gabrielle said nothing and Luc contemplated stepping in front of her and blocking her from the older man's view. As it was he reached for her hand and twined his fingers in hers. Whatever she needed from him, whatever she wanted, all she had to do was say the word. Stay. Go. He would take his cue from her. Gabrielle glanced at him and sent him a tiny, grateful smile before lifting her chin and turning back to Etienne, her hand still firmly clasped in his.

'I never thought I'd live to see a woman more beautiful than your mother,' said Etienne. 'I have now.'

'I never thought to see an older version of my brother sidle up and smile,' said Gabrielle baldly. 'I hope never to again. What do you want?'

'I see you inherited your mother's charm as well,' said Etienne.

'You leave my mother out of this!' snapped Gabrielle. 'What do you want?'

'A phone number,' he said. 'A contact address. For my son.'

'You could have gotten that any time during the past thirty years,' said Gabrielle. 'You don't need me for that.'

'An introduction,' he said next.

'Not from me,' said Gabrielle.

'So like your mother,' he murmured.

'I am *not* like my mother,' she said through clenched teeth. 'I swear I will slap the next person who implies that I am. My *mother* has spent half her life considering herself to be of no significant value to anyone because of you. Not good enough, not polished enough, not rich enough or beautiful enough. For you. Whereas me…I don't care what you think. I know my worth. And I know yours.' Gabrielle speared Etienne with ice-filled eyes. 'Rafael already has a father, thank you. One he loves very much. One who loves him. He doesn't need you.'

'But I need him,' said Etienne.

'I really don't care,' said Gabrielle and turned her back on Etienne dismissively. 'Seven this evening,' she said to Luc. 'I'll see you there.' And with another icy glare for Etienne, she stalked away.

LUC WAITED UNTIL Gabrielle had gone before turning his attention back to Etienne. The older man was sharp. Too sharp for Luc's liking.

'She knew who I was,' said Etienne thoughtfully. 'You told her?'

'No.' Not entirely true in the strictest sense, but he would not discuss Josien and Simone with Etienne. Not now. Not ever.

'Would I be right in assuming that Josien told her about me?'

'No.'

Etienne sighed. 'It doesn't have to be this difficult, Lucien. I intend no harm.'

That was a matter of opinion. Lucien waited in silence. Etienne sighed again.

'And Rafael...does he still know nothing of me?'

This question Luc would answer. 'Rafael believes that Harrison Alexander is his biological father. No one has ever told him otherwise.'

Shadows crossed the older man's eyes and he looked away; Luc followed the direction of the older man's gaze. Gabrielle had made her way to the door and was speaking with the auctioneer. Simone was with her, and together they seemed bent on reducing the auctioneer to a blushing morass of flattered middle-aged manhood. A dangerous combination, those two. Luc would have to figure out some way of reining in the wilder schemes they were likely to come up with once Gabrielle settled into his life. That or direct them to his advantage. He predicted great changes to the running of the House of Duvalier in the coming months. Changes that would benefit them all.

'So like her mother,' said Etienne, and Luc returned his attention to the matter at hand.

'No,' he said simply. 'She's not.'

'I still think you and I were bidding for the same reason,' said Etienne. 'You wanted to purchase the vineyard for Josien's children, *non*?' He smiled wryly. 'So did I.'

'Why now?' said Luc, echoing Gabrielle's question. 'All these years you've been content to watch from afar. Keep tabs on your son from a distance. He needed you when he was a child, they all did, but you never came. Why turn up now?'

'My wife died last year,' said the older man with a smile that contrasted starkly with the sadness in his eyes. 'She never bore me any children although heaven knows she tried.'

'I'm sorry for your loss,' said Luc curtly.

'As am I,' said Etienne. 'I remained faithful to the wife that had been chosen for me for thirty years, no matter what the temptation. She was a good woman, a fine companion, and I grew to love her.' Etienne turned those vivid blue eyes on him and the memory of Rafael's eyes stabbed through Luc. 'I'm dying, Lucien, and my wife can no longer be hurt by revelations of my youthful indiscretion. I have no legitimate heirs. I wish to acknowledge my son. There is the matter of succession.'

Luc shook his head and suppressed a bitter laugh. As a child Rafael had needed a father badly. And this man had stood back. 'My kingdom for an heir.'

'All I'm asking for is an introduction,' said Etienne.

'I can't help you.' Luc quelled the faint stirrings of pity he felt for this man; for the duty-bound prince he'd once been, for the solitary king he'd become. 'It's not my introduction to give, and nor is it Gabrielle's. It's Josien's.'

'I NEED YOUR HELP,' said Gabrielle to Simone as together they dragged her two large suitcases across the gravel courtyard towards the kitchen door.

'You're getting my help,' said Simone as she hauled on the suitcase and shifted it another three feet closer to the door. 'Is this gravel driving you nuts? Because it's driving me nuts. Crunch, crunch, crunch, and weeds popping up all through it. I'm thinking pavers.'

Gabrielle was thinking surrender, but she took the time to make a detour for the sake of a lifelong friendship. 'Pavers would be good,' she said. 'Pavers would allow suitcase wheels to function. I need your help with selecting a wedding dress.'

'A what?' Simone dropped the suitcase she'd been dragging, dusted off her hands, and smiled broadly. 'Simone is At Your Service,' she said. 'This day just keeps getting better. Luc can get these cases in for you later. Let's go to Paris.'

'Not a *Paris* wedding dress. An instant wedding dress. As in something from out of my suitcase that looks vaguely weddingy and virginal. I need it by tonight.'

Simone's hands went to her hips and thunder-clouds gathered in her eyes. 'You're marrying Luc *tonight*?'

'I'm not marrying him at all at the moment,' muttered Gabrielle, sweeping past Simone and making a grab for the handle of the suitcase Simone had dropped. 'Let me rephrase. Tonight is a very important night for me. An all or nothing night. It may not *be* an actual wedding night but that doesn't mean a woman can't prepare for it as if it were one. I need a frock a man will remember with pleasure. I need my hair up so he can take it down. I also need a shot of courage. Possibly Dutch, preferably French.'

'You need to stop teasing me like that,' said Simone as she came up and reclaimed the suitcase she'd been dragging along earlier. 'You also need a brides-maid. But first things first. Where's he taking you?'

'Nowhere,' said Gabrielle loftily and then went and spoiled her bravado by blushing like a school-girl. 'I'm meeting him in the caves.'

THE CAVES BEHIND the Chateau des Caverness had been used for many purposes over the years. During times of war they'd hidden people and their belongings, given them shelter and given them ease. So many names carved into the soft grey stone walls. Names of the people who had worked here and played here, names of the wines. Gabrielle had carved her own name into these walls as a child. If she looked in that corner she would find her name there, written in childish scrawl, all the more childish for being so carefully carved. A record of her passing this way all those years ago. A witness to what had passed between her and Luc all those years ago as well.

Gabrielle made her way along the narrow corridor, lit only by the occasional beeswax candle. She knew the way, knew exactly where Luc would be. The tiny grotto where they'd begun to walk this path all those years ago. The tiny ancient grotto with its shelves of old wine and its hundreds of tiny tea-lights nesting in the walls. The little room with its black wrought-iron door and its worn wooden table in the corner—the kind that had endured for centuries.

She wore an ivory linen dress with wide shoulder straps and buttons all the way down the front. Her shoes were cream too and her hair was pinned up loosely. Cool air parted before her, caressing her skin as she drew ever closer to the place where it had all begun. This wasn't about seduction and it wasn't about sex, although the need for both burned fiercely through her. It was about finishing what she'd started, coming full circle. Candlelight drew her through the last of the big caverns towards the little grotto, soft yellow light, and she let it guide her as she had let it guide her all those years ago.

He was waiting for her, as she'd known he would be, his clothing dark but not as dark as his hair or his eyes. He stilled when he saw her, every muscle in his strong beautiful body tense and predatory. What would she find in her lover this night? What would he give?

What would *she* give in order to be with this man?

She closed the distance between them, stopping only when they shared the same shadow, when all she need do to touch him was sway a little closer. 'Always so still,' she murmured. 'So very careful around me.' She spoke the words she'd spoken seven years ago, speaking them boldly, speaking them true. 'They tell me you're a danger to me.'

'I am.'

'Why?'

'Because of what I want,' he said huskily. New words to replace the silence that had once been his only answer. 'Because of what I would give in return.'

'What do you want?'

'Everything.'

'And what would you give for it?'

'Anything.'

'Some might call that obsession.'

'It is.'

'Some would call it possession.'

'It is.'

'Some might even be scared of such a love. Such

an all-consuming, crazy kind of love. But not me.'
She walked around him in a slow circle, staying
close, trailing her fingertips up and over the broad
expanse of his shoulder, the base of his neck, more
shoulder, and then finally his heart. If seduction was
war she commanded a conquering army. If seduction
was a duel her blade would have drawn first blood.
But this wasn't seduction. It was truth. 'I want what
you have to offer. All of it.'

'The deed to Hammerschmidt,' he said huskily.
'It's yours.'

'Rafe warned me you'd say that,' she murmured
and set her lips to the strong cord of his neck. Lightly.
Lovingly. Such a still and waiting night. The heavy
expectant stillness that came before an almighty
storm. What would she bargain? And what would
he give? She pulled back to study him, her breath
catching at the raw magnificence of this man in the
flickering light of a hundred candles. 'I propose a
partnership. A new company. Something sticky and
entwined. Something that's not yours or mine. Something that's ours.'

'I accept,' he said.

'You mentioned marriage,' she whispered, bringing her fingertips up to trace the perfect curve of his
lips. He did not reach for her, though he shuddered
hard. So much control in this man, such perfect control. 'And I had to think hard about that. I worried
what others would think. I wasn't sure I was worthy of you or of the Duvalier name and all that came
with it. And then it occurred to me that you didn't

care what others might think and neither should I. All that mattered was whether I loved you. And I do.'

'Marry me,' he said.

'I accept,' she replied with a smile Luc would doubtless learn to be wary of. 'There is…one more thing. All that formidable control when I'm naked in your arms. All that careful restraint when I'm burning up inside for love of you,' she said delicately as she traced a path from his chest to the formidable bulge in his trousers. 'It has to go.'

An unholy light crept into his eyes, a wild and challenging hunger that called to her and always had. 'Then make it go,' he said.

She started with the buttons on his shirt, slowly easing them from their holes. Then she began in on his belt and his trousers until they too sat loosely in place. His shirt came off and dropped to the ground. She left his trousers where they were. For now.

'It would help if you kissed me,' he murmured.

She expected hunger from him. She craved the dark edge of need he brought to their lovemaking. But the kiss he shared with her was different again. Better again, as he showed her his soul, a soul filled with such purity and sweetness that she prayed his kiss would never end.

'I love you,' he murmured as his hands went to the pins in her hair. There were only a few of them, carefully placed, and moments later her hair tumbled down for him in waves. He stroked it with his knuckles, threaded it through open fingers and finally, finally his eyes grew black with desire as he wound it round his hand and made a fist. This time the sweetness in his kisses gave way to a fierce and uncontrollable need. 'I'll never hurt you,' he muttered.

'I know.' Night, the household staff had always called him, because of the shadows on his soul and the fierceness of his passions, but he was *her* night and always would be. She did not fear his hunger, and never had. 'This time you ride the storm with me,' she whispered as she slid her hands in his hair and dragged his lips closer. 'I'll be your lighthouse.' She touched her tongue to the side of his mouth, darkly pleased when a groan escaped him and he trapped her within the circle of his arms. 'I'll be your guide, and you need to trust me.'

'I do trust you.' If seduction was a war, Luc's kisses reminded her that even if she did have a conquering army at her back, this man commanded the skies. She wanted him naked. She wanted him wild.

'Surrender to me,' she whispered as she called up the storm. And he did.

* * * * *

We hope you enjoyed reading

AFTERSHOCK

by *New York Times* bestselling author

JILL SHALVIS

and

XPOSED: MISBEHAVING WITH THE MAGNATE

by reader-favorite author

KELLY HUNTER

Both were originally Harlequin series stories!

For more glamorous, passionate romances,
look for the **Harlequin Presents** series!

⊕ HARLEQUIN®

Presents®

xperience glamorous settings, powerful men and
assionate romances with **Harlequin Presents!**

ook for eight *new* romances every month from
Harlequin Presents!

Available wherever books are sold.

Find us at Harlequin.com

NYTHR0714

* * *

His expression shuttered, and his dark eyebrows came dow
into a scowl. "His surname, however…"

I sighed. "I thought you might want to change that. B
don't worry." I gave an awkward smile. "I won't hold you
your marriage proposal."

His eyes were dark and intense. "What if I want you
hold me to it?"

My lips parted in shock.

"What?" I said faintly.

His dark eyes challenged mine. "What if I want you
marry me?"

"You don't want to get married. You went on and on abo
all the women who tried to drag you to the altar. I'm not o
of them!"

"I know that now." Leaning his arm across the baby se
he cupped my cheek. "But for our son's sake, I'm starting
think you and I should be…together."

"Why?"

"Why not?" He gave a sensual smile. "As you said.
already broke one rule. Why not break the other?"

"But what has changed?"

"I'm starting to think…perhaps I can trust you." His eyes met mine. "And I can't forget how it felt to have you in my bed."

Something changed in the air between us. Something animal, dangerous. I felt the warmth of his palm against my skin and held my breath. As the limo drove through the streets of London, memories crackled through me like fire.

I remembered the night we'd conceived Miguel, and all the other hot days of summer, when I'd surrendered to him, body and soul. I trembled, feeling him so close in the backseat of the limo, on the other side of our baby. Every inch of my skin suddenly remembered the hot stroke of Alejandro's fingertips. My mouth was tingling, aching….

"That's not a good reason to marry someone. Especially for you. If I said yes, you'd regret it. You'd blame me. Claim that I'd only done it to be a rich duchess."

He slowly shook his head. "I think," he said quietly, "you might be the one woman who truly doesn't care about that. And it would be best for our son. So what is your answer?"

* * *

What will Lena Carlisle do when pushed to her limits by the notorious Duke of Alzacar?

Find out in
UNCOVERING HER NINE MONTH SECRET
August 2014

HARLEQUIN®

Presents®

Save $1.00 on the purchase of

UNCOVERING HER NINE MONTH SECRET

by Jennie Lucas,

available July 15, 2014,
or on any other Harlequin® Presents® book.

Available wherever books are sold, including most bookstores,
supermarkets, drugstores and discount stores.

Save $1.00

on the purchase of
UNCOVERING HER NINE MONTH SECRE
by Jennie Lucas
available July 15, 2014
or on any other Harlequin® Presents® book.

Coupon valid until September 17, 2014. Redeemable at participating retail outlets
in the U.S. and Canada only. Limit one coupon per customer.

Canadian Retailers: Harlequin Enterprises Limited will pay the face value of t
coupon plus 10.25¢ if submitted by customer for this product only. Any other
constitutes fraud. Coupon is nonassignable. Void if taxed, prohibited or restric
by law. Consumer must pay any government taxes. Void if copied. Millenniu
Promotional Services ("M1P") customers submit coupons and proof of sales
Harlequin Enterprises Limited, P.O. Box 3000, Saint John, NB E2L 4L3, Cana
Non-M1P retailer—for reimbursement submit coupons and proof of sales dire
to Harlequin Enterprises Limited, Retail Marketing Department, 225 Duncan Mill
Don Mills, Ontario M3B 3K9, Canada.

U.S. Retailers: Harlequin Enterpri
Limited will pay the face value of this cou
plus 8¢ if submitted by customer for
product only. Any other use constitutes fra
Coupon is nonassignable. Void if tax
prohibited or restricted by law. Consumer n
pay any government taxes. Void if copied.
reimbursement submit coupons and proc
sales directly to Harlequin Enterprises Lim
P.O. Box 880478, El Paso, TX 88588-0
U.S.A. Cash value 1/100 cents.

® and TM are trademarks owned and used by the trademark owner and/or its licensee.
© 2014 Harlequin Enterprises Limited

Caitlin Crews brings you an explosive tale of seduction and passion in the sultry desert heat.

Innocent Cleo Churchill is exactly what Khaled, Sultan of Jhurat, needs—a convenient yet beautiful bride to unite his warring country. He'll offer her diamonds and riches but nothing more.

Yet as their marriage plays out in the darkness of the night, the passions unearthed threaten to consume them both!

UNDONE BY THE SULTAN'S TOUCH
by
Caitlin Crews

**Available August 2014,
wherever books are sold!**

HARLEQUIN®

A *Romance* FOR EVERY MOOD™

Stay up-to-date on all your
romance-reading news with the
Harlequin Shopping Guide,
featuring bestselling authors, exciting new
miniseries, books to watch and more!

The newest issue will be delivered right to you
with our compliments! There are 4 each year.

Signing up is easy.

EMAIL

ShoppingGuide@Harlequin.ca

WRITE TO US

HARLEQUIN BOOKS
Attention: Customer Service Department
P.O. Box 9057, Buffalo, NY 14269-9057

OR PHONE

1-800-873-8635 in the United States
1-888-343-9777 in Canada

Please allow 4-6 weeks for delivery of the first issue by mail.